ESTHER

ELLEN GUNDERSON TRAYLOR

Author of 'John, Son of Thunder'

HARVEST HOUSE PUBLISHERS
Eugene, Oregon 97402

Other Books by Ellen Gunderson Traylor

Song of Abraham
John—Son of Thunder
Mary Magdalene
Noah
Ruth—A Love Story
Jonah
Mark

ESTHER

Copyright © 1988 by Harvest House Publishers
Eugene, Oregon 97402

Library of Congress Catalog Card Number 87-081246
ISBN 0-89081-604-2

Printed in the United States of America.

To Eric,
who loved beauty.

Contents

Thy lovingkindness, O Lord,
  extends to the heavens,
Thy faithfulness reaches to the skies.
Thy righteousness is like
  the mountains of God;
Thy judgments are like a great deep.

Psalm 36:5,6 NASB

A Note to the Reader

In a tiny hall of the Oriental Institute Museum, on the campus of the University of Chicago, there is an enormous artifact—the 20,000-pound black stone head of a guardian bull. Transplanted from the grounds of Persepolis, the ancient Persian ceremonial capital, this cold creature stares down upon tourists and scholars with centuries-old aloofness. Could it speak, it would doubtless tell fabulous tales of the grand empire which once ruled half the world.

Having embroiled myself in the study of Esther, the biblical queen who was for a time first lady of that empire, I was overcome with feeling when I first set eyes upon this heartless creature. Esther herself, fairest woman on earth and pure of heart in devotion to her Jewish heritage, had most likely passed before this very statue, and the sightless rock had glowered down on her, just as it now did on me.

In an instant, I sensed a personal link with the young girl whom I had studied, understanding for the first time how frightened she must have been when carried away to become wife of the despot, Xerxes.

Esther's name does not show up in any secular chronicle. Herodotus, the most meticulous recorder of Xerxes' life and of the Greek-Persian Wars, mentions Amestris (probably the biblical Vashti), who was the rightful queen. Only the Bible tells of Hadassah, the orphaned Jewess who rose to the throne, unhappily taking on a pagan name and filling the place where the first noble lady should have remained.

Although overlooked by secular historians, the tale of Esther is crucial to the story of Israel. For Esther was a savior to her people, raised for a purpose higher than worldly acclaim.

"What was she like?" I would have asked the great bull, if I could. "When you and your brothers in Persepolis and Susa loomed above her, did she tremble?"

Only a novelist's imagination could assist me toward the answer. The Scriptures, though telling us all we know of this obscure queen, are typically scant in revealing the heroine's heart. We see the plot, but must interpret the character's motivations and emotions with the aid of prayer and intuition alone. This is true not only for Esther, but for Vashti, Xerxes, and the host of other people who fill the pages of God's Word.

Fumbling as our reconstruction may be, we will not go far wrong if we remember that these were folk of flesh and blood, who once loved and cried and laughed. And that they, like we, were guided through their steps by the Sovereign God who rules all history and governs each life for his ultimate purpose.

If we can apply this principle as we read of those who lived so long ago, we also can apply it to ourselves. No one's circumstances, no matter how mysterious or confounding, are outside God's grand design. Our Father knows the end from the beginning. Despite our frustrated attempts to understand, he will always be proven the Master Architect of all things.

May you find encouragement for your hard times and the laughter of the Lord in all your triumphs.

—Ellen Traylor
Grants Pass, Oregon

ESTHER

PART I

The King and the Prince

1

Purple dusk had settled over Persia's western desert. A rush of cool wind swept through Susa on its way to the Gulf, bearing the scent of lilies across the housetops.

It was Spring. Tomorrow would begin a new imperial year.

Amestris Vashti, daughter of Otanes, shivered and glanced south toward Persepolis, the distant ceremonial capital, where the revelry of New Year's Eve would be even more boisterous than in this northern citadel.

Vashti's private balcony afforded an expansive view across Susa's southern wall, and in this sanctum of her father's home she was free for a moment from the din in the streets beyond the river.

One of the mansions of the seven noblest families in Persia, the house of her childhood stood safely tucked atop Susa's acropolis. Rarely had Vashti found it necessary to mingle with the commoners who lived in the shadow of the royal mount, but New Year's Eve required it.

Vashti, along with her royal sisters (girls born to the highest homes in the land), had ridden through town this day in open carriages, bearing long-stemmed lilies in their hands and wearing pink irises in their hair. Though they had been cheered and praised by adoring masses, Vashti had not enjoyed it.

She would have preferred to accompany her cousins, the young princes of King Darius, to Persepolis.

But that journey was for boys alone.

Pushing slender fingers through a tousle of long black curls, she lifted her face to the wind and let the cool air spill over her bare arms. As she wrapped her fringed shawl about her shoulders, she remembered that Prince Xerxes had once stood with her upon this very balcony.

They had been mere children and very innocent. But when the chamberlain had found them, he had rebuked them soundly. "It is dark, and you are alone!" he had glowered. "This is indiscretion!"

At the time, being but a young girl, she had not known what "indiscretion" meant. It must be something dreadful, she deduced, and so did Xerxes when they spoke of it in the garden the next day.

That had been a decade ago. Vashti was 16 now, and most of her training for the past ten years had been concerned with discretion and indiscretion. She had come to love being a lady and behaving the part.

And she had come to love Xerxes too, if indeed she had ever *not* loved him.

In truth, she could not remember ever feeling neutral toward the third son of Darius. And she could not recall ever feeling anything for him but admiration.

Certainly her circle of childhood playmates and adolescent companions had been carefully chosen. She had known only a few boys in her growing-up years—sons of nobility and sons of Darius. Well before she had reached puberty, she had been limited in socializing even with these.

But Xerxes had won her heart before she knew she could give it. And being rarely allowed to see him had only bound her to him more surely.

Closing her eyes, she leaned against a fluted column of her lofty porch and tried to envision what he might be doing just now. In a few hours it would be midnight, the first day of the new year, and twelve years since Xerxes' ascension to the office of viceroy. He was 18 now, but he had stood behind his father's throne since he was less than half that old.

Though he was not the monarch's eldest son, he was the first since his coronation. Hence he would one day succeed to the throne.

And should all go as planned, Vashti would be queen.

At midnight in Persepolis the sacred dice would be cast, the "purim," which would determine the appointed dates of special events for the empire's coming year.

"The priests, when they cast the dice, will speak of you and me," the prince had promised her. "On New Year's Eve they will decide our wedding day."

It was fully possible that a quirk of the dice or an interpretation of accompanying omens could throw the date into a later year. But Vashti and Xerxes had prayed to Ahura-Mazda and had taken a second drink from the cup of haoma, pleading that no such delay would take place.

Rarely since their earliest days of childish play had the prince been alone with Vashti. As a small boy and girl they had touched often, had held hands, and had skipped through the mammoth hallways of Susa's palace.

But their encounters were more guarded now. Those fleeting occasions when the prince had brushed her arm in passing or had touched her fingertips at a banquet table were stored in her memory like hallowed gems.

Bronze-skinned and tall, he was a striking figure now—a man and not a boy. Were he to bend over her with his strong neck and able arms, she would tremble, she knew. For she had done so this very morning, when in a stolen moment he had kissed her.

Had that been indiscretion? The chamberlain would have said so. But Vashti was Xerxes' betrothed, his soon-to-be-wife. No one could have kept him from seeking her in the garden and pressing his promises to her.

Vashti opened her eyes. The din in the streets was clearly audible now, even at this far side of the mount. Below wound the Shapur River through the center of town, and beyond the city wall stretched the night-cold desert.

Small strings of light here and there along the sandy expanse marked feudal villages, where proud farmers and craftsmen derived a tolerable living from the irrigated soil. Though Susa was dominated by Persians, every nationality in the empire, from Indian to Ethiopian, composed its population and its suburbs. Tonight the people were free to come and go through the city's open gates, and a constant line of traffic traced the highway between the citadel and the nearby Gulf.

Vashti had often tried to comprehend the enormity of Darius' realm. Susa was only a small fraction of the whole, of the dominions which stretched over three thousand miles across the world and which included 127 provinces from India to Africa.

All this would one day belong to Xerxes. The greatest names on earth, from Babylon to Egypt, bowed the knee to Persia.

And if Darius had his way, even Greece would eventually succumb.

Greece, alone of all civilized nations, had managed to resist tribute to Darius. Its native tongue had not yielded to the Aramaic language. Even Xerxes, properly known as Ahasuerus, was called by the more popular Greek variation.

One day, Darius was determined, he would usurp Grecian hold over southern Europe. He would bring away captive Greek slaves, just as his Babylonian predecessor, Nebuchadnezzar, had done with the Israelites.

But that was *Darius'* plan. *Vashti's* was to marry Xerxes. This was all she cared for.

She would have closed her eyes again, to contemplate him, had her gaze not been caught by certain pedestrians along the desert highway.

Hundreds came and went upon the road, all in festive mood, singing, dancing, reeling from drink.

But the little group which caught her attention was strangely huddled, bent about an elderly man and the bundle he carried in his arms. A couple and a younger fellow walked with the old one, intent on helping him along and watching the little parcel with care.

"Peculiar," Vashti thought; "always they are peculiar."

She had recognized them immediately as Jews, and designated them strange not only because of their dress but because of their typically somber attitude.

Though all Persia partied tonight, these folk, like many of their race, kept to themselves, observing the holiday independently and quietly.

These, of all the folk in Persia's realm, were hardest for her to understand. She neither loved nor hated them, but found them curious oddities.

Were she at hand, she might have asked them why they behaved so strangely, and what was concealed in the wrapper.

But when they disappeared through the city gate she forgot them, and her eyes grew heavy with the dark.

Turning for her chamber, she slipped to bed and hoped the midnight cacophony would not rouse her.

She wished to dream of Xerxes.

2

When the little band of Jews entered the city, they did not turn toward the center of common festivity, the marketplace, but instead crossed the elegant bridge leading toward the acropolis.

Along the foot of the mount stood fine homes amid imperial office buildings and treasuries. These houses and apartments were not so elaborate as those of the Persian nobility but were more handsome than the box-shaped residences of the lower class. These fine homes spoke of success and upward mobility. If a Jew lived in Susa, it was not unlikely that he would live here.

The close-knit folk whom Vashti had observed from her balcony traversed several broad avenues fronting such abodes. The youngest of the group, a slender fellow with smooth features and well-trimmed beard, seemed most anxious to move along but was hindered by the eldest, who was not so spry as he.

"We are almost there, Uncle," the young man spurred him. "Just around the next corner."

"You have done well for yourself, Mordecai," the elder observed, studying his surroundings with proud eyes. "To dwell in a foreign land in finery—that is a task for a Jew. And you have accomplished it!"

The idea of Persia being a "foreign" place, after more than two centuries of his ancestors' residing here, had always struck Mordecai as strange. But he nodded graciously, having heard such assessments all his life.

True, the ancestral Israelites had not come to Mesopotamia willingly. They had been taken captive by Nebuchadnezzar 200 years before—"exiled," as they put it, by the hand of God. But Cyrus the Great had emancipated them. There were no longer Jewish slaves in Babylon or any part of Persia. They had been

16

free to return to Israel, just as all captive people of the realm had been free to return to their homelands.

Since then, of course, other slaves had been taken by Cyrus' successors—but never again the Israelites. The many Jews who had chosen to remain in Persia were free to pursue all the empire had to offer, and they, being industrious and creative, had carved many niches of success for themselves.

Certainly in Susa, as in every Persian quarter, there were ghettos—impoverished, hovel-lined pockets where less fortunate Hebrews dwelt. Perhaps Abihail, the elder, had envisioned such a neighborhood when Mordecai had encouraged him to come for a visit. But he was seeing now, as he surveyed these well-kept housefronts, that his nephew was not among the poor.

"I tried to tell you that Mordecai has climbed high in Susa," the young woman of the group objected. With a worried sigh she reached for the old man's bundle, which wriggled now in his arms. "Please, Uncle, let me carry the baby," she pleaded. "You could stumble . . . you could . . ."

"It is all right, Leah," said her husband, Moshe, who steadied the elder's uneasy gait. "Do not press him."

Abihail had been a farmer all his life, in one of Susa's small village suburbs. So had his son, as well as his brother, both of whom had died of plague many years before. Left with no family of their own, Abihail and his wife had taken in the brother's orphaned children, Mordecai and Leah, rearing them as offspring of their own love.

Never had they dreamed that the five nephews and nieces born to Leah, and whom they loved as grandchildren, would not be their last "gifts from the Lord." Like Sarah of old, who had given Abraham his Isaac, Abihail's wife became pregnant in advanced age. The swaddled infant in the wrapper was the result.

Just seven days ago the old man's wife had died while giving birth to the child. Had Abihail not seen hope for tomorrow in the newborn's perfect form and face, his heart would have died as well.

"A daughter of Israel," he whispered as he cradled the tiny girl to his bosom. "Is she not a myrtle blossom?" he crooned as he peeked between the folds of the homespun blanket, his long patriarchal beard tickling her chin.

"Hadassah," he had named her: "Myrtle," for her creamy skin, white like the bush's fragrant flowers, and her shock of deep-brown hair, dark as evergreen boughs.

Mordecai wondered at the elder's fond behavior. He had always marveled at the old man's love of tradition and heritage. Now that he saw it had a forward thrust, as well as a backward, he marveled all the more.

As for himself, if Mordecai esteemed Israel it was for personal advantage. He had learned in youth that the line of Kish, from whom he was descended, had been Hebrew nobility. Nebuchadnezzar had imported the cream of Israelite society, bringing the highest leaders and families into exile with the Jewish king, Jeconiah. The line of Kish could be traced back to King Saul himself, and many men of the clan had been notable administrators, scribes, clerks, and accountants in Israel and Judah.

Educated in the village synagogue school, Mordecai had been praised at a young age for his finesse with figures and mathematics. He would be a financial wizard, he had decided in his youthful dreams. He would sit one day in the palace gate at Susa or Persepolis, where all the greatest consultants sat. And he would make himself famous for brilliant manipulation of the market.

But Mordecai was not without a sentimental side. Though he had been promoted beyond the village walls and had now come to reside in the city, first as a merchant's bookkeeper and now as his executive stockkeeper, he had not forgotten his kin. He loved them all devoutly, and when he thought of Judaism, he considered it best expressed by close attachment to his people.

Abihail wished he saw it more spiritually than that. He had rankled when his brother named the lad Mordecai, after Marduk, god of storm. The brother had insisted that it meant nothing to do so—that he simply liked the name, and that it was a common one in the land.

"But there is much *meaning* in a name," Abihail had insisted. "The Scriptures bear this out. The lad will have much to overcome with a name like that."

To this day it rolled awkwardly off Abihail's tongue. Though proud of his nephew, he still wished the young man had an Israelite name.

The infant was beginning to whimper. Mordecai saw his sister reach anxiously for her, accustomed to mothering as she was. It had been for this very reason that he had insisted Abihail and Hadassah stay with him for a time. Leah had too many mouths to feed and too many little ones to tend. An aging and bereaved uncle along with a tiny newborn would be an unwieldy burden.

"There are women servants at home, and we are almost there now," he reminded her. "I even hired a nurse to suckle the child. Never you mind."

Leah sighed again and shook her head. She could not imagine a confirmed bachelor like her brother long enduring the trouble a baby would bring. She had tried to warn him of the nighttime crying, the colic, the diaper changes. But he had insisted.

"Abihail needs a shift of scene," Mordecai had determined. "If he grows homesick, he will return to you. But give him a few weeks."

Fireworks imported from the Indus Valley lit the New Year's sky. It was close to midnight as the little family turned the last corner for home. The palace gate was not far from here, and folk in royal chariots were descending the winding road which led from the king's house toward town. Since the king himself, his sons, and his closest companions celebrated in Persepolis, and since women of the court would not leave the acropolis at night, the ones hastening for the market square were underlings, administrative assistants, household eunuchs, and valets. They would not miss the climax of merrymaking which would follow the light display at midnight.

Most of them were already half-drunk. The little group of Jews stepped into the shadows as they went by, watching them quietly. Mordecai's lips curled in a covert smile at their frivolity. He had known a share of high times himself since abiding in Susa, but he was careful not to let Abihail know about it.

When the courtiers were nearly past, and only a band of rowdy stragglers followed, Mordecai led his people back into the street.

Perhaps it was the Jews' simple garb, shawled heads, or downcast eyes, but something in their demeanor enraged the besotted gang who stumbled into the trail of the regal parade. Mordecai would not have recognized them had they not called to him. When they hissed his name, following it with a racial epithet, he instantly knew their voices.

Assistants to the king's grand vizier, they were. Assistants to Haman, highest counselor in the land. Mordecai knew them because his own master had enrolled him in accounting courses at the vizier's royal academy.

They had never lived up to their respectable positions. Mordecai often wondered why Haman had selected them for himself. But, of course, they were very bright—and it did not hurt them that they came from monied families.

He would have ignored the racial slur, but they would not allow it. Stopping directly before his group, they impeded passage down the walkway and began to hurl more insults at him.

"Jew boy," they taunted. "Sheep trap, sand flea!" Then, spying the elderly one behind him, as well as his attractive sister, they made crude gestures with their hands.

"What's in the bundle, old man?" one laughed. "A little lamb for New Year's dinner?"

"Of course, Drusal!" another shouted. "It wouldn't be a pig. Jews don't eat 'unclean' beasts!"

The rowdies elbowed one another, doubling over with guffaws, and Abihail shielded the baby anxiously.

"Ah!" a third cried, seeing his protective action. "It must be a treasure! Let's see, Grandpa!"

When the young men grasped at the bundle, Leah shrieked and her husband pulled her to him.

"Leave us be!" Mordecai growled. "This is nothing to you."

But suddenly, spurred to violence by hours of drink, the men shot forward, pushing Leah's husband aside and pressing Abihail to the wall.

Held tightly to her old father's chest, the baby began to cry, disclosing the secret of herself. With wicked leers the men reached for the bundle, laughing "Jew baby!" and seeming ready to toss her from hand to hand.

Abihail slumped to his knees, still clutching the infant, as Mordecai and Moshe did their best to ward off Haman's boys.

Though they had no love for Jews, in a more sober mood they never would have harmed these people. The leader would never have thrown the piercing kick to the old man's head which sent Abihail sprawling to the pavement.

Leah shrieked again and grabbed the baby, who now lay squalling on the curb. The two Jewish brothers rushed at the attackers with clenched fists.

Suddenly another chariot could be heard coming down the acropolis hill. It would prove to be only the vehicle of a tardy courtier, racing to catch up with those who had passed by earlier.

But Haman's assistants, fearing the authorities, scrambled down the avenue. Though they were drunk, they were not so addlepated as to be caught in a street brawl.

Mordecai and Moshe bent down to help the uncle to his feet. Blood trickled from the old man's forehead, and an ugly bruise throbbed at his temple.

"Help is on its way," Mordecai assured him. "A chariot approaches."

But the Persian vehicle did not slow as it drew near. If the driver even noticed the stranded Jews, he did not stop to help.

There were fireworks to see, and wine to drink in the center of town. The tall white horses shot past, pulling their regal passengers to the sting of an eager whip.

Nothing could be more important than a party.

3

A princely wedding was like practice for a coronation. It would be nine more years before young Xerxes took the throne, but his prayer to marry Vashti before another 12 months elapsed had been granted. It was an auspicious occasion, calling for all the grandeur and pomp the empire could muster, and it evoked images of the day he would be crowned.

Processionals featured the elitist corps of Darius' army, machines and weapons of war, flower-strewn carriages, bevies of dancers and high-stepping horses, orchestras and bands, and wagons of gifts for the bride and groom.

The festivities would last for weeks. Though only the most privileged friends of the palace would actually witness the nuptial rites, Darius had proclaimed a reduction in taxes, release of all but the most criminal of prisoners, and a six-month rest for his troops in training.

But Mordecai was not prone to celebrate. In the darkened chamber which had once been his own bedroom, his uncle lay in a fitful sleep, unable to walk steadily or even sit for long since the blow to his head.

The accountant had seen to it that the best physicians outside the palace of Susa were made available to Abihail. But the man was old, and had only recently sustained a great loss. Though he had much to live for in his new daughter, without his wife life was bitter. The jolt of a head wound made recovery unlikely.

Leah and Moshe had returned reluctantly to their village, leaving Mordecai in charge of both the ailing uncle and the infant. But considering their limited resources, they knew Mordecai was better able to carry the burden.

Blasts of trumpets from a marching band roused Abihail. As always, his first waking thought was of Hadassah.

"She is well," the nephew assured him. "She is with the nurse."

"She should be with her mother," the elder groaned. "God above, why has my little one been put in such a strait?"

Mordecai rarely addressed the Almighty personally. Religion was best left to the rabbis and the synagogues, he reasoned. His uncle's bold conviction that Jehovah really heard, and furthermore cared, had always intrigued him. But it was good that Abihail had his faith, since he had little else in this world.

The nephew stepped near the elder's bed. Noting his perplexed glance toward the window, he was quick to explain the sounds rising from the street.

"Prince Xerxes is getting married today," he said with a smile. "All of Susa celebrates."

Abihail was not impressed with the events of Persian royalty. "A marriage of convenience, I suppose," he muttered. "Some nobleman social-climbing on the head of his daughter."

"Not this time, I hear," Mordecai laughed. "It seems that Xerxes truly loves his bride. They have been betrothed since childhood."

Abihail leaned his head back with a sigh. "Well, and what of you, son?" he asked. "Have you ever loved a woman?"

"Not to my knowledge," the bachelor grinned. "I have had no time for such things."

"You should marry," Abihail insisted. "It would do you good. And Hadassah . . . she needs a mother."

Mordecai knew he alluded to the possibility of her being orphaned. He had tried not to admit the eventuality. He had tried not to think of his own responsibility toward the child should she be left alone.

Changing the subject, Mordecai referred to the men who had put the child's future in jeopardy.

"I have reported to the palace police what happened on New Year's Eve, Uncle. I am assured that they will look into the matter, although since the culprits were Haman's boys we may never see justice."

The old man was not surprised. "It is futile to hope we could. Tell me, who is this Haman?"

"The highest of the king's advisers. And yet he is not even a Persian, I hear. He is an Agagite, a crafty one, who has won his way to the top through many lucrative decisions."

Abihail sat up suddenly, pricked by something in the revelation.

"An Agagite?" he scowled. "He calls himself this?"

"Yes," Mordecai shrugged. "He seems proud enough of the fact."

Wondering why Abihail should take the information so seriously, he listened as the old Jew recounted a bit of Israelite lore.

"King Saul, your ancestor, once had a run-in with an Amalekite named Agag. Do you recall the incident?"

Mordecai shook his head, hoping that the history lesson would be brief.

"The father of the Agagites, Haman's ancestor, he would be."

Again the younger Jew nodded. The story would be a long one, he feared, and how it could possibly bear on their own time he could not imagine.

"The Lord Jehovah had told Saul to utterly destroy the Amalekites—men, women, children, cattle, and all. But Saul took mercy on Agag, their king, and even took the spoil from the vanquished enemy—something which God said he must not do."

Mordecai stifled a yawn. The day was very hot, and he wished he might be with the other Susaites, observing the parade outside the window.

As the musicians of Darius' court marched past, row upon row of them, Abihail's voice droned on, mixing with the rhythmic drums and lulling Mordecai half asleep.

"No end of trouble have the Amalekites been all these years!" he insisted. "The blood-feud has never ceased, except for those who do not remember."

The young accountant supposed he referred to his like, for he had never known this tale. Most Jews of his generation cared little for such matters. Only Abihail and his kind, the rabid orthodox, clung to such particulars as though they still mattered.

"I doubt that Haman knows the story either," he objected, rising from his lethargy. "So what difference does it make? If the animosity is gone from both camps, there is no war."

"Ah," Abihail argued, "but there you are wrong! This shows your shortsightedness. For Jehovah sees things in a timeless frame. He has never forgotten His promises to Abraham, though many of Abraham's children have done so. Nor has He forgotten that he swore enmity against Amalek, and that Israel is obliged to stamp him out."

Mordecai frowned incredulously. "Can you possibly believe that the command given to an ancient Israelite king devolves to his descendants?" he marveled. "Saul is dead, and Agag is dead. So it is ended!"

But Abihail was not dissuaded. Rising up from his bed, he declared, as though it were self-evident, "Saul failed! Therefore the order has been unfulfilled."

Mordecai paced the room now. Such reasoning was preposterous—the product of senility. But he would not argue impersonal theology with a sick old man.

"I think I hear the baby crying," he lied. "Rest, Uncle. The parade will be over soon, and you will be able to sleep."

With a knit brow, Abihail watched Mordecai's exit. Even in the hall beyond the darkened room, the young accountant could feel the elder's sad gaze against his back.

4

Slaves with large feathered fans stood in each corner of Darius' sumptuous council chamber, trying to keep the heat at bay. No breeze had passed between the columns of the porch all afternoon, nor had any movement of air parted the long linen curtains framing the sunlit veranda.

This was the king's private consultation room, one of several palace sanctums devoted to discussions of state. Today he and two of his generals, along with his vizier, met without his other ministers being present.

His son, Xerxes, was with them, however, just as he often was when they spoke of Persia's future. The prince sat erect in a straight-backed chair, hanging on every syllable of the conversation. For today Darius spoke of Greece.

While their great ancestor, Cyrus, had made an unprecedented move to wrest the Middle East from the Medes and Babylonians, consolidating the empire under one banner and founding what would become the greatest dominion on earth, Darius' genius lay in the fact that he completed the organization of the realm created by his predecessors.

From the extremities of the East to the rim of the Mediterranean he had expanded the empire, constructing a canal from the Nile to the Red Sea and even sending an expedition down the Indus to explore the Indian Ocean. For the first time ever there was a commercial waterway linking India, Persia, and Egypt, so that Darius' sovereignty was more vast than any which had gone before.

It was therefore fitting that he was known as "Darius, one king of many, one lord of many, the great king, king of kings, king of the countries possessing all kinds of people, king of this great earth far and wide."

But he was not content. He never would be until the Aegean and the Hellenistic world lay at his feet.

Some said a demon drove Darius. His forerunners had been great warlords. Cyrus had died fighting a savage Eastern race, and Cambyses had made bold attempts against Ethiopia. But Darius had been the first to invade the West.

Trekking into the Danube territory 22 years ago he had made the first historic attack of Asia on Europe. Sweeping through the Balkan hinterland, he crossed the great river on a bridge of boats, and though revolt among his own men ended the campaign in failure, the Greeks and Scythians could no longer consider the Persian dynasty a slumbering dog.

The men in the room today were privileged with a view of the harem courtyard, spread directly before them at the veranda's foot. Few men on earth were allowed to view the king's women. It was supposedly against the law for anyone to look upon his queen. But, though dozens of concubines and secondary wives sported in the pools and garden, the men rarely glanced their way.

Intensely involved in conversation, the generals leaned forward, riveted by the king's ambition. Otanes, Vashti's father, and Mardonius, the mightiest of Persia's military advisers, had much to gain by being here. And Haman, whose expertise lay not in war and weapons but in finance, could advance himself even further in the emperor's graces by wise contributions regarding the state of Persia's economy.

Years before, Otanes had proven his indispensable worth as a warlord when he had subdued Byzantium and her sister cities, securing the entire border between the Asian and European continents and bringing Persia's frontiers within easy distance of Greece.

In the meantime, several forays at Sardes, Miletus, Cyprus, and Caria had thrown victory from hand to hand between the Persians and Greeks. When a surprise nighttime maneuver had destroyed the entire Persian force at Caria, generals and all, the Westerners won a two-year respite by land and sea. Defeat of the Persian fleet at Cyprus and the army at Caria had forced the Persians into a palsied stance, and months had passed with no retaliation on Darius' part.

Perhaps today's meeting heralded a revival of courage on the king's part. Mardonius was hot for blood, and Otanes itched for the feel of the spear.

"How do you see the Greeks these days?" Darius asked his generals. "What are the reports from the Aegean?"

Mardonius cleared his throat and rubbed his hands upon his tight trousers. "The Greeks lack leadership. They are disunited," he replied.

Otanes nodded, adding eagerly, "They have not used their time well during these two years. There are no signs of movement against the sea. They seem to have been simply resting all these months."

The king smiled and leaned back into his throne. The consultants almost laughed with him, but they would not presume to do so just yet.

"They are at rest? But they won the last skirmish. Why would *they* need to recuperate?"

"Our successes have consistently outnumbered theirs, Your Majesty," Mardonius reminded him. "Their victories have been short-lived, or by surprise advantage. They know we could crush them if we had half a mind . . ."

Otanes fidgeted uneasily at this and Mardonius caught himself before he said too much. His suggestion bordered on the discourteous. No one dared impute cowardice to Darius.

Of course, all present knew the question should not have been why the Greeks had been "resting," but why Persia had made no offensive in the same length of time. This was Darius' matter alone, but all suspected that he had taken his fill of beatings at the hands of the Greeks, and was only now recovering.

The emperor scowled at Mardonius, and the general cast his gaze to the floor. When the king addressed Haman next, the warlord's flushed face began to cool.

"The treasury is adequate to an expedition?" Darius inquired.

Such a question! Did the emperor really wonder if the wealthiest coffers on earth could sustain a venture against the West? The generals glanced at one another covertly as Haman joined the talk.

Of course they knew the vizier had been invited only to give the final seal to the king's desires. Everyone knew there was no financial trouble in Persia. But Haman must make good his reason for being here.

"Your Highness has recently reduced taxes," he began. "They may need to be levied at the higher rate once more."

Xerxes shot a keen look in Haman's direction. The citizens of Persia had been granted a break in tribute and celebration of the prince's recent wedding. Was the vizier suggesting that the court had made a mistake?

Otanes, whose daughter was the object of the celebration, liked the insinuation no more than Xerxes. But he dared say nothing, as Haman was the king's favorite.

Darius did not always agree with Haman, however. Studying the young bridegroom fondly, he shook his head. "Taxes shall remain untouched for the time established," he asserted. And Otanes nodded to Xerxes, very pleased.

Haman kept his silence as Mardonius dealt with matters more important to the moment.

"We can engage a Phoenician fleet," he asserted, "and we can call upon contingents from Egypt, Cilicia, and Cyprus to invade Greek waters. All we need is time."

Xerxes' blood boiled with ambition as the commanders plotted their course. Perhaps one day, when he entered upon the throne, he would rule the Western world as well as the Eastern.

Surveying the harem through the consultants' bent heads, he imagined Vashti crowned with the jewels of Greece and Rome, Athens and Carthage.

He would give her half his kingdom. Whichever half she desired.

5

Mordecai, the Jew, stood upon his little veranda watching as the troops of Darius returned from war. He could see just enough through the narrow grates of his barred gate to tell him it was a sorry scene in the street tonight.

Hadassah, his adopted daughter, played at the feet of her governess, pulling at the tall stalks of lilies bordering Mordecai's modest garden. The music of the small fountain which babbled in his court was drowned out by the slow tramping of soldiers and the rhythm of funeral-like drums proceeding down the avenue. But the little girl, now three years old, was oblivious to the great dishonor received by Persia's troops at the hands of the Greeks.

Her father, were he still alive, would have told her that Darius had been retributed by the hand of God, that it was Jehovah who had seen to Persia's defeat due to its greed and materialism.

He would have told her that the 6400 Persian dead at Marathon, versus only 192 lost on the Greek side, was reminiscent of the battles of the Hebrews at Jericho and Abraham at Dan. He would have told her that such things do not happen without supernatural intervention. After numerous victories in the Aegean region, and the taking of whole cities of Greek slaves, the Persians had seemed invincible. God had a way of laughing last, Abihail would have told her. The old man had died shortly after coming to Susa, however. So now there was no one to teach Hadassah the deepest things of Judaism.

But the fact that Mordecai was weak on religious training was no indication of his feelings toward the child. The tiny girl had filled a spot in the stubborn bachelor's heart which he had not known was vacant. With the passing months, as he had seen her take her first steps and learn her first words, his affections had expanded.

Along with this came a distinct antipathy toward Haman, the man whose underlings had orphaned the child. When, as Abihail had predicted, nothing was done by the palace police to bring justice against the young men, Mordecai had found himself increasingly doubtful of Persian policy toward the Jews, and especially skeptical of the grand vizier. Though generations ago King Cyrus had emancipated the Hebrew people, it seemed that justice was still elusive.

Nonetheless, Mordecai rarely considered Abihail's adamant assertions concerning the "sons of Agag." The old man's view of history and nations was too ludicrous to be taken seriously.

The only heritage of value given him by his uncle was the curly-haired child who clutched now at his robe. In her tiny dimpled fist she held forth a long-stemmed lily, offering it to Mordecai.

"A scepter befitting a queen," he said with a grin, as he reached down for her and lofted her to his shoulder. Pointing to the bedraggled spearmen who marched past the gate, he teased, "Poor, poor warriors. Perhaps if you had touched them with your wand, Hadassah, they would have come home victors."

* * *

King Darius longed to revenge the rebuff at Marathon. He longed to annex Greece. His most restless neighbors would have made his most useful subjects. But the king whose empire had spread as far as possible to the east, north, and south would not live to recoup his Western losses.

Five years after the defeat in the Aegean, Darius was dead. Whether he was a good or an evil man would remain forever open to debate. As for Xerxes, he would do well to emulate his father in many things. And from the start, as he watched the funeral procession of the fallen monarch, he determined to do so.

The 27-year-old prince rode this evening in a golden carriage behind the black-shrouded wagon which bore his father's corpse into the Zagros Mountains. Far behind lay the glow of Susa, coral in the setting winter sun. Beside him sat his wife, her hand resting lightly upon his knee.

Before Darius' body would be interred in the ancestral tombs at Persepolis, his spirit would be committed to Ahura-Mazda, god of the sky.

It had to be said of Darius that, though he was devoted to this one deity, he gave amazing latitude to the other religions of his diverse subjects. Imitating Cyrus, he even saw to it that the temples and worship of all gods were subsidized by the state.

But when it came to his private devotions, the god embraced by Zoroaster, famed and obscure prophet of the Zagros, was his sole focus. His religion did not call for much art or architecture. No soaring temples lifted the minds of the faithful to the deity. Sufficient were small fire altars atop lofty peaks in the untamed wilderness of Persia's barbaric ancestors.

Through the dusk Xerxes and Vashti could see the curl of gray smoke ascending from one such pyre lit at the crest of the jagged, snow-covered horizon. The flash of burning coals was visible, and behind the pale light, which intruded even at this distance into the darkness, they could make out the silhouettes of the magi, men of the priestly caste, who would offer up Darius' soul.

Certain elements of Persia's religion lingered from the time before Zoroaster's teachings, from the time of the Aryans, ancient animists who had once inhabited the hinterland. Though Zoroaster had recognized no nature worship, some customs died hard.

In keeping with those old traditions, therefore, Darius' body would be exposed to the mountain frost until sunrise, while the magi spread the flesh of a small sacrifice upon a carpet of herbs and burned it to the chant of a theogony.

Already the haunting drone of the hymn was borne on the cool wind descending from the peak. Xerxes felt a chill cross his shoulders, but would not admit to his wife that he found the priests and their rituals an eerie combination.

The shadow of a hawk crossed the icy moon directly above the prince's path as the carriage driver urged the horses higher. A good omen or bad? he wondered. The priests, who studied such matters, would have known, for they saw omens in everything.

Xerxes lifted his regal face to the mountain. Pale silver light illumined his noble features and played against his crimped beard like the hoarfrost of venerable age. He was, in fact, feeling far older than 27 tonight. The knowledge that tomorrow he would receive the imperial crown was a weighty burden. Perhaps with daylight he would feel the joy of power and prestige unequaled in the world. But tonight, grief and responsibility pressed him down.

Cradling Vashti's small hand in his own, he glanced down at her supple fingers, the warmth of her touch strangely saddening him. Dependent she was, as a bird. His most prized possession, though he possessed all things.

As the refrain of the priestly chorus reached them, tears rose to his eyes.

"Ahura-Mazda, who upholds the earth and the firmament," it rang, "who causes the moon to wax and wane, who yokes swiftness to wind and cloud, who creates light and dark, sleeping and waking, morning, noon, and night . . ."

If there were a god in heaven, a father-god, he would surely fit this description, Xerxes believed. But tonight he knew only emptiness. On the eve of his coronation he felt inadequate to his calling.

At last the little processional reached the zenith of the hill. With careful hands the priests pulled back the dark shroud which concealed Darius' prone form, and then, in memory of the days when a corpse would have been left for the dogs and vultures, they ceremonially tore his neckline.

Xerxes stared into the air above his father's frigid body, almost hoping to see the spirit thus released. Such thoughts he kept to himself, shamed by their childishness.

But when the chant began again, and when the flames of the sacrifice leapt renewed into the coolness, his throat was tight.

"Ahura-Mazda," the chorus swelled, "who created this earth, who created yonder heaven, who created man, who created welfare for man . . ."

Scarcely could he bear to hear more. Though it was not dignified to do so, he clung to Vashti's hand and lifted it to his lips. The nearness of her at this needy moment, the availability of her love, filled him with hope.

Perhaps he could be what he must be.

The priests and the entourage of courtiers were fixed on the spectacle of ritual and invocation. They would not see if the prince were to hold her close.

Pressing her head to his breast, he touched his lips to her soft dark hair.

"Precious," he whispered. "My most precious possession."

PART II
Pride Before a Fall

6

"A tax farmer!" Mordecai bellowed. "I have heard it with my own ears. Haman is a tax farmer!"

Leah stood over the pan of dirty cups and utensils, cleaning up after yet another meal. Her children, all teenagers or nearly so, had accomplished their afternoon chores and had taken off for various parts of the village. She, looking forward to an evening of adult conversation, listened eagerly to Mordecai's palace gossip.

Her brother, within the first two years of the new administration, had risen from merchant's stockkeeper to executive of inventory in the royal house. She had always been proud of Mordecai, but never more than now.

"So how did you learn this?" she marveled. "Do you have access to Haman's books?"

"Not directly," he explained. "But there are few secrets among the management. Haman weasled his way into Darius' graces years ago by buying up provincial concessions."

"He is a tax collector, then," she sneered.

"More than that. A tax *farmer* actually pays an annual lump sum for the right to bleed the public. He does not just earn a commission. He pays such a high rate for the privilege that he is allowed to keep the entire collection! Can you imagine the returns? Enormous!"

Mordecai slapped his thighs and threw his head back. "Tens of thousands of talents!" he sighed.

Leah shook her head. "Then our tax monies, given by the sweat of our brows, do not even go to the royal treasuries?"

"Oh, be assured, the king makes a haul off the bidders. He does not sell the concessions for a song. With several sharing the rights to each province, he makes as much as or more than the taxes would bring in. And the competition between the concessionaires . . ." Here he pounded a fist into his open palm. "They would kill to beat one another out."

Leah pulled the wet dishes from the suds and rinsed them in another bucket. "Folk have been known to murder for less."

Mordecai knew she referred to the wanton violence directed against Abihail. Rising from the low stool in her kitchen, he walked to the little window which looked across the fields east of the village. The snow-capped Zagros Mountains loomed majestic and protective above the sweeping valley.

Mordecai loved Persia, but often, as Hadassah had grown, he had found his mind turning to the teachings of his uncle, especially to his tales of Israel, passed down from his own father and his before him.

He wondered if Israel were as beautiful as the land of his birth. And he wondered if he had missed out on something wonderful by passing off his heritage so lightly.

In the flowered field beyond the low town gate, village children played. Hadassah, now ten years old, ran with the smallest as they mimicked the adult game of goat-drag, riding sticks like horses and hauling a stuffed burlap bag from stake to stake on a miniature playing field. Never was the girl happier than when she visited her second cousins, the energetic offspring of Mordecai's sister.

As the accountant watched her run through the ankle-high grass, her slender legs kicking up dust and her long raven curls bouncing, he knew he would do best by the child to afford her more exposure to the Jewish community.

"She is nearly a young lady . . ." he mused.

Leah, surprised by the new topic, glanced with him out the window. "You are only now noticing?" she teased. "Look over there," she pointed, indicating her 15-year-old firstborn son, who leaned against the gate cavalierly. "David has certainly noticed already."

Mordecai nodded, a smile working at this lips. "I would like to bring her here more often," he requested.

"Of course!" Leah offered. "You know we all enjoy her!"

"Then it is settled," the brother determined. "It would be good for all of us to keep closer ties. I would like her to visit at least twice a month. She would be no trouble. I will pay you . . ."

"Nonsense!" Leah protested. "*Pay*, for *family*? I won't hear of it. And, of course she is obedient! Docile as a doe!"

Turning for her dishpan again, she bustled to finish her work before sunset, shaking her head and muttering exasperation about brothers and about men in general.

* * *

Indeed David, the eldest of Leah's children, *had* noticed Hadassah. She had always been a comely child, and now, as she approached young womanhood, her charms were of another sort.

Sitting cross-legged on the ground, his back against the gate-post, he watched her keenly as she sported with the younger children of the neighborhood. Mordecai had never allowed her to wear her hair twisted and fettered, as so many of the haughty girls of Susa wore theirs. For this David was never more grateful than at this moment as it swung free in the breeze, glancing against her rosy cheeks and caressing her back with brown-black waves. Where the descending sun caught it, auburn-to-red tones revealed themselves amid the curls tumbling about her shoulders.

Nor had Mordecai ever allowed Hadassah's hair to be cut. Though it was trimmed fashionably about the face, it flowed to her midback and bore no ribbons or pins.

Pale lavender gowns were unusual in the small hamlet where David had been raised. The fact that Hadassah's simple dress was out of this hue, and was girded with a fine linen rope, marked her as one of Susa's upper middle class. Whenever she came to visit the village, younger children stood in awe of her as much for this fact as for her unusual beauty.

Always their star-struck gazes mellowed to open smiles, however, when the gentle girl took them by the hands and began to play with them.

Just now, as the stuffed burlap bag (the pretend goat) was carried by an opponent toward the enemy's goal, she raced after the rider, not as quickly as she might, but fast enough to give him a challenge. From behind came another opponent on chubby legs, grasping for her to take her to the ground.

He succeeded only in snapping the belt about her slender waist, breaking the clasp on her fine-carved alabaster buckle.

Squealing, Hadassah wheeled about and confronted the challenger, feigning more offense than she felt.

As she bent over to pick up the broken treasure, David leapt to his feet and ran to her. "Let me see," he offered, touching her lightly on the arm. When she rose to find her cousin brooding over her, a blush rose to her cheeks.

Handing the buckle to him, she said nothing. As he turned the ornament over and over in his hands, she was struck by the glints of gold within his azure eyes.

"This is a very fine piece," he marveled.

"Papa gave it to me," she said, finding her voice.

David nodded. "It must be a pleasure to give you fine things," he said.

Hadassah was not too young to detect the admiration in his tone. But not being trained in worldly ways, she did not know how to respond.

"It is a Greek design, is it not?" David observed, still contemplating the jewel.

"I believe so," Hadassah replied, surprised at his apparent knowledge of such things, and not really certain herself of the artistic origins.

"We have Greek blood in our veins as well as Jewish," he went on. "Did you know this?"

Hadassah recalled Mordecai's allusions to the family's mixed roots. "Such a thing is not unusual," she replied.

"No," David agreed.

But when Hadassah saw that he was proud of the fact, she quickly added, "Of course, you have acquired the look as well as the blood."

The young man straightened his shoulders and lifted his strong chin. He had hoped she noticed, and that she approved. Blond hair and blue eyes were rare in Persia, and had won him the admiration of many village girls.

"I think I can fix this for you," he asserted. "I am an artist in my own right, though I shall likely always be a farmer."

Hadassah was touched by his youthful frustration. "Papa left the village to work in Susa," she reminded him. "Aunt Leah says you are gifted with carving and painting. Perhaps . . ."

"No," David said again. "I am needed too much here."

The girl looked at the brothers and sisters who had congregated at David's back. They had come out from the house to call the two cousins home.

Darkness was descending quickly now, as it always did in the desert. As the family walked toward Leah's warmly lit house, Hadassah knew that David spoke the truth. His parents would require his assistance for a long time. He might never be able to pursue a career beyond the village gate.

Though she was very young, Hadassah felt a peculiar stirring in her as she followed David's manly lead back to the cottage. It was not the first time she had felt it. She had not failed to notice his ruddy strength and field-hardened physique. His golden hair and eyes only added to his appeal.

He still held the buckle in his artistic fingers. She watched him study it as they walked. No words passed between them, but Hadassah stayed close to his elbow.

7

In following Darius' love of Ahura-Mazda and his prophet, Zoroaster, Xerxes had departed from his father's ways in one unusual respect: He had chosen to have no harem, but to honor a monogamous relationship with his beloved wife, Vashti.

Zoroaster had taught that the highest good was symbolized between humans in faithful love for one's spouse. Where Persian kings turned from this injunction, they deviated from the noblest path.

As soon as Xerxes had taken the throne, he set about to send the women away, seeing to it that they were endowed with gifts of precious metal, fabrics, and spices so that they might have means of support. He could do nothing about the fact that many of them, no matter how lovely they might be, would never find a husband. Virginity was highly prized in a bride, something none of them could claim. And to have lived under the same roof as the king, though supposedly an honor, had marked them as "soiled" women.

Harem girls, once turned away, would not even qualify as widows, but would be considered "scorned" women, rendering them even less valuable.

Still, Xerxes could not help this. It was better to remove them, he reasoned, than to maintain secondary wives against the teachings of his faith.

Hadassah had been allowed this morning to enter the outer rim of buildings in the palace area. Mordecai was in charge of an inventory tour through the storehouses of the acropolis, and he had brought his adopted daughter with him for the day, leaving her to enjoy the sights as he escorted his young accountants about their assignments.

Never had the girl been privileged to see the inner workings of the royal compounds. Of course, nothing private to the king's family transpired in the utilitarian courts enclosing the monarch's private palace. Nonetheless, it was an honor for her to be here.

Mordecai was presently inspecting the second floor of the royal warehouse where the king kept his most prized gold pieces. Resting in cases of velvet were tiny trinkets shaped like striding lions, miniature bulls, and birds of prey. Each was worth more than its weight in artistic beauty alone. Thousands upon thousands of delicate chains, bracelets, rings, and earrings sat unused in cedar boxes, the containers themselves worth a fortune.

Once a year the inventory must be recounted, valued, and polished. This was not the rule of a miser, but rather the wisdom of a long line of Persian kings who, despite their wealth, kept careful books. For the managers of the coffers, the day the accountants came around was a tense time. If any treasure was missing, even the slightest piece, it could mean their lives.

Of course, Hadassah was not privy to her uncle's work. She had been permitted to ascend to the second story, but had been left outside the labyrinth of doors barring strangers from the treasury rooms.

The glory of even the limited area she observed, however, was enough to occupy her for hours. The shiny marble balcony, wide enough for two chariots, and the intricate carvings of the turquoise-inlaid mezzanine filled her with wonder. A small garden below, leading to the outer gate of the compound, dazzled her with poppies, irises, flamingos, and fountains. Were she never to see another inch of the acropolis, her memory would be entertained for a lifetime.

When the sound of soft voices caught her attention, she stood poised at the rail, marveling at beauty even more splendid than the surroundings. Half-a-dozen women had entered the little gateway garden. In flowing silken gowns they passed beneath Hadassah's gaze, slender as flower stalks. The girl had seen lovely ladies in Susa's streets, but none so glamorous as these. Soft hair of various hues framed faces that no artist could have conceived. Yet great art was evident in arched eyebrows, blushed cheeks, and red lips. Paint accentuated eyes already large by nature, shading and highlighting flawless complexions.

While each lady had individual charm, they were more alike than not. Hadassah was not too young to realize that these must be women of the king's harem, all selected to suit the taste of one man.

Long of limb and graceful as willows, most of them were quite tall. In carriage and in form they could have passed for sisters, though their skin tones told that they were of different nationalities. The young girl did not know much about the world, but she had heard of Babylon and Africa and India, and figured that these women represented such farflung places.

Captivated, she observed them with the same fascination that the village children exhibited whenever she herself graced their humble town.

But, while she would have expected great happiness to accompany such beauty, these ladies appeared anything but cheerful.

Tears smudged charcoaled eyes and heavy sorrow contorted winsome lips. A few of the women had locked arms, as though for support, and muffled weeping rose from the group.

As the klatch of women crossed the garden, drawing near the door to the outer world, several began to wail miserably. On the instant, a stern-looking character entered behind them.

"Such clatter will not be tolerated!" he growled, his bald head flushed crimson from ear to ear. It seemed he would strike at them, and Hadassah knew he could send them all sprawling with a blow, for he was a big, meaty man, his bare biceps sporting bracelets which would fit a harem girl's waist.

Falling against each other, the ladies cried out and then stifled themselves.

Suddenly the sound of quick footsteps approaching from the corridor halted the bully. The women dried their eyes, falling to their knees, just as he did.

The footsteps heralded the approach of another woman, who stood now in the doorway. Hadassah, peering down between the banister posts, could not have imagined anyone more beautiful than the girls who huddled together. Yet the newcomer to whom they made obeisance was even more ravishing.

"Your Majesty . . ." the hulking fellow cried, "live forever!"

The young spectator deduced immediately that it was the Queen of Persia who stood beneath her gaze. And her small-girl heart tripped with awe.

All her life she had heard of Vashti. She had heard of her great beauty, but she had never dreamed she would one day see it for herself.

It was not Vashti's clothing, nor the style of her hair, nor the flair of her cosmetics which set her apart. Rather, it was her bearing, her noble demeanor, her look of certainty, which elevated her.

Ignoring the fawning man at her feet, she hastened to the cowering women, whose tears for now were fearfully contained.

"Stand, sisters," she commanded.

The ladies, confounded, did so. Then the queen glared at their keeper, who had not dared to look up from the floor.

"Angus!" she confronted him. "Have I not spoken with you about your handling of the harem? You shall treat these women with the same respect they merited when Darius was their lord."

Since the behemoth was being addressed, he knew he must rise and face the queen. How to account for himself he knew not. Vashti realized that any vulnerable female was a temptation to his cruel nature. But he had been raised to his position, keeper of the concubines, by Darius. And, while this station would terminate as soon as the women were removed, only Xerxes, and not Vashti, could send him from the palace.

Nonetheless, he must treat the queen with respect or else lose his head, if not further employment.

"Your Majesty, the women are contrary," he lied. "They require a firm hand."

At this the ladies, who had done nothing amiss, turned defensive eyes to the queen.

"I think they have done no wrong," Vashti interposed. "See that *you* do nothing but your proper job."

Then, clapping her hands, she went toward the hall door and summoned a small train of servants.

Once again the girl on the balcony had reason to marvel as a cohort of slaves entered the garden, each bearing a trayload of luxuries.

Flasks of jasmine, gold necklaces, cakes of myrrh and aloe, sachets of spices, and jeweled bracelets were piled upon broad silver dishes. Hadassah did not know much about the worth of such finery, but she was sure Mordecai would value it at a very great price.

The women, awestruck as each was handed her own trayful of treasure, reacted as though the offerings were worth a lifetime of acquisition.

Trembling, some of them refused the gifts, scarcely believing the queen could mean such generosity. But at last, as Vashti implored them, they conceded, tears dripping down their faces.

"These should stand you in good stead until you can establish yourselves," she explained.

Establish themselves? Hadassah thought. *They should never have to lift a finger the rest of their lives!*

"Though the king has foregone more than one wife," the queen went on, "he would not send you forth into poverty."

"But, Your Highness," one of the girls objected, "these are from your *own* storehouse! They are not a man's treasures."

"Hush, Darla," another softly warned. "You have not been addressed."

But the queen took no notice. Clapping again, she sent the servants away.

"Take them forth now, Angus," Vashti commanded. "See that they all find lodging, and see to it that their treasures are put in safe keeping."

By this she referred to the fact that the poor women, unlearned in matters of investment, might abuse their endowments or, even worse, lose them to thieves within hours of leaving the grounds.

"I am your servant, Majesty," Angus replied, bowing as he led the ladies through the outer door.

Hadassah sat very still upon the balcony. The beauty of the women and the glory of the gifts had riveted her so that she could not pull away.

When Vashti had sent the slaves back down the hall she stood alone for a long moment, looking toward the door where the ladies had departed. Tears glimmered along her lashes, and the girl on the balcony held her breath, deeply moved by the queen's compassion.

What drew Vashti's gaze upward, toward the mezzanine, she would never know. But suddenly the sad eyes were upon Hadassah. The girl trembled, not knowing what punishment her eavesdropping might deserve.

Soon enough it was apparent, however, that the queen would dismiss the child's indiscretion. In her expression was only bemused surprise, as though she wondered how the young girl had come to be spying.

And then the expression turned to wonder. But Hadassah could not interpret this, for she did not fully appreciate her own charms.

Vashti did. The queen knew what loveliness was, seeing it every day about the courts and possessing it herself. The queen knew that, had this child been older, and a member of the harem, the king would have found it very hard to disown her.

8

Vashti observed the banquet preparations with mixed emotions. For a full three years Xerxes had been obsessed with plans to invade Greece. Once he had taken the throne, set his administration in order, and sent the harem away, he had turned his mind to the West with a vengeance that frightened his queen.

Now he was about to launch his expansionism, and to celebrate he had sent invitations to the 127 provinces under his rule, calling for the chief leaders and noblemen from throughout his empire to attend a six-month party in Susa.

Already thousands were arriving for the festivities, which would begin in a few days. 40,000 anticipated visitors would stay for varying lengths of time, arriving and departing throughout the festival.

Of course, the event would be honored by the entire city, as hostels and homes were opened to accommodate the influx. Local merchants rallied to prepare for the boost that such an event would be for the economy. People worked day and night to produce wares for purchase by the incoming tourists. From shoe merchants to jewelers, from bakers to perfumers, all made ready.

As for the palace itself, the inner court, or pavilion, would be the scene of the king's banquet. This open, colonnaded garden could be intensely hot in summer, but Xerxes planned to station a hundred slaves about the garden's numerous fountains, where they would fan the guests with imported ostrich plumes day and night.

Vashti stood upon the upper deck of the court, gazing across the sumptuous arboretum. Servants scurried amid flowering bushes and trees, arranging furniture and spreading pristine linens upon the tables. The colors decorating the extravaganza were of cool hues: Curtains of white, green, and blue were fastened to silver rings upon the marble pillars and were bound together by cords of royal violet. Chaises in the same fabrics were placed along the tables, their gold and silver frames resting upon decks of purple, blue, white, and gleaming black marble.

Xerxes had recently squelched insurrections in Egypt and Babylon. He had inflicted harsh penalties upon those states, leveling the Babylonian temple and melting to bullion their 1800-pound statue to Marduk.

These successes had piqued his appetite for further conquest, drawing his energies toward the West.

His wife, chief treasure of his heart, received less and less of his time as he pursued his dreams. It had begun in small things—tardiness to a rendezvous, the overlooking of an anniversary. Now their stolen moments were fewer and fewer, his attention span more fleeting.

Vashti had just come from the women's court, where her own banquet was being prepared. Only women of the palace, wives and daughters of the invited noblemen, would be attending her feast, which would likewise last for days. But it would be a tame, ladylike affair, unlike the boisterous and ribald merrymaking which would dominate the king's strictly male festivities.

As the headwaiter emerged from the palace's enormous pantry, leading a bevy of slaves, Vashti grew uneasy. Each slave hauled a small wheeled cart, piled high with gold drinking horns, every one of a different configuration, from winged griffins to strutting bears. This would be a drinking orgy unlike any held here before. And she hesitated to think of the excesses it would inspire.

Her husband had been busy all day with the governor of the feast, looking into the man's plans and adding to them. Vashti had not expected to see him this afternoon, and when he entered the court, across the way, she thought he might at last have a moment for her.

But it was not to be.

"Leave room along here," he was saying as the governor followed behind him. "Move in this row of tables so that my treasures may be paraded."

"Just so, Your Majesty," the governor agreed, clapping his hands and sending servants to reposition the furniture.

"The finest riches of the warehouse shall be brought forth for display, borne aloft upon silver trays or hauled in gilded barrows," Xerxes continued, his voice trailing down the hall.

Could he mean it? Vashti marveled, wondering at his compulsive pride. Such an exhibition could take weeks!

Once, she recalled, she had been considered his most precious possession. But today he had not even seen her standing alone, waiting for him.

Sadly she turned for her chamber, fearing another night without him.

9

Lights danced in the court of King Xerxes, potted candles on bobbing trays borne high on the shoulders of slaves, who dipped to serve as they wove between tables and couches.

It was the last week of Xerxes' feast, the evening of the seventh day. At least a thousand men had been served in the garden since morning, congregating in shifts to celebrate the culmination of half a year of merrymaking.

This was the final spate of excess, capping the previous six months of orgiastic feasting and drinking which had entertained notables from about the empire. And this week was reserved for the king's own, those who served his personal and state needs, from janitors to cabinet officials, in the palace itself.

As the candles spun a hypnotic web about the guests, the music of pipes and lutes and timbrels evoked enchanting delirium.

Of course, so did the wine. By pitchers and casks and buckets it flowed—into the golden chalices shaped in many shapes, down the mouths and throats of ten hundred laughing men.

"To Xerxes!" the toast rang, followed by clanking rims of tankard on tankard. "To Persia!" "To Mardonius!" "To Otanes!" "To War!" chased by clinks and gulps and cheers.

Jokes flowed too, and dares and taunts and jibes. From time to time, females imported from about the king's immense realm danced and teased and cavorted. They were not women of the palace, the king having removed his harem, and the ladies who now graced the ground of Vashti's banquet, wives and daughters of palace officials, would have been offended at such an invitation.

The fleshy bouquet of scantily clad dancers greeted an increasingly lusty crowd each time they were summoned, their presence stirring the room to ever-higher pitches of demand and appreciation.

Between the pageantry of the women appeared precisioned jugglers, hilarious clowns, and dexterous acrobats for the audience's pleasure. All the while, as the wine flowed and the delicacies of the king's kitchen were gorged upon, the treasures of the monarch were paraded in the background—furs never worn, cutlery and weaponry never brandished, diamonds and jewels never sported, fabulous works of art, and rare birds and animals from every corner of the empire.

For half a year these valuables had been displayed through the court, and now as the party was winding down, the king, besotted, gazed upon the end of their procession with heavy-lidded eyes.

He was deliciously relaxed as he lay back upon his chaise, high upon the uppermost deck of the court. But his closest valets, who knew him best, could see that he grew restless.

His plans to go against the West, hinted at numerous times in the previous six months, had finally been heralded privately before his own palace cohorts. Now he seemed anxious for action.

As clearly as he could think in his drunken condition, he tried to imagine some very spectacular way to climax this final evening of the most elaborate celebration which the world had ever seen.

His valets, middle-aged eunuchs with smooth faces and boyish voices, congregated at his back, sensing his regal agitation.

As the monarch rose upon one elbow, resting his pensive face upon his fist, he gestured for Mehuman, his chief valet, and the gaunt fellow hastened forward, bowing to the ground.

Xerxes, scarcely looking at him, stroked his head and patted him upon the cheek. "These are all my very best friends," he slurred, tears in his royal eyes as he scanned the loud revelers below.

"Yes, Your Majesty," Mehuman agreed.

"I have done so little for them," the king remorsed, weaving a bit upon his bed.

"But, sir," Mehuman objected, "you have reserved the finest for these folk. This week has been the highlight of the year."

"No, no," Xerxes insisted, flicking a long hand in the eunuch's peach-clean face. "They deserve more—something I have done for no one else, and shall never do again."

By now the other valets, nervous over the king's unhappiness, had gathered behind Mehuman. Biztha, Harbona, Bigtha, Abagtha, Zethar, and Carkas pressed close to the chief eunuch's bowed form, and each in turn received a stroke upon his bent head from the unusually affectionate emperor.

"What can we do for His Majesty?" they inquired, seeing that he was determined to have something.

"His Majesty desires to grace these revelers with some extraordinary benevolence," Mehuman explained. "He has shown them his treasures and bestowed upon them royal gifts, the finest wines and rarest delicacies from his larder. Yet he wishes to do more."

"Such is the nature of His Majesty's generous spirit," Harbona purred.

"Most Benevolent Lord," Zethar offered, "perhaps a tour of your grounds . . ."

"They have all seen the grounds!" Mehuman quickly corrected, seeing Xerxes' furrowed brow.

"Rings for their fingers," Carkas suggested.

"He has given fine jewelry to them all!" Mehuman replied, gesturing to a thousand braceleted arms and necklaced breasts.

In a huddle, the valets continued to confer but came up with nothing. At last Mehuman, frustrated, shrugged and said, "Your Highness, we can imagine nothing which you have not already given. You have bestowed food for their lips, wine for their hearts, song for their ears, women for their eyes . . ."

At this Xerxes lurched forward, his crimped beard quivering as his head shook. "No, no!" he cried. "I have been selfish! There is yet one thing I have withheld from my friends, from those who would give their life's blood for me!"

The king exaggerated, not about his generosity but about the loyalty of his companions. However, Mehuman dared not challenge his wine-dazzled estimation.

"All the women in the world would not be enough to honor my dearest allies," Xerxes enthused. "Had I given them my harem, it would not have been sufficient!"

Xerxes rode high on the excitement of six months, on the daring of future campaigns and on the praise of his plans for expansion. He soared on wings of wine and the sound of laughter swelling up from the court.

His multitude of comrades did not attend to him just now, for they were busy with the licentious freedom of the seven-day fling. Never would they or his valets dream that he was about to break one of the most stubborn taboos of his ancestors for their sake.

"Only one woman can do justice to the king's desire. Only Vashti herself, my chief treasure, is good enough for such friends!" Xerxes declared.

Mehuman drew a sharp breath.

"You cannot mean . . ."

"Bring her forth!" Xerxes commanded.

Suddenly a pall of silence overtook the eunuchs. The guests below, ignorant of the proposition, went on with their hilarity unimpeded. But the valets were appalled.

"Your Highness," Harbona dared to remind him, "it is the law that no man apart from the emperor himself is to look upon the queen."

Yes—this was the law. It was impossible that she would be spared the gazes of all men whatsoever, exposed as she was to life in the palace, but the spirit of the injunction applied against men looking upon her to lust after her.

Still, Xerxes darted a threatening glance at the disapproving Harbona.

"Am I a child, that my eunuchs are my counselors?" the emperor snarled. "I said, 'Bring her forth!' "

"Your Majesty, how shall we summon her? What shall we say?" Mehuman hedged.

"Say, 'Your husband desires your presence in the garden!' " Xerxes replied, his tone tinged with sarcasm. "What do you suppose you should say?"

"Do you simply wish for her to appear? And nothing more?" the valet hoped.

Xerxes, reading his apprehension, grew impatient. "What evil do you imagine of me?" he said with a glare. "Tell the queen to place the royal crown upon her head, so that all the men may gaze upon her beauty! She is a very beautiful woman!"

Mehuman bowed, agreeing utterly with his assessment, but still uneasy over the results of such an appearance before this disorderly mob.

"If you feel this is wisdom . . ."

"Are you questioning my sagacity or my sobriety?" Xerxes smirked, leaning cavalierly upon his pillow. "Go now!"

Mehuman glanced at his fellow eunuchs, his face full of doubt.

But, failing to dissuade the king, and knowing that he dare not try again, he bowed and left the chamber.

The other six eunuchs did likewise; following their master, they scrambled for the hall.

"Can he mean it?" Abagtha marveled.

"He means it," Mehuman sighed. "And we shall comply, though I fear going before the queen with this request more than I fear defying the king."

10

With nearly as much expense and finery, Vashti had entertained the ladies of the kingdom since the beginning of the year. This final week, she, like her husband, designated the celebration for the palace workers as well as for the wives, daughters, sisters, mothers, and grandmothers of the men who reveled in Xerxes' court.

But her banquet and her festivities were of a different sort than the wild abandon which characterized the men's party.

The ladies feasted on the daintiest of foods, the rarest of wines. But the temperament of the women's garden was marked with ladylike restraint.

The displays which the queen paraded for their viewing pleasure were not calculated to inflate their estimation of her own glory or wealth. She had scheduled dancers and musicians as well as jugglers and clowns and acrobats, just as had Xerxes, but their acts did not appeal to prurient interests and the occasional fashion show which edged the court was not a display of the queen's own garments and jewels but had been put together by experts who wished to show the latest in womanly attire for the interest and entertainment of the guests.

None of what Vashti presented was intended to arouse jealousy or to pique her own pride.

Nor would her guests dream of humiliating this sovereign lady by drinking to excess or by gormandizing on the delicacies she provided. Often she encouraged them to display their own talents, inviting this one to sing for the group or that one to tell a fetching story.

All in all, the scene in Vashti's court was a far cry in color and demeanor from that promulgated by her husband.

And the queen enjoyed it immensely. If any heavy thought tinged her pleasure, it was the realization that Xerxes had changed, the knowledge that what went on in his pavilion would have embarrassed herself and her guests had they been privy to it.

Just now she strolled with several of her companions along an arbor path, the scent of hyacinths and roses making a heady climax to a satisfying evening. Several hundred women lounged around the fountains of her retreat, listening to the entrancing notes of a flute and observing the fluid movements of a young dancer decked in trailing scarves. Surges of soft applause brought a smile to Vashti's lips as she conversed amiably with her closest friends, wives of prominent noblemen, daughters of the seven highest houses in the land, and sisters of her childhood.

When a slave came running, announcing the appearance at the garden door of Xerxes' eunuchs, Vashti was not a little surprised.

"They say they have a request for you, from His Highness, your husband," the messenger explained.

The queen's face lit with enthusiasm. It must be, she reasoned, that Xerxes wished to meet her after his grand celebration for a private rendezvous.

When she went to the door to receive the eunuchs, therefore, she was troubled to see their uneasy countenances.

"Your Majesty, live forever!" Mehuman cried, falling on his face before Vashti. The other valets, likewise bowed themselves to the floor, and when the queen asked them to rise, Mehuman's face was red.

"Queen Vashti," he stammered, "Our Lord Xerxes wishes us to convey an invitation . . ."

"Yes?" the woman spurred him.

"He wishes you to come before him . . ."

Aha, she had supposed right! He wished to have her private company this night.

". . . with the royal crown upon your head . . ."

The queen studied Mehuman in amazement. She never wore the heavy ornament except to make public appearances.

"Go on," she whispered.

". . . so that he might show you to his companions."

Vashti, scarcely believing her ears, surveyed the man with contempt.

"Say again," she commanded.

Mehuman summoned as much diplomacy as he could muster, and cleared his throat. "He wishes to bestow upon his friends the gift of your beauty, My Queen. He would have you appear before his servants and noblemen, that they may . . . gaze upon you."

The eunuch sighed. Try as he might, there was no graceful way to dispense with this duty. And when the royal lady evinced incredulity, her poise a poor covering for utter horror, he looked away shamefaced.

At this pronouncement Vashti's lady friends began to mutter among themselves, and quickly their astonishment caught the attention of others in the court, until the entire company of guests grew apprehensive.

The music ceased, the dancer stopped in her steps, and silence descended.

No queen of Persia had ever been placed in such a predicament. No matter how Vashti responded, her integrity was at stake.

It was beyond comprehension that a royal spouse would ever defy a king. Yet it was also inconceivable that a regal lady should expose herself to a crowd of drunken, leering males, be they friends of her husband or gutter vagabonds.

A queen was expected to be the epitome of wifely duty and purity. What she chose to do spoke to all women of the realm, and were she to disobey her lord and master, her actions could easily be misconstrued as condoning the undermining of male authority everywhere.

Indeed, Vashti was in a most uncomfortable and irresolvable dilemma.

The silence burned her ears as the scrutinizing gaze of a thousand eyes seared her back.

As she looked upon the man with the bowed head, time seemed to stand still. Her next words could mean life or death to her. Were she to actually refuse the king's invitation, she could lose everything.

Memories of Xerxes' coolness toward her, of his unthinking rejections over recent months, still haunted her. And she had no way of knowing just how cruel he might be if she were to resist his summons.

Yet it was a certainty that an appearance before the inebriated mob in his court would forever mar her own selfhood, stripping her of a dignity even more precious than Xerxes' esteem.

"Tell the king I shall *not* appear," she replied.

A rush of whispers and a rattle of shaking heads and conferring voices followed her words.

Some denied that she had said what she did. Others insisted that she had.

Mehuman himself, who had heard the words directly, trembled with wonder.

"Your Majesty?" he marveled.

"Tell the king I shall *not* appear," Vashti repeated.

Indeed, she *had* chosen disobedience! Like a flurry of chortling doves, a chorus of awe-filled commentary rose through the roofless air.

Gathering her silken robes in calm hands, Vashti departed the garden, her head held high, her back straight as an upright spear.

11

"She what?" Xerxes growled, leaping from his couch of pleasure and glowering at Mehuman.

Despite the loud partying which went on in the court below, guests turned in surprise at this sudden movement on the king's part.

Only the seven eunuchs knew the reason for his volcanic reaction. Only Mehuman and his cohorts knew of the ludicrous summons sent to Vashti.

"The queen refuses to appear," the chief valet repeated, cringing as though he himself might receive the full force of the king's anger.

Indeed, such a thing was not out of the question.

Messengers had been known to die at the whim of a dissatisfied monarch for bearing less sorry news than this.

Xerxes' fury pushed past his drunken lethargy, pulsating in clenched fists and throbbing temples. Face red, the emperor paced to and fro before his couch until every eye in the room was on him and not a sound of music, laughter, or even of breathing broke the air.

The eunuchs to Mehuman's back stood with bowed heads, cowering together like a pack of desert dogs, fearing that their fate, like Mehuman's, hung in the balance.

Meanwhile, seven other fellows, the king's legal counselors, began to draw near. Thinking that there must be some matter of politics, injustice, or threat against their master, they were eager to assist him.

"Your Majesty," their leader intervened, "what troubles you? May we help in any way?"

Xerxes, too flustered and wine-soaked to readily reply, only continued to pace his porch. At last Mehuman answered for him.

"Our Lord sent a summons to his queen, requesting that she appear at his party . . . so that all of the men might . . . gaze upon her."

Mehuman's own embarrassment was evident, though he tried to conceal it. And the attorney, Memucan, was caught in a hard place.

Not quite as inebriated as the emperor, he instantly understood the queen's reticence to comply. But at the same time he knew he dare not call the king's commandment into question.

Looking awkwardly at his fellow lawyers, he sought some suggestion, but they only shrugged, not wishing to touch the matter.

However, it was too late to withdraw an offer of assistance. And when Xerxes turned to them, his bloodshot eyes full of ire, it was their turn to cringe.

"So what shall we do about this situation?" the emperor demanded. "What penalty does the law provide for a queen who refuses to obey the king's orders, properly sent through his aides?"

Again Memucan looked to his fellow counselors. Did the emperor want an honest answer? In his drunken state, did he have any idea what he was asking?

The drama was now open to a thousand observers. What was decided here today would play heavily upon families throughout the empire. Most important to those present, it would play on the image of the king and the status of men throughout the realm.

Surely, were Xerxes in a more rational condition, matters would not have gone this far. Nevertheless, it was Memucan's responsibility to handle the king's legal affairs. Though this time he was not dealing in matters of criminal justice or interprovincial legislation, he had been asked a direct question. And it concerned issues perhaps equally as great as ones of imperial policy.

Shuffling uneasily, he fumbled for a reply. In truth, there was no specific injunction regarding this dilemma, and no precedent in Persian history, for no queen had ever thus defied her husband.

Naturally, uppermost in the counselors' minds was their own welfare. The advice they framed must appease the king's anger and bring them the best advantage.

Noting his retributive countenance, they knew that no soft action would suffice to save his pride. Vashti could be reprimanded and undergo some loss of privilege, but what if she were to disobey him in the future on some other matter? Surely the attorneys would pay dearly for not recommending a stiffer penalty. Furthermore, they were aware of the careful scrutiny which their advice would receive from other noblemen of the realm. If it were too gentle, it could appear to favor the undermining of men's authority in general.

Therefore, looking to their own futures, it was clear that their decision and their counsel must take a hard line.

They discussed this only briefly among themselves. All of them saw the implications of mercy all too well, and therefore their conference was brief.

While the emperor still paced his deck, wringing his hands and scowling at the courtiers who lined the walls, Memucan addressed his question adroitly.

"Your Majesty, live forever," he said, bowing before Xerxes. "My friends and I have considered the crime and have reached a conclusion."

"Speak!" the monarch bellowed, weary of delay.

"Queen Vashti has wronged not only the king, but every official and citizen of your empire. For women everywhere will begin to disobey their husbands when they learn what Queen Vashti has done."

At this a murmur of agreement arose from the besotted crowd, and so Memucan took courage.

"Before this day is out, the wife of every one of us will hear what the queen did and will begin to deal with her husband in like manner. There will be contempt throughout your realm."

Again a chorus of consensus rang from the court, and Memucan began to swagger with confidence.

"Therefore," he declared, "we suggest that, subject to your agreement, you issue a royal edict, a law of the Medes and Persians that can never be revoked, that Queen Vashti be forever banished from your presence and that you choose another queen more worthy than she! When this decree is published throughout your great kingdom, husbands everywhere, whatever their rank, will be respected by their wives!"

Because Memucan was more aware at this moment of the reaction of the crowd than of the king, he swelled with glory. He did not note the emperor's sudden halt, nor did the twinge of grief which passed over Xerxes' face reach his inflated spirit.

Few, in fact, heeded the monarch's mood, so taken were they with Memucan's daring.

Perhaps the valets, intimately acquainted as they were with their master, thought they read a less-than-enthusiastic expression on his face. But not one of them encouraged a rebuttal, fearing the authority of the counselors.

Of course, Memucan's advice was founded on the most bizarre logic. That every wife in the realm would begin to despise her husband based on Vashti's actions was pure paranoia, and that the crowd could embrace such an assumption was classic evidence of their alcohol-altered mentality.

But then, such was the mood of taverns late at night, the coveys of negligence and excess where men supported one another and where women were warned against. Such was the potential reasoning wherever wayward husbands gathered, and wherever families were scorned by guilt-ridden souls.

All of this might be clear in the light of day, when the haze of alcohol lifted and the clarity of sober thinking descended. But it was not clear now, and *now* was when the decision would be made.

Xerxes, though appalled by the advice, would never admit it under these circumstances. Though he could see its folly, even through besotted eyes, he could not speak against it before a thousand comrades.

He was a man, a man's man, a man of men. To soften now, even for the sake of Vashti, his "most treasured possession," was unthinkable.

As the company in the court looked to him for his reaction to the attorney's counsel, his face was a mask of unwavering strength. Behind it was the soul of a young boy, the one who had once stood with Vashti upon her father's balcony, who had promised always to cherish her, who had reveled in her love and thrilled to her caress. But the mask would win tonight, the love of men's approval, the insecurity which drove him always to conquest.

Hesitating only briefly, he looked at his valets, at the counselors, and at his many assistants. Not one gave argument against Memucan, and each, when pressed, colluded in the deception that he agreed, giving assent with a nod.

"Let it be," Xerxes said, his voice huskier than he wished.

And with this he turned for his private chamber for the comfort of another wine goblet and for the sanctuary of sleep.

12

As morning sun filtered past the heavy blinds of Xerxes' chamber, he rolled over with an ache in his chest. His head throbbed after days and nights of drinking. But the dull pain in his heart was more troubling than the hangover.

At first, as he struggled to sit erect, propping himself against his pillows, he could not recall why he should feel such heaviness. But as wakefulness replaced drugged stupor, recollection pierced him like a physician's scalpel.

"Vashti!" he groaned, staggering from his bed.

He was alone with the dim reality of what he had done the night before. As it settled over him in waves of irrefutable certainty, as the growing illumination that it was no dream, no nightmare, crashed in upon him, the ache in his breast brought tears to his eyes.

Limping to the window, he pulled back the curtain and stared into a high-noon desert. He had slept too long. His commandment would already have been fulfilled, and Vashti would have long ago been shunted from the palace.

Exiles of Persia could be sent to any number of wild and isolated places. In his besotted condition the night before he had made no formal selection of a site for her banishment, and he knew now that her fate had been left to the whim of whoever hauled her away.

"Almighty Ahura-Mazda!" he cried, falling to his knees. The bleak wilderness of the uncharted Zagros haunted him, beckoning with blunted fingers across miles of steamy mirage. "Where is she? Where is my beloved?"

But there was no retracting his judgment. There was no

reversing his command.

The one who had waited for his attentions night after night would wait no longer. For she could never be his again.

ESTHER

PART III

Descent of a Kingdom

13

Hadassah stood outside the village gate, gazing across the swaying grainfields. It neared sunset, and she knew that her cousin David would soon be returning from his daylong labor of scything ripe barley into sheaf-ready piles. She would wait here in the harvest gloaming, enveloped in twilight until he returned.

The sickles of a hundred workers had raised a fine dust through the evening air. The sun's setting was therefore a crimson blush, billows of coral clouds reflecting the same color that sailors see when they watch the golden orb descend through a veil of fog.

But there was no sea here—only endless miles of hot earth, fertile in the Zagros valley, but nevertheless a desert.

As Hadassah watched the returning laborers, their sweat-streaked bodies glistening in the pink light, many of them nodded to her, passing through the small town gate with words of greeting. No man among them failed to appreciate the fresh beauty of the teenaged girl, and it was safe to say that each bore a bit of envy for David, knowing that it was he who held her heart.

"He is not far behind," one elderly fellow acknowledged, smiling as she blushed and looked away. As soon as he was gone, however, she was on tiptoe, seeking the figure of her cousin in the suspended haze.

When at last she spied him, one of the very last to arrive, her heart stirred eagerly, though not without a twinge of sadness. Too often she read growing frustration in David's face. Eighteen he was, and bound forever, it seemed, to work the soil. His artist's soul had not died, though at times he surely wished it would so that he might find contentment with his lot and not continually wish for broader opportunities.

It had not escaped her, however, that when David was with her, the sadness lifted. Such was the case just now, as, coming upon her, his countenance lightened and a smile touched his lips.

Though Hadassah knew he resented his lot, she always considered him most beautiful when he returned from the fields. Always he was her golden boy, gold of hair and eyes, but never more than when he had put in a day beneath the sun, his skin bronzed and the fine chaffy silt of harvest clinging to his torso.

"Hello, Blossom," he greeted, lifting his heavy scythe higher on his shoulder, his free arm scooping her into a playful embrace. The term was one of endearment, playing with the meaning of her name, "Myrtle." As much as David was her goldpiece, she was his priceless flower. And though neither of them had ever revealed in words the depth of their caring, every action and every expression betrayed it.

"Cousin Leah says supper will be ready any moment," Hadassah said, laughing as he hugged her.

"We will be there in time," he replied. "Sit with me a while."

Drawing her aside, he guided her to a grove of gnarled palms which shaded a corner of the town wall and bade her rest with him in the little oasis.

"But aren't you very hungry?" she marveled, knowing that he usually rushed home for dinner like a starving prodigal.

"I am," he agreed, "and thirsty." At this he pulled from his belt a skin-bottle of warm wine and swigged it eagerly. Capping it, he sighed, "But I have not seen you for days. That is more important."

Hadassah had not visited the village for several weeks, for her papa was busy with the inventory of Vashti's abandoned possessions, stored in the queen's warehouse during this full year since her banishment.

It was a sad task, one put off all these months since her going, in deference to the king's wishes.

"I suppose the queen's inventory *could* take a while to count," David smirked, showing his disdain for the royal household.

"Yes," Hadassah nodded. "But Vashti was a good queen," she insisted. "A very good woman."

David noted the defensiveness that Hadassah always manifested when she spoke of the grand lady. Many times she had recounted the occasion when she observed Vashti's kindness firsthand. It had made a lasting impression upon her young mind, and David knew she admired the queen's refusal to accommodate the drunken king.

Mordecai had not been present at the banquet when Vashti was deposed, having attended during an earlier shift. But in his growing love of Judaism and skepticism of Persian politics he conceded that Jehovah would have honored Vashti's choice, and that her exile was a crime for which Xerxes would pay dearly.

"Where do you suppose she is?" Hadassah sighed, gazing wistfully across the desert.

David, sensitive to her tender feelings, knew the question reflected sincere concern for her heroine.

"I have heard there is a great highway," he replied, "running all the way to India—the silk route, plied by kingly caravans and fabled merchants. Have you heard this?"

"Yes," Hadassah answered, warming to the poetry in David's speech.

His eyes took on a faraway look, and she knew he pondered not just the queen's fate but also the many distant places which he could visit only in daydreams.

"She could have been taken that direction, to any of a hundred outposts along the way. Or," he continued, studying the bleak range which hemmed the valley, "it is said that years ago the royal house sent Greeks into the Zagros, captives taken by Darius when he passed into Europe. Perhaps the queen was sent to dwell with them."

Despite the heat Hadassah shivered, considering the irony of such a possibility. "But Xerxes plans war on the Greeks," she objected. "Surely he would not send his wife to live with the enemies."

David smiled fondly at the girl. "Can you think of a better punishment?" he asked.

Hadassah kicked absently at the dirt. "What a dreadful man the king must be!" she exclaimed, her face contorted with anger.

But David, wishing to lighten her mood, drew nearer, directing her to study the vast valley floor.

"On the other hand, "he offered, "perhaps she plays with the Quasqui."

"The Quasqui?" she repeated.

"Nomads of the plain," he said. "I saw them once when I was a small boy. My Papa took me on a trip to Ecbatana and we saw their encampment one evening, near the oasis where we slept."

His romantic soul surged at the memory, and he pulled Hadassah close as he recounted it.

"They live like kings in their own right, you know—summer homes and winter homes, mountains in the heat, valley in the cold. And they eat like kings, on roast wild partridge and grilled lamb livers, wafer-thin bread and fragrant tea, yogurt and skewered quail. They sleep on downy quilts and sing to guitars . . ."

Hadassah was breathless as he wove these images, entranced as much by his mesmerizing voice as by the word pictures he painted.

"I heard them sing a love song that night while they were camped about their fire. Beautiful it was!" he declared, taking Hadassah's hand in his.

" 'The tribe has left, the dust remains,' " he sang, his voice liquid and mellow. " 'The sun has gone, the yellow glow remains; I never kissed those dark eyes . . . the sorrow remains . . .' "

As he recited the last phrase, he gazed into the girl's open countenance with a strange sorrow, a sadness for which she could not account.

And her fingers trembled in his grip.

The sun was sinking fast, dark coming upon them all too quickly. Eyes closed, Hadassah tilted her head back. For a long moment David studied her supple lips, but then he suddenly stood, pulling her to him and bending over her with a hesitant sigh.

"We must be going now," he whispered, resisting the urge to kiss her. Turning, he led her back to the village.

After all, he told himself, she was a child of status and he was but a poor farmer. He thought it best not to love her.

14

Xerxes had spent four years preparing for his invasion of Greece. Shipbuilding alone had taken nearly a quarter of the imperial budget.

One thousand seaworthy vessels were launched from the eastern shore of the Mediterranean and the north shore of Africa when at last he went to war. His forces, the most numerous ever to traipse the earth, were led by his three brothers, the sons of Darius with whom he had dreamed his greatest dreams since childhood.

Arsames was placed in charge of an enormous Ethiopian contingent, and Achaemenes and Anatrigines shared the leadership of the navy. As for Xerxes himself, he took the admiralty of the Phoenician fleet, fulfilling an ambitious vision for a man reared in Persia's landlocked interior.

This afternoon a balmy breeze swelled the sails of his trireme as 600 oars pushed the sleek vessel across the Thracian Sea toward the Greek mainland. He had traveled by camelback up the royal Persian highway from Susa through the Taurus Range, and after entering the Cicilian Gates he had crossed the Hellespont by two bridges of boats. Awaiting Xerxes in the Greek towns of Asia Minor (which his father, Darius, had conquered a dozen years before) had been standing armies levied for his purposes against their European compatriots. He had enlisted some of them as sailors and had left the rest to his generals for invasion against the Hellespont's western shore.

Darius, more bent on reconstruction than revenge, had established democracies in the Ionian towns. Therefore it was with mixed feelings that the Greek forces met the emperor, some of

73

them grateful to Persia for its fair treatment but others, especially the older ones, still full of resentment against their conquerors.

Xerxes had spent the winter at Sardis before advancing on Ionia. Ahead of him he had sent supplies, and now stores of corn for his infantry were accumulated at intervals leading all the way into Europe.

In all, nearly two million foot soldiers and sailors composed the force that Xerxes brought with him from Mesopotamia and points east. As they were joined by contingents from about the empire, he would be advancing upon Europe with over five million men, the most awesome horde ever to practice battle.

His dream this day as he stood at the helm of the warship, observing the pilot's dexterous work and listening to the chanting slap of the vessel's oars, was that all the West would be his. As the sleek bark passed island after island along the Dolopes chain, his pulse skipped.

This was, he reasoned, where a man's heart ought to be: in war and its implements, in power and command. Nothing short of this was worthy of attention, and surely not of grief.

Vashti should have come to him when he called for her. Did she not know that matters of marriage and love could not always be of grand importance? Not to a king, anyway.

In the cold heights of the Asian mountains, as he had slept in his guarded tent, he had often reminded himself of this. On desert nights when he slept beside his spear, and wondered where Vashti was, he had taken comfort in the conviction that such questions were beneath him.

As he had ridden high in his camel's swaying canopy, leading his millions toward the goal of glory, he had forced his queen from his mind, drugged by the call of destiny and the praise of his comrades.

In time, he told himself, she would cease to haunt him. When he owned Europe and held the entire world in his grip, she would fade forever from memory.

Just now, scanning the advancing shore, the coast which cradled Athens and Sparta, he girded his spirit for adventure—adventure craved by his forefathers but never tasted.

Where Xerxes set foot, Persia set foot. As Persia prospered, so would his soul.

This he told himself when Vashti's sweet face darted across his conscience. It worked to quell his guilt, to appease his yearning for her touch—sometimes.

15

For several months Xerxes' millions had been positioned at various sites throughout the Aegean and Thracian Seas. When 180,000 of them went against the Athens-Sparta alliance, they were met by only 10,000 Greeks and 300 ships.

On their way to Athens the Persians had encountered unprecedented victory at Thermopylae. When they easily overtook the Greek capital, besieging the acropolis and setting the temple of Athena aflame, the horrified Athenians bowed to eastern occupation with chagrin.

For the first time in history an Oriental power not only invaded the West but held its most prestigious city in a stranglehold. Xerxes had, therefore, fulfilled more of the Persian expansionist dream than any of his predecessors, and after sending word of victory to Susa he headed for Salamis, plotting to take over the entire Dorian sector of the Hellenistic world.

It was September 23, over a year into the emperor's European experience. What he had only imagined in fantasy was spread before him as he sat beneath a striped umbrella high atop a hill at the head of Piraeus Harbor. A soft southern breeze wafted up from the Myrtoum Sea, bringing the scent of clashing steel and the sound of bloody cries across Salamis Isle.

This was the gateway to all points west. If Xerxes won this round, nothing could stand in his way. Though the forces were fairly equal, the Persians, having demoralized the Greeks at Athens, were enjoying the advantage.

Xerxes straightened the silken folds of his lavender gown and rested his flared sleeves upon the arms of his portable throne. Sunshine glinted off his upturned face as his secretaries raced back and forth with word of his captains' exploits. Dozens of ships representing both sides of the fray expressed their differences in the narrow slit of water separating Salamis from the mainland. While presently the battle was quite balanced, the emperor was confident.

His Phoenician navy was an awesome contingent, not only for expertise but also for appearance. Its squat, flat-bottomed boats, propelled by two decks of oars, denoted divine retribution with their huge idols of the stocky god, Baal, leaning threateningly from each prow and with sharp-nosed battering rams pushing ominously through the water.

The Greeks' more curvaceous, streamlined vessels appeared fragile by comparison, and although the goddess Athena was often depicted as a warrior, in crested helmet and full armor, her likeness did not adorn her ships.

Despite the huskiness of the Phoenician craft, however, the Greek ships proved themselves a formidable force. About dusk the scales began to tip in favor of the Europeans, and Xerxes' secretaries hesitated to bear the discomforting tidings to their king.

Nevertheless, it was increasingly apparent that, while the Phoenicians were masters of the open seas, the more slender and maneuverable Greek barks were better able to cope with the restricting canal. The Hellenists, accustomed to the narrow shoals and treacherous conditions of island waterways, managed to lure the Phoenicians into straits beyond their ken.

Perhaps Xerxes need not be told the worst. He could surely see for himself the broken wreckage of several Persian vessels floating in the canal. And along the rocky shore wounded sailors swam, clambering up the beach toward the village of Psyttaleia.

Soon, from the vantage point of his sheltered throne, Xerxes could see that nearly the entire Persian garrison scrambled ashore, thousands upon thousands abandoning floundered ships and dragging wounded comrades across bloody sands.

Close on their heels followed the enemy, shooting down those who ran and falling upon the disabled as they hacked them to pieces with broadaxes.

Those still manning the faltering ships retreated now, trying to flee the scene of battle, the waters strewn with hulks and corpses and flailing swimmers. Few would escape, taking with them the memory of comrades clubbed to death by the enemy's oars or spitted like tunny on steamy lances.

The slaughter continued until nightfall. Two hundred Persian ships were lost in the Salamis strait to only 40 Greek vessels. While the emperor's fugitives fled to Phalerum, the chagrined monarch sat like a statue upon his regal chair.

As the sun dipped over the westland, which he still longed to possess, tears trickled down his cheeks. And a Mediterranean breeze, warm but not conciliatory, dried them.

* * *

Winter was approaching. Xerxes and his defeated troops limped back to Susa along the same route they had followed into Europe.

Though he was not utterly abandoning dreams of westward expansion, the emperor must give his demoralized and disorganized forces time to recuperate. Those who retreated with him would be sent home, most of them too badly wounded to fight again. The larger part of his army, that which had not seen action at Salamis, had been sent north to await spring. Under General Mardonius they would seek alliance with Athens, and though Xerxes had lost command of the sea, a fleet now guarded the Hellespont, plotting another foray into the hinterland.

The dream was tentative, however. As Xerxes withdrew into Asia, word came from other parts of Greece that his brothers, all three of them top commanders, had given their lives in his cause.

How swiftly ambition had turned to ashes, dreams to dust! Somewhere in the foothills of Cicilia, Xerxes laid his royal head upon a lonely pillow and remembered Persepolis, the ceremonial halls where he and his young brothers had been trained for war.

Little was left to him now of human love. Father, wife, and kin were gone. Only the adoration of his subjects remained, and unless he took the West, even that hollow consolation could fade away.

16

Xerxes, Emperor of the East, trembled as he knelt in his private chapel before the frieze of his god, Ahura-Mazda. In stone relief the winged deity hovered above him, its wheeled craft soaring, aloof, yet unmoving.

For weeks all of Susa had sat on edge as news from Greece fluctuated between victory and defeat.

Mardonius, left with the best of Xerxes' troops to complete the work begun in Attica, had failed to achieve an alliance with the trampled Athenians, and so had occupied the city since spring. Recent word was that the Greeks had at last taken the offensive, and so the general had burned the capital to the ground, thus procuring an empty retribution by destroying the greatest prize of the emperor's campaign and evacuating Attica itself.

While there was strong Persian fighting here and there throughout the Greek isles, just today a messenger had brought tidings that Mardonius and his troops were huddled behind a wall of felled trees at Plataea, and that their situation was very precarious.

Nearly a full year had passed since the battle of Salamis. In all this time Xerxes had slept little, eaten little, and fretted much, living only for the sporadic reports which filtered to his palace from the warfront.

The three battle points which counted most were at Plataea, Mycale, and Sestos. If Mardonius lost Plataea, one-third of Xerxes' remaining hope would die. And so he prayed today in the small sanctuary adjoining his bedchamber—pleading with his god to give his generals wisdom, his admirals craftiness, and his armed men strength.

Every day of his life he had practiced prayer, but the last time he had done so with such determination was when he begged

Ahura-Mazda to hasten his wedding to Vashti. The god had granted that request. Perhaps he would grant this one.

But as Xerxes knelt before the carving of his beloved deity, he doubted whether his petition would be honored. Fasting and agonizing until his face was gaunt and lined, he wondered if the god who had blessed him with the girl of his dreams could ever again look kindly upon him after he had sent her away.

Soon enough his doubts were confirmed. A rap upon the chapel door lifted him from his knees.

"Enter," he called hoarsely.

Pushing open the door, the chamberlain admitted three young boys, all dusty and windblown, having traveled hundreds of miles and each bearing word from the European forces.

Quickly the news was dispensed as the youngsters fawned and shivered before the mightiest man on earth. Mardonius and his troops had been slaughtered like sheep at Plataea, the fleet at Mycale had been destroyed, and the garrison at Sestos, being reduced to eating their bedstraps, had abandoned the town by night.

Xerxes, receiving the messages numbly, could have called for the execution of the three lads. Instead, after gazing upon them mutely, he dismissed them and turned again to his prayers.

"Mighty Ahura-Mazda, you who answer when I call, *so* you have answered," he wept.

Burying his nails in his scalp, he mourned—for himself as well as for those who had given everything for him.

17

The seven eunuchs—Mehuman, Biztha, Harbona, Bigtha, Abagtha, Zethar, and Carkas—stood outside the king's council chamber, peering past his guards and consulting among themselves.

"For days he has sat thus," Mehuman whispered, his face furrowed with concern. "He mutters to himself a great deal, and whispers Vashti's name too often."

The eunuchs studied the king's slumped form as he rested upon his throne, and they shook their heads sadly.

"It is not only his defeat in Europe which haunts him," Biztha surmised.

"I think it is less that than anything," Mehuman agreed. "He shall rally from that in time, for there are always more lands to conquer. But Vashti he shall never forget."

"It is our responsibility to lift His Majesty's spirits," Zethar announced, his chin jutting in determination. "We must think of something!"

The others murmured agreement, and through a process of elimination they began to arrive at a plan.

"Riches are not the answer. We should make no suggestion which could inflate his coffers," Carkas reasoned.

"Right," nodded Abagtha, "nor would a round of parties or entertainers do the trick."

"I agree," said Harbona. "And we have already ruled out conquest."

Bigtha shrugged. "A *woman* has been his downfall; perhaps a woman can *save* him!"

All eyes were on Mehuman, awaiting his response to this astute observation.

For a long moment he contemplated the matter. Then a smile tugged at his lips.

"Very well," he assented. "I can see no other way. We must provide the king with a romance, something to surpass what he had with Vashti."

The others nodded enthusiastically. But then, one by one, their faces fell.

"How can such a thing be accomplished?" Carkas stammered. "His love for Vashti was a rare thing. And there are no women from among the seven royal families to compare with her."

Carkas' referred to the injunction that no queen was to be taken from outside the seven highest houses in Persia, a law established by Darius in order to honor the seven men who had been loyal to him during an insurrection.

"This is true," Mehuman conceded. "But our king's health is failing. Something must be done. And this law was made years ago. It is reversible under a new administration."

The eunuchs raised their eyebrows at this, but would not question Mehuman's interpretation of the edict. Indeed, there was no formal stipulation regarding an emperor's contradicting the decisions of a former ruler.

"Still," Carkas objected, "where are we to find a woman worthy of Xerxes?"

Biztha jumped on this. "Why, we should seek high and low for her. We should bring beauties from all about the king's empire, and let him choose for himself!"

At first the suggestion seemed so absurd that the others laughed—all except Mehuman. And when he seemed to be thinking upon it, the snickers subsided.

"You cannot actually take such a notion seriously!" Harbona cried. "Why, this is tantamount to calling for a new harem—something Xerxes would never condone. Did he not just recently divest himself of such pleasures, sending hundreds of women from the palace?"

Mehuman did not reply quickly, but peered in at the king, who sat lethargically in his solemn chamber, tipping a goblet of red wine back and forth and gazing upon its contents.

"A man in His Majesty's condition could consider almost anything," he concluded. "Give him a few more days, and then we shall approach him."

18

Hadassah sat up in bed and peered toward the dim yellow light glowing beneath her chamber door. In rooms down the hall her female cousins, Marta and Isha, breathed in contented sleep beside their husbands. But voices in the parlor had jolted her awake.

Anxiously she leaned over the edge of her low pallet and tried to make out the words of Mordecai, Leah, and Moshe in the room beyond.

At first she could not believe her ears when she heard Mordecai in the house. He had not intended to come to the village until later in the season, giving her several more weeks of her seventeenth autumn to spend with her dearest companions. Why he should be here now, and in the middle of the night, she could not imagine. But she was not eager to return home. As much as she loved her adopted father, she much preferred to be with her cousins . . . especially with David.

As she pieced together snatches of the conversation, however, it seemed that Mordecai had not come to fetch her home, but was instead enlisting his sister's aid to continue maintaining her here.

Past a sleepy haze now, she managed to pick up the idea that some news from the palace greatly troubled her papa. As she concentrated on fragments of his story, she realized that he feared for her safety.

"'Let there be fair young virgins sought for the king,'" she heard him expostulate, as though he quoted some royal edict. "Can you believe that Xerxes would stoop to such indulgence?"

Leah's voice followed this, with a heavy sigh. "Well, though he has been known in the past as a moral man, Brother, he *is* a pagan, after all. He does not worship Jehovah. And remember that even certain of Israel's own kings kept harems—David . . . Solomon . . ."

"Yes," Mordecai granted. Despite his growing love of Judaism, he could be embarrassed by certain aspects of its history. "Still, it is disillusioning."

"Only if you expected better things," Moshe shrugged.

"So, go on," Leah urged him. "Surely you have come here at such an hour with more than courtroom gossip."

"I have," Mordecai acknowledged, rubbing his hands together anxiously. "Word in the palace is that the king has appointed officers in all the provinces to seek out and bring to Susa hundreds of young damsels. From among them, Xerxes shall choose a queen to replace his lost Vashti."

His eyes were wide as he spoke, and when his relations only studied him impersonally, he shook his head in frustration.

"Can't you see what this could mean? Are you blind, or am I the only one who has noticed my daughter's beauty?"

Suddenly, with a pang of recognition, Leah's breath came sharply.

"Hadassah!" she groaned, glancing toward the girl's chamber.

Her motherly heart raced protectively. Though there were other lovely maidens in the village, she knew that Hadassah outshone them, and that any procurator sent here would snatch up the willowy lass with the raven curls.

Nor need Mordecai go into detail as to how the king would sort through the hundreds brought to him. Moshe, drawing his manly shoulders into an indignant square, imagined the sweet child herded into Xerxes' bedchamber, to be exploited and then tossed aside.

"What can we do?" he whispered, almost afraid that the sniffing hounds were in the street at this very moment.

Mordecai paced the floor of the tiny parlor. "You must try to keep her from daylight until this misery passes. She must remain with you, and you must keep her from view."

"But," Leah gasped, "how are we to explain this to Hadassah? Surely it would terrify her to know the truth."

"Indeed," Mordecai agreed. "She is very innocent about such things. A good girl, she is. You know?"

"Of course," Moshe assured him. "We know her as well as you do."

"Then," the guardian declared, "tell her whatever you must. But keep her secluded."

At this the voices tapered to a solemn whisper. Hadassah leaned back upon her pillow, her hands clutching at her blanket, and her whole body aquiver.

19

When the eunuchs had presented Xerxes with the proposed "solution" to his loneliness and depression, he had grasped at it. Of course, as at the party where he had deposed Vashti, his decision to seek a new queen had been made through a wine-soaked fog. There would be times throughout the ensuing months when he would feel the guilt of this choice, just as he felt remorse over the loss of his wife. But he would manage to push it aside as day after day lovelies were paraded before him.

It took only a few weeks, following his acceptance of the advice, for the harem quarters to be refurbished and for hand-picked virgins to begin arriving at the palace, first from points closest and then from provinces along the farthest reaches of the empire. Soon the king's manly blood was stirred by the presence of innocent beauty in his courts.

Access to the damsels would be postponed, however, for what became an excruciatingly long time as the girls were put through a routine of cleansing rituals and beautification, taking a full 12 months from the time of their arrival. The king's desire, piqued by this anticipation, began to alleviate his former depression, replacing it with energies he must release in creative ways.

Mehuman, the eunuch, had foreseen this. When Biztha had proposed the procurement of a new harem, he had quickly realized the effect that a bevy of women on the palace grounds would have upon the emperor. And as Xerxes began to take up administrative duties with a vengeance, channeling his aroused and unrequited passions into business, politics, and parties, the valet smiled with private gratification. "As good as a physician's prescription!" he reasoned. "Our king is himself again."

It was the month of Tebeth, "mud" month of midwinter, four

years after Vashti's deposition and more than a year since Xerxes' defeat at Salamis. Even in Susa, the weather was cold.

Hadassah worked in the smoky kitchen of Leah's little cottage, chatting gaily with her cousins. Her seclusion, which had begun three months before, did not seem so strange once the weather turned bad. Until the muddy time, Leah and Moshe had expected to be questioned often by their niece as to why they found so much for her to do inside and kept such close track of her whenever she went outdoors. But, to their surprise, she had accepted the peculiar isolation quietly, and had not once complained when Mordecai sent word that she should remain with them through the winter.

Though the guardians never suspected that the girl had overheard their midnight conversation with Mordecai, it was not long before news of the king's edict was public knowledge, and so Leah sought opportunity to caution the pretty girl.

Moshe, David, and the young husbands of Leah's two daughters were away from the house this evening, working beside the other men of the community to lay out fresh straw upon the empty grainfields, a duty required several times during the winter to prepare the muddy ground for spring planting.

The women labored over piles of onions and carrots in the dimly lit kitchen, peeling the vegetables for stews and soups. An aromatic broth simmered on the brick oven in the center of the room, and though it was chilly outside, the ladies wore light frocks in the steamy quarters.

Leah nervously broached the subject of the edict, addressing her daughters rather than Hadassah. "I hear there have been a good many coaches and carriages passing under the gates of Susa lately, bearing guests for the palace," she said.

"Guests?" Marta laughed. "Why, mother, you know all those young girls cannot be guests!"

Leah glanced at Hadassah, expecting her interest to be aroused. But the girl only kept her head bowed, intent upon the task of slicing cabbages.

"Well, then," the mother went on, "if we all know who the young ladies are, and why they have been taken to the palace . . ."

"Taken! Yes, Mother! They are *taken*, against their will, aren't they?" Isha cried. "How awful!"

"We are lucky we are married," Marta chimed in. "At least we needn't worry . . ." But then she caught herself, her hand flying to her mouth. "Oh, I am sorry," she groaned, gazing at Hadassah with round, sad eyes.

At this the girl at last looked up from her work, her own eyes moist with tears. Leah flew to Hadassah's side, throwing her arms about her.

"Dear child!" she wept, seeing unconcealed terror in the innocent face. "You have known all along, haven't you?"

The girl did not reply, but nestled her dark head upon her cousin's shoulder.

"Then I needn't warn you more strongly," Leah insisted, lifting Hadassah's chin and studying her perfect countenance. "You must be careful. Continue close to home. Do not go out in the daylight, or linger, as you often do, near the gate when David comes back from the fields. Do you hear me?"

"I hear you," Hadassah stammered, frightened all the more by Leah's curt tone.

Softening, the woman held her close and looked anxiously at her daughters. Drawing near, they embraced their cousin, and together the women stood in a huddle, listening to the wind outside and wishing their men would return.

20

The flame of the candle on the window ledge fluttered uneasily as a rainy breeze pushed through the half-open reed blind. Soon David, Moshe, and the other girls' husbands would be coming in from the fields. Surely, Hadassah reasoned, it could not hurt if she sat in the little hall of Leah's entryway and watched for them in the street outside.

This had always been a safe little hamlet. Folk did not cover their windows with grates or slats, as in the city. Only in inclement weather did they even lower flimsy shades like this one, which admitted the winter wind.

Feeling quite secure within the house, Hadassah rested her elbows upon the sill and leaned her chin on one hand. A slender moon glanced between heavy clouds, and she remembered the night that she and David had sat in the little oasis beyond the town wall.

She was of marriageable age, and had never met a man more to her liking than David. Having lived much of her life in the royal city, she had seen many a handsome and wealthy fellow. But David was a kindred soul.

A good man he was—committed to his family despite the fact that such service frustrated his desires to pursue his artistic leanings. Yet he did find ways, even in the village, to express the creative side of himself. Many a night he sat beside the parlor fire, spinning glorious yarns in song and poem, of mountains, bedouins, and distant kingdoms. When a spare moment granted the luxury, he painted or carved his imaginings upon small shards of pottery and hunks of cast-off alabaster.

From the parlor, the orange glow of Leah's little firepit blended with the flame of Hadassah's window candle. Trickles of gentle rain dashed against the sill, and her mind drifted out toward the fields, toward the one she loved.

A stir down the street seemed to say that the men were coming in from the evening's labors. Eager voices from many doorways called out greetings.

Hadassah leaned her head out the window, straining for the sight of David rounding the dark streetcorner.

The flash of torches verified that a company passed into town. Had she not been anticipating her cousin, she might have paid more attention to the accompanying sounds, for housewifely hellos were suddenly muffled, and cries and weeping followed.

Too soon for her preoccupied heart to heed this change, the approaching torchlight blazed rudely across the housefront. Before she could duck inside, the disconcerting glare revealed faces unfamiliar to her. As though made to seek her out especially, one of the flares was brandished in her direction, lighting up her countenance like a miner's torch.

"Aha!" someone laughed. "Here's a pretty one!"

And then other voices joined in as Hadassah shielded her eyes.

"Pretty, indeed! She's a beauty!"

Lurching backward, Hadassah grappled with the blind.

But it was too late.

Leah came running from the kitchen just as the front door was kicked open and strong men in hard leather armor forced their way inside.

"This is your daughter?" the leader asked, grasping Hadassah by the arm.

"Why, no . . . yes . . ." Leah fumbled.

"Whatever," the official shrugged. "She now belongs to King Xerxes."

Crazed, the girl shrieked, and Leah clung to her until the guards beat her away.

Into the street Hadassah was thrown, her lavender dress torn at the shoulder and her pale face spattered with muddy rain.

Marta and Isha shrieked with her, holding onto one another as their favorite childhood playmate was thrust upon a waiting horse, and the horse was whipped into a gallop.

As the throng of thieving soldiers raced back toward the town gate, they took with them half a dozen girls of the village.

But the leader of the pack kept a keen eye on Hadassah. She was the evening's prize—perhaps the prize of his career.

He had done himself proud tonight.

21

Morning sun gleamed through a dreary blanket of fog over the palace of Susa. Mordecai the Jew sat in the gate of the royal house, behind his accounting table, and tried to keep his mind on the business of figures and ledgers.

On most days such preoccupation came easily to him despite the traffic of executives and officers who came and went upon the spacious stairway from the avenue out front. He was accustomed to the klatches of conversing courtiers and servants in the shady recesses of the gate's multistoried complex. But lately concentration came hard.

More young women had been arriving today than ever before, being escorted toward the harem quarters in the palace's most private sanctum. Mordecai's nerves were kept on edge as cluster after cluster of girls passed by his station, and as he surveyed them carefully, praying that his daughter not be among them.

After months of this surveillance he was still unaccustomed to it. And though to this point he had been spared the horror of Hadassah's capture, concern never ceased to possess him.

More than fear haunted him today, however. Haman, the king's vizier, was doing business in the gate, his boastful voice and ostentatious presence goading the Jew since morning.

It was not that Haman meant especially to offend Mordecai. Rarely had he ever paid much mind to the slight accountant in all the years he had served this administration. Day in and day out the grand vizier passed by the unassuming fellow who sat at the inventory bench. Day in and day out he disregarded him, interacting with the Jew only on those infrequent occasions when their business overlapped.

The only times that Haman seemed to actually have focused on Mordecai were when he had worn his fringed mantle to work, the one which designated him a member of the Jewish race. During Mordecai's early months of duty at this post he had not worn the garment. But as he had become progressively more involved with his heritage, and as he had fallen more and more in love with the teachings of Israel (scorned and avoided though they were in his youth), he had become more comfortable with those symbols which identified him with the despised ones.

It did not surprise him that Haman took note of him when he was so distinguished. Instinctively he had known the vizier would do so. So perhaps he was goading Haman subtly and quietly as much as Haman inadvertently goaded him.

Indeed, Mordecai's antipathy toward the Agagite, the Amalekite, was deep and strong. Though Haman had no idea that the old man whom his underlings had assaulted in the streets long ago was Mordecai's adopted father, he was not blind to the coolness of the Jew's greetings or the edge of bitterness which tinged their dealings.

When the accountant wore his shawl, as he did today, the Jew's antipathy was more distinct, for Mordecai himself was more distinct.

Haman did not like Jews. Though many of the race held prominent positions in Persia, the vizier looked upon them with suspicion. He did not like the way they kept to themselves, the way they attended to their own laws and customs. Strange they were, to him and to others. And sometimes he wondered how loyal they could be to the empire when they served from a divided heart.

The fact that Jews were rarely disobedient to Persian authority served only to confuse people like Haman. They were notoriously scrupulous citizens, and this in itself cast a question over them.

Be that as it may, Haman cared little what Mordecai thought of him. Jew or not, he was a fellow of small importance to the empire. As long as he did his job, Haman ignored him.

Mordecai observed the prime minister's pompous swagger as he strode here and there across the steps, giving his opinion on this matter and that, sending his valets flying on errands and commissioning his executives with various tasks. Accompanied by his closest consultants, Haman approached a broad banister which hemmed the stairs. Perched upon it was a huge stone lion, one of two which guarded either side of the entry. The Jew watched with a gimlet eye as the vizier cavalierly leaned against the royal statue. And he clenched his teeth in private disgust.

His disdainful revery was short-lived, however. Another bevy of young beauties was being brought for the king's scrutiny. As always, they were marched up the stairs, huddled and quiet. As always, they received the leering glances of a hundred onlookers. But, unlike times past, Mordecai's worst fear was realized.

He was certain he saw Hadassah. She could not be mistaken— there in the center of the little group, taller and more striking than the rest.

Anxiously she surveyed the gateway, doubtless knowing that her papa would be seated here. But before she could spy him he ducked his head, fumbling for some nonexistent object upon the floor.

Once she had been led away he rose up again, fighting back tears. Haman still reclined upon the banister, representing all that was alien. While Mordecai had publicly embraced Judaism, he felt it best for now to shield Hadassah from such a connection.

Until this calamity be past, she must not be called a Jew.

22

Hadassah walked with her dozen sister captives through the palace's echoing halls, forced along at spearpoint by a group of rigid guards. Like frightened does, the young women hung close together, fearfully eyeing their surroundings.

Soaring pillars, narrow of girth and widely spaced, lent an airiness to the enormous compound, which opened out onto vast gardens and sparkling pools. From every cornice and column top small bulls' heads stared down upon their passage, and friezes along broad staircases told tales of kings and conquerors, slaves and tribute, impressing all who traversed the grounds with the grandeur and power that belonged to rulers of this dynasty.

Crossing several colonades and entering vestibule after vestibule, the girls passed many an archway and closed door, each leading to some private sanctum of the king's courtiers and governors. Straight-backed soldiers protected every entryway, but their attire indicated that they were meant more for show than for combat. In blousy pantaloons and silken shoes, the toes upturned, they hardly looked threatening. Nonetheless, Hadassah and her companions avoided their cold gazes.

Across expansive porches the women's footsteps rang, and where they were muffled by thick Persian carpets—red and blue and gold, fringed and intricately patterned—the sound of cascading fountains, the cries of strutting peacocks, or the music of caged birds and minstrels' lyres filled the air.

It seemed a century of distance separated the queue of girls from the outside world. Ahead was a scalloped archway leading to three lobbies, each descending after the other toward a sunlit court. Soft-shoed fellows again stood bastioned alongside this portal, but by their smooth cheeks and shining chins it was clear that they were eunuchs, not warriors.

As the ladies were ushered into the first and largest of these lobbies, they were greeted by the aroma of a heavy, bulbous smoking pipe which sat upon a low table surrounded by laughing men. Propped upon embroidered pillows, they passed the pipe's hose from mouth to mouth, playing a game of dice without looking up until one of the escorts cleared his throat.

The host of the jolly party glared at the intruder.

"Another lot for the king's harem," the guide announced.

"You know where they go," the gambler sneered, flicking a hurried hand. As he surveyed the knot of girls, Hadassah took a sharp breath. She had never forgotten the angry countenance of Angus, the man who had so callously commandeered a group of harem wives the day she watched them being evicted from the palace. She had rarely thought of him during the intervening years, the memory of Vashti being the stronger image from that long-ago day. But one glimpse of his round, gloating face brought back the incident as though no time had elapsed.

Quickly the soldiers led the girls forth, through the little vestibules and toward the harem's sunstreaked court. The mocking aroma of the men's smoking pipe blended with the heady fragrance of perfumes and bath oils as the women proceeded through the last arch. Overcome with anxiety and fatigue, Hadassah doubled a fist against her stomach.

The final portico, opening on a sumptuous arboretum, framed an elegant scene. Bowers of roses and lilies, slaves with broad, feathered fans—all seemed calculated to inspire romance and a sense of luxury.

Across the pool, at the far side of the garden, the harem apartments rose in several tiers up from the court floor. They were a pretty sight at first glance, fronted by narrow catwalks and decorated with hanging plants, vines, and statuary. But on closer inspection they resembled the wall of a hive. In contrast to the open airiness of the palace compound, the quarters of the harem girls were so many claustrophobic boxes stacked atop one another.

As it dawned upon the klatch of newcomers that these were the living quarters which came with being "chosen" women, they were hushed with horror.

Hadassah wiped her palms upon her torn gown, recalling the annual village fairs she had attended with Leah's children. Just like the cattle stalls where farmers brought animals for breeding and for slaughter, so were the rooms of the harem girls.

Somewhere in the small huddle of virgins, soft weeping broke tense silence. Last night, after the girls had been led captive from several villages near Susa, they had been herded into an encampment outside the city walls. None had slept well. Certainly not Hadassah. And to face a night—endless nights—in the confines of these narrow cells was too much to contemplate.

Tears forced their way to her eyes and spilled over her flushed cheeks.

She wondered where her papa was, and why he had not been seated at the palace gate. The young Jewess sorely needed his prayers now, for he was a man of God, and he understood Jehovah's ways more than she.

23

Hadassah lay within her narrow cell, upon an even narrower cot, her head toward the back wall. It had been 24 hours since she was transported from the encampment outside Susa to this little chamber. Not once since she had arrived had any official greeted the newcomers or explained to them what was to come.

All night long she had dreamed of David, trembling into wakefulness over and over as he had turned from her in her shame. Barely could her conscious mind consider her purpose here without the most horrid fears enveloping her. Repeatedly she told herself that some salvation lay directly before her, that surely God could not mean for the king to touch her, for her life to be irrevocably sullied and her future dismissed.

Soon, she reasoned, her uncle would hear of her imprisonment. Perhaps he could bring some influence to bear . . . some plea for her release. But even as she hoped for this, her throat grew tight. She knew very well that Mordecai was no great man in the palace. Likely, the king did not even know his name.

As dawn filtered through the court's latticed ceiling, spilling past vines and laces of flowers, women up and down the hive stirred awake. Throughout the night's bleak hours, soft sobs had drifted through the thin wall of Hadassah's chamber from the adjacent room. They had quieted just before the first gray rays of morning, but now they resumed.

The neighbor was a girl of Leah's village. Close in age, Hadassah and Maryam had known each other since childhood, and the Jewess wondered how her friend would endure this misery. Maryam was a delicate child, diminutive of stature, unlike the long-legged females generally selected for the harem. Pretty as a field flower, she was painfully shy and the ordeal had already taken a murderous toll on her.

Hadassah sat up in bed and leaned around the front edge of the partition. Like a tortured convict, Maryam hunched against the wall of her room, her knees updrawn fetally, her face ravaged.

The cell to the other side of Maryam's was occupied by a Phoenician beauty. Dark and hearty, like the heathered hills of her seacoast nation, this young woman had been brought to Susa several weeks earlier. Familiarity with harem life, however, could not account for her indifferent attitude.

She sat upon the narrow walkway, her legs dangling casually between spindles of the balustrade.

Dressed in the briefest of garments, her shoulders covered only by a mass of black curls, she glanced toward the weeping newcomer with a callous sneer.

"I hope we can get some sleep tonight!" she said, loudly enough that several other girls, sporting in the pool below, responded with sly smiles.

These, like the Phoenician, evinced a careless air, and must have been her favorite companions.

"Yes—it would be nice," one replied, and the other swimmers laughed.

Hadassah bristled, creeping into the cubbyhole where her fellow villager sat.

Placing an arm about Maryam's shaking shoulders, she whispered, "Please stop crying. Everything will be all right."

"Certainly it will!" the Phoenician shrugged, poking her head into the little chamber. "Did you know that when you are at last sent before the king, you will be given your choice of dowries? Silks and jewels and precious ointments! A fortune will be yours!"

At this Maryam only wept louder, and Hadassah studied the intruder with amazement. Clearly, a passion for luxury had thus far sustained the foreigner. And perhaps such greed was what it took to endure this imprisonment.

But Hadassah had known luxury all her life. Though she was very young, she knew that such things ill served the heart.

"What of family?" she softly challenged. And then with a wistful sigh, "What of love?"

Again Maryam sobbed, and the Phoenician glanced away with a fleeting grimace. Just as quickly, however, her careless ambiance returned, and she stepped away.

"I cannot send my mother or my 12 brothers and sisters love in a bucket!" she sneered. "But they will be happy to buy food for their stomachs!"

Hadassah drew Maryam close and watched the Phoenician's determined retreat.

There were various ways to handle heartbreak, she deduced. Weeping and wailing was one, and haughtiness was another.

24

Mordecai paced the floor of his bedchamber, sleepless for the third night with thoughts of his poor Hadassah.

The house was very quiet, the servants having retired hours ago. The silence was almost oppressive as Mordecai slipped into the hall and drew near the room where his uncle, Abihail, had spent his dying days.

This room was Mordecai's study now. A large table occupied the place where Abihail's bed had been, and spread upon it were not only ledgers and accounting tables but scrolls of the Jewish Scriptures, his most prized possessions.

Softly he went to the broad desk and sat down where his servants so often found him. Since he spent more time in this place than in any other room of the house, the chambermaid knew that it was her foremost duty to keep the master's reading lamp always full of oil, his quill sharpened, and his ink bottle full.

With the passing years Mordecai had come to devote as much energy to meditating upon the Torah as to his bookkeeping. Mordecai was not an old man, but as he increasingly preferred the look of a Jew, his beard had grown patriarchally long. Streaked with silver, it gave him an appearance of age beyond his 42 years, and his shoulder-length hair lent another Hebrew touch. Yet he was still in touch with Persia, and as he walked the courts each day, he sensed more and more the disparity between the two cultures.

Tonight, restless and anxious, he tried to collect his thoughts and focus them on prayer, for he knew he was powerless to help his daughter by any human means. Yet every time he attempted to intercede for her, the image of Abihail, prone upon the bed which had sat in this very place, haunted him.

Never before had such a phenomenon interrupted his meditations. Night after night he had studied in this room, and never had the memory of his uncle interfered.

"Strange . . ." he whispered, his brow knit. "What is it?"

It was only to himself that he asked this question, but as he did, the memory of Abihail's warning, the ancient story of King Saul and Agag the Amalekite, leapt to mind.

Despite Mordecai's increased love of Israel and her traditions, Abihail's interpretation of this tale had remained gibberish to him. Suddenly, as he pondered it afresh, his skin crawled and a pervasive sense of dread enveloped him.

Rising, he stepped to the chamber window and gazed out toward the acropolis, toward the palace gate where he sat each day beneath the shadow of Haman and his cohorts.

The impression was very strong, as though imparted by the night's dark silence, that Abihail had been right. Evil stalked the royal house of Susa, evil alien to Persia as well as to Israel. Until Jehovah's will was done, it would fester, bringing misery to both cultures.

* * *

The instant dawn broke over the royal compound, Mordecai made his way through the palace gate.

All night long he had meditated upon the meaning of Abihail's warning. And though he did not yet understand just how it might involve Hadassah, concern for her well-being obsessed him.

Accountants, even of the highest stature, must have good reason to venture past the treasury rooms of Xerxes' residence. But Mordecai had a plan, one borne of the genius which darkness and solitude can generate.

"I would speak to the Keeper of the Dowries," he announced, rousing the guard from his morning post outside the harem court.

"To what purpose?" the sentry asked. "And who are you?"

"Mordecai, Chief Accountant of the Treasury. It is required that an inventory be made of the harem storehouse."

"Who requires it?" the guard challenged, wondering at the odd timing.

"I do," Mordecai simply said. "It will take several days, and we will begin straightway."

"But . . ." the guard objected, "the keeper is asleep. Can't it wait?"

Feigning impatience, the Jew looked up at the gray sunlight and sighed. "Very well. We will not waken the keeper. Only lead me to the storehouse and I will begin without him."

"But . . ."

"He may join me as soon as he likes," Mordecai snapped, rushing past the guard's objection.

Befuddled, the sentry lowered his spear and looked over his shoulder.

"I suppose it will do no harm. . . ."

"Hurry, man," Mordecai spurred him. "I haven't all day!"

Doubtfully the guard led him down the back hall of the harem. "The women are all asleep," the guard said. "See to it that you are gone before they take their morning walk. No man is to intrude upon their privacy."

"Of course," Mordecai sniffed, seeing an opportunity here. "Uh, when did you say that would be?"

"Three hours past cock crow," the guard replied. "See to it that you are nowhere near their passage."

"Certainly," Mordecai said with a bow.

They stood before the storehouse door now. Nervously the guard worked the key in the lock and let Mordecai enter the dark room. Setting a flame to the single oil lamp upon the interior wall, he stepped back and cleared his throat.

"The keeper will be informed of your presence here as soon as he wakes," he announced.

"Don't worry," Mordecai said, facing him with a condescending smile. "I am his superior. You have done well."

Bowing away, the guard softly clicked his heels together and left Mordecai to himself. The Jew beamed with private victory and began the task of counting ointment jars, his ears attuned for the sound of girlish voices in the hall.

25

Well into his "inventory" of the storeroom, Mordecai found his patience rewarded.

Girls by the dozens were emerging from their harem cells, to be herded down the hall into the morning light. They would be led to the outside garden which hemmed the palace compound, where they would enjoy one of two daily constitutionals.

Eagerly Hadassah's adopted father peered through the crack of the door, which he had purposely left ajar. He knew that the regimen of court life would repeat this spectacle again tomorrow morning. Therefore he waited to spy his daughter and to follow her beyond the wall—only to know her routine, and not, this time, to contact her. If he were successful in tracing her steps, he would venture to do so again tomorrow, and would pray for the chance to speak with her.

When at last he identified Hadassah toward the end of the line, he stifled a little cry. How sad she looked! Though she carried herself well, after the manner of her upbringing, her youthful dignity was poor compensation for the sorrow in her eyes.

Keeping close in the corridor shadows, Mordecai trailed the throng, avoiding detection by the guards who marched behind the girls.

Just as the outer garden became visible through the hallway's last door, however, Mordecai was called to a halt.

"What are *you* after?" a voice arrested him.

Wheeling about, the Jew found himself confronted by a portly lady dressed in the simple gown of a servant and bearing a tea tray.

"I . . . I . . ." he stammered.

"Yes?" the woman demanded, trying to show disapproval despite the twinkle in her eye. "You had business in the cloisters, and you saw the girls go by. It has happened here before." Then, growing very serious, she leaned near. "While your appreciation of their beauty is understandable, you must know that it is against the law to hang so close."

Waving a chubby finger under his nose, she warned, "I could turn you in, you know." With that she bustled past him. "You'd best be gone straightaway!" she called over her shoulder.

Mordecai grimaced, but something in the servant's mercy encouraged him.

"Madam," he replied, his tone anxious, "please stay a moment. I must speak with you."

Bewildered, the woman glanced back at him.

"You are very kind," he asserted, joining her near the door. "I should be forever in your debt if you might indulge me further."

The servant said nothing, but curiosity shown on her face.

"I am not what I seem," Mordecai insisted. "I am not some lecherous fool, here to spy on the maidens."

"No?" the woman said, skeptical.

"No," the Jew asserted. "I am guardian to one of those lovelies—her adopted father. You must believe me, for this hardship is very great."

The servant, knowing that such a tale could have little purpose as a lie, listened with more sympathy.

"I must know how she fares, my lady," Mordecai pleaded. "It would be worth a great deal to me."

The emphasis placed on this last statement sparked warmer interest.

"Indeed?" the woman whispered. Peering through the garden portal, she sighed, "Very well. Which child is she? And how may I serve you?"

Mordecai smiled. All morning he had counted treasure, but none of it was so valuable as this encounter.

* * *

Hadassah sat upon a bench at the nearest end of the outer court.

The helpful servant who had met Mordecai in the hall, and whose name was Dorca, assured him that the girl often sat there alone, and that he could usually find her there when the women were led to the garden.

He had waited until the second day to venture down the hall again. Now he stood within fetching distance of his daughter, trying to work up courage to call her name.

She looked thinner than he liked to see her. Surely the king's harem was afforded the finest cuisine. Was Hadassah failing to eat?

Surveying the corridor, Mordecai saw that he was alone. Leaning his head out the garden door, he saw also that there were no keepers near his daughter.

"Child!" he whispered. But his voice was lost in the sound of breeze and splashing fountain.

"Child!" he tried again.

Hadassah turned about, not certain of what she heard. And when she saw her papa, her hand flew to her mouth. Tears welled in her wide eyes, and Mordecai hushed her with a gesture.

Then, beckoning, he pleaded that she join him in the hall.

Hadassah fearfully peered about, and finding that she could do so without notice, she slipped discreetly from the bench.

Falling into her papa's arms, she quietly wept upon his shoulder.

"My Dove," he sighed, "my Myrtle Blossom. You are so thin. Are you ill, my child?"

Hadassah shook her head but continued to tremble in his embrace.

Question after question followed this as he sought to know how she was treated, how she slept, what she knew of her future.

"Tomorrow we are being sent to Hegai, Keeper of the Women," the girl informed him. "Since we arrived, we have been kept in a lesser court until he could receive us. Others have gone in already, but tomorrow my sisters and I are to go before him."

"Your sisters?" Mordecai puzzled.

"The girls with whom I entered. Hegai receives each group in its own turn."

Mordecai nodded, but grew more concerned than ever. "You must eat, my daughter. It will not go well for you here if you do not care for yourself!"

Hadassah shook her head. "But, Papa, you have taught me that certain foods are not fit for a Jew to eat. Even Leah and Moshe taught me this. There is little among the king's delicacies which is lawful."

Amazed, the Israelite studied her sincere expression. "Dear girl," he marveled, "you have always been an obedient child. But this . . ."

Words failed him. She was right, of course. Although he had not been a rigid Jew himself when Hadassah was born, he had grown more scrupulous in his observance of kosher law as she had grown. Since she had been quite little, both he and her closest kin had taught her "clean" from "unclean."

Faltering, he continued. "You are in a Persian house now. As long as Jehovah has brought you to this place, it is your duty to live according to what is provided."

He could not look at her as he said this, uncomfortable with his own logic. When she suddenly pulled away, aghast, his face burned.

"Papa!" she cried. "How can you even suggest that Jehovah has brought this trouble upon me?"

Mordecai knew all too well the reasoning which must have been hers these long days since her abduction: that surely Jehovah would not willingly subject a daughter of Israel to such humiliation, nor expect her to cooperate in any way toward its consummation.

Never had his own faith in the oracles of Mosaic law been so tested. What counsel had he for this innocent one?

A dreadful moment followed as he fought for guidance. But it was Hadassah who at last broke the silence.

"Perhaps," she softly wept, "perhaps I have done something wrong and am being punished. Perhaps I have been an evil girl, and this is my reward!" Bitterly she stared into her papa's desperate countenance. "Yes, that is it! You have told me the stories of Jehovah's vengeance—how He recompenses evil with evil!"

Flushed, she buried her face in her hands, trying to contain her tears.

Grasping at her, Mordecai clutched her to his bosom.

"You have done nothing amiss, Hadassah!" he insisted. "Even

in the moment of your capture, you honored the law."

Bewildered, the girl looked up at him. "I did?" she asked.

"Indeed!" he asserted. "Leah told me so—how you cried out in the house and in the street as you were taken."

More puzzled than ever, Hadassah shrugged. "Any girl would have done so."

"Most likely, yes," Mordecai replied. "But do you not see? This is all the law of Moses requires. When a young woman is forced into disgrace, she is absolved before God and man if she cries out. This is all that is necessary, for it is all a girl can do. Beyond this, nothing is expected . . . except that she go on living!"

Trembling, Hadassah absorbed his confident assertion. As he reached up to wipe a tear from her cheek, she clasped his hand to her lips.

"I am not wicked, then?" she whispered.

Mordecai smiled broadly and shook his head. But just as quickly he hushed her.

"I must be going," he said. "But I shall walk near the harem each day. Though I may not see you for a time, I have ways of knowing how you are. And I shall pray for you constantly. Only . . ." Here he paused, looking about warily. "One thing you must promise me."

"Yes?" she asked, picking up his careful tone.

"Have you let any of your keepers know you are a Jew?"

"I have not been asked," she said.

"Very well," he nodded. "You must keep your race a secret. Tell no one. Do you hear?"

"But, Papa, why . . ."

"It is not for shame that I say this, Daughter. It is to save your life, just as all my counsel is. Will you obey me in this?"

The girl did not understand, but complied. "I have always obeyed you, Papa," she answered.

Content now, Mordecai stepped back as though he would be going. But his daughter had fresh tears in her eyes, and reached for him pathetically.

"What is it child?" he inquired.

"David . . ." she stammered, the very word causing her to

quake. "What must he think of me now? Oh, Papa, will I ever see him again?"

Gazing upon his beloved with a heavy heart, Mordecai tried to address her gravest fear.

"Trust David to God," he said. "Trust everything to God."

ESTHER

PART IV
The Ascending Star

26

Otanes, father of Vashti, stood on the balcony once belonging to his daughter, from which she as a child had often watched the distant highway and the bustling city below.

For some months now he had known of her whereabouts, having received the information from Angus, guardian of the new harem.

Angus and Vashti had not always seen eye to eye. From the time she had been a little girl in the courts of Darius, she had resented his treatment of the king's women, and he had resented her interference, her constant suggestions and counterpoints. But the callous fellow had a soft spot for the princess in his brutish heart, and since her banishment and the reinstatement of the harem, he had turned his resentments toward Xerxes.

Otanes had been present at the banquet on the night that his son-in-law had, in besotted stupor, cast Vashti from the palace. Ever since, he had sought to know anything he could about her.

General Otanes had opted out of Xerxes' Greek campaigns, unwilling to serve Darius' successor once he had betrayed the queen. As head of one of the seven most privileged families in Persia, he had the right to bow out of military service, and he did so in spite of the fact that he had long lived and breathed to incorporate Greece into the empire.

From the night of the banquet, seething hatred of Xerxes had grown in him, festering into unrequited desire for vengeance. With the acquisition of the harem, and now talk of a new queen, he was bent fully on revenge.

Yes, he knew where Vashti was. And his skin crawled at the thought of her lonely, outcast existence in the wilds of Zagros, in the prison camp of Persia's enemies.

Since the time of Darius' forays into Europe, captured Greeks had been exiled in the stark and snowbound region east of the desert. Otanes had once seen their village, no more than a tract of wooden huts and mud houses. He had deposited a wagonload of prisoners there years before. It had been spring, and though the narrow valley was covered with cedar and mulberry trees, and wildflowers graced the rugged steeps, melting snows had left the rutted street a torrent. Sewage flowed down every path, and sickness stalked the doorways.

He could imagine his gracious Vashti, his aristocratic daughter, taunted every day, persecuted for her relation to Xerxes. He could imagine her sitting in some dark cabin, her once-royal garments long ago fallen into disrepair, and herself obliged to don the habit of strangers.

Greeks were a volatile race. He knew this, for he had observed them firsthand, both in war and as an occupying officer in their Ionian district. While they were also a merry lot, "descendants of Dionysus," god of wine, they were also captious and restive. He could imagine them dancing around his daughter, laughing and deriding as she sat unwilling beside their evening fire.

With their tight-braided hair, heavy black robes, and tattooed hands and faces, they would be leering at her. They would be swaying about her, arms raised, as pipe and drum echoed their hilarity. A thousand clacking cowrie shells, strewn upon their belts and dangling from their headdresses, would mimic their derision. And Vashti—hopeless, alien, exile of exiles—would endure the humiliation alone.

How Otanes hated Xerxes! The lad he had once loved like a son, who had grown up beside his daughter, whose alliance with her had been a coveted thing, was now the object of his fondest loathing. If he could but find a way to bring him down, to make him suffer the way Vashti surely suffered!

But he would need help. Though he was a man of influence, treachery against a king required careful planning and collusion.

Turning from the balcony, he raked his memory for faces and names of those in power who might feel antipathy toward Xerxes. It need not be antipathy of the same intensity he felt, nor for the same reasons. But if there was a seed of it anywhere, he could help it sprout and blossom.

Whether it was a good or an evil spirit which presented the suggestion to him, he knew not. Neither did he care. Indeed, it was genius which reminded him of Haman, the man currently closest to the king.

He recalled, as though it were yesterday, the little cabinet meeting held in Darius' chambers as that monarch plotted his ill-fated escapade into Greece. He recalled how Haman had disapproved the tax break given the citizens in celebration of Xerxes' upcoming marriage to Vashti.

How petty it had seemed that anyone could think a war venture required such stinginess as he proposed.

Otanes had hated Haman then. He had despised his casual disregard of Vashti and her happiness, of Prince Xerxes and his betrothed.

But now he saw Haman's resistance in a different light, in the light of his own loathing. Although Haman had risen high in the service of Xerxes, being one of his closest advisers, perhaps a shred of his former attitude remained. Perhaps Haman was not as devoted to the king as he seemed.

A smile lit Otanes' lips as he reclined upon his daughter's childhood bed. For a long time he stayed in her chamber, pondering possibilities.

27

The murals and frescoes lining the walls of the women's hall depicted a harem life unlike that which Hadassah experienced. Today, as she and her sisters were ushered away from the hive to meet Hegai, Keeper of the Women, the young Jewess wondered what artist had conceived such carefree scenes.

The pictures were from the era of Darius and his predecessors. They supposedly related to events and themes from a previous time. But Hadassah did not believe them. She did not believe that women of any harem spent most of their time laughing and dancing and sporting about. She did not believe that women who would never again see their families, women who would never have husbands of their own choice, women, who, unless the king especially delighted in them, might never twice be called by him, could be happy.

As the girls shuffled down the polished corridor, hesitantly obeying the voice of the guards, Hadassah could not imagine them ever joyous over being here. If some long-ago artist had come upon a scene of merriment and sisterly abandon, he perceived it wrongly. Perhaps he had seen girls frolicking in the pool, splashing one another and giggling, as girls will do. But he had not known their deepest hearts. Perhaps he had found them, from time to time, given to the rhythm of a pipe or tambourine. But he did not understand that they danced around heavy hearts, vainly trying to bury their misery in the moment.

If he saw the other side of their existence, he did not portray it. Such a thing would not have satisfied a king when he came to gaze upon his women. Such a thing would have cooled the ardor of a hungry monarch, passing this way to indulge his senses and select a beauty for the night.

Xerxes had not yet entered this hall, for the women were still in preparation for him. The year of his yearning for a bride was not yet over, and the selection process had not yet begun. But soon enough it would begin, as evidenced by several servants just now kneeling in the corridor with paintbrushes and putty, filling in chips, refurbishing faded colors, and updating the frescoes.

Tears threatened to spill over Hadassah's stony face as she plodded behind her sisters. She wondered if Hegai, Keeper of the Women, would interrogate her today, if he would ask her nationality or her family name. She prayed that he would not, for she did not know what she would say, and she was determined to honor Mordecai's request for secrecy.

They waited outside Hegai's door for what seemed a very long time before a portly woman came to fetch them.

Hadassah could not know that Dorca was Mordecai's "connection." But Dorca knew who Hadassah was, and she smiled especially kindly on her as she guided the virgins into the chamber.

The girls were all dressed alike, in simple cotton smocks, their street clothes having been taken from them—to be burned, they were told. Dorca understood, as they might not, that they were dressed simply and uniformly so that when Hegai looked upon them for the first time he would be able to judge them on fundamental beauty alone. No extravagant clothing, coiffure, or adornment must distract his eye from its discerning purpose.

For Hegai was seeking not just a quantity of women who would please the king, but that one special girl worthy to be queen.

Hadassah had expected Hegai to be another Angus. She was therefore very surprised when a little wisp of a man emerged from the office and came forth to greet the girls.

While Dorca introduced Hegai as the one who would manage them during their preparation, he circled the group, round and round, his hands rubbing together and his beardless chin studiously wagging this way and that.

"Uh-hmmm," he intoned, over and over, "Uh-hmmm."

Nervously, the virgins clung together as he surveyed them up and down, much as a housewife might inspect the meat hung out at market.

Yet there was much of the artist in his eye, the experienced critic. It was obvious that he knew beauty and imperfection, and could have turned away from the entwined huddle with a firm memory of each dimple, each freckle, each sweaty little hand.

Hadassah's heart pumped rapidly as he stopped near her elbow. Once more he circled the group, and then returned to her, observing her more pointedly than the others.

As he did so, his eyes brightened. And then he drew back, thoughtfully stroking his shiny chin.

"All right, all right, Dorca," he demanded in a boyish and impatient voice, "line them up."

His gaze was on Hadassah until she grew uneasy, but she followed Dorca's command and fell in line against the chamber wall, side by side with her sisters.

"Disrobe," Dorca ordered.

At this, indignant gasps arose from the little group, and the girls clung modestly to their smocks.

"It must be done," the servant insisted, trying to be callous.

Dorca had not been doing this long. She had not worked for the harem of Darius, and this routine was still uncomfortable for her. Her expression betrayed more sympathy than she liked.

As the girls shielded themselves, observing Hegai in horror, Dorca whispered, "He is a eunuch, after all. There is nothing to fear."

If the keeper heard this, he did not comment, only standing impatiently by and leafing through a sheaf of fabric samples.

When he glanced up, he again focused on Hadassah, who fumbled with her gown.

One by one the young ladies complied and cringed in shame under his scrutiny.

But it was all done quickly, and red-faced, they donned their clothes again.

Hadassah's cheeks burned and her fingers were palsied as she tugged her short tunic over her head, drew it down to her knees, and stood shaking against the wall.

"They will do," Hegai crooned.

Dorca nodded. Like so many humiliated sheep, the damsels were herded from the room until Hegai's voice stopped them.

"This one," he called to Dorca, "this one—speed her up!"

The servant followed his pointed finger and studied Hadassah with him.

Perhaps she too had seen what Hegai saw in the girl. It seemed not to surprise her when Hadassah was singled out.

"I shall," she agreed.

The young Jewess could not imagine what design they had in mind. She only crossed her arms and huddled against the back of the line.

As the virgins exited, led back to their hive, she was sure she would always feel naked. For the rest of her life.

28

Mordecai wrung his hands as he glanced between the pillars of the harem corridor. Dorca was late. Normally she met him in the hall, with word of his Hadassah, before the women's midday repast. But it was already early afternoon, and she had not come yet.

When the shuffle of her slippered feet caught his ear from behind, he wheeled about nervously.

"Madam," he greeted with a short bow, "the guard is growing suspicious. My 'inventory' work must terminate soon, and I will not be able to meet you here."

Dorca nodded. "I have expected that. But if you wish me to continue in your service, I can find a way."

The Jew smiled relief. "I do wish this," he asserted.

"Then meet me each evening in the entrance garden. I can arrange to be there after dinner," she offered.

Mordecai knew she referred to the large lobby just inside the main gate of the palace. This would be convenient to Mordecai as he sat all day upon the porch, doing his ledgers.

"Fine, fine!" he exclaimed. "The garden is open to officials of my rank. I will not attract undo notice."

Dorca's smile was reticent. "I have news today which would please most men of ambition. But in your case . . ."

"Yes," he spurred her. "It regards Hadassah?"

"She has been promoted."

Mordecai's eyes brightened reflexively. But just as fast the twinkle vanished.

"What does that mean?" he hesitated.

"Hegai sees something special in the child," the servant replied. "I just left her with the matrons where she is to enter

preparation immediately. Tradition requires a full year of puri-
fication and beautification, but your daughter's time will be
overseen with particular detail, as she is a rare find." Color fled
Mordecai's face. His middle-aged hands trembled.

"You are not proud," Dorca observed. "I feared this."

"I shall not see Hadassah after I leave this place," he sighed.
"So long as I have worked in the harem storeroom, I had the
chance to glimpse her."

The servant put forth a plump finger and stroked his sleeve.

"Perhaps the next time you see her she will be a woman in
regal splendor. My friend," she whispered, "try to see this as an
honor. Hegai is a connoisseur of beauty, and in Hadassah he has
found something rare and wonderful. The girl has been greatly
blessed."

But Mordecai only looked at the lady sadly.

"Blessed . . . or cursed?" he pondered. "I am not certain
which."

* * *

Hadassah sat upon a ledge of her private pool. Cooling fountains splashed into silent, lily-laden waters as her personal maids,
seven in all, bustled about to the commands of the head matron,
Dorca.

Here one young woman poured a flask of frankincense into
the girl's fragrant bath, and there another mixed a beautifying
paste of flour, mustard oil, turmeric, and saffron according to a
recipe recently received from India.

After Hadassah's third dip of the day into the perfumed
waters, the paste would be applied to her face and she would
sleep through one more aromatic night, still unused to the
pungent smells of her heady lair.

The evening before, a Bengalese mixture of sandalwood and
aloes had been administered, leaving her cheeks atingle, and
when it had been removed this morning, a stubborn flush had
remained part of her complexion for hours.

But all of this was supposed to perfect her—to make her more
beautiful than any other woman in the empire.

She wished that she might feel some enthusiasm for the project, which had already extended over three months. She knew that many of her harem sisters would have traded places with her at any opportunity.

The Phoenician was one of her handpicked helpers. Dorca had let Hadassah have some say in which girls were taken from the hive to assist in her personal preparation. She had selected the dark beauty from the coastland out of compassion, though the proud girl would have scorned the notion.

As for Maryam, her fellow villager, she envied Hadasssah not at all. Tender pity marked her attendance on the Jewess, for she knew Hadassah would never have chosen this "honor." She was only glad that Leah's young cousin had not forgotten her, once gone from the lower harem, and she was grateful to serve her.

Two other girls fumbled through a pile of silks and velvets, giggling and trying on today's collection of fashionable gowns, all made to complement Hadassah's natural glory to best advantage. "Oh, my lady," one exclaimed, "you will love these! Why, they are the best yet!"

Dorca, with a gesture, flicked the girls away from the rack. "The lady's linens must be changed," she barked, ordering them to the boudoir where Hadassah would recline for the night. Quickly they scurried away to change Hadassah's bedding for the second time since morning, since she had napped upon the couch, soiling it with the pastes and oils applied earlier to her skin.

Everything about this private chamber, the most indulgent in the harem, was pure luxury. Countless girls would have found life here beyond their wildest fantasies. But Hadassah had never longed for such attentions.

When Dorca set a tiny tray of stuffed prunes and iced apples before her, she only sighed. And when the matron turned away, a tear trickled down Hadassah's cheek, streaking the face cream spread upon it.

Maryam bent over her, stroking her dark curls.

"The king was seen from the harem wall today, riding with his attendants along the river," she whispered. "His royal parasol tipped back, Hadassah, and some of the girls saw his face . . ."

The Jewess did not respond.

"Oh, Hadassah, they say he is very handsome!" Maryam went on, trying to cheer her.

Still the favored one said nothing. Memories of David's golden eyes haunted her, and in her heart she walked beside him through the wheat fields.

29

Xerxes sat on the edge of his bed, staring through the twilight which crept with desert dawn through his chamber window. His huge feather pallet, elevated from the floor on golden ram's feet and enclosed with gauze draperies, cradled a young woman. Upon her face his regal gaze lingered.

He could not recall her name. He would forget her as soon as he sent her from the room. And he would never request her again.

For three months the king of the Eastern world had enjoyed the company of a new girl each evening. But he could remember only a handful. When he especially admired a certain female, he commanded her name and a brief description to be registered in his private chronicle so that he might summon her again.

Thus far the list in the royal book was quite short. And he had not bothered to request a girl a second time.

Upon dismissal from the king's chamber, each young lady was ushered to the house of the concubines, to live out her life on the chance that she might be useful in the future. Most would face years of loneliness and despair, their youthful beauty fading, their isolation prison-like despite its luxuries.

Most girls, however inexperienced, could tell after their first night whether or not they had pleased their "husband." For Xerxes was developing a volatile temper, and some of the women were thrust from the chamber before the moon had fully risen, their virginity still intact.

The sweet and simple child who now lay sleeping beside him would not encounter that side of the king. It ebbed and flowed unpredictably, and she had come to him when he was in a conciliatory mood. Nor did most of those who were rebuffed know what they had done to incur his wrath, being often among the loveliest and most charming of the "brides."

Beyond the bedroom door two guards stood, waiting on the emperor's emergence, waiting to escort the girl to the Keeper of the Concubines, the Shaashgaz, who was in charge of the second harem.

The guards had come by their work ironically. Having once served as Vashti's sentinels at the door of her private chamber, they were promoted to serve the king when she was sent away.

Their new station did not please them. They had loved the queen a long while, being her attendants when she was a child and having served her in Otanes' house. Sorely did they resent the lady's banishment, and it distressed them each time a new "bride" arrived to consort with the king.

When the door to Xerxes' chamber was at last drawn open, and the most recent "wife" stepped shakily into the corridor, they bowed rigidly toward the room's dark shadows.

They could not see the king, nor did he speak to them. Without a word he had dismissed the lady, and she stood now with the sentinels, wondering what was to come.

"You take her back," Teresh said, nodding to his companion. "I tire of this."

Bigthan, the other guard, sighed sympathetically, turning toward the errand with stooped shoulders.

Their brief interchange did not go unobserved. Otanes, father of Vashti, was rarely so near the king's chambers, especially this early in the morning. But family business had brought him at dawn to this sector of the palace, and as he passed by the emperor's quarters, he overheard the unhappy murmur.

Eager as he was for names to add to his ledger of malcontents, he registered their identity in his mental file.

These two fellows might be advantageous to him—a snare to the king.

30

Mordecai paced through the porch before the palace's garden gate, darting glances through the portal.

"Late again!" he muttered, wondering what could be detaining his contact, Dorca, this time.

The sky above the open porch was dark with thunderclouds. It was "mud month" again, a full year since Hadassah had been abducted to the harem. Anxiety had been growing in the girl's adopted father as the anniversary of her imprisonment drew near. Daily he raised earnest petitions to Jehovah, pleading for the child's release, for some miracle of intervention which would spare her from shame.

It was dinnertime throughout the palace. Most of the executives and hired help who lived outside the king's house had gone home for the evening. Mordecai would have been among them except that he had an arrangement to meet Dorca at this time each day. So far no one had questioned his lingering after hours. But he feared that sometime his "late work" might be suspect, should anyone find him pacing the open air of the garden.

The longer Dorca took, the more fidgety Mordecai became, until he heard her quick shuffle in the entry.

"I am sorry, sir," she apologized, coming upon him with her own anxieties, "I could not break away from Hegai. He kept me late tonight, preparing our dear lady for the morrow."

Though this announcement was given without hesitation, her face showed lines of regret.

"Hadassah . . ." Mordecai whispered.

"I fear so, my friend. But you must have known it was inevitable. Tomorrow is one year to the day since she was brought here. Hegai will not delay sending her to His Majesty."

"Tomorrow evening?" he said, his voice tremulous.

Dorca only nodded, and Mordecai stared at the floor through tear-filled eyes.

Hope lay in shattered shards at his feet, faith peeled itself from his heart. For 12 months he had prayed for Hadassah's salvation, finding it incredible that Jehovah could allow an innocent child to undergo such defilement.

Perhaps, he thought, perhaps he should have taught her to rebel, to risk her young life to escape the evil design. Perhaps he had been woefully remiss in suggesting to the girl that Jehovah could have brought her here. Perhaps he should have told her that she had the right to save herself regardless of the cost.

Suddenly reality clutched at him with cutting claws. Nothing he had assumed seemed apt to prove itself. Nothing he had dreamed would come true.

Dorca stood uneasily in his presence, waiting for her pittance of payment, the daily drachma of wage received for her secret service.

When Mordecai appeared to have forgotten her, she did not press him.

She said something about meeting him another day, but he did not hear her, and after she had departed he stood for a long while, staring blankly at the swirling floor.

It was not until another set of feet shuffled into the silent garden that Mordecai glanced up from his sad preoccupation. When his gaze fell upon Haman, his blood ran cold.

Stealthily he turned from the arboretum, and with a chill across his shoulders he hurried home.

Had he remained, he might have witnessed yet another rendezvous within the twilight court. For it was Otanes who had requested Haman's presence here, and moments after the prime minister's arrival, the general joined him.

The plot they discussed was private unto themselves. But in time the simple bookkeeper, the Jew who had long suspected Haman's capacity for treachery, would be their unwitting foil.

31

Hadassah stood before a long brass mirror in her private dressing room. Her seven personal maids surrounded her, their faces smitten with awe.

After four hours of helping their mistress to dress and undress, to try on one gown after another, it seemed that the most radiant combination of raiment, accessories, and hairstyle imaginable had been struck upon. Surely the keeper, Hegai, would be pleased this time when he came to inspect their handiwork. Had he not, after all, personally selected every piece of this ensemble? His temperamental taste had driven him to rage more than once this day when he had come to approve their choices. Nothing, nothing had pleased him. But surely this time there was no improving upon the lady's appearance.

Indeed, Hadassah herself was stricken speechless as she gazed upon her likeness in the mirror. Despite her fears and the dreaded ordeal which lay ahead, she could not repress a smile of surprise and delight as her reflection stared back at her.

Hardly did it seem possible that this was she! Hadassah had never been blind to her own beauty, but the regal glory of the female in the glass was beyond any she had ever witnessed before.

A lump caught in her slender throat as she turned slowly this way and that. Raising her hand to her mouth, she held back a little cry of joy.

Her keeper had chosen the most complimentary of colors for his favorite damsel. The gown, of purest linen, had been dyed a pale lavender and was cinched to her tiny waist by a broad cummerbund of royal scarlet. The scarlet, in fact, verged on magenta, with every tuck and hem piped in deep purple.

Upon her small feet were slippers of velvet, likewise of magenta hue, encrusted with gleaming rubies, violet sapphires, and amethysts. The slightly upturned toes sported tinkling bells, so teeny that they would be heard only when she walked upon the deep carpet of the king's silent chamber.

But even as she peered down at the silver ornaments where they glinted against the velvet, her heart quivered, and she could not retract the tear which gleamed upon her cheek.

David should be the first man to see this glory. Yes, David, her love—and not a Persian despot.

With numb fingers she brushed the betraying tear from her face and tried to smile again. However, when she looked once more into the glass, the image of her beloved had transposed itself over her own, with sad and hurt-filled countenance.

None of her companions saw the phantom in the mirror, and no one seemed to notice her sorrow. Save for Maryam.

As the other women laughed and giggled about her, holding the broad train of her dress to their own cheeks and dancing, her little friend came close and placed a sympathetic hand upon her shoulder.

But Maryam had no time to speak a comforting word, for suddenly the chamber door opened and Dorca bustled in, chatting excitement to Hegai, who followed with an anxious step.

"See," she exclaimed, "see! Is it not as I told you? How can she be better? She is the beauty of the world!"

The maids, who had worked so hard to achieve the effect which Hegai would now assess, held their breath as the eunuch drew into the lamplight and beheld Hadassah.

For a long while he said nothing, his face vacant. And the girls were more nervous by the minute.

Their lady was due to go before the king this very evening. If the keeper did not appreciate this work of art . . . they feared the consequences.

Slowly he circled the Jewess, uttering not a word, until even Dorca became apprehensive.

When the keeper suddenly fell to his knees, bowing over and over before Hadassah, everyone drew back in wonder.

Except for Dorca. Her expression, while one of amazement, was mixed with relief, and she nodded her head, smiling to herself.

As for Hadassah, she observed the eunuch fearfully, pondering the meaning of his strange behavior.

"My Lady!" he cried, lifting wet eyes to the Jewess, "surely you are Vashti! Surely you are the dear queen!"

Hadassah looked about her, more terrified yet, seeking an explanation.

Instantly Dorca was at her side, bowing from the waist.

"Hegai is right, my child," she agreed. "How you resemble our banished Lady!"

Recalling the one time that she had been privileged to look upon the queen, when as a child she had peered between the spindles of the garden balcony, Hadassah turned again to the mirror and with hesitation surveyed her reflection.

A chill passed down her spine and she grasped her skirt with a trembling hand. Long ago as it had been, the recollection of Vashti matched that in the glass, and Hadassah braced herself against vertigo.

But now Hegai was standing, and as the girl studied the mirror, Dorca handed the keeper the cape which he had designed for this ensemble.

Stepping behind the Jewess, the eunuch tenderly draped the stole around her shoulders and gazed with her into the glass.

"It is a miracle!" he cried.

And it was. The purple stole, embroidered with pink and lavender irises, drew the entire outfit together, lending Hadassah an unmistakable look of royalty.

Feeling faint now, the girl put forth a hand, and Hegai held her upright.

"It is fitting that you should have a new name," the eunuch pronounced. "A new name for a new life. You shall be called 'Esther,' for you are worthy of nothing less."

Hadassah clutched his hand more firmly, her breath coming anxiously. Esther? No more dreadful designation could be applied to a Jewess, for Esther, or Ishtar, was the most pagan of goddesses, the Astarte of the Canaanites, the Aphrodite and the

Venus of the Greeks. Goddess of fertility and sexuality, she was a demeaning label for any girl who loved Jehovah.

Shaking her head, Hadassah wished to cry aloud. But, remembering Mordecai's injunction to keep her race a secret, she choked back her horror.

And now Hegai was standing before her, placing a fresh orchid in her raven hair and weaving its short stem between the intricate waves.

Bidding her take his arm, he turned her about and led her forth from the chamber.

She would not remember the long walk down the palace's cold corridor. She would not notice the awe-filled faces of all who saw her, nor would she hear the gasps of wonder which followed her bleak passage.

She walked into a void, mystified that faith should have failed her.

32

Esther stood within the king's dimly lit chamber, the door having been closed behind her.

Xerxes, Emperor of the East, master of the greatest empire on earth, had not yet acknowledged her presence, but only sat brooding at his northern window. He had no reason to pay this new "bride" any more mind than he had paid the dozens brought before.

It was true that Hegai had personally escorted Esther to his door rather than sending her with a guard. It was true that the eunuch had, upon introducing her to the bridal suite, emphasized her new name. And if anything should have piqued the king's interest, it would have been this.

For though the emperor was a devout adherent of the one god Ahura-Mazda, the name "Ishtar" in any language had a way of thrilling the blood of most men.

It had troubled the keeper when Xerxes had ignored the introduction, receiving Esther with a flick of the hand and failing to even turn his head toward her. But Hegai had shut the door upon the couple, confident that when the king did glimpse the girl he would succumb to her humble charms.

And humble she was. This too might have troubled Hegai. He might have wondered just how adept the young virgin could be at seduction. But he passed off the concern. What need had such beauty of experience or of effort? The fact that any female so designed was flesh and blood, and not a statue conceived by wild fantasy, would be enough to secure her place in Xerxes' favor.

For no man could fail to love her. No man could ignore her, Hegai was certain. Even he, stripped of his masculinity, rendered impotent from birth that he might serve the palace with docile single-mindedness—even he was moved in his own way by this girl.

So Esther stood, unspeaking in the shadows, awaiting whatever lay ahead.

Never had she prayed so fervently as during these moments. If Jehovah intended to intervene, He must do so now. For weeks she had, in hours of fear, rehearsed the childhood lessons of Judaism learned upon Mordecai's lap, memorized at Leah's knee. Tonight, however, they eluded her, and she found herself cast helplessly upon blind trust.

Somehow, though it made no sense to her, she must accept whatever should happen here. Having done all she could to please Jehovah, she must abandon herself to any tyranny that God might permit.

With an empty sigh she looked down at the garment that Hegai had prepared for her. Each girl was allowed to choose the outfit she would wear upon her "wedding" night, heeding or disregarding Hegai's advice as she wished. But Esther had not quibbled, having determined ahead of time that she would accept the eunuch's advice. Truly his taste was impeccable, and he had done well by her.

The garment symbolized the end of life as she had known it. It was, in fact, all she had in this world. Every young woman, upon the day she went before the king, was allowed to take from the harem whatever she wished. Most girls had given this privilege much advance thought, gathering up enough jewels, gold, spices, and fine fabrics to secure their futures and the futures of their loved ones beyond the palace walls for years to come. But Esther had requested nothing but the clothes upon her slender frame.

This was all she needed. Material goods would never cheer a future without family . . . without David. . . .

It seemed she waited in the shadows for an eternity, though by the wintry glow of sunset beyond the king's window it had been only moments since she arrived.

Quivering, Esther surveyed her intended. Though he was in silhouette against the ruddy night, she could see that he was a tall man, and strong. His features, framed by the departing light, were regal; his hair, where it spilled in waves to his shoulders, was lustrous and dark.

Still, until she could see his eyes, she would know little about him save what rumor had imputed to him. And rumor had painted a fearful picture—one of capriciousness and cruelty.

Through the window's scalloped arch the famed Zagros mountains loomed, distant and austere.

Was the emperor at prayer? Esther wondered. The faraway mountains were sacred to the Persians, she knew, especially to those who followed the teachings of Zoroaster.

But, then, she reminded herself, Xerxes was the man who had sent his queen into exile. Could such a creature bear a bone of religious devotion in his body? Ahura-Mazda, she had heard, was very much like Jehovah—God of the universe, a kind and just deity. If it were possible that the Persians received some spiritual light from their worship, Xerxes had surely turned from it.

It must have been the descending dark which spurred the king to turn at last from the window. When he did, he did not immediately focus on the girl in the shadows. It seemed, in fact, that he had forgotten her very presence. And Esther was surprised to note that his eyes, now visible in the lamplight, bore a heavy sadness. Far from indicating a cold heart, they betrayed a wounded spirit, taking Hadassah aback.

"Well, let us see what we have here," the emperor suddenly commanded, gesturing her forward, though still not looking upon her.

Cautiously the virgin Jewess stepped into the lamp's exposing glow, and at last the king glanced up from whatever wistful thoughts had held him.

As he did, his expression grew from one of apathy to one of incredulity. Gripping the bedpost, he held himself steady and slowly sank to the mattress, sitting palefaced as one who witnessed an apparition.

"Lord Ahura-Mazda," he gasped, "can it be? Vashti, my bride!"

Esther, rigid with fright, dared not contradict the king.

Finding strength to rise, Xerxes approached her, his lips trembling.

"Thank you, Ahura," he was whispering over and over. "Thank you."

Reaching for Esther, he enfolded her in strong arms, repeating Vashti's name in her ear.

Terrified, the girl struggled in his embrace. But he allowed no resistance.

"My child," he groaned, "bless me. Do not deny your king . . . your husband. Let me believe in miracles."

Pressing his lips to her neck, he drew her cape from off her shoulders, stroking her bare arms with gentle hands.

Dizzy from his persistent caress, Esther closed her eyes, and the lamplight yielded to the night.

* * *

Somewhere deep in the Zagros, Vashti, deposed Queen of the East, lurched upright on her bed of animal skins.

Her face, still lovely despite the lines which loneliness and alienation had traced, peeked through the darkness toward her distant royal city.

Something had roused her from near slumber— some dread awareness.

She was alone in her wooden hut. Everyone else in the village was asleep. But there would have been no consolation even in brightest daylight. Had she spoken fluent Greek, none of her fellow exiles would have cared for her plight.

Lying down again, she listened to the beating of her solitary heart. Somehow she knew that Xerxes was not alone. Somehow she sensed the rising of another star.

ESTHER

PART V

For Such a Time as This

33

The sky over Susa was a rainbow of color. Phosphorescent greens, blues, and vermillion lit up the night in explosive auroras.

Xerxes had spared no expense in celebrating his marriage to Esther. Within a week of her coming to him a holiday had been declared, imperial gifts in the form of reduced taxes had been given the provinces, and people had exchanged lavish presents.

The wedding itself, held in Persepolis, was unparalleled in Persian history. And immediately following, the king announced a banquet in Susa's royal house. "Esther's banquet," he called it, a reception second in grandeur only to the many-month celebration at which he had banished Vashti.

Fireworks had been displayed each evening for a week, igniting the sky above the acropolis with symbolic splendor, because the emperor, after years of disappointment, misery, and futile endeavors to find happiness, was experiencing life once again.

Daily he called his new queen to dine with him in his private suite, and nightly he loved her with an ardor unknown since last he had lain with Vashti.

He assumed that Esther must be as happy as he was, though not once had he asked her. In fact, he knew nothing of Esther's heart, reading in her only what he wanted to read. And what he wanted to read was that she was the answer to prayer, the closest thing to Vashti returned to him.

There was another man, however, who wondered how Esther felt. She had never been out of his thoughts since the night she was abducted to the palace.

David stood at his village's western gate, watching the bursting aura across the desert.

Hope had died when Hadassah was taken to the king's chamber.

David had known what evening that was. He had counted the dawns and sunsets leading to it, 365 of them.

As he stood tonight at the low village wall, studying the celebrating flashes, each explosion sent a spear through his heart. He was no warrior. He had no weapon with which to fight back—only the farmer's hoe upon which he leaned. And the acropolis, bathed in azure and scarlet, mocked his poverty.

Should he wonder any longer how Hadassah felt? Was she not the owner of an emperor's embraces, pride of a sovereign's heart, wealthiest woman on earth?

David gripped the handle of his hoe in a stranglehold. Perhaps he should wrap the long tool in fancy paper and send it to the palace, he thought cynically. It was all he could offer as a wedding gift. It was all he possessed.

Glancing heavenward again, he shrugged and dropped the hoe against the wall. Downcast, he plodded home, pushing against the weight of a hollow heart.

34

Clouds of nearing spring swept over Susa's acropolis. Queen Esther, hastening through the inner court, glanced skyward but did not see the cottony tufts, her mind speeding higher, seeking Jehovah in earnest prayer.

She would be with her papa in a few moments. Using her regal position to advantage, she had arranged to "interview" the bookkeeper for a position as her private accountant.

She had let no one know of her relationship to the Jew, in accordance with Mordecai's wishes. It was only under the guise of business that she could even properly be seen by any male other than her husband. But she had made certain that no one else would be present, sending all her maids off on errands and scheduling the "audience" in an unguarded alcove.

"Let nothing hinder this stolen moment," she pleaded as she hurried toward the rendezvous.

Passing through the final vestibule before the garden, she came to a frozen halt, a deep shadow having fallen across her path.

High above, upon a fluted pedestal, the enormous black stone head of a sacred bull stared down upon her. Fully as great in length as the lady's own height, and half as wide, it hovered over her like a disapproving giant. And across the broad aisle was its partner, equally brooding.

Though she was queen, she had not been trained for the part. She was still a humble Jewess, quiet daughter of a quiet man.

The bulls threatened her, doubting her ability, suspecting her.

For a long moment she hesitated beneath their austere gazes. Gleaming in the brilliant sun, they leveled dark questions at her, their cold, polished eyes and heavy brows deflecting all signs of weakness.

Quietly she eased past them, entering the garden and the alcove through a haze of self-castigation.

But when she saw Mordecai, her countenance brightened.

"Papa!" she cried, flinging her arms wide and flying to him. Mordecai drew back, shaking his head and bowing.

"My Queen," he hailed.

Horrified, Esther stared at him, hot tears rising to blind her.

"Papa?" she returned. "It is I, your Hadassah."

But Mordecai could only gaze speechlessly upon her.

Did he disapprove as well, she wondered? Did he recoil from the stain upon her life?

In agonized silence the girl turned her face to the floor, and Mordecai, seeing her distress, at last found words.

"Hadassah . . ." he whispered. "It is only that you . . . you are royalty now. And a woman, a beautiful woman . . . not a girl. Hardly would I recognize you, did I not know you so well."

Though this acknowledgment bore a sting, a smile parted Esther's lips, and with a sigh she reached for him again.

"It has been so long . . ." Mordecai cried, returning the embrace. "Can you still care for this old man—this . . . commoner?"

"Papa!" Esther rebuked him. "Do not speak so!"

But it was Mordecai's turn to smile. And clinging, they wept together.

Just as quickly, however, the Jew held her at arm's length, his face etched with urgency.

"Child," he whispered, "bear with a bit of whimsy, if you will. There is something I must tell you."

Esther studied him quizzically, wondering at the anxious mystery in his tone.

"Of course, Papa," she nodded. "What troubles you?"

Casting a wary glance over his shoulder, he continued, "There is evil afoot in this place. I have felt it for months, and today, on my way here, I witnessed it firsthand." Then, bowing again, he seemed to beg her indulgence, and she spurred him.

"Papa, I am your Hadassah," she asserted. "Please go on."

"Perhaps it was my imagination . . ." he hesitated. "But as

I came down the main corridor, I passed by two men who consulted together, dressed like guards—royal guards. Both were tall, and very strong, as though . . ."

"The king's doorkeepers," Esther guessed. "Dark and bearded?"

"Yes, yes!" Mordecai enthused. "You know them, then?"

Esther's mind flashed to the night she had first been introduced to the king's chamber, and she nodded with wistful sadness.

"Then I am not mistaken!" the Jew determined. "The king is in danger!"

Quickly reciting the conversation overheard in the hall, he warned the queen that this very evening Xerxes' life was at stake. "'When he is asleep, after the chamberlain puts out his light . . .'" he quoted them. Then, rubbing his hands nervously together, Mordecai continued, "Oh, child, they thought they were alone, and when I suddenly rounded the corner, coming upon them, they covered their plot with idle chatter."

Esther's face grew pale, and drawing close, she confirmed Mordecai's fears. "There are many who hate the emperor," she agreed. "Many loved Vashti, and I have sensed jealously for that lady in the air since the day I took the throne. . . ."

"Then, my child," Mordecai cringed, "you also could be in danger!"

Esther shivered, and placed a cold hand on her papa's arm.

"You shall be rewarded," she commanded him. "I do not know the king well, but I know he honors his friends."

Mordecai glanced at the tiled floor, an ironic smirk working at his lips. "I, a *friend* of Xerxes," he laughed. "I dare say, I love him less than anyone could."

Gazing into Hadassah's sympathetic eyes, he shook his head. "There is more . . . much more than I have told you," he insisted. "There is more evil here than a plot between bedroom guards."

The queen awaited an explanation, but he could give none. It was an intuition of the blood which told him—an insight of the spirit giving warning.

"In time we shall see it all," he said. "For now I know nothing."

Esther felt the pallor of his prophecy, and did not question it. Recalling the dark gazes of the garden bulls, the black gleam of their marbled eyes, she knew he spoke the truth.

The palace of Persia was a battlefield, and the opponents played a contest more profound than politics.

35

The incident with the king's guards was to be only the first skirmish in the supernatural battle staged in Persia's royal house. Of all the people in the land, only Mordecai the Jew saw it as something more than a human battle. And even he could not foresee the part it played in the greater drama.

Otanes and Haman certainly did not perceive the working out of a higher plan. To Otanes, the attempt to overthrow Xerxes was a justified act of retaliation. To Haman, whose assistance Otanes had promised to reward, the goal had been personal advancement.

When the general and the prime minister lost the first round, they determined even more sincerely to work for Xerxes' demise.

In the executive courtyard they met this afternoon, beneath the swaying shadows of two corpses, the bodies of Bigthan and Teresh, suspended from the gallows of Xerxes' wrath.

"Who revealed the plot?" Otanes snarled, disappointment heavy beneath his breath.

"A minor executive," Haman replied, "the Jew who now keeps the books for Queen Esther."

His loathing of the race readily surfaced, and Otanes shrugged. "The one who used to sit at the gate? Head of inventory?"

"The same," Haman smirked. "One can never be too careful."

"Careful?" Otanes sneered. "The fools must have heralded their plan upon the palace roof!"

"Well, it is done now," Haman sighed, glancing up at the dead men on the gallows.

Otanes said nothing, deep in thought. Then, having struck upon a new idea, he eagerly pursued a different tack.

"Haman, how would you like your reward *now* . . . before the deed is done?"

The prime minister studied the general, incredulous. Leaning forward eagerly, he dreamed of glory.

* * *

Trumpets blared in the gate of Susa's palace. Haman was entering, and everyone prepared to do him homage.

Xerxes, prey to the blindness common to the powerful which renders them insensible to dangers directly beneath their noses, saw Haman as a loyal adviser, a man of duty and accomplishment who had served his father well and who served his own administration admirably. When Otanes came before the king praising the prime minister and suggesting that some great honor be heaped upon him, Xerxes, wishing to appear magnanimous, elevated the Agagite, establishing his position as second in command of the empire. With this, he went so far as to require all servants and princes of the royal house to bow down whenever the man passed by. Refusal to do so would not only merit Haman's disapproval but would invoke the wrath of the emperor himself.

In reality, the "advancement" carried little political clout. Haman was already grand vizier. But this public commendation on the part of Xerxes raised his prominence in the eyes of all, forcing them to render obeisance, however begrudgingly.

Haman was not a popular figure. He had few admirers and fewer lovers. But since the king's edict had been enacted, it could be suicide to ignore him.

Therefore, it was with incredulous wonder that the palace servants, bowing as Haman entered the gate, observed Mordecai's rebellion.

The Jew would not bow. The Jew would not pay homage to an Agagite.

Stiff and austere, the gray-bearded Hebrew sat behind his accounting bench upon the public porch, unyielding as the prime minister passed his way.

Until Mordecai foiled the assassination attempt, Haman had brushed elbows with the Jew on numerous occasions but had paid him little mind. He was, as he had told Otanes, a "minor executive," and a Jew at that.

But this day, when Mordecai drew attention to himself through blatant disrespect, Haman had more reason than ever to notice him. In an instant the Jew leapt from obscurity to public prominence.

Haman, stopping directly before the bookkeeper's table, said nothing, waiting for his compliance. But Mordecai's behavior was not the product of oversight. Directly he stared back at the prime minister, refusing to bow, until Haman's face flushed crimson with anger, and amazed whispers fluttered about the court.

Had Haman only rebuked him, the Jew's position might not have seemed so precarious. But when the Agagite turned for the palace door, entering the royal house without a word, retribution was all the more imminent.

Once Haman was out of sight, the spectators gathered around the quiet Hebrew like astonished gossips.

"Why are you transgressing the king's command?" they queried.

Mordecai, a very private man, had never drawn so much notice. But an answer was ready on his tongue.

Stroking his frosted beard, he framed the reply with dignity. "Because," he said, "I am a Jew."

36

Haman paced the king's council chamber, counting the alabaster tiles with his toes, his face etched with feigned frustration.

"How your royal patience must have been strained all these years, Your Majesty! I do not know how you have endured it," he exclaimed.

Xerxes leaned forward upon his throne, his own expression one of bewildered scrutiny.

"Say again, Haman," he implored. "These folk to whom you refer—they have been party to sedition?"

"Indeed, Your Highness. But you must know it. Surely—oh, I see . . . How clever of you to test me, Sire. You wish a fuller disclosure of their activities?"

Xerxes, not wishing to appear unaware of the supposed dissension within his kingdom, only nodded.

Haman, with a sigh of deep concern, ceased his pacing and rubbed his hands together. "O King, live forever!" he intoned. "You know that there is a certain people . . ." And here he peered about him, as though concealing their identity was of critical importance to the safety of the realm, ". . . a certain people scattered abroad and dispersed among the folk of all the provinces of your kingdom. And their customs are different from everyone else's. Nor do they keep the king's laws," he lied. Then, with a quick and deliberate pronouncement, he concluded, "Therefore it is not for the king's profit to allow them to continue!"

The emperor sat back, studying Haman blankly. Dare he let on that he was less informed than his key adviser regarding such widespread subversion? And dare he question the very man whose reputation he had so recently secured, whom he had just publicly endorsed as second-in-command of his entire empire?

He knew not of whom Haman spoke. He did not know that this tax pirate had a personal vendetta against a single Jew, a modest bookkeeper. He did not know that Haman's wounded pride could prompt him to appeal for a pogrom against an entire race.

Xerxes had his own struggle with pride. Therefore, rather than admit to ignorance, he would affirm Haman's stand.

Swallowing hard, he considered the prime minister's intentions.

"What do you wish of me?" he asked at last.

A gleam flashed through Haman's eyes. "If it please the king," he said with a low bow, "let it be written that these people may be destroyed."

He hesitated to look upon Xerxes. Quickly he added, "I will pay 10,000 talents of silver to the mercenaries who carry out the business . . . for the king's treasuries, of course."

Haman, still in a bowed posture, remained that way for some seconds as the king surveyed him with a drumming heart. When Xerxes finally spoke, a thrill of certain vengeance shot through the Agagite.

Taking his royal ring from off his finger, the one with which he sealed all documents of law, the emperor handed it to Haman.

As the prime minister held forth a sweaty hand to receive it, Xerxes grasped at a show of power. "Keep the silver," he flaunted. "Go and do as seems good to you."

37

Xerxes ambled through the court of his harem, luxuriating in the fleshly beauty of half-clad women who, on cue, sported before him in their garden pool.

Never let it be implied by blushing cheek or hesitant gyration that any girl upon whom he gazed was obliged to tease him. The flirtatious cavorting must always be spirited, as though prompted by ardent love.

After all, were not his visits to this sanctum very rare? Especially since he had taken Esther to wife, he had seen little reason to grace this court with his regal presence.

As compared with previous Persian monarchs, Xerxes' attention to his concubines was becoming more and more casual. In fact, now that he had married the lovely Jewess, his lifestyle bordered on monogamy.

It was true that he still allowed his underlings to continue bringing beautiful young virgins to his palace, and that he had at his disposal an entirely new bevy of maidens ready for initiation into the house of wives. But he had virtually ignored them.

As he passed through the garden this evening, it was with only cursory interest that he lingered over them. He was headed for Esther's suite.

Usually he met with his bride in his own chamber. But he had tired of that, and now wished for new surroundings. What he did not anticipate was that meeting Esther upon her own ground would reveal a side to her that he had not yet seen.

Indeed, there was much about his wife which was unknown to him. For months now he had freely called her "Vashti," reveling in her embrace as though it were the embrace of his first love. Many times Esther would have addressed this fact; she would

150

have challenged her "husband" regarding his illusions. But she had never found the strength, had never felt it her place to do so.

Tonight, as she waited in her room, in lonely anticipation of the king's arrival, some seed of self-assertion awoke within her. Perhaps it had cracked open days before, sending forth a shoot of courage when her papa had spoken of the evil in this place. But tonight it struggled for expression, and as she heeded its demands, she steeled herself against Xerxes' touch.

When he appeared in her doorway, however, he was his commanding self, the sovereign who had forced her obedience months before. His striking frame nearly filled the entry, his handsome bronze face irresistibly appealing.

Had his eyes not beseeched her, she could have been angry with him. But in his face she read his humanity—the vulnerability which allowed him to be wounded as much as he had wounded others.

As he approached across the room with admiration in his gaze, she could almost believe that he loved her—*herself*, Esther . . . Hadassah.

If, as it seemed, she was destined to remain forever with him, she must believe this. Life would be unending torment otherwise. And though she did not love him, she might be persuaded to try . . . if only . . .

But when Xerxes spoke, she knew again the truth.

"My Lady," he said, sighing a smile, "you are, of all women, worthy of this chamber. Only such great beauty as yours should enter here."

Esther had not risen from her seat beside the fireplace. Sadly she studied the shadows between the flames, the amber light betraying her heavy spirit.

"Sir," she whispered, "you often say such things, thinking they do me honor. And so they do. But they also prick my heart."

Xerxes had never heard her speak so. In fact, in all these months of marriage her heart had remained a closed scroll, nor had he attempted to read it.

Stepping close, he leaned over her, passing a gentle finger across her cheek.

"You are not yourself tonight, my dear," he crooned.

Esther pulled away and surveyed him quizzically.

"I suppose that depends upon who you think I am. If you refer to me, Esther, I am indeed myself," she asserted. "If you think of me as Vashti . . . I am not."

There. It had been said. Xerxes was incredulous—not at the revelation, for he knew he clung to illusion. But at the girl's newfound courage he was taken aback.

Still, Esther took a deep breath and added, "Is it not true, My Lord, that you did not admire *me* when you entered the room, but your memory of Vashti as she once graced this chamber? And is it not true that you still love her, and have never loved me?"

Xerxes did not readily answer. Lowering his eyes, he shunned her observation.

"By the faith of Ahura-Mazda," he swore, "I have loved you!"

At this Esther stood and faced him squarely.

"You claim the blessing of your god upon our union?" she challenged. "Do you not call him God of the Universe, King of Heaven?"

The emperor could have been offended by her tone, but instead he nodded solemn agreement.

"Then," the young Jewess declared, "he never countenanced the treachery which sent your first queen from you, and which brought me to your bed. He did, perhaps, allow all this for some cause unknown to us. But he did not ordain it. And he will not suffer the lie forever."

Esther's pulse quickened with the confrontation, and for a long moment Xerxes stood confounded by her discernment.

Longing to draw her to him, he at last turned for the door, leaving the room with stooped shoulders and wondering if he should ever hold her again.

38

The rackety clatter of large bone dice was muffled by the thick Persian carpet in Haman's council chamber.

Three young men, longtime servants of the prime minister, were huddled about a circle of goat hide upon which were mystical designs and a chart of the houses of the heavens. Over and over they rolled three "purim," the bone counters, against the leather map. As the pieces took their places upon the star chart, the men chanted out the weeks and months of the year.

For the chart was not only an astrological map but a calendar, and the bone dice chose not only certain celestial positions but their corresponding dates as well.

Night after night, the men had met to carry out the strange ceremony, and night after night Haman had watched them, pacing anxiously along the carpet and asking the interpretation of their findings.

He had chosen these fellows to perform this rite because they had always served him well. Having been his students years before in the accounting school, they had risen with him in imperial administration.

The sacred "purim," obtained by Haman from the palace priests, were used to determine the times and seasons of special events. Such dice had been rolled when Xerxes and Vashti awaited the pronouncement of their wedding date, and they were being rolled now to set the date of the pogrom against the Jews. Normally only the priests would have handled the "purim." But the case to be decided here was a matter of national security, Haman claimed, and government officials could be ordained to determine the times for such things.

As the servants tossed the counters again and again, brows

153

dotted with sweat from the hours-long ordeal and throats rasping from interminable chanting, they rocked to and fro upon their heels, their knees sore with chafing against the woolly carpet.

At last, however, one of the men gave a cry.

"We have a match!" he declared.

"A match?" Haman repeated, hesitant to enjoy the possibility.

"It is definite, Master!" another confirmed. "The number of our throw corresponds perfectly with the number on the dice, and it has fallen upon the same number upon the calendar."

"Yes . . . yes . . . what is it?" Haman demanded, weaving his fingers together.

"The twelfth month, the month of Adar," the servant replied.

Haman was delighted to have an answer, but somewhat put off by the fact that Adar was yet 11 months away. Nevertheless he asserted, "Very well. And now, what of the day?"

"By tradition, sir," the third reminded him, "the day is always one number larger than the month. We need not throw the purim to decide this."

Haman's eyes brightened. Of course he remembered this.

"Then," he reckoned, "the annihilation of the king's enemies is set for the thirteenth of Adar."

"Indeed," replied the first. "Now, sir, may we know against which people we have been performing this duty? Who exactly are these enemies of the king?"

Haman was not a very superstitious man, but he would not risk the goodwill of the purim by prejudicing his servants in the performance of their task. Therefore he had not told them just whose lives were at stake in the coming purge. Now that the date had been established, however, he could let them in on the secret.

Drawing them to him in a tight circle, he whispered, "Do you recall, years ago, how I spared you from judgment in the matter of an old man's death—an old fellow you challenged in the streets one New Year's Eve?"

Thinking back, the men did recall an incident in which they had in youthful frolic done bodily injury to an elderly gentleman. Unfortunately, the old man had been too frail to survive their exuberance, and had died shortly thereafter.

"We recall, Master," they acknowledged.

"Well, he was not the last of his race to receive a kick from you."

Haman's toothy grin sent chills down the servants' spines. Though they admired their master, something about him could chill the coldest heart.

"He was a Jew, was he not?" one asked.

"You have a keen memory, Drusal," Haman commended him. "A sneaking, money-grubbing Jew. The kingdom will be better off without his kind."

Drusal and his companions surveyed one another silently. Through each of their minds flashed the image of Abihail, the innocent one whom they had shamefully attacked.

He had not seemed a wealthy man. Had he not been dressed in a farmer's rags?

And he had not appeared bent on any treachery that long-ago night as he carried his wriggling bundle through the dark street.

But they would not correct Haman on these points. Their duty had been done. It was now left to them to deal with their consciences, to find ways to sleep each night for the next eleven months.

39

Mordecai the Jew sat in the public square outside the palace of Susa, sifting ashes through his fingers and pouring them over his head. The ashes mingled with the silver streaks of his already-gray beard and clung to his eyebrows. Ashes covered his shoulders and the pathetic garment of sackcloth which he had donned.

Upon the ground he sat, rocking to and fro, as all about him Jewish brothers and sisters from all parts of Susa—from the fine mansions lining the Shapur River to the filthy ghettos on the far side of town—chanted the horrid tale of Haman's hate.

This very day the edict, sealed with the king's own signet ring and declaring the destruction of their entire race, had been delivered by courier throughout the capital. Even now copies were being sent to every province of the empire, declaring the date for the annihilation of the Jews.

Confusion reigned, among Gentiles as well as Hebrews. For this pronouncement had not been preceded by any warning, and there had not been any escalation of bias against this group of people. For decades, Jew and Gentile had coexisted peacefully, with only occasional spates of racial tension coloring their interaction.

Certainly everyone knew that the Jews were an odd lot. They themselves were fond of acknowledging that they were a "peculiar people," having their own brand of history, their own slant on imperial politics, and even their own code of religious laws and traditions. However, they were known to be quiet folk, generally honest and reputable citizens of the kingdom. Few could think of any reason for this sudden turn of policy on the part of the emperor.

But Mordecai knew the reason, and there were others who suspected that it was due to his refusal to bow to the prime minister that Haman had set the king's heart against the Hebrews. Even those who suspected this, however, were amazed that Xerxes could so lightly be moved against such a large portion of the population.

Had they known that Xerxes had signed the edict without even inquiring as to the identity of the targeted group, they would have been even more chagrined at their sovereign's shallow nature.

Tapping into palace rumor, Mordecai had learned more than most about the details of the case. In fact, because he was so personally involved, friends brought him every word they heard from the interior. And so he knew even the amount of money that Haman had volunteered to pay for the extermination.

It had been noon when the edict was posted in Susa's square. By early evening, thousands of horrified Jews and their sympathizers had crowded into the square outside the palace.

No one was allowed inside the King's Gate while dressed in mourning, but the cries of protest and pleading which filled the dusky air had surely reached the ears of Xerxes, who, it was reported, sat at wine with Haman himself.

Of course, word of Mordecai's likely involvement in all that had come to pass had spread throughout the Jewish community. He could have been the most despised man among his brethren. But instead, his refusal to accommodate the pride of unpopular Haman had become a symbol of racial integrity, and Mordecai had in a few short hours been catapulted to the prominence of an ethnic hero.

As for Mordecai, there certainly had been moments since news of the edict when he had regretted his rebellion, wondering if Jehovah had been with him. It was true that the proposed move against the Jews was still nearly a year away, but no amount of time would save his people. Were they to gather together in force even now, they could not succeed against the entire empire of Persia.

However, in the presence of this reassuring company Mordecai found his faith uplifted, and felt hope in the midst of hopelessness.

As he sat, eyes closed and head tilted back, imploring heaven, he felt a tap on his shoulder. Peering above, he found a grandly attired fellow bending over him.

By his appearance he was a eunuch, bald and clean of face, decked in pure linen embroidered with gold. In strange attitude he bowed to the Jew, holding forth a bundle of even finer clothing in his arms.

"Mordecai?" he greeted.

"I am."

"Our Lady, the Queen, has sent me to you, pleading that you take these garments and cease your mourning."

Mordecai stared at him in mute consternation.

"You are Mordecai, the bookkeeper to the Queen, are you not?" the servant repeated.

"I am," he replied again.

The eunuch, maintaining his dignity despite uneasiness at the task he had been given, went on.

"Our Lady's maids brought her word of your condition, saying you were in this square. The queen begs you to take off your sackcloth and accept her gift."

Straightening his back, Mordecai insisted, "Does the queen not understand the reason for my grief? Has no one told her?"

The servant, unused to questioning a royal command, could only shrug. And Mordecai, clearing his throat, answered, "Tell Our Lady that her lowly employee appreciates her concern. But . . . I cannot accept her gracious gift."

Stunned, the eunuch stepped back, looking awkwardly at his bundle.

But seeing that Mordecai was intent upon his decision, he bowed slowly once more and retreated toward the palace.

All about the bookkeeper a huzzah of astonishment rose as folk observed Mordecai's daring. His status as hero grew on the instant, his name becoming a chant which filled the sky above the court.

"Mordecai, Mordecai," it rang, the syllables exciting the twilight. As dark descended, the name continued to mark the moments until the Jew, sitting calmly in an attitude of prayer, was again roused by someone's hand.

Looking up once more, he found yet another eunuch standing above him, this one even grander than the last.

"I am Hathach," the servant announced, a hush coming over the crowd, "one of the king's eunuchs, appointed to Her Majesty."

This man's demeanor was more challenging than that of the last. Had Mordecai not learned the confidence of faith, he might have trembled before him.

"Her Majesty, Queen Esther, wishes to know the meaning of your behavior this day, and the purpose of this . . . gathering."

This last word, preceded by an aloof glance about the court, was said with a sneer.

But Mordecai cared not for Hathach's assessment. Gathering his dusty garment to his chest, he looked upon the eunuch with equal condescension.

"Can it be, sir," he inquired, "that Our Lady is not privy to the news of Persia? Does the palace so insulate her that she has not heard of the king's edict? And is it possible that such a notable as yourself can likewise be ignorant of affairs affecting thousands across the world?"

Hathach, taken aback, had no ready answer, and was about to repeat the queen's command when Mordecai rose to his feet and grasped him by the arm.

Hundreds watched in silent admiration as their hero guided Hathach across the court, talking all the while about what had transpired between himself and Haman, and the exact amount of money offered by the treacherous prime minister in return for the lives of the Jews. Leading the bewildered fellow through the crowd until they stood before a public notice board, he turned him about to face the masses.

Then, reaching for the hideous parchment which had been posted that noon, he ripped it from the billboard and waved it beneath the eunuch's aquiline nose.

"Here!" he shouted. "Take this to the queen, and read it to her. Plead her forgiveness for the embarrassment heaped upon her, for the hypocrisy which expects her to rule without knowledge!"

Hathach, face red, tried to stammer some defense, but Mordecai would hear none.

"When you are done explaining this horror to the queen," the Jew demanded, "charge her to go to the king, to entreat Xerxes on behalf of these folk and to supplicate for their lives!"

Charge the queen? Such a notion was unthinkable.

But Mordecai, seeing Hathach's hesitation, shouted again as he walked away, "Our blood be upon you, and upon Our Lady, if you do not what I say!"

Stumbling across the congested pavement, Hathach scurried toward the palace, eager to be free of the mocking throng.

In his hand was the parchment, tightly crimped and awaiting the queen's scrutiny. As he disappeared behind the golden doors, the crowd's laughter turned once more to chanting, the name of Mordecai heralding the emergence of the moon.

40

Esther stood upon her balcony, listening to the chants which rose from the distant courtyard. She could not see the people who by blood were her kindred and who wrestled with the fate mapped for them. But she shared their agony, for she too faced the possibility of death.

Tears glimmered along her lashes as she turned a small parchment over and over in her fingers. It was a letter from Mordecai, and its contents bore the gravest challenge of her young life—a prospect even more frightening than eternal imprisonment within these palace walls.

To Mordecai's plea that she entreat the king on behalf of the Jews, she had sent word reminding him that no one could go into the king's court without his personal summons. Not even she, his queen, could do so without risking execution. Only if he were to extend his golden scepter to her might she be received. And though most would expect that she, of all people, would be welcomed into his presence, she had neither seen nor been requested by her husband for 30 days.

All this she had told Mordecai. But perhaps he had not believed her. Who could believe, having not heard her last conversation with Xerxes? The royal couple's most intimate servants had doubtless noted the distance between the king and his bride. But likely they assumed he had simply tired of her, that the growing harem was of more interest these days.

Esther, however, knew the true reason for her husband's aloofness. She knew he had been pained by her rejection, and that the rebuff merited his regal indignation. Indeed, it was a wonder he had borne the humiliation so calmly.

In her brief reply to Mordecai she had revealed none of this.

161

But as she surveyed his response, she knew it would have made no difference.

"Think not that just because you are in the king's palace you will escape," was his unwavering directive. "If you keep silent, deliverance will rise for the Jews from another place, but you and your father's house will perish."

The warning stung her, forbidding all complacency. *Had* she come to trust in her newfound privileges? *Had* the station into which she had been thrust become less than loathsome to her?

Gazing about at the fine furnishings of her boudoir, she shook herself. Mordecai's injunction had drawn the knife of conscience, making her cringe beneath its exposing gleam.

"No," she asserted. "I am *Hadassah*."

The name still felt at home upon her tongue, and she knew she still loved her heritage. Always she had been Israel's child. Why, even her challenge to Xerxes had come from a heart miserably entrapped within these Persian walls.

To others she was Queen of the East. To herself she was yet Hadassah.

Still, fear was her companion. Her defense to Mordecai had been fitly framed. She *would* be taking her life in her hands to step unbidden into the emperor's stateroom.

Trembling, she listened to the chants pushing up from the courtyard. Fumbling once again with the parchment, she contemplated its closing words.

"Who knows," it said, "but what you have come to the kingdom for such a time as this?"

For such a time as this . . .

The phrase beckoned, repeating itself over and over.

As though it were yesterday, she recalled her conversation with her papa when he had first met her in the harem hall.

"Jehovah has brought you to this place," he had deduced. "Trust everything to God."

How she had hated those words at the time! But now, telescoping into the present, all the unthinkable events which had led to this moment seemed suddenly capable of interpretation.

Perhaps, after all, she had been drawn into Persia's royal life for a high purpose—a purpose far greater than that of being queen. Perhaps she could be a servant—savior of her people.

A quiver of awe thrilled through her. Hardly did she feel worthy of such an assignment.

But as the chants outside grew more insistent, she suddenly raised her chin. Wheeling about, she clapped for a maid, sending her off to find a scribe.

And when the scribe arrived, she gave quick instruction. "Draft a note to Mordecai the Jew," she commanded. "Tell him to gather together all the Jews of Susa, that they may fast for me. They must neither eat nor drink for three days and nights. I and my maids will also fast. Then I will go in unto the king, which is against the law. And if I perish . . . I perish."

ESTHER

PART VI
The Triumph

41

Esther the Queen left her chamber in the strength of prayer. Robed in purple, her royal crown upon her head, she stepped into the hallway for the first time in three days.

Early she had risen, calling for her maids to prepare her bath, and eagerly they had complied, having been denied access to Her Majesty and having done her no service since her meditations had begun. Bewildered, the maids had filled their time in trivial employments during the queen's self-imposed isolation. They did not understand her ordeal of private prayer, or her command that they fast for three days along with her. They knew she prayed for the Jews, who still chanted in the public square. But her seemingly inordinate concern for their welfare was a mystery.

Esther had kept her devotions private, just as she kept her race and her faith a secret. Her servants did not know the God to whom she prayed, and so she had faced this test alone.

Now, however, as she emerged from her cloister decked in regal attire, her face barely showing the strain of hunger and fatigue, folk gathered about her in amazement.

Dorca was there, as well as Hegai, waiting in the hall and worrying. Her seven chambermaids, her devoted friend Maryam, and countless palace servants clustered in the corridor, gazing upon her and restraining the questions which hammered to be spoken.

"Your Highness," Dorca said with a bow, "we are so pleased to see you! We have been gravely concerned, My Lady, for your welfare."

"I am fine," the queen replied, smiling, her chin lifted in a determined angle. "I have been upheld by the prayers of many people."

The plump servant studied her vaguely, wondering at the statement. Whispers passed among those gathered.

"But I have one request of you," Esther added.

"Anything, Your Majesty!" Dorca replied, her face radiant.

"Prepare a table in my dining room. Three wine goblets and a carafe of fine wine."

"Yes, Your Majesty," the servant said, squelching her curiosity.

No one asked the reason for this assignment, nor for the queen's monastic behavior during the past days. It was not proper to question royalty. But when Esther lifted her skirts and turned toward the king's stateroom, a murmur of fascination, and then of fear, filled the onlookers.

"His Majesty is in his receiving hall, is he not?" she inquired.

At this Hegai drew near, his face white.

"He is, My Lady," he answered furtively. "Always on the third day of the week . . ."

"Very well," Esther nodded. And with a placid countenance she continued on her way.

"But, My Queen . . ." the eunuch objected.

"I am well," Esther assured him.

Passing through vestibule and lobby, she attracted a train of awed followers, but offered no further consolation.

* * *

Esther stood outside the emperor's audience hall, the elegant Apadana, whose princely columns, though 36 in number, were so narrow of girth that they barely intruded upon the vast space.

As the airy lightness of the stateroom collided with the shadow of the outer court, the queen's tamed fears clawed to assert themselves. At her back a dozen personal aides pleaded that she reconsider.

"Your Highness," they reminded her, "you know the penalty . . ."

"I know," she insisted. Walking up to the guards at the stateroom door, she stood silently, peering between their spears.

Beyond, she could see her husband seated upon his throne, a ledger of appointments in his hand, and his seven aides at his side.

"Our Lady," one of the guards whispered, his spear quivering in a sweaty hand as he recognized her intentions. "Do you mean to enter here?"

For a long moment Esther said nothing, only studying Xerxes as he casually chatted with his valets.

"I do," she replied at last, taking a deep breath.

Glancing at his fellow guard, the sentinel hesitated, feeling that to raise his long weapon and admit the queen was tantamount to decreeing her death.

But his partner, nervously complying, warned him with a look that they must obey their lady's wishes.

Ever so slowly they turned their spears upright, allowing Esther to step into the stateroom light. Fearing for their lady's safety, they could not bring themselves to announce her, but only stood aside like impotent shadows.

Silent as a statue she stood, waiting for the emperor to look upon her. Her pulse counted the minutes with a stammer, as her life hung on the king's response.

It was Mehuman, the chief eunuch, who at last spied the queen standing at the edge of the court. Eyes wide, he turned to his master and whispered in his ear.

Lurching erect, the emperor stared across the room, puzzled at the sight of his wife.

The instant Xerxes saw her, Esther lowered her head and bowed in a deep curtsy, her knees nearly touching the floor, a gesture befitting a queen only in deference to her husband. And for a long while she held this position, not daring to glance up, her heart drumming.

As the eunuchs conferred together, wondering at the woman's motives, the king only leaned forward in amazement, studying his daring bride.

Beautiful she was, in her courage, in her humility—as beautiful as ever he had seen her. How she reminded him, again, of Vashti—not only in appearance but in spirit!

His hand tightened upon the arm of his chair as he recalled, as though it were yesterday, the night his first queen had challenged him. Her self-assertion had exiled her as he in his pride had retaliated.

Once again, a lovely woman was laying her very life at his feet. But this time he could not imagine the purpose.

As he pondered the mystery, however, an explanation much to his liking suddenly dawned upon him. Perhaps, his fond heart told him, perhaps Esther, heartsick at his monthlong rejection of her, had come to plead for his husbandly attentions. Yes, he counseled himself, the love she had experienced in his kingly arms must have been a treasure sorely missed. Indeed, she regretted her unkind words when last they met. Life had lost all meaning without him, and therefore was worth risking, if only he might be hers again.

As he considered the countless females whom he had spurned, the harem wenches and concubines who had lain with him only once, forever after to live in solitary widowhood, a glib smile pricked his lips.

Lifting a hand, he reached for his scepter, and Mehuman, who had witnessed his abuse of Vashti, handed it to him fearfully. The eunuch knew that whatever Xerxes did with the royal wand would decide Esther's fate. If the emperor thumped the floor with the scepter's foot, the queen would die. If he extended it, she would live. Not having a clue to the king's heart, Mehuman quietly joined his brethren behind the throne.

Whether it was compassion for this lady, or guilt at the remembrance of Vashti, not even Xerxes could have said. But something softened his despotic nature as he gazed upon the queen. Her loveliness alone could have worked the miracle. But more than physical winsomeness worked for her this day.

When the monarch raised the golden shaft, a hush thrilled through the court. And when he extended it, pointing the glistening head toward his queen, a great sigh of relief ascended.

Scarcely believing what her ears told her, Esther found strength to lift her head. Tears nudged at her lashes as she saw the beckoning orb. Rising, she crossed the room, bowing again when she reached the throne, and touched the scepter's top with careful fingers.

"What is it, Queen Esther?" Xerxes said, his heart pounding now as the gentle woman stood before him. A quaver of manly emotion colored his tone as he proclaimed, "What is your request? It shall be given you, even to half of my kingdom."

Standing, Esther smiled. But though he tried desperately, Xerxes could not interpret her feelings.

"If it please the king," she replied, her voice sweet and supple, "let the king and Haman come this day to a dinner that I have prepared."

Quizzically, Xerxes sank back upon his throne. Haman? Why Haman?

But of course, he reasoned, she was being coy. She would win him cautiously, in the presence of another.

Not taking his eyes off her, he gave a condescending nod. Flicking a careless hand toward Mehuman, he commanded, "Fetch Haman quickly, that we may do as Esther desires."

At this the queen curtsied again and backed away from the king's platform. Turning, she hastened toward the door.

Smitten by the woman's self-possession, the emperor watched her departure. When she disappeared from sight, he shook his head, chuckling with delight.

42

Haman doffed his leather skullcap to every servant, every chambermaid, every doorman as he sidled through the palace halls, his head light with wine and his heart merry. Smugly smiling to himself, he reveled in the irony of the honor just heaped upon him.

How Otanes would laugh with him when Haman told him he had just come from dinner in the queen's hall! He, Haman, coconspirator for the death of Xerxes, had just sat at private banquet with the emperor and his lady. He who had only recently been publicly elevated, obliging obeisance from all who saw him, had now been received by the queen—an award only rarely bestowed. In fact, he could not recall such an honor ever being given a palace official during Darius' reign or since.

Not only this, but he had been invited to dine with the royal couple again tomorrow evening! The prestige was almost more than he could bear.

He could not imagine what he had done to deserve either invitation. He could accept the thought that he was a stunning fellow, brilliant and charming. Perhaps this was enough. And perhaps, he snickered, not even his plan to overthrow the king could be thwarted.

His step lively, he ambled through the court on his way home, recalling with fond satisfaction the luxuries of Esther's hall. How lovely the queen had been! Reclined upon her dinner couch, her linen gown the same lavender as the lounge's linen upholstery, her hair and eyes black as the marble tiles bordering her porch—she was a memorable sight.

The conversation had been airy and carefree. Matters of state did not intrude as the empress spoke of the weather and asked caring questions about his wife and family.

Proudly he had told her of his ten sons, and if her eyes darkened at this, he knew not why, nor did he notice.

Toward Xerxes she had shown the same casual ease. Haman had not attempted to interpret her feelings toward her husband. Her gracious hospitality toward himself was all he absorbed.

His blood glowed with the wine's caress as he headed toward the palace door, eager to share his good fortune with plump and comely Zeresh, his wife of a quarter-century.

But just as he entered the outer porch, near the king's gate, the chanting of the Jews in the public square reached his ears, and a chill ran through his veins.

Ahead sat Mordecai. Having removed his sackcloth and having washed himself, he had taken his station behind his accounting desk. Though it was night, he had perched himself there, awaiting Haman's emergence. And the instant the prime minister saw him, Mordecai's eyes locked on his with a knowing twinkle.

When the Jew neither rose nor trembled before him, Haman seethed with indignation.

Restraining himself, he passed by without a word. But his glorious day had been ruined. Utterly ruined.

*   *   *

Haman entered his house with a bowed head. Zeresh, who had eagerly anticipated his homecoming all evening, rushed to him with open arms. But seeing the dark cloud upon his face, she faltered.

"My Lord," she fawned, stroking him on the shoulder and removing his cape with solicitous hands, "I trust it went well— your dinner with the queen."

"Call Otanes," was all he could say. "Call my friends, my confidants."

Bewildered, Zeresh would have inquired more deeply, but knowing her husband's determined personality, she hastened to comply. Sending her servants through the neighborhood, she saw to it that all her husband's associates were summoned, and then she sat with him by the fire to await their arrival.

"It did not go well?" she managed.

"I will tell the tale when I have an audience," he curtly corrected, though Zeresh probed his expression for further clues.

Shortly the house filled with Haman's executives, who gathered doubtfully, wondering why they were required to leave home and hearth at so late an hour.

When at last Otanes arrived, seating himself across from Haman's ten sons, the grand vizier began to pace the floor.

"You are all aware of the honor I received this day . . . that I did dine with the emperor and his wife in the queen's hall," he said.

Murmurs and nodding heads confirmed this.

Then, with dramatic tears in his eyes, he recounted the trophies of his life.

"You all know that I am a wealthy man, that no one in the kingdom surpasses me for financial security."

Again, everyone agreed, though not without resentment.

"I have fathered ten sons!" he cried, throwing his arms wide, and caressing his heirs with proud scrutiny.

Zeresh beamed, and Haman's friends condoled that this was indeed true. The fact that they did not feel as much warmth for their superior as he imagined would not trouble him.

"Furthermore," he went on, "everyone knows how I have been honored by His Majesty . . . his public endorsements of me . . . the promotions I have received in sight of all the empire!"

Heedless of his associates' growing uneasiness, he did not consider the affront which Otanes might feel at this self-aggrandizement. Nor did the memory of Otanes' personal involvement in his "promotion" faze him.

"Why," he boasted, "I have been advanced above all the princes and servants of the king! Even Queen Esther let no one come with the king to the banquet but me!"

Any applause now elicited was given only out of duty. But Haman accepted it with condescension.

"And tomorrow also I am invited to dine with the queen and king! Yet . . ."

Here he paused, his voice cracking and his face falling.

"Yet . . . all this does me no good as long as I see Mordecai the Jew sitting at the king's gate!"

At this Zeresh stood and rushed to his side, begging him to seat himself, to calm his heart lest it break.

After a hesitant moment, one by one the advisers began to console him.

"Truly, Master," they sympathized, "this monster, Mordecai, would be a thorn in any man's side. Such patience you have shown in enduring his insults!"

Haman kept his head bowed, gazing into the fire with contorted countenance. But how he loved their forced support!

For a long while Otanes studied his partner in crime. He had no great love for Haman. In fact, he despised the pompous braggart. But Haman was the most useful pawn to the general's vendetta against Xerxes. The prime minister's recent intimacies with the royal family could only hasten the fulfillment of Otanes' plot. If Mordecai were dampening Haman's spirit, he must be done away with.

A cold-blooded warrior, one who enjoyed the sport of power, Otanes would just as soon kill a man as put up with any inconvenience he might pose.

His voice smooth as honey, he called Haman's name and crossed the room, embracing Zeresh as though he treasured her. "Dear friends," he began, "I cannot express the sorrow I have at the sight of your discomfort. I think we all agree that this is a serious matter, calling for immediate action. For you, Haman, are our brother as well as our superior."

No one dared deny this as syrupy smiles graced each conciliatory face.

"Therefore, after due consideration, I have a plan which, with your indulgence, Prime Minister, I will address."

Haman glanced sideways at Otanes. Feigning deference, he bowed.

"Let a gallows 50 cubits high be built," Otanes coolly suggested. "And in the morning, tell the king to have Mordecai hanged upon it. Then go merrily with Xerxes to the dinner."

How simply the matter had been resolved! How easily death became the answer!

Here and there a face went white, but no one spoke contrary to Otanes.

Zeresh, her lips wet, planted a firm kiss on Haman's wan cheek.

"Oh, my husband!" she cried. "Heed our beloved Otanes! Free yourself of this plague, of the cloud which hangs over you, and be our merry Haman once again!"

Nothing but endorsement issued from the little gathering. Haman had his answer—an answer which set well with his callous spirit.

"Thank you, friends," he smiled, a polished tear reflecting firelight on his face. "It shall be done."

43

That night Xerxes found sleep impossible to achieve. Each time he came near dozing, the sight of Esther, gracefully reclined upon her dinner bed, invaded his masculine heart.

He had never thought of her as a seductress. She had not needed to play such games with him. But he was certain that today's invitation to the dinner, given at peril of her own life, was an attempt to woo him. Even buffering the encounter with the presence of a third party, Haman, was doubtless part of her strategy.

How coolly she had handled things during the rendezvous, focusing more on Haman than on himself—asking all those idle questions about the vizier's career and family, chitchatting about the weather and the delicacies of the table!

Certainly her tactics were effective. She had captivated him, and his thoughts had been on her alone all evening.

Wide awake, he paced his room, glancing out at the desert moon over and over. Thoughts of Vashti and thoughts of Esther blended into one, as always they had done since the girl had come to him. Deep inside he knew that Esther's accusation of him had been valid—that he saw his first wife in her more than he saw herself. But perhaps today's encounter had been her way of telling him that she could live with the fact. That she would take him—indeed, craved him—regardless.

As he stepped onto his balcony with the dawn, having paced and tossed and turned all night, a strange sound, intermittent and persistent, intruded upon his reveries. It seemed to be a hammering of some kind, as though a construction job were underway upon the acropolis.

Generally Susa was quiet at such an early hour. Though the labyrinth of palace corridors and walls could deflect vibrations

177

at misleading angles, he was sure the pounding came from the direction of Haman's house. As he cocked his head to listen, he noticed that the odd chanting which had filled the public square for days and nights had ceased, as though the hammering had replaced it.

Persians could be a hot-blooded race, and the many diverse nationalities comprising Susa were a volatile combination. Protests or sit-ins were not a rare sight in the public market. Xerxes had not bothered to ask just what the most recent discontent regarded. If it concerned his edict against Haman's alleged foes of the state, he knew it would pass. After all, he was certain the accused people must be only a minute fraction of the population, having done nothing to attract his attention before Haman clued him to their subversion.

Glad he was that his prime minister was so in touch with the citizens. Surely no king could have a more efficient adviser.

But glad he would also be to sleep.

In times past he would have called for one of his harem girls to distract him, to soothe his body and tire him enough for slumber. Now, however, he would have been content with no one but Esther. And he knew the timing was not right to have her. She must play out her winsome plan, and he must indulge her scheme.

Meanwhile, as his heart drummed to thoughts of her, and as the mysterious hammers chattered through the twilight, he grew irritable.

Clapping his hands, he called for Mehuman, who appeared the instant the guards opened the king's door.

"Mehuman!" Xerxes snapped. "What is that infernal pounding?"

"Hammers, Your Highness," the eunuch said with a bow.

"Of course it is!" the emperor growled. "I know it is hammers! But why—why at this hour?"

"Some project of Haman's, Your Majesty," Mehuman replied. "A gallows of immense proportions. I am certain he will inform you . . ."

"Yes, yes. Very well," Xerxes nodded, raising a limp hand to his throbbing temple. "I have not slept all night."

Mehuman, whose duty it was to anticipate the emperor's every need, quickly offered to send word commanding quiet in the acropolis. But Xerxes only quipped, "It would do no good now, since the night is already gone. My spirit is restless."

"Perhaps, Your Highness, if someone read to you . . ."

Xerxes had suffered often from insomnia, especially since sending Vashti away, and sometimes his troubled mind was calmed if someone lulled him with a reading.

His tired eyes brightening, the king grasped at the idea.

"Send for the Book of Memorable Deeds," he cried. "Yes, yes . . . I do enjoy that!"

He referred, as Mehuman knew, to the royal chronicles, a scrupulously maintained record of all the valorous and complimentary things done in the empire by folk of all stations. If a general pulled off an amazing feat in battle, if a commoner performed some especially heroic act, if an inventor notably contributed to the empire's technology, or if a physician advanced the cause of medicine by discovering some valued cure— any such achievement would be noted in the chronicle.

Of particular honor were acts of benevolence directed toward the king's personal welfare. And periodically Xerxes enjoyed being updated as to the contents.

Two scribes appeared quickly with the priceless volume, bowing through the door. To the monarch's delight, they began to recount the story of how a certain Jew had once saved the emperor's life.

"Mordecai, you say?" Xerxes mused. "Of course, I remember. He revealed the plot of my treacherous guards, Bigthan and Teresh!"

"Yes, Sire," the readers confirmed. "It says here that he reported the scheme to your queen, and she to you."

Xerxes' eyes again brightened at the thought of his wife. And fondly he contemplated the tale of Mordecai.

"He is a palace accountant?"

"Head of inventory," the scribes reminded him.

"And what honor or dignity has been bestowed on Mordecai for this kindness?"

The readers scanned the pages, their fingers tracing the scroll line by line.

At last, shrugging, they replied, "Nothing has been done for him."

* * *

Somewhere beyond the palace wall a morning cock crowed.

And with the twilight, hastening footsteps rang through the king's receiving hall.

"Who is in the court?" Xerxes asked as he sat upon his stateroom throne. To his right, on a low table, sat the Book of Memorable Deeds, and upon his lap was a roster of items to be considered this day, judgments to be made, and visitors to be entertained.

"Haman is here, Your Majesty, asking to see you," Mehuman replied.

"Good, good," Xerxes smiled. "Let him come in." Then, glancing at the book of deeds, he enthused, "I could use his advice!"

Promptly Haman entered, eager to speak to the king regarding his planned execution of Mordecai, and ready for the quick consent which was always given his wishes. When the emperor interrupted him with a spirited inquiry, he was caught off guard.

"Good morning, friend," Xerxes called as Haman approached. "What shall be done to the man whom the king delights to honor?"

Assuming that this was a mere pleasantry, Haman only bowed. But when the king repeated the question, the vizier gave it more thought. Of course Xerxes must be referring to the prime minister himself. Whom, after all, would the emperor delight to honor more than himself? Had not Xerxes already heaped acclaim and dignity upon him? It seemed there was no limit to the king's generosity toward those he loved.

Haman cleared his throat. "Why, Sire," he chuckled, feigning embarrassment, "for such a man let royal robes be brought, which the king has worn, and the horse which the king has ridden, on whose head a royal crown is set." Gaining more boldness with each selfish syllable, he continued, "And let the robes and the horse be handed over to one of the king's most noble princes. Let him array the man whom the king delights to honor, and let him conduct the man on horseback through the open square of the city, proclaiming before him, 'Thus shall it be done to the man whom the king delights to honor!' "

Leaning back on his throne, Xerxes laughed with Haman. "Ah-hah!" he cried. "Marvelous! Make haste, my friend. Take the robes and the horse, as you have said, and do so to Mordecai the Jew who sits at the king's gate. Leave out nothing that you have mentioned."

44

There was no parade in the Susa streets, but folk from all quarters lined the viaduct before the king's palace. There was no military processional or train of acrobats and actors to draw a crowd. But thousands had turned out to observe two men's passage down the royal avenue.

The rumor of the king's command to Haman had spread through the palace court like wildfire, and by the time Mordecai had been summoned, an amazed throng awaited him.

When he appeared upon a white, prancing charger, upon whose noble head was set a shining tiara, the crowd was delighted. Mordecai himself was dressed in a blue gown of purest silk, his silver beard lying gloriously against it. Not only did Jews line the avenue, but supportive Susaites of all sorts. And when it was seen that *Haman* had been commissioned to parade the bookkeeper through town, hilarity was the order of the day.

In fact, the hilarity had begun at court, when Haman set about to fulfill the king's commission. Calling for Mordecai, he was obliged to deck the Jew, firsthand, in the royal apparel. Then, leading the regal horse to his enemy, he bowed in chagrin as the accountant mounted the beast.

Now, of course, his humiliation was unbounded as the thousands who had chanted hatred for him watched, hissing and spitting, while he conducted their hero through the streets.

Mortified, he kept his eyes to the ground as Mordecai was lauded, wondering how this irony had come to be, and how the man he had planned to execute on this very day could be his sudden superior.

When he reached the public square, he was obliged to make the pronouncement which he himself had ordained: "Thus shall

182

it be done to the man whom the king delights to honor," he cried, his voice a rasping croak.

Over and over he shouted the words, until he thought his tongue would bleed for shame.

And all the while Mordecai said nothing, only reveling in the victory of Jehovah.

* * *

Zeresh swabbed her husband's perspiring brow with a damp cloth. Red-faced and close to weeping, he had come home with his head covered, not needing to tell his sorry tale, for his wife, along with all Suṣa, knew of his humiliation.

Nevertheless, the grisly details spilled forth in a torrent of shame and self-pity as he recounted to her, to his household servants, and to the advisers who lived on his estate the horrid events of the day.

"With my own hands I was obliged to drape the royal cloak about that scoundrel's shoulders!" he wailed. "With my own hand I was forced to lead him forth through the streets! Oh, my friends," he bellowed, "how shall I ever live it down?"

Zeresh tried to calm him, but it was no use. One by one his counselors, who had themselves encouraged him to take vengeance against the Jew, offered worthless comfort.

"Lord," they reasoned, "surely Xerxes was unaware of your hatred for this man. Perhaps he did not even know Mordecai is a Jew. Had he known," they insisted, "he would never have elevated him."

Haman sank into his chair, shaking his head. He could not admit to his friends that Xerxes was unaware of more than this—that Xerxes did not even know that the edict so recently published against the "subversives" was against the entire Jewish race.

But as the counselors considered their master's unhappy state, another concern formed in their minds.

Whispering together, they contemplated a new side to the dilemma, and Haman, observing their knit brows, leaned forward anxiously.

"What is it?" he demanded.

"Uh, sir," one spoke, clearing his throat, "it occurs to us that your humiliation may only be beginning."

"How so?" he inquired.

"Why," the adviser said softly, "if Mordecai, before whom you have begun to fall, is of the Jewish people, and if Xerxes knows this, the king may begin to side with the Jews. And you will not prevail against Mordecai, but will surely fall utterly."

The possibilities were too horrible to contemplate. Loss of influence, perhaps even of position . . . or of life . . .

When Xerxes began to put all the facts together, seeing that Haman had no just cause for the edict, there would be no salvation!

Quaking, Zeresh drew close to her husband and cried, "They are right, of course! How can you stand before the king?"

But there was no time for answers. At that instant messengers from the palace arrived at the mansion, summoning Haman to the feast prepared in Esther's hall.

Turning helplessly to his wife, Haman stood on shaky legs as Zeresh handed him his cloak and studied him with mournful eyes.

Feeling as though he were headed for his own execution, the man who had just last night commissioned a gallows left the house.

45

Today's banquet was even more festive than yesterday's, confounding Haman.

If he had been confused by Xerxes' commission to heap honor upon Mordecai, he now began to suspect that the king and Esther were playing games with him.

Yet if it was a game he had no choice but to play along—to hope that his past status as the king's favorite would carry him above the mixed messages he was receiving. He must not mention the morning's humiliation. He must draw no further attention to Mordecai, in conversation or in attitude, lest the king pursue the issue.

Perhaps, after all, Haman was still the emperor's most esteemed prince. Perhaps the incident with Mordecai was a fluke, and his own fears were unfounded.

Stretching his lips into a smile, he followed the messengers into the queen's hall. He tried not to register surprise at the sumptuous array upon the long table, or at the elegant decor which had been lavished on the place. Yet it was evident that Esther had spared no expense in making the room and the meal even more luxurious than yesterday's feast, surrounding the little gathering with immense bouquets and calling all her servants to serve.

As he bowed to the royal couple—the king, who sat upon a high pile of ornate pillows, and the queen, who reclined majestically upon her couch—his chest ached with anxiety. When he took his own seat, he hesitated to study their faces.

What he saw when he did so gave no clue to their view of him. Xerxes, after a cheery greeting, seemed to focus all attention on his queen, so that Haman began to wonder if his presence were a hindrance to their bliss. Esther, on the other hand, attended to Haman with a persistence which made him equally uneasy.

Not once did she allow his cup to run dry or his plate to go bare. Not once did the conversation lag, though he sensed a peculiar scrutiny in her eyes and an ironic lilt to her voice.

Just as he was thinking he might enjoy her attentions, however, Xerxes drew her away.

Hoisting a fluted goblet, the king toasted his lady's beauty. Then, almost groaning, he suddenly declared, "What is your petition, Queen Esther? It shall be granted you! And what is your request? It shall be given you, even to half of my kingdom!"

Servants ceased their serving, slaves lowered pitcher-laden trays from their shoulders, and the men who guarded the chamber stood rigid with surprise.

Such a statement made by a king was not unheard of. Xerxes had spoken this very thing to Esther yesterday. It was usually reserved for those who had performed some great feat in service to the empire, and it was never to be taken literally. Still, it was an incomparable honor, and to be spoken twice in two days to a woman, even to a queen, made it even more noteworthy.

If the offer were amazing, however, so would be the queen's response. No one anticipated that she would so boldly pursue Xerxes' generosity—not the king himself nor any of the onlookers.

Esther felt a flush rise to her cheeks, and every fiber of her being tingled with the opportunity afforded.

Hammered and honed by palace life into a female of power and prestige, Esther was no longer the meek Jewess who had been dragged into the harem. A few weeks earlier she had boldly confronted her "husband" with his unfair use of herself and Vashti. Then, wielding the weapon of faith, she had risked her life to enter his stateroom, seeking help (unbeknownst to him) for her people.

Now in a compulsive moment he had fulfilled her deepest longing, unwittingly granting her the chance to attain salvation for the Jews.

As she studied the floor, framing in her mind just how to speak her wish, Xerxes wondered at the interlude.

Indeed, he had opened the world to Esther with a few words. But surely she must not make so much of it! Was she so unschooled in Persian protocol that she knew not the typical response? Would she not simply smile and calmly thank his lordship, fawning over the treasures of her chamber and the glories of his love? Would she not simply say that she had everything a woman could ask, and that to receive more would overwhelm her?

Still, she pondered her answer until even the servants grew embarrassed. Then, as she turned scalding eyes on Haman, boring through him with a vengeful stare, whispers filled the room.

At last, tears trickling down her hot cheeks, she slid from her couch and fell to her knees, burying her face in her hands.

"Oh, My Lord!" she cried. "If I have found favor in your sight, O King, and if it please the king, let my life be given me at my petition, and my people at my request! For we are sold, I and my people, to be destroyed, to be slain, and to perish. If we had been sold into slavery, I would have kept silent, for such a thing would not be worthy of the king's attention."

Unprepared for this strange turn of events, Xerxes beheld his lady with amazement. "Of what do you speak, my dear?" he marveled.

The queen, rocking back on her heels, at last revealed her long-kept secret. "I am a Jewess," she declared, "the daughter of Mordecai, whom you have honored this day. But I and all my people live in fear for their lives!"

"Who would do such a thing?" the king demanded, scowling about the room. "Where is he?"

Esther leaped to her feet, abandoned now to the liberty of the moment, and pointed a revenging finger at their guest. "A foe and an enemy!" she cried. "This wicked Haman!"

Utterly bewildered, Xerxes digested the accusation, his volatile nature seething with indignation. So, Haman had pressed an edict against an entire race, even to the life of his own queen!

Rising from his bolsters, the emperor glowered down upon the cringing vizier. No word escaped his lips, but his countenance was livid. With a clenched fist he stalked from the banquet hall, exiting into the adjacent garden.

Mortified, Haman turned to the queen, his own face now covered with tears. Esther, having returned to her couch, scorned to look upon him until he, a crazed fool, threw himself at her feet.

"Oh, Your Majesty," he wailed, "Take mercy upon me. Speak unto the king on my behalf, My Lady, I beg of you! For my life surely is in your hands!"

When Esther only recoiled, drawing her skirts up from the floor, he grew even more desperate. In an attitude of utmost despair he scrambled toward her, flinging himself across her dinner bed and weeping like one of the damned.

"Will he even assault the queen before my very eyes?" Xerxes shouted, reentering from the garden. At this the eunuchs scurried forth, draping Haman's head with a cloth for shame, and dragging him into the center of the room.

There he sat, rocking to and fro, wailing like a skewered hog, until Harbona, one of the king's attendants, reminded Xerxes of the gallows which Haman had built only the previous night.

" . . . made for Mordecai, who saved the king's life!" he revealed.

"No, you cannot mean it!" Xerxes spat.

"Indeed, it is so," Harbona declared. "This fiend would have killed the Jew for no matter greater than his own pride."

Even in his escapades against the Greeks, when he would have taken the Western world, Xerxes had never felt a desire for revenge more strongly than he did this moment.

Pointing a spasmed finger at the cowering Haman, he roared vindictive judgment.

"Hang him on it!" he commanded.

With this the guards hurried forth, jolting Haman to his feet and carrying him from the room. Xerxes, his face contorted with bombarding emotions, took Esther's hand, lifting her to his bosom and holding her close to his heart.

46

"Oh, Papa! How wonderful you look!" Esther declared, studying her adopted father's reflection in her hallway mirror. "A more distinguished fellow has never come before the king's throne!"

Mordecai gazed upon his dapper likeness, not concealing a broad smile. For his daughter had just draped about his shoulders a robe once belonging to the king. And his tunic, given him only yesterday by Haman, was the one he had worn as the prime minister led him through the Susa streets.

"Are you not splendid?" Esther laughed. "I am proud of you, Papa!"

Mordecai turned about, grasping the queen's hands. "Why has the king called for me?" he wondered. "Has he not already honored me?"

Esther perceived his anxiety at the notion of standing before the despot. Trying to reassure him, she nodded, "Xerxes has his gentle side, Papa. And he is very generous, once he takes a liking to someone."

"And swift to retribution when someone crosses him," he added, remembering the vizier's quick demise.

Hung on the gallows prepared for Mordecai, Haman had met his death only last evening. And just as quickly, at the king's command, the dead man's house and all his wealth had passed to Queen Esther.

"But in his eyes, Papa, you are a hero. You once saved his life. Remember?"

"I have sometimes questioned the wisdom . . ." he grinned.

"Hush, Papa," Esther giggled, glancing warily down the hall. "Now, come! He waits for you!"

189

As the bookkeeper entered the lobby, the king's eunuchs stood ready to receive him. Hastening, they took the queen and her adopted father to the stateroom.

The reception would be quiet this time, but very dignified. When Xerxes, seated upon his throne, had extended his scepter to the couple in the presence of all his princes and advisers, he stretched forth his open palm, upon which was perched his signet ring.

"This I took from the hand of your enemy, Haman," Xerxes explained. "It is my own ring of law, by which your enemy did seal the death of your people. So now receive this, my friend, as a token of apology, and in honor of your kindness to me."

Mordecai stared mutely at the gift, hardly daring to consider the implications. Glancing at his daughter, who only nodded enthusiastically, he at last reached out and took it.

"Behold, my new prime minister!" Xerxes announced, gesturing toward the humble Jew with a dramatic sweep of the hand.

Trumpets blared and applause rang through the court. But scarcely could Mordecai believe his ears until Esther herself bowed before him.

Rising, she took from one of the king's aides a small pillow upon which was the key to Haman's house.

"With the emperor's approval, Father, I pass the wealth of your enemy into your keeping," she declared, placing the cushion on his hesitant hands.

Again celebration filled the air.

Wonderful as all this was, however, the queen's heart was not wholly joyous. She must speak again, and that without delay.

Turning to her master, she appealed to his generous mood, falling to her knees and releasing all the pent-up stress of past days.

"O My Lord," she cried, "surely the good you have done this day is only the beginning of your kindnesses. My people still fear for their lives due to the edict of Haman!"

Xerxes had known she would address this matter. He was learning to anticipate her bravery.

Extending to her his scepter once again, he bade her rise and speak her mind.

Smoothing her linen gown, she phrased her words with care, words rehearsed in the night.

"If it please the king, and if I have found favor in his sight, and if the thing seem right before the king, and I be pleasing in his eyes," she began, "let an order be written to revoke the letters devised by Haman the Agagite, the son of Hammedatha, which he wrote to destroy the Jews who are in all the provinces of the king. For how can I endure to see the destruction of my kindred?"

Her concentration on this little speech was so deliberate that she dare not contemplate the emperor's face until she was done. But when she at last allowed reflection, she found his countenance soft toward her.

In his eyes was the warmth of love, and she cared not now how genuine.

"Behold," he addressed both Esther and her father, his own voice husky with feeling, "I have given Esther the house of Haman, and have hanged him on the gallows, because he would lay hands on the Jews. And you may write as you please with regard to the Jews, in the name of the king, and sealed with the king's ring. For an edict written in the name of the king and sealed with the king's ring cannot be revoked."

47

Esther stood once again at her chamber window, where so much agonized prayer for her people had been lifted. She turned over in her hands a piece of parchment similar to the one on which Mordecài had challenged her to go before the king.

This paper, like that one, bore the handwriting of her papa, but these words were not for her eyes alone. They would be duplicated by countless scribes and sent to all parts of the empire, for they were the first edict of the new prime minister.

Persians were fond of saying that the laws of their kings, sealed with the royal signet ring, were irrevocable. But no dynastic ruler who reigned over half the world could truly be subject to such a restriction. While no subordinate official nor any uprising of the people could revoke an emperor's command, the emperor could not be his own slave.

Out of deference to his image, however, Esther and Mordecai had worded the new edict to accommodate the original. They would not do away with the planned day of assault against the Jews, but would instead send word throughout the empire telling the Jews to arm themselves.

Of course, there was more behind their decision to do this than honor for the king.

Esther felt a chill crawl up her arms as she dwelt on Mordecai's reasoning. All her life he had raised her in the ways of Israel. But tonight, for the first time, he had shared with her the tale told by Abihail, her departed father—the story of King Saul and the wicked foe, Agag.

"I thought Abihail was a foolish old man when first he spoke of the ancient tale," Mordecai had said. "But now that we have seen the wickedness which Haman devised against our people, I know that Saul was remiss in not stamping out the Amalekites."

Amazed, Esther had listened to the story, overwhelmed with the personal involvement of God in her own life. "So," she had replied carefully, "are you saying that Jehovah is using us now to right that wrong done so many years ago?"

At this Mordecai had risen from the queen's desk, where he had been penning the edict, and had gazed out the night window. Far away his mind was carried to the land of Israel and the distant time of King Saul his own ancestor.

"God never lets His purposes go unfulfilled," he answered softly. "All the world is hallowed ground, and years are of small consequence to Him. In His good time and in His chosen way He always brings about His will. Only we poor humans are bound by the frustrations of how and when."

"But why *me*?" Esther marveled. "Why has God chosen me, an orphan and a commoner, to perform this thing?"

Mordecai gazed lovingly into her awe-filled face.

"Why did He choose Rahab? Why Ruth? The women who mothered king David were of humble birth," he asserted. "Often God has raised up salvation for His people from the most unlikely places. Why," he mused, "who knows but what the mother of Messiah Himself shall be a girl of low station?"

Esther raised her hand to her mouth, stifling a giggle. And her papa, drawing her close, whispered, "Did I not tell you when you first came here to be anxious for nothing? Trust God, my dear Hadassah."

The last word had infused the young woman with zeal.

" 'Hadassah,' " she repeated. "I am still Hadassah, aren't I, Papa?"

"You never were anyone else," he assured her, bowing low and bidding good night.

That had been two hours ago. The queen should have been asleep long since. But, her heart still full of wakeful contemplation, she found sleep impossible.

The new edict, as Mordecai and she had agreed, would not only honor the king but would help to establish the people of God. While a simple revoking of Haman's command would have saved countless lives, the call to defense would secure the peace of the Jews by revealing who their enemies were, and who their friends. Like Saul should have done generations before, the Hebrews would now be able to stamp out their foes.

If the Jews were allowed to arm themselves, so would be their sympathizers. It had become quite obvious during the growing unrest over Haman's edict that there were many more who would side with Israel than not, given the opportunity. Mordecai's order would free them to aid their Jewish neighbors, and so the tables would be turned, resulting in a purge against the anti-Semites.

It seemed to Esther that she was being carried through these events on a supernatural wave—by a force outside herself. Never had she become accustomed to her role as queen. Perhaps, she thought, even that role was only a garment which she had donned for higher purposes. Inside, where her spirit dwelt, she was still a young girl standing at the village gate, tripping through the wheat fields, watching for her beloved David. And such memories lifted her above the present distress.

A knock at her door roused her from poignant reveries, and brushing a tear from her cheek, she went to answer it. In the hall's shadow stood her master, Xerxes, his ruddy face flushed with long-suppressed feeling.

"My Lady . . ." he whispered, bowing his head.

Esther's throat tightened. "It has been a long time, My Lord," she softly replied.

"Too long," Xerxes sighed. "May I come in?"

It occurred to Esther that this man could do as he pleased, entering and exiting at will through any door on earth. That he should humble himself in this way touched her.

Stepping away from the portal, she assented, but as he walked to her couch, removing his cloak and draping it over the foot, she hesitated to follow.

His gaze passed over the room, and she knew that, as always he thought of Vashti, who had once dwelt here. But his eyes fell on the parchment which Esther had set upon her desk, and for a moment she expected he might ask about the new edict.

Instead, however, he seemed to study her sadly, and she hoped he would not speak of love.

When he did begin to talk, she was surprised at the direction the conversation took.

"So," he said patting the seat beside him and bidding her draw near, "I have taken a Jewess to wife."

Esther nodded, sitting down. "Does this please or displease you?" she inquired.

"Nothing about you displeases me," he replied with a smile. "You are only a source of continual delight."

Esther blushed and looked away. It was not the blush of a virgin, for she was that no longer. Rather, it was the result of unvoiced longings, unmet needs.

"No," he went on, barely sensing her frustration, "I have nothing against the Jews. They are an odd lot, no doubt, but good people. And Mordecai is a popular man."

Then, reaching out, he touched her hand. "But I have not come for this, My Lady," he asserted tenderly. "Haven't you missed me all these weeks?"

Part of him still hoped that her recent advances toward him indicated more than a yearning to save her people, and he still dreamed she might crave his embrace.

Yet she was unyielding.

"You know, My King, that I have never belonged to you," she insisted, looking bravely into his face. "Since you know that I am a Jew, you must understand this now more than ever."

Something like a shudder passed through Xerxes as the long-avoided reality was addressed.

"And you have never truly been mine," she went on.

"This is not so," he objected. Then, more uncertainly, "Not so . . ."

Esther rose from the couch and stepped to the archway. For the first time he saw in her the attitude of the caged doe, of the wild thing in captivity, as she watched the distant fields and the dim-lit burgs of the peasants far beyond.

Xerxes was capable of sympathy. He was not an utterly heartless man. And he also knew, as he had known in Salamis, when he had lost and when to retreat.

"I could demand your love," he sighed, joining her at the window.

"No one can demand another's heart," Esther countered. "You have not even been able to force *yourself* to love *me*. Don't you see? It has all been a wicked game, My Lord, one which Jehovah has miraculously turned to His own ends."

Her tone was rising with her courage, but she caught herself short of disrespect. "My soul belongs to the God of Israel," she softened, "and my heart to yet another."

Xerxes bristled at these last words, his fists clenching. "Another? Do I know him?"

"He is a poor man, My King. Not mighty, not monied. But a prince nonetheless."

Xerxes would hear no more.

"What can I do?" he sighed. "I would give you anything . . . unto half my kingdom . . ."

For a long while their eyes locked on one another. Rigid body confronted rigid body until Esther dared reply.

"Let me go, then, My Lord. And restore Vashti to her rightful place."

Dumbfounded, Xerxes could say nothing. Was this child, this humble orphan girl, suggesting once more that he should reverse himself?

"You have the power, O King," she insisted. "Nothing is too hard for the Monarch of the World."

Possibilities swirled through Xerxes' head. But he resisted them. Had he not rejected Vashti? Had he not commanded a harem and slept with countless women since? Never could he bow to such humiliation as this slip of a female suggested.

Yet . . .

"If you reversed Haman's edict, sealed by your own signet ring, why cannot you do this?" Esther continued.

"Stop!" the king suddenly shouted. "How dare you . . ."

Gently, Esther drew near and took him by the hand.

"Follow your heart, Majesty. What is it you wish? You may have it with a word," she reminded him. "Or you may concede again, to pride, and lose all hope forever."

Staring at the floor, Xerxes stood with stooped shoulders. But gradually a smile conquered his downturned lips.

"Are all Jews as headstrong as you, my dear?" he asked.

"We are a stiff-necked people," she laughed. "A peculiar people."

Dawn was creeping over the Zagros. The king glanced toward the hazy realm of the East, and his heart seemed suddenly to drop its fetters.

"A glorious people!" he cried, sweeping the girl into his arms. "May your God be blessed, as you have blessed me, dear child!"

48

It was a time of fulfillment.

Such liberty and grace had not been experienced by the exiled Jews since their taking away into captivity, more than 200 years before. In a matter of two days, the thirteenth and fourteenth of Adar, the twelfth month of the year, the Jews had overcome their enemies.

Throughout Persia's vast empire, governors and deputies had risen to the aid of the "peculiar people," and those who had dared come out against them had been slain.

In Susa 800 enemies had been killed, testimony to the slim number who took such a stand and to the vindication of the Hebrew race. Elsewhere, over 75,000 met their deaths at the hands of the Jews and their sympathizers.

Even the ten sons of Haman had been destroyed, run through with Jewish swords, and then, at Esther's suggestion, hanged from the very gallows upon which their father had died.

"Let it be a testimony to the fulfillment of God's will," the queen had said. "Agag and his descendants are gone forever!"

Only the Jews could fully appreciate the meaning of this. And only they understood why, in observance of Jehovah's counsel to King Saul, they were allowed to take no spoil from their enemies.

Yes, it was a time of fulfillment—and it was a time of returning. All along the roads of the empire, Jewish warriors traveled to their homes from scenes of victorious battle. Having gone wherever the need was greatest, they had fought in town after town in every province across the map. In two short days they met the centuries-old command of their God to obliterate the Amalekites, and now they would celebrate.

Esther drew her lavender shawl across her shoulders and peered into the eastern sunset. Tonight, in Leah's village, as in all cities and villages of the empire, there would be great merry-making, and she would be with her family, for the first time since her abduction, to join the party.

She passed beneath the gate of the royal palace riding in a queenly carriage. This would be her last time to enjoy the luxury of such a conveyance, and the last day she would ever be called "Queen Esther." Granting her fondest request, Xerxes had agreed to return her to her people, once the "Day of the Jews," as he called it, had passed.

And such a time it was, of victory in war over the Israelites' foes. On the thirteenth and fourteenth of Adar the Jews of Susa were allowed to fight, and on the thirteenth the Jews of the smaller villages prevailed over their enemies.

Just this morning Esther had stood with her papa, Prime Minister Mordecai, upon the king's porch before all the people of Susa. There, together, they had proclaimed their blessing upon the ensuing holiday, enjoining all their brothers and sisters to remember the Hebrew glory from that generation forward in annual celebration of "Purim." For the dice, the purim, cast by wicked Haman to determine the date of the Jews' annihilation, had selected the very date on which Jehovah gave His people victory over their enemies and established them as citizens of the world.

Such happiness there would be in the old hometown tonight!

Hadassah, humble daughter of Abihail and beloved of Mordecai (whose name was now great in the earth), turned her dark eyes one last time toward the palace as it retreated behind the gated wall.

To her delight, Xerxes had stepped onto his chamber balcony, watching her departure with a sad smile.

Lifting a hand, she waved goodbye to him, and he, feeling many things, returned the gesture.

But then it seemed his gaze was caught away. And when Hadassah scanned the roadway, wondering what attracted him, she felt her heart leap to her throat.

Another noble carriage, this one heading toward the city, was just now passing hers on the highway. As it drew within the torchlight of the sunset wall, it favored Hadassah with a view of the interior.

There, barely concealed by a gauze curtain, was the unmistakable face of Vashti, a bit older than the girl remembered her, but beautiful as ever.

The returning queen was riveted by the sight of her beloved at his high balustrade. And her heart was full, it was clear, of love and forgiveness. In the king's embrace she would revel this night, and he in hers.

Vashti did not see Hadassah as she passed by. For this the younger woman was glad. She would rather not be known.

But if the lady had glimpsed the Jewess, she might have remembered the lovely child who had peered down on her from the garden rail so long ago. She would have seen the image of herself, and would have understood her husband's clumsy attempt to love another.

ESTHER

EPILOG

Better is the little of the righteous
Than the abundance of many wicked.

The Lord knows the days of the blameless;
And their inheritance will be forever.

Psalm 37:16,18 NASB

The lights of Leah's village square warmed the dark night as Hadassah wound her way through the merrymakers.

No one had yet recognized her as she passed through the dancing townsfolk and through the musicians who frolicked the night away.

She had slipped from her cab quietly, bidding sad goodbyes to Dorca and Maryam, who had ridden out with her. And she had privately entered the town gate.

She sought among the laughing villagers the faces of Leah and Moshe, and her cousins, Marta and Isha. But most especially she sought David. Her ears were atuned for his voice amidst the sounds of celebration, and her eyes focused for the hue of his hair and the angle of his chin.

But her cousins saw her before she identified anyone. And their squeals of delight drew the crowd's full attention to the newcomer.

Hadassah had always been a star to these folk. Since she was a child, she had captivated old and young alike. Now she was a regal celebrity.

No one had anticipated her homecoming. Vashti's resumption of the throne was news not yet delivered to the empire, and no one had looked for Queen Esther to be leaving the palace. That she should appear unannounced in this little place upon this festive occasion was a fantasy hardly credible.

As the reality of her presence dawned upon the locals, silence overcame the crowd, the music ceased, and awe marked every face. Leah, upheld by Moshe's strong arm, advanced toward the long-lost girl, tears spilling over her cheeks.

"My child!" she cried. "Can it be you?" the woman stammered, afraid to touch her, and bowing reverently before Her Majesty.

"Stand up, Cousin," the star smiled. "Call me not Esther. I am your Hadassah."

Leah turned hesitantly to Moshe, who could only shake his head. "We do not understand," he marveled.

"All in good time," Hadassah laughed, her dark eyes sparkling. "God's time is always perfect."

Nobody questioned her further, but Leah studied Hadassah's furtive glance about the square, and knew what occupied her heart.

"You seek David?" she guessed, drawing close.

"I do," was the simple answer.

The newcomer could see from her cousin's somber expression that all was not well.

"He went off days ago to fight at Ecbatana."

"Yes—yes," the girl replied, recalling how David had once spoken of the fabled city, and of the nomads who sang in the desert.

"We have not heard from him since," Moshe stepped in.

Hadassah's pulse quivered, as she feared to contemplate the meaning.

"Have others returned from that battle?" she spurred him. "Is David the only one missing?"

"Most have come back, but not our son," Leah sighed.

The younger Jewess hesitated, but then bravely insisted, "Of course not!" Then, trying to calm the quaver in her own voice, "He would have seen matters through to the end."

"We hope so . . ." Moshe agreed.

"How can you doubt?" Hadassah cried. "He is coming! He must come!"

With this she tore herself away from her friends, heading for the town's northern gate. Leah would have restrained her, but Moshe held his wife in check.

"Let the girl go," he soothed. "God is her strength."

* * *

Hadassah stood on tiptoe outside the low village wall, straining her vision up the highway which led to Ecbatana.

Overcome by memories, she trembled, gripping the rough slats of the gate and pulling herself as tall as she could stretch. How often she had done this very thing as she waited for David to come home from the fields! But tonight there were no homecoming workers to greet her, no friendly winks or nodding heads.

For long hours she stood, watching as darkness deepened, and as the villagers in the square danced and sang. She stood vigil until her legs ached and her eyes burned, and until the heat off the moonlit desert cast a shadowy mirage across her gaze.

Sometime past midnight her weary eyes were caught by a movement near a plot of palms which marked a bend in the highway.

Thinking perhaps she had dreamed it, she shook herself alert and focused on the spot. The more she concentrated, however, the more she was certain someone traveled toward her.

David, her soul pleaded.

But this man did not have David's walk. This man had a strange, limping gait—as one who had been . . . wounded.

Suddenly, as she absorbed the implication, she grew rigid. *Lord, could it be?* Before her intellect received the word, her heart knew. And when the moonlight reflected off his golden hair, she was charged with certainty.

Flying across the fields and the dry plateau beyond, she hastened after him.

The bone-tired soldier, the plowboy who had traded a hoe for a sword, fearfully studied the oncoming phantom. Something in the grace of the form was familiar, but not until he heard her call his name would he ever have dreamed it was Hadassah.

Even when she was upon him, flinging her slender arms about his neck, he could not accept what his eyes told him.

"My lady?" he marveled. "Are you a desert angel? Or have I passed on to Abraham's bosom?"

"Neither, my dear, dear David," she replied, laughing and crying at once. "It is I—your Hadassah. Like you, I have come home this night."

"Home?" he sighed. "To me?"

"Yes," she insisted, still clinging to him.

Suddenly he could bear no more, and thrusting her from him, he glared at her in torment.

"You mock me!" he groaned. "What have you to do any longer with a peasant?"

At this he staggered on toward the village, leaving her alone.

"You are hurt," she cried, seeing plainly now his bandaged leg and twisted foot. "Let me help you."

Rushing to his side, she pulled him closer, drawing one of his strong arms across her shoulders.

"Why have you left your palace, my queen?" he quipped. "Have you come out to play with the poor folk?"

"Enough, David," she returned, stopping still in her tracks. "You have not seen me for years. Is this how you greet me?"

The young veteran studied her quizzically, his pride more badly wounded than his leg.

"I will have a hero's welcome when I reach home," he said. "I need no greeting from the acropolis."

"And you shall have none," she answered. "I no longer live there."

The wounded warrior feared to contemplate her fevered eyes. Barely could he tolerate the hope her words instilled.

"Tell me no lies," he pleaded.

"Call me not your queen, then," she sighed, "unless I am queen of your heart. For I am no longer Queen of Persia. I am not Esther, but Hadassah. And I love you."

David's mind raced with questions.

"I am a poor man," he objected. "You have possessed a king's caress, you have owned an emperor's embrace . . ."

"I was his prisoner, David, not his lover."

"You have had everything . . ."

"Nothing—nothing without you," she insisted.

Tears quivered along the young man's lashes. The moon set fire in his golden eyes.

"Hadassah?" he whispered.

"Say you love me," she pleaded. "You have never said it."

Bending over her, he drew her to his bosom and breathed into her hair. His sigh said it all, and his lips met hers, to the soft sound of dancing beyond the village wall.

Dear Reader:

We would appreciate hearing from you regarding this Harvest House book. It will enable us to continue to give you the best in Christian publishing.

1. What most influenced you to purchase *ESTHER*?
   - ☐ Author
   - ☐ Subject matter
   - ☐ Backcover copy
   - ☐ Recommendations
   - ☐ Cover/Title
   - ☐ _____

2. Where did you purchase this book?
   - ☐ Christian bookstore
   - ☐ General bookstore
   - ☐ Other
   - ☐ Grocery store
   - ☐ Department store

3. Your overall rating of this book:
   ☐ Excellent ☐ Very good ☐ Good ☐ Fair ☐ Poor

4. How likely would you be to purchase other books by this author?
   - ☐ Very likely
   - ☐ Somewhat likely
   - ☐ Not very likely
   - ☐ Not at all

5. What types of books most interest you?
   (check all that apply)
   - ☐ Women's Books
   - ☐ Marriage Books
   - ☐ Current Issues
   - ☐ Self Help/Psychology
   - ☐ Bible Studies
   - ☐ Fiction
   - ☐ Biographies
   - ☐ Children's Books
   - ☐ Youth Books
   - ☐ Other _____

6. Please check the box next to your age group.
   - ☐ Under 18
   - ☐ 18-24
   - ☐ 25-34
   - ☐ 35-44
   - ☐ 45-54
   - ☐ 55 and over

Mail to: Editorial Director
Harvest House Publishers
1075 Arrowsmith
Eugene, OR 97402

Name _____

Address _____

City _____ State _____ Zip _____

Thank you for helping us to help you in future publications!

DARK COUNTRY

DARK COUNTRY

BRONWYN PARRY

LARGE PRINT

Oxford

First published in Great Britain 2010
by
Piatkus
An imprint of Little, Brown Book Group

Published in Large Print 2010 by ISIS Publishing Ltd.,
7 Centremead, Osney Mead, Oxford OX2 0ES
by arrangement with
Little, Brown Book Group
An Hachette UK Company

British Library Cataloguing in Publication Data
Parry, Bronwyn.
    Dark country.
    1. Police - - Australia - - Fiction.
    2. Romantic suspense novels.
    3. Large type books.
    I. Title
    823.9'2–dc22

ISBN 978–0–7531–8728–9 (hb)
ISBN 978–0–7531–8729–6 (pb)

For my sisters:
We each hear different drummers,
but still find music to dance together.

CHAPTER
ONE

He shouldn't have come back. Gil's hands tightened on the steering wheel as he approached the bend in the road where everything had fallen apart, half a lifetime ago.

For an instant he took his foot off the accelerator and considered turning around, driving through the night and the rain to get back to Sydney and far, far away from his past. He should have taken it as a bad sign when the direct route to Dungirri was closed due to flooding. He'd had to take a long detour, looping an extra two hours' drive through Birraga to come into Dungirri from the west, passing the place where one set of nightmares had ended, and another begun.

The tall gum trees bordered the road, ghostly white trunks catching the headlights, twisted branches like fingers reaching out as menacingly as the memories.

He gritted his teeth. He would not let memories affect him now. He'd just go to Dungirri, do what he'd set out to do, and leave again.

He took the bend slower, cautiously, exhaling a pent-up breath when the road proved clear. No kangaroo this time. In the shadows just off the road, he could barely see the eerie shape of the tree, but his mind's eye filled with the vivid image of another time. The tree standing immoveable, a vehicle wrapped around it, the drooping branches scraping over the roof and the strobing lights of emergency vehicles surreal in the once-peaceful darkness. His gut clenched tight, and the recollection of the sharp, nauseating scents of blood, petrol, eucalyptus and alcohol came to him again, the mix permanently scarred into his nostrils.

He stared ahead, determined to keep his brain as focused on the road as his eyes were. Twenty kilometres to go. Fifteen minutes at most, as long as the rain didn't get heavy again.

The shadow of Ghost Hill rose to his left, as ethereal in the lightning and rain as its name, and the road curved around to nestle into its base. As the road straightened out, a vehicle parked ahead began to flash blue and red lights. He glanced down at the speedometer and swore. Just his damned luck — seven kilometres over the speed limit, and the Dungirri cops were ready with a welcoming party, especially for him. If he'd needed any confirmation that coming back was one hell of a mistake, he'd just got it.

The cop, swathed in reflective wet-weather gear, stood in the middle of the road with a torch and signalled him to pull over. He wound down the window but kept his eyes forward, telling himself not to respond to the triumphant look on the old sergeant's face when he recognised him.

He jerked his head around when a female voice said, "Sorry to pull you over, sir. I was hoping you were of the locals. Were you by any chance planning to stop in Dungirri?"

"Yes," he replied slowly, searching for the sarcasm in her voice. After flicking the light quickly around the interior, she turned the torch sideways, so that it didn't shine in his face, yet provided some light for both of them. Under the dripping brim of her hat he caught a glimpse of lively blue eyes and a few wisps of red hair around her face. Not a face he knew, which shouldn't have surprised him, given he'd been away so long.

"Oh, good. Would you mind doing me a favour? Could you get someone to phone my constable and tell him the patrol car's bogged out here? Just ask anyone — they all know him."

He stared at her, trying to make sense of her unexpected request. "You can use my mobile, if you like."

She grinned an open, friendly smile that he wasn't used to seeing from a police officer. "If it works out here then your phone company performs miracles. It's a notorious dead spot; Ghost Hill's between us and the towers, and blocks the phones and the police radio. Which is why I flagged you down."

He glanced at his phone in its holder on the dashboard. Sure enough, no signal.

"I could give you a lift into town." Hell, had those words come from his mouth? He'd avoided police as much as possible all his life, and for good reason.

She smiled again, shook her head. "Thanks, but I'll be fine. If you could just make sure the message gets to

Adam — Constable Donahue — I'll wait here until he comes."

Despite the perfectly reasonable logic, her refusal gouged across the old internal scars that he hadn't realised he still carried. Yeah, well, what did you expect, his inner voice taunted him.

"No offence intended," she added quickly, as if he'd frowned.

Something about the way she smiled at him, like an equal, kicked logic back in again. No sane woman would get into a car with a strange man, far from anywhere, even if she were a police officer with a gun on her belt. He knew he looked like someone you'd definitely avoid in a dark alley, and he'd been in enough dark alleys in his life to know he lived up to that impression. In his black T-shirt and well-worn leather jacket, he certainly didn't fit the image of a safe, respectable citizen — more like the type that most cops itched to arrest, without bothering to ask questions first.

He understood her refusal, yet the idea of leaving her here, alone in the dark and out of radio contact, didn't sit comfortably on his conscience.

"Maybe I could help you get your car out?"

"Thanks for the offer, but it'll need the four-wheel drive and a winch. It's in a ditch, and the entire left side is axle-deep in mud." She gave a rueful shake of her head. "You'd think that after years in the bush I wouldn't be stupid enough to swerve to avoid a kangaroo on a wet night, but I did. At least I didn't hit a tree."

4

He turned away quickly before he betrayed his shock. The parallels brought the other memories crowding back, halting his breath in his throat.

Yeah, coming back to Dungirri had definitely been a bad idea.

Kris caught the instant of bleakness in his shadowed eyes. So, the granite-faced man had some emotions, after all.

Already off-kilter from the shock of running into the ditch, the thought of waiting out here in the dark and rain another hour or so longer didn't appeal. She didn't dare sit in the patrol car; it felt too unstable, as if it were on the verge of tipping over into the mud. So, stand alone in the darkness and rain on jelly legs for fifty minutes or more, or risk going in a car with a guy who made James Dean look like a choirboy?

A flash of lightning above heralded a smashing of thunder that made her duck her head instinctively. Just her luck that she'd skidded the car into a ditch on the one night thunderstorms were interrupting the drought.

The man yanked the keys out of the ignition and thrust them at her through the window.

"Take my car. I'll wait here till you get back."

Maybe the thunder had befuddled her brain, because she couldn't for a moment work out what he meant, but realisation came as he opened the door and got out of the car.

In the torchlight he looked tall and dark and potentially dangerous, six-foot of muscle, with an unsmiling face that had seen more than a fist or two over the years. Even a knife, if she read the scar on the side of his cheek right. Eyes dark in more than just colour met hers, and his scowl suggested one really bad mood. Not a man to mess with, and sure as heck not the average guardian angel.

Yet, in some bizarre way, she trusted him. He stood a non-threatening metre from her, shoulders hunched against the rain, water already dripping from his black hair onto his leather jacket.

"I can't do that."

"Yeah, well I'm not going to leave a woman out here alone without radio or phone, cop or no cop. So take my damned car."

Light exploded nearby, with an instantaneous crash of thunder so loud it jarred every bone and muscle in her body and pounded her eardrums. A tree a hundred metres down the road flared a brief light before smoking in the heavy rain.

"You all right?" He reached a hand out, touched her on the arm. At least she wasn't the only one shaking. That crack of lightning had been way too close for comfort.

She gave a nervous laugh. "I will be, when my heart starts again. Okay, you can give me a lift into town. I don't plan on becoming a human lightning rod. Have you got room in the back for a couple of boxes? The senior sergeant at Birraga will kill me if the new computer gets drowned in mud."

The two computer boxes were on the near side of the patrol car, held in place by less precious boxes of stationery, so she didn't have to wade into the muddy ditch to retrieve them. The guy took the heavier one from her and stowed it in the boot of his car while she carried the smaller box.

Wherever he was going, he was travelling light, her observant cop eye noticed as she slid off her wet jacket, shook it out and folded it so it wouldn't drip water everywhere. A slightly battered kit bag lay on the back seat, a laptop case on the floor, and that was it. No maps, no fast-food containers, no CDs, no general bits and pieces that might accumulate on a trip or in daily use. Probably seven or eight years old, the car was clean — not sparkling rental-car clean, more not-used-often-at-all sort of clean.

She scrambled into the passenger seat, out of the rain, putting her jacket onto the floor at her feet. He shucked off his leather jacket, too, before he got in, tossing it over onto the back seat. He wasn't fussy about a bit of water on his seat, then.

"Thank you, Mr . . .?"

The interior light was still on, and she saw something wary flicker in his eyes.

"Just call me Gil."

Oh, yes, she knew an evasion when she heard one. So why would a man offer her his car, but avoid giving a surname? He could have just driven off when she'd first asked him to contact Adam, and she wouldn't have even taken his registration number.

"Thanks . . . Gil." She emphasised his name enough to let him know she hadn't missed the evasion. "I'm Kris Matthews."

He pulled his door shut properly. The interior light flicked off so that she could no longer see him clearly. Only a profile silhouette, stark and sharp.

"Buckle up, Sergeant Matthews," was all he said in response to her introduction, and he clicked his own seatbelt into its clasp before he twisted the key in the ignition.

So, Mr Cool and Distant had recognised the sergeant's stripes on her uniform shirt after she'd taken her jacket off. Sharp of him. And Mr Cool and Distant wasn't overly fond of police, it seemed, for all that he'd offered to wait in the rain while she took his car.

Too bad for him. He was heading into her town, and these days she was pretty damn protective of it.

"You're not from around here?" she asked.

He put the car into gear, pulled out on to the road before he answered. "Not any more."

One of those who'd left over the years, then. Dungirri had been bleeding its population for decades, dying the slow death of many rural communities. The closing of the timber mill, and the long drought, meant there were few jobs left, and now only three hundred or so residents, most struggling to make a decent living. Tragedies in the past two years had torn the town apart even further, and on bad days Kris had her doubts that it would ever recover. On good days, she hoped the recently formed Dungirri Progress Association might have some success in rebuilding the community. Good days didn't happen too often.

"Have you come back for the ball on Saturday?"

An eyebrow rose. "The ball?"

"The Dungirri Spring Ball."

No, he'd obviously not heard of it and, come to think of it, she really couldn't imagine this man in the Memorial Hall, mixing with Dungirri's citizens. It would be like throwing a panther in with a cage full of chickens.

"No. I'm just here to see someone on . . . business."

He didn't explain further — another evasion. He'd lived in these parts, knew that everyone knew everyone else, but he mentioned no names, gave no hint of his business, as a local would have.

Not a good sign.

They came out of the shadow of Ghost Hill, and within two minutes his mobile phone bleeped in its holder. Perhaps because of her presence, he grabbed the headset draped on the phone with one hand and slid it on before punching the answer button.

"What's up, Liam?" He listened for a moment. "Fuck." Definitely bad news, by the harshness of the word and the way his jaw clenched tight. Another pause. "She's all right?" A gruff note touched his voice, a hint of real concern.

Kris tried not to watch him, to give him a semblance of privacy, but in the silence as he listened, she saw out of the corner of her eye his fingers gripping tight on the steering wheel, and although he didn't stop driving, he slowed a little.

"Look, take Deb away with you for a few days' break, okay?" he said. "To that eco-lodge she wanted to check out, or somewhere like that. Tell her it's a surprise bonus from me for the two of you. Charge everything to the business account." Another pause, and his tone hardened again. "I've already dealt with Marci. You look after Deb. Might be best if you get her away from there tonight. I'll call you tomorrow."

He ended the call, muttering another curse under his breath as he dragged the earpiece off.

"Bad news?" she enquired. She couldn't pretend she hadn't heard his side of the conversation.

She counted to four before he eventually said, "One of my employees was attacked by an intruder at her home."

She had the distinct impression that while that might be the truth, it wasn't the whole truth.

"Is she hurt?"

"Only shaken. She has a black belt in karate."

"So the attacker came off worst?"

In the dim light from the dashboard she saw the corner of his mouth twitch, a suggestion of a grin, for just an instant. "Yeah. Something like that." But his mouth firmed again straight away, and he stared ahead, tapping a finger on the steering wheel, his expression tense and shuttered.

And although she wondered, she didn't ask why a man would send two of his staff away for an all-expenses-paid break just because one of them was shaken up. Or what sort of business he ran that was profitable enough to give generous bonuses, and that had brought him back to Dungirri for a meeting. Or what the rest of the bad news was, news that had made his mood even darker than when she'd met him a few minutes before.

10

She didn't ask because she suddenly had a strong suspicion that she might not like the answers.

She let her head fall back on the headrest, closing her eyes in weariness. They were almost at Dungirri, and if the guy had dastardly intentions towards her he would have acted on them by now. Her trust that he'd get her there safely seemed well enough placed.

But then again, that proved nothing. She'd been neighbours with a murderer for years and never twigged. "Just-call-me-Gil" could be a dark angel straight from hell, for all that she felt safe, just now.

If he planned on staying around, she'd have to damn well ask those questions and find out, one way or another.

She just hoped he didn't plan on staying around. "Safe" wasn't a word that was likely to stick to him, long term, and Dungirri had had more than its share of visits from hell already.

Gil silently worked through every single swear word he knew, and made up a few more when they ran out.

There had to be something about this damned road. The last time he'd been on it, his plans for a new life had been smashed to smithereens and now, tonight — almost eighteen years later, and the first day of what was supposed to have been another new start — Liam's news had brought that all crashing down.

Damn Vincenzo Russo for getting himself shot in the chest last night. It was lousy timing for Vince's personal security to fail him, as far as Gil was concerned. With Vince on life support, his son Tony would waste no time in moving to take control of the Russo family operations — and Tony had neither reason nor inclination to honour the agreement that had kept Vince out of Gil's affairs for years. Gil's plans of being long gone from Sydney by the time Tony eventually took over had just been screwed, well and truly.

The sergeant had gone quiet, stopped asking her questions. With her head back, eyes closed, a hint of vulnerability underlay the confident cop persona she'd shown earlier. Wayward curls of red hair framed her face, and a few wet ends curled against the pale skin of her neck, just above her shirt collar. For some reason, that sight gave him a sharp, hot kick in the guts.

He turned his eyes back to the road. Oh yeah, lusting after a *cop*, in *Dungirri* of all places — that was truly the definition of stupidity.

Christ, he hadn't even given her his surname, because even if she hadn't heard of him, she'd have made the connection between his name and that of his old man, and those blue eyes would have turned cold, lumping him with the same label as his mad bastard of a father.

And if the locals had told her about him, or if she'd heard the other end of that phone call . . . well, she'd sure be doubting the wisdom of getting into a car with him.

And what did it all matter, anyway? In just a few minutes he'd drop her off at the cop station, and he'd never see her and her lively blue eyes again. He'd go and call on Jeanie, do what he'd come to do, and then leave Dungirri. He'd get back on the road to try to sort out the god-awful mess his life had just become, before Tony Russo took his vendetta out on people who didn't deserve it, like Liam and Deb.

The dim lights of Dungirri appeared, and he shifted down a gear as he came to the first scattered houses. Another landslide of bad memories tumbled out thick and fast from the dark places in his mind, catching him unawares, jumbling on top of his current worries and making his gut coil tight.

Damn his memories. Damn this town. Damn that stupid conpulsion that pushed him back here to finish once and for all with his past before he moved on. Dungirri held nothing for him but bitterness and nightmares.

As he drove into town along the deserted, mostly dark main street, a line from something he'd once read suddenly came into his mind like some bleak premonition and drummed again and again in his head: *The wheel has come full circle; I am here.*

Well, he might be here, but he wouldn't be for long.

The old police station hadn't changed much. A new keypad security system, a phone link to connect straight through to Birraga for when the local cops were out, and a coat of paint were about the only differences Gil could discern as he walked up to the steps. When the sergeant opened up the station and he carried the larger of the computer boxes in for her, he saw that the 1950s wooden chairs in the small reception area had been replaced by 1970s orange plastic chairs. So much for progress.

She pushed open the door to the interview room. "In here thanks, Gil. I have to make space in the office first before I can set it up in there."

Hell, it would have to be the interview room. Definitely a place he had no desire to revisit. He slid the box onto the table in the small room and made for the door again, without checking whether it was the same wooden table he'd had his face smashed into.

On the veranda, he sucked in a breath of fresh, damp air.

"Are you staying at the hotel?" the sergeant asked from behind him. "Can I shout you a drink later, to thank you for your help?"

He turned to face her, and the light from the porch illuminated her in the doorway. Not a classically beautiful face, yet attractive in her own way, and small lines around her eyes revealed that under the aura of relaxed competence she carried tension and concerns. Well, if she'd been in town longer than a year or so, she'd have had more than enough stress and worry. Two abducted kids and several murders couldn't have been easy for any cop to deal with, let alone one who seemed to have a whole lot more soul than the old sergeant had ever had.

Kris Matthews. A woman with a name and a history, not just "the sergeant" as he'd called her in his mind — since there could be no point in thinking about her as a real person.

"I'm not staying," he told her.

She stepped out, directly under the light, so that it glinted in the red-gold of her hair, but cast her face into shadow.

"Oh. Well, thank you for the lift. I do appreciate it. And drive safely, wherever you're going."

He raised a hand in acknowledgement, took the three steps down from the porch in one pace, and strode to his car.

He drove back down the main street, past the empty shops and the few businesses still struggling to survive, past the council depot and the pub, and pulled into the empty parking area of the Truck Stop Café. It was only eight o'clock and lights spilled from the café, but other than a couple of teenage kids laughing at the counter, he could see no-one inside. Jeanie might well be in the kitchen, or in the residence upstairs.

He pushed the door open, and both kids watched him enter. The girl, maybe sixteen or so, wore a blue "Truck Stop" apron over a black goth-style skirt and top. The lad, sweeping up behind the till where customers paid for petrol, might have been a year or two older. So, Jeanie was still giving employment to Dungirri's youth.

The girl smiled. "Hi, there. I'm afraid the kitchen's closed, if you were after a meal, but I can still do coffees and there's pies and sausage rolls left."

The mention of food made his gut do an uneasy somersault. It had been a while since he'd eaten, but his appetite had disappeared somewhere on the road to Dungirri.

"No, that's okay. I was looking for Jeanie Menotti, actually. Is she around?"

"I'm sorry, she's out tonight. There's a meeting to finalise the ball arrangements. She won't be back until late."

Of course — the ball the sergeant had mentioned. As incongruous as a ball in Dungirri sounded, if there was going to be one then Jeanie would be involved in running it.

It just put a massive spanner in his plans to be out of here tonight. For a brief moment, he contemplated leaving an envelope for her with these kids, but he ditched the idea straight away. Jeanie would be more than hurt if he went without seeing her, and Jeanie, of all people, didn't deserve that sort of shoddy treatment.

"What time does she open in the morning, these days?" he asked the kids.

"Six-thirty. I'm opening up for her tomorrow, but she'll be around not long after that," the girl answered, and something about the way she smiled struck him with a vague sense of familiarity. Probably the daughter of someone he'd once known. Although, in his day, Dungirri kids hadn't worn multiple studs in their ears and nose. A touch of the city, out here in the outback.

"Thanks. I'll call in tomorrow, then."

Out in his car again, he thumped the steering wheel in frustration. He'd be spending the night in Dungirri. He could sleep in the car, out on one of the tracks that spider-webbed through the scrub east of town . . . no, not a good idea. All day in the car had been more than enough for a tall body more used to standing than sitting, and he had the return journey to make tomorrow.

He reversed out and swung around to park in the side street beside the hotel, away from the half-dozen other vehicles parked randomly around the front.

Harsh weather and neglect had worn away at the century-old hotel. The external timberwork cried out for a coat of paint, and the wrought-iron railings around the upstairs veranda were more rust-coloured than anything else. The "For Sale" sign tied crookedly to a post had faded in the weather, too, adding another forlorn voice to the visible tale of lost glory.

He yanked his bag and his laptop from the back of the car and went in through the side door, purposely avoiding the front bar. The back bar was dark and empty, as was the office. He tapped on the servery window into the front bar, keeping out of the line of sight of the customers. He had no desire to meet up with any familiar faces from his past.

A bloke in his early twenties in a work shirt and jeans finished pulling a beer for someone and strolled over to him. Not anyone he recognised.

"Have you got a room for the night?" Gil asked.

"Sure, mate." He reached into a drawer, passed a key and a registration book across the counter. "Room three, upstairs. Just sign here. You wanna pay in the morning, or fix it up now?"

Gil paid cash, signed the book with an unreadable scrawl the guy didn't bother looking at, and headed up the stairs. The room was basic, as he'd expected, relatively clean but with worn-out furnishings that had seen a few decades of use already.

He dropped his bag on the floor, lay flat on his back on the bed and stared up at the old pressed-metal ceiling. A few creaking springs warned him that it wouldn't be the most comfortable of nights. He'd coped with far worse.

Staring at the ceiling only let his brain wander to places he didn't want to contemplate, and his body clock wouldn't be ready for sleep until at least his usual time of two or three in the morning. He swung his legs back over the edge of the bed, hauled out his laptop and set it up on the small, scratched wooden table in the corner, draping the cord over the bed to get to the single power point. The room had no phone line or wireless network — the twenty-first century hadn't made it to Dungirri, yet, it seemed — but he connected his laptop to his mobile phone and went online.

For an hour he worked, tidying up the loose ends of the inner-city pub he'd just sold, checking and sending email, making payments to creditors, transferring funds between accounts. And all the time, the half of his brain that wasn't dealing with facts and figures tussled with other questions — like who the hell might have had the balls and opportunity to shoot Vince, and what the response of his various rivals would be.

Maybe Tony would be too caught up in fighting for power to pursue his long-desired vengeance on Gil. Gil dismissed that hope as quickly as he thought of it. Tony would view getting even with him as a sign of his new

18

authority, and a message to anyone who might stand in his way.

Somewhere around nine-thirty, the single light bulb in the room pinged and went out. A light still burned outside on the veranda. Just his bulb blowing then, not a loss of power. Reluctantly, he headed downstairs to ask for a replacement. In the corridor behind the bar, an older guy swung out of the gents' just as Gil passed, almost knocking him with the door.

The bloke turned around to apologise, and Gil stifled a groan as they recognised each other. His bad luck was still holding strong. Of all the people in Dungirri to come face to face with.

The man's face whitened. "You . . ." He seemed to struggle for control, pain and rage contorting his face, then lost it. He raised a fist, took a step towards Gil and roared, "You murdering bastard."

CHAPTER TWO

Kris took the call on the radio just as she and her constable, Adam, drove back into Dungirri, towing the damaged patrol car on a trailer behind the police four-wheel drive. A fight at the Dungirri Hotel, police presence requested.

"We're right outside," she told the dispatcher as Adam slowed down to pull in opposite the hotel.

"I've been on duty fifteen hours already today, and I am so not in the mood for this," she grumbled, flicking her seatbelt off and thrusting the door open.

"Well, if it's the Dawson boys again, you can make good on that threat to throw them in the old cell, and force-feed them your cooking," Adam teased, as they crossed the road at a jog.

"Watch it, Constable Performance-appraisal-tomorrow," she retorted, her grin reflecting the easy friendship they'd built over the past three years. They worked well together, and if she had to go and break up yet another pub brawl, there were few she'd feel more comfortable with having at her side.

The fight had already spilled out in to the courtyard behind the hotel, judging by the shouts. Pub fights were rarely serious here — usually just a mix of too much

20

drink and testosterone, and a few lousily aimed drunken punches.

This one, she saw when she pushed through the gate into the courtyard, was different.

The outdoor lights clearly illuminated a dozen men who stood by watching while four others laid into one man with fists and kicks. The victim — it was *him*, Gil — seemed to be aiming to block blows rather than fight back. And the only one trying to help him was Ryan Wilson, out there in his wheelchair, dragging at the arm of one of the fighters. And strong ex-boxer though Ryan might be, the odds weren't in his favour.

For an instant, an image of a body, beaten beyond recognition, flashed in her memory. No, *that* wasn't happening again. Not in this town.

Bellowing an order to stop, she charged in on a surge of adrenaline and determination, Adam beside her. She caught one guy's arm as he lifted it to punch again, wrenched it up behind his back before he realised what was happening, and dragged him out of the fight, handcuffing him to one of the big wooden tables. Adam pulled another away and clicked handcuffs on him before going back to help Ryan. The fourth man managed to get in one more punch before Kris made it to him, and Gil staggered under the blow to his head and stumbled against the fence, while she pushed the guy down against a table and held him there.

And then it was quiet, but for some heavy breathing, and Kris looked up to see some of the watchers starting to sidle out the gate.

"Nobody move," she ordered at the top of her sergeant's voice. "If any of you try to leave before I get to the bottom of this, I will throw the whole damn charge book at the lot of you. Do you understand me?"

She glanced around at Gil, straightening up to lean against the fence, already digging in his pocket for a handkerchief to wipe the blood from his nose. *Not as bad as Chalmers, thank God.*

Ryan wheeled across to him.

"Does he need an ambulance, Ryan?"

"No," Gil replied for himself. "I don't."

She pulled up the guy she held — Jim Barrett — and dumped him on a chair. She did a quick look round the other men involved. All Barretts. Not the usual troublemakers. Adam still held Jim's brother, Mick, a morose guy in his sixties who normally propped up the corner of the bar and hardly said anything to anyone. And the two others were Jim's boys, in their mid-thirties.

She glared at the entire group, including Gil.

"Right. Which one of you is going to tell me what the hell is going on here?"

"That's Morgan Gillespie." Jim pointed an accusing finger. "He killed Mick's daughter, Paula."

Oh, shit. Her stomach dropped into her boots.

"It was an accident," Ryan interjected, before she'd had time to draw in a steadying breath. "The conviction was quashed."

"He got off on a bloody technicality," Jim spat back.

22

"A rigged blood-alcohol report is hardly a technicality," Ryan argued. "And he spent three years inside because of it."

Her brain whirled. So, Gil — *Morgan Gillespie* — had been to prison for some accident involving Mick's daughter, way before her time because she'd not heard about it. Until now.

Well, she knew Ryan better than she knew Jim, and if Ryan was prepared to stand up for a person so strongly, she'd lean towards trusting his judgement over Jim's. Ryan was a decent man, and with a cooler head than Jim.

The two people most concerned stayed silent. Mick stood, stooped in Adam's grasp, face downcast, tears running down his cheeks. And Gil had slid down to sit on the paving of the courtyard, still leaning against the fence, his head tilted back and eyes closed.

She crossed to him quickly, reaching to check his pulse automatically. "Are you okay, Gillespie?"

Dark, near-black eyes opened and looked straight into hers, alert and piercing, and the pulse in his wrist drummed strong and strangely hot against her fingers.

"I'll be fine."

Split lip, bloodied nose, bruised face aside, his pulse and breathing seemed good, and there were no signs of dizziness or disorientation in the sharpness of his gaze. She figured he might be right, although she'd take him up to the station and check him over properly very soon. With the ambulance — and the nearest doctor — at least forty minutes away in Birraga she wouldn't call them out straight away, but she'd keep a close watch on him.

She let his wrist go, sat back on her heels and looked straight at him. "Anything you want to add to what they said?"

"No."

No excuses, no denials, no explanations. She wasn't sure whether to respect him for that, or throttle him in frustration. Throttling the lot of them held a certain appeal, right now. But she still didn't know exactly what had happened.

Satisfied that Gillespie probably wouldn't collapse and die right there, she stood up and glared at the gathered crowd, with no attempt to hide her anger and disgust.

"Right. Gillespie's coming with me for some first aid and then some questions. Adam, you keep this lot under a close watch and take statements from all of them. I want some answers. Davo, close up the bar. The only thing you're serving for the rest of the night is strong coffee while they give their statements. And if I hear of any of you talking together to concoct some story, I'll have you up on a charge of conspiracy so quickly you'll be in the Birraga lock-up before you know it."

"I won't press any charges, Sergeant." Gillespie spoke from behind her, loud enough for everyone to hear.

Damn the man. She wasn't in the mood for heroics, or for letting anyone off the hook.

24

She snorted loudly. "You'll change your mind when the bruises start hurting. And if you keel over and die from a brain haemorrhage, your body will be sufficient evidence to charge the Barretts with murder and the rest of these bloody idiots with being accessories." She dropped her voice to a barely audible hiss. "So shut up and make it look good and let this lot stew on their frigging stupidity."

Community policing as it *wasn't* written in the manual, but she didn't give a damn. The people who wrote the manual hadn't worked for five years in an outback town that had been disintegrating long before a psychopathic resident had begun abducting local children and murdering witnesses. Nor had they seen what a frenzied mob could do to an ageing, defenceless suspect, or ridden in the back of an ambulance with the critically injured colleague — and friend — who'd tried to protect him.

So she'd handle this her way, because she was one of them now and she knew them and this wasn't just a hot-tempered pub brawl. And she'd damn well make sure that this lot contemplated — *sweated over* — the possible consequences of their idiocy.

It had to be the blows to the head that were making him feel dizzy, because the physical proximity of the fiery sergeant shouldn't be doing it. Not when she was as seriously pissed off as she was.

This close to her he could see the anger, tightly controlled, but the intensity of it almost made him take a step backwards. The sort of anger with its roots in deep emotion, not some mere bad mood.

Make it look good. She wanted him to limp away from this as though he'd been really hurt.

Ryan Wilson wheeled his chair a little closer and studied him. Ryan, the only one of the lot of them who'd tried to help him. Gil's irregular school attendance had become even more irregular when high school meant having to get into Birraga each day, but on the rare occasions he'd been, he'd hung around with Ryan and the other rough-edged Birraga larrikins. Time and circumstance might have smoothed Ryan's roughness slightly — he'd apparently ended up marrying one of the shyest, nicest girls in Dungirri — but there sure as hell was nothing *meek* about the man.

"He's not actually looking too good, Kris," Ryan said. "I think we should call the ambulance after all."

Gil started to object, but the words halted in his throat when he caught the conspiratorial gleam in Ryan's eye. He choked his objection into a cough and winced as the movement sent searing pain across his ribs.

The sergeant, hands on her hips in typical cop stance, didn't look in the slightest bit amused. "Yeah, that cough doesn't sound good. He could have broken a rib and punctured a lung. In which case the ambulance will take too long to get here. I'd better get him in the car and meet it half-way."

She was beside him in two strides, her arm around his back. "Can you make it as far as the car, Gillespie?"

"I don't . . ."

She cut off his protest. "Lean on me."

A flare of masculine pride warred for a moment with pragmatism, and lost. It didn't matter to him what these blokes thought — he couldn't fall any lower in their estimation, anyway — but getting an angry police sergeant any more off-side would not be a good move.

He put his arm around her shoulder and pretended to lean on her as they walked slowly across the courtyard, as if he were dizzy. And he did his damnedest to ignore the very *female* feel of the woman beside him, which walking hip to hip with her reminded him with every step.

"Adam, get the rest of these bozos inside," she instructed the constable. "If any of them try to leave before you have their statements, arrest them. Or shoot them. I don't particularly care which."

Ryan followed them out, swinging the gate shut behind him.

Gil began to draw away from Kris as soon as they reached the street, but her firm grip around his waist didn't budge. "Keep going. They'll still be watching."

"I don't have any broken ribs," he told her. "I've been there, done that before, and I know they're not broken this time. And my head's fine."

"Good. Because if I have to drive to Birraga again tonight, I'll be seriously pissed off."

She didn't drop her arm from around him until they'd crossed the road to the police vehicles.

"Get in. You're coming up to the station for first aid and questions."

"Do you want me to ask Beth to come and check him over, so you can go back and help Adam with the statements?" Ryan offered.

"No. She's busy with the meeting. And if I go back in there just now my blood might boil." She exhaled an exasperated breath. "If you can give Adam some moral support, I'd appreciate it, Ryan. Feel free to tell gory stories from your boxing days and scare the shit out of them. I want them worried sick, because then they might get the damn message that mob violence is not going to happen again in this town."

"I suppose I should thank you," Gil said into the silence as she drove the two blocks up to the station.

"You should grovel and beg forgiveness for ruining what was supposed to be my first quiet evening at home for a week."

"Would it work?"

"No." She rammed the vehicle down a gear to pull in at the front of the police station. "What were you thinking, Gillespie, letting them at you like that? You don't strike me as a turn-the-other-cheek kind of guy."

Yeah, she had that right. He'd have merrily ground Jim Barrett's face into the ground when he and his sons had joined the fight. But he'd learned over the years to pick his battles. It had happened — shit, it had been almost inevitable, once he'd set foot back in town — and he understood the reasons why.

"I figured if swinging a few at me helped Mick Barrett get some long-held anger out, I could deal with an old man's punches."

28

She switched off the ignition and yanked the keys out. "Yes, well it wasn't just Mick, was it? Were you going to let the four of them continue to use you as a punching bag?"

"No. But I read the crowd, just as you did. If I'd fought back it would have been a dozen rather than four. Four I can handle. More than that and the odds aren't great."

And as he said the words, he remembered the news he'd heard a couple of years back, and her anger and reaction to what had happened suddenly began to make sense. A mob of locals had bashed an old guy to death when they'd thought he was responsible for the abduction and murder of the little Sutherland girl. It had been the first in a string of deaths that had haunted the place while a killer played his twisted games.

"Yeah, you're right," she muttered, with a soul-weary sigh. "Come inside and we'll do something about your face."

She led him not into the station itself, but into the residence behind it. Her personal space. Her home. Flicking on lights in the kitchen, she shoved a pile of books and papers on the pine kitchen table to one side and motioned for him to sit at the end.

"I'll get the first-aid kit," she murmured and disappeared down a corridor. He took the chance to glance around the room. The place was lightly cluttered with the signs of a busy life. The books and papers she'd shoved aside, a small pile of unopened mail, a coffee mug with remnant grounds in the bottom, a handful of dishes piled in the drainer.

One bowl, one plate, one mug, he noticed. If she shared this place with anyone, they didn't eat much. Like it was any of his business, anyway.

He was only here because . . . because cooperating with the police made for less trouble, that was why. Not because she'd come raging in like some damn Valkyrie to break up the fight, outnumbered but undaunted, dealing with the situation without resorting to any of the weapons on her belt. Packing all that power and authority into her slight five-foot-six frame.

She came back into the room, dropped a police service first-aid kit on the floor beside the table, and rummaged in the freezer for an ice-pack. Sliding a chair around in front of him, she sat down and began to check his face.

She was all professional and impersonal, but underneath her competent composure he sensed she was distracted, on edge, *distant* — as though only her professional self paid any attention to him. He, on the other hand . . . well, it had been a while since he'd been up close and personal with a woman, and having this one only inches from his face was reminding him of that fact, in no uncertain terms.

Cool, deft fingers swiped antiseptic over the cut on his lip, and under his cheekbone where he'd caught one, hard. The sting contrasted sharply with the light intimacy of her touch.

"You said you weren't staying," she said, and he grabbed on to the opening to reel his thoughts away from dangerous ground.

30

"I didn't plan on it. The person I came to see is out tonight."

"Who?"

"Jeanie Menotti."

"Oh." Surprise registered in the single syllable, as if she'd been expecting him to meet with one of Dungirri's more dubious characters, instead of an elderly widow. She raised a wary eyebrow. "She never mentioned you were coming."

"She isn't expecting me."

"Hmmm." She finished with his face, and he breathed a little easier when she moved away from him to toss the wipes in the rubbish bin. But the ease lasted only a few seconds before she said, "Take off your jacket and T-shirt."

After a moment's hesitation he complied, although agreeing to sit there half-naked while she put her hands on his body probably ranked up there with crossing the Russos on the danger stakes.

She leaned forward, and he caught the scent of damp, sweet-smelling hair as she ran her hands over the reddened skin where the Barretts' blows had landed. Surprisingly gentle for such a fiery, strong personality.

"When was the accident with Mick's daughter?"

Oh, yeah, *that* question sure dragged his thoughts away from inappropriate territory and back into cold reality. Of course she'd ask about it. She was a cop, doing her job.

"Eighteen years ago in December."

"You must have been young."

He shrugged. "Eighteen."

Her fingers touched a painful spot. He gritted his teeth but didn't flinch. He'd have a whopping bruise by tomorrow, might even have cracked a rib, but he wasn't letting her know that. There wasn't much she could do, anyway, other than assure herself that he wouldn't become a corpse on her watch. And since he'd be heading straight back to Sydney in the morning, he'd be out of her way before long. Compared to Tony Russo's probable plans for him, a few bruises from the Barretts were the least of his worries.

"Was Ryan right? Did someone tamper with the blood-alcohol report?"

"Tampered with" wasn't the description he'd use. More like "created an entire bloody work of fiction". But as he had no intention of going over any more old history than necessary, he merely answered, "Yes."

She shot a cutting glance his way. "Full of details, aren't you, Gillespie?" She frowned suddenly, sat back and regarded him, her eyes shadowed. "Oh, shit. *Gillespie*. Des Gillespie was your father, wasn't he? I'm sorry about his passing."

Gil reached for his T-shirt, yanked it over his head and thrust his arms into it, ignoring the sharp pain just as he ignored her sympathy. "Did you know him?"

"We'd met a few times," she acknowledged.

"Then don't pretend you're sorry he's dead."

His eyes had turned dark and cold, a universe of emptiness in their chilling depths.

"Not even a mean, vicious bastard, like he was, deserves to be murdered," she said quietly.

"Just a 'mean, vicious bastard'? He must have mellowed in his old age." He spoke carelessly, without emotion, as if it weren't his own father he spoke of.

And if she hadn't known Des Gillespie, that disconnection would have worried her. But she had known Des, and Gil would have had to have emotionally disconnected to have survived a childhood with his father, then three years in prison, and whatever else life had thrown at him. He carried the hard-edged wariness of a man who knew what it was to fight for his life, and the scar on his face wasn't the only one — she'd seen two more long, ragged scars on the side of his chest.

Yet he'd let a grieving old man throw punches at him, without striking back. Not an easy man to understand, this one. Layers and complexities and too much hidden under that cool exterior.

He picked up his jacket, hooking it over his shoulder with a finger.

"If you've finished your questions, I'll head off."

"Oh, sit down, Gillespie, and put the ice-pack on your face. Otherwise you're going to have one heck of a shiner before too long. You're not going anywhere until I say so."

He didn't sit. Not that she'd expected him to. Just stayed where he was, narrowed eyes watching her. "Am I under arrest?"

She cocked her head to one side and gave him back look for look. "For being a pig-headed, stubborn, pain in the neck? Unfortunately, it's not against the law. Nope, you're just staying put until I'm sure you don't have concussion or worse, and to make sure that anyone else who wants to punch you doesn't get the chance tonight. Since there aren't any other options, that means that you're sleeping in my guest room, and I'm checking on you every hour for the next eight hours."

"That's not necessary."

"In my judgement, it is. Humour me, Gillespie. Otherwise I'll spend the whole night imagining you dead or brain-damaged, or standing guard over the Barretts, to make sure they don't go after you again."

He made neither comment nor move, and his guarded expression gave no indication of his thoughts. But at least he hadn't walked out.

She snapped the catches on the first-aid kit and rose, picking it up with one hand, tossing him the ice-pack with the other. He caught it deftly.

"Look, I'm not going to jump your bones, if that's what you're worried about. Even if I was interested, I've been working double shifts for two weeks and I'm too frigging tired to remember how. So you're quite safe here."

She caught a flicker of something — amusement, maybe — on his face. Yep, underneath the layers of granite, there definitely lurked a human being. A physically attractive one. Possibly even a decent one. Not that a guy like him was likely to admit it.

And yes, if she had any libido left he'd quite probably tickle it, but she *was* too tired to even follow that train of thought, and he'd be gone in the morning. A quiet night with no more worrying was all she wanted, and

34

Gillespie had given no sign he'd even think of trying anything. And if he did, well, he'd find out quickly enough that years of policing in the rugged, masculine environment of the bush had given her a whole lot of skills that made the police self-defence training redundant.

As she headed towards the office, she tossed over her shoulder, "Did I mention that the guest bed is extra long, and the mattress is at least a decade newer than the ones at the hotel?"

Two seconds passed before his laconic drawl floated down the passageway after her. "Well, you sure know how to tempt a man, Blue."

Gil jammed the ice-pack against his aching face and mentally kicked himself. Hard.

No. That's what he should have said. *No thanks, I can sleep in the car out in the scrub.*

Instead he'd not only called her by the traditional bush nickname for anyone with red hair, he'd made a damn stupid comment that could well add bruised balls to the rest of his injuries.

There had to be a law against flirting with cops. And if it wasn't in the statute books, it definitely was inscribed in his personal rule book, up there on page one, right next to "Thou shalt not let the Sydney mafia rule your business".

He heard a door close, then the firm tread of her boots back along the wooden floor.

But when she appeared in the doorway, she didn't look pissed off, just bone-weary. Like a woman who'd been working too many hours, and caring too much, for way longer than just a couple of weeks.

Guilt twisted in his gut. If it weren't for him, her day would have ended at least an hour ago.

"So, this is where you tell me that the guest room is the one with the bars on the windows and the steel door, right?"

She leaned against the door frame, arms folded, her strained smile hardly touching her eyes. "It's only used for storing old files these days. Just don't make me cram you into a filing cabinet, okay, Gillespie?"

"I won't cause you any trouble, Sergeant."

"You already did," she said simply, without any rancour, but the truth of it still made him feel like a bastard. "Adam's walking the Barretts up from the pub now, so I'd better go and deal with them."

"What will happen to them?"

"Since you won't pursue charges, they'll get the thermo-nuclear death-glare. They'll be reduced to piles of radioactive dust on the floor within minutes."

She didn't smile, and he almost felt some sympathy for the four Barrett men.

"Sounds like charging them might be kinder."

"For them? Probably. For me — a heap more paperwork." She shrugged, a pretence of uncaring that he didn't fall for. "Help yourself to any food if you're hungry. You might be lucky and actually find something in the fridge that hasn't mutated into an alien life-form."

She shoved her hands into her pockets, about to go, and without thinking he asked, "Have you eaten?"

36

She paused, a frown lacing her features as if she was trying to remember. "I'll make a sandwich later," she muttered, then turned on her heel and was gone again.

Not a good sign when someone couldn't remember when they'd last eaten. Maybe he should make something for her . . .

He shoved the ice-pack against another ache on his face and wondered what — other than the Barretts' fists — had hit him and scrambled his sanity so thoroughly.

If he had any sense, he'd leave a note on the table and disappear out the back door. Except then she probably *would* be awake all night, worrying about him, and that was one thing he didn't want to add to his conscience.

He pulled a chair out with his foot and sat down, leaning his head against the wall, shifting the ice-pack to his jaw, and closed his eyes, resigned to a night under the sergeant's roof. With a headache the size of Mount Kosciusko. And knowing that in a few minutes he'd get up, raid her fridge, and see what sort of meal he could fix for them both.

The alarm beeped its way into her consciousness, and Kris dragged herself awake with a groan and fumbled for the off button. Early daylight dulled the glare of the electronic numbers. Six o'clock. For the sixth time in as many hours, she dragged herself out of bed, yanked her robe on, and stumbled to the spare room next door.

He was already up, rummaging in the bag that Adam had brought from the hotel last night, and he must have heard her footsteps because without turning, he said dryly, "It's Friday, I'm Gil Gillespie, this is Dungirri, and I don't have concussion, Sergeant."

Pretty much the same thing he'd said the last four times she'd been in to check him. Except those times, he'd been in bed, covered by the blanket, and now he stood wearing only his T-shirt and jocks, and she should have been checking his eyes for responsiveness, but instead she found herself checking over his legs — long, muscular, *naked* legs — and his large, beautiful, equally naked feet.

Lack of sleep must be fusing her brain and drying her throat, because she'd seen plenty of men's legs over the years without those effects occurring.

The feet turned towards her, and a yawn gave her the excuse to close her eyes and keep them closed until she could look at eye level, and not at anything in between. Professional. Impersonal. Like she was supposed to be.

She was too tired to read the lightning-flash of emotion in his eyes before the granite settled again. Pain, probably. Those bruises had to hurt.

"I've got a jar of ointment that Beth Wilson swears by for bruising. I'll find it for you." She blocked out the thought of touching his face again to tend to the bruises. She'd get the damn jar, leave it out for him, and then she'd go and take a shower. A long, cold one, to wake up her brain and cool down her body.

By the time she'd showered, ironed a clean uniform shirt, dressed, and dragged a brush through her hair, he'd had his shower and was moving around in the kitchen.

The aroma of coffee jolted another two brain cells awake before she entered the room. He leaned against the bench, mug in hand, in black jeans and T-shirt as he'd been wearing last night, although the T-shirt was a tighter cut, sculpting his body more closely. His bags stood by the door, the leather jacket draped across them.

"I made coffee," he said, nodding towards the plunger on the table.

"An omelette last night, coffee this morning — have you got a halo I didn't notice, Gillespie?"

"Not me, Blue. Just a caffeine addiction." The closed expression never changed, but something about that "Blue" softened it. Or maybe that was just her imagination.

He drained his mug, then rinsed it out under the tap while she poured her own coffee.

"I'll head off. I want to catch Jeanie early, then get back to Sydney."

"Oh." The mug she'd just lifted shook in her hand, and she lowered it to the table again. Of course he was going. He had no reason to stay, and she had no reason to detain him.

He paused at the door as he picked up his gear and looked back at her, "Thanks."

That low rumble of his voice *was* a fraction softer. Oh, yeah, like basalt was softer than granite.

She mentally kicked another brain cell into action. "All the best, Gillespie. And make sure you avoid the Barretts."

He nodded once and then he was gone, pulling the door shut behind him. A chilly draught from outside swirled around her, and for a moment she stood motionless, not able to think, before she reached for the coffee again and drank a long, strong slug of it.

She had to get moving. She had a hell of a day ahead, a mile-high stack of paperwork, and with the senior sergeant in Birraga away on a course, she'd be lucky if she made it home before midnight.

And there'd be no-one to care if she ate dinner or not.

Gil walked down the main street, staring ahead to avoid eye-contact with the few locals about, but all he could see in his mind's eye was a beautiful, sleepy woman, with tousled hair, heavy-lidded eyes, and a cotton robe that entirely failed to hide her curves. Strength and vulnerability and dedication and attitude all wrapped up in a body he'd dreamed about in the rare minutes he'd managed to sleep between her hourly visitations.

Shit. He dragged his thoughts away from remembering those dreams. Talk about a waste of mental energy. In an hour, he'd be out of Dungirri forever. And then he had Russo to deal with, and how he'd do that he still had no idea. He had no leverage, as he'd had with Vince. Chances were he'd end up at the bottom of Sydney Harbour, breathing seaweed.

All the more reason to make things right with Jeanie, first. And now that he saw Dungirri in daylight, he figured that Jeanie might need what he intended giving her. In the years since he'd left, economic decay had eaten through the core of the town, and only a handful of the businesses remained. Across the road, empty shopfronts gaped between Ward's Rural Supplies and the hotel on the corner, and on the side of the road he walked along, the Pappas's small corner store seemed to be the only business still open, even the old council office and depot beside it were padlocked and boarded up. Dungirri had shrivelled to a dry, dead husk, and he couldn't imagine any business managing to do well here, even an essential one like Jeanie's.

He reached his car, dumped his gear in the back seat, and crossed the road to the café, pulling his jacket tighter against the morning chill as he walked. The café was open, but there weren't any breakfast customers about.

"Gil!" Jeanie's face creased into a huge, welcoming smile as soon as he walked in, and he didn't know which surprised him more — the rare experience of a genuine welcome, or the stark reality of how much she'd aged. The once-grey hair was white, her hands misshapen by arthritis, and she seemed smaller, frailer, *fragile* beside him.

Yet her eyes still held their sparkle, and the hands she clasped around his were warm and surprisingly strong as she tugged him towards a table and made him sit down.

"It's so good to see you, Gil, although not with those bruises, Ryan was in not long ago. He said you were back, had run into some trouble last night. Are you okay?"

"I'm fine, Jeanie." Although the sense that he was walking on unsteady, unfamiliar ground made him grit his teeth and move straight to the point of his visit. "I came to repay what I owe you."

"Owe me?" Her puzzled frown seemed entirely genuine. "You don't owe me anything, Gil."

"Yes, I do." He drew in a slow breath, determined to acknowledge what she wouldn't even consider a debt. "You paid for the lawyer for my probation hearing, and for his work proving the falsity of the blood-alcohol report and having the conviction overturned. Until a month or so back, I never knew that you did that — I thought it was on Legal Aid. But the lawyer happened to come into the pub one day, and he recognised me. We got talking."

Jeanie clasped her hands on the Formica table-top. "You needed proper legal representation, Gil, and the lawyer they sent from Legal Aid for your committal hearing was a raw graduate without much sense. I never begrudged a cent of the money."

"You were saving for that trip to Italy. To search for your husband's family. You never went, did you?"

"No. That was just a dream — not as important as getting you released."

But she twisted her wedding ring on her finger, probably without even realising she was doing it, and the small, typically Jeanie gesture made him all the more determined. He pulled the cheque he'd written earlier out of his jeans pocket and slid it across the table.

"Well, you can go now. Take a friend. Do a world tour, if you want."

She stared at it, looked up at him and pushed the cheque back across the table. "Don't be silly. That's ten . . . twenty times more than the lawyer cost."

"Jeanie, just take it. I sold the pub. Prices have gone sky-high, and I've got more money than I know what to do with. You, of all people, deserve some share of that." And if he ended up breathing seaweed, she would get a big share of the rest of it. That was already signed and sealed in his lawyer's office.

"I can't take that much from you," she protested, her stubbornness as great as her generosity. "You've worked for every cent of it."

"And now I'm spending it how I want. Jeanie, it's not just the lawyer's fees I owe you." Damn the rock in his throat. He needed to say this. "You gave me a chance, gave me a job and trusted me, when almost nobody else did. And later, in prison . . . I never knew how to say —" Shit, he still didn't know how, and the rock in his throat was a boulder, and all he could do was push out some words he hoped she'd understand. "Your visits, they made a difference for me."

Her hand closed over his, gentle, just as it had all those times she'd been to see him and he'd been silent, unbelieving, too unfamiliar with kindness to trust in it.

"I just wished I could have done more for you."

"You did more than enough." He squeezed her fingers, disentangled his hand from hers — yeah, okay, so he still didn't know how to deal with *that*, either —

and glanced around for something, anything, to change the subject.

The girl he'd seen last night came in from out the back, carrying a box of drink bottles, and she smiled across at him and Jeanie before she went to stock the fridge in the far corner.

"Another one of your strays?" he asked Jeanie.

"Yes, I guess so. Megan's had it tough. Her adoptive parents died in an accident a few years back, and Community Services eventually let her contact her birth family. But her mother had died of cancer already, so now Megan's only got her grandparents. Do you remember the Russells? Barb would have been your age. She got pregnant straight after she finished high school, but she never told anyone who the father was."

Barb Russell. The memory, long buried, slammed back into his consciousness. A hot summer night, and a bunch of teenagers gathered at the swimming hole, celebrating their final exam results. He'd been passing by and Mark Strelitz, friendly as ever, had called him over, handed him a beer, and invited him to join the party.

On the fringes of the group, Barb and he had got talking, and then she'd started crying for some reason, and he'd put his arms around her, clumsily trying to offer some sort of comfort, and one thing had eventually led to another . . .

Gil turned sharply to look across at Megan, who was laughing with a young man who'd come in to pay for petrol, flicking her straight black hair back from her face with long, fine fingers.

He stared at her face, and the reason she'd looked familiar last night hit him harder than the Barretts' punches. Her features were softer, more delicate, but he saw damned near the same brows, eyes and cheekbones every morning in the mirror.

He heard a chair scrape back against the tiles, realised vaguely that it was his, but the need to escape roared in his head and without even a goodbye he walked out of the café, away from Jeanie's too-perceptive gaze, and away from his daughter.

The mechanic sent out from Birraga to check the roadworthiness of the patrol car didn't arrive until after eight-thirty. Adam had the four-wheel drive out already, responding to a theft report east of town, which left Kris stranded at the Dungirri station half the morning, unable to leave for Birraga. At least it gave her a chance to reduce the accumulated pile of paperwork — not a task that improved her mood, however.

The mechanic finally gave the all-clear to drive the patrol car, and she backed out of the driveway just before ten o'clock, giving way to and then following an old truck that kept her to a crawl along the main street.

The slow pace gave her time to glance down the side street beside the pub, and she quickly flicked on her indicator and swung left.

Two guys stood by Gil's car, peering in. Despite their neat jackets, she didn't read that as a good sign. A newer sedan was next to Gil's car, probably their vehicle, and she parked beside it, studying them as she got out. The jackets and polished shoes screamed "city", and their confident returning of her gaze said "detective" just as loudly.

"Can I assist you, gentlemen?" She kept her voice cool and polite — a whole lot politer than "What the hell are you doing here, without even the courtesy of notifying me?" — but the guilty discomfort in the older guy's expression told her he'd read the unspoken question. The younger one barely managed to hide a smirk.

"I'm Detective Sergeant Joe Petric, from State Crime Command." The more senior officer showed his ID, and so did Mr Cocky — Constable Craig Macklin. "We're investigating a woman's disappearance, and looking for a man by the name of Morgan Gillespie to . . . assist with our enquiries. I believe this is his vehicle."

Shit. She nodded, not quite trusting herself to speak. What was Gillespie involved with? *Assist with our enquiries* — yep, that usually translated to "prime suspect". *In a woman's disappearance* — and he'd spent the night in her home. Yet all she could think was that she'd felt safe.

"It is his car," she confirmed.

"You know Gillespie?" Petric asked. "Do you know where he is?"

"I met him last night. Wait here. I'll see if I can find out where he went."

She crossed the road towards Jeanie's. Three hours. Close on three hours since Gil had left this morning. Would he still be at the café?

Jeanie met her at the door, a frown creasing her face as she gestured to the men by Gil's car.

"Is something wrong, Kris? Is Gil all right?"

"He's not here?" Other than Megan, hovering nearby, Kris could see the café was empty.

"He was here about seven, for a while," Jeanie said. "Maybe half an hour. But then he left, just walked off down the Birraga road. I'm worried about him, Kris. I don't think — I don't think he quite knew what he was doing."

"You think he was ill?" Another cause for concern layered on top of the detectives' insinuations. Gil had seemed quite okay this morning. But what if, after all, one of the punches to the head had done some real damage?

"No, but he was upset, shocked, about something I'd told him."

"Something to do with his father?"

"No. It was . . . a private matter." Jeanie clammed up, her face set. And although Kris wondered, there was no sense pressing for anything more — if Jeanie held a confidence, she was immune to any pressure. "We've been watching for him, watching his car, but he hasn't come back. Those men — who are they?"

"Police officers. They just want to ask him some questions." *About a missing woman.* She kept that to herself and spoke calmly, as if everything was fine. "I'll drive out to his father's old place, see if he's there. Call me if you see or hear from him, please, Jeanie."

She returned to where the detectives waited, had just reached them when some instinct made her glance around, and there was Gil, walking along the road in front of the café, shoulders hunched, hands in his pockets. He saw them and slowed, his eyes flicking past her, over the two officers, back to her again. For just a second, he stopped.

Out of the corner of her eye, she saw Macklin's fingers flex, move to his waist.

But Gil didn't run. He continued walking towards them, slow and steady, watching the two detectives as if he'd seen that slight movement of Macklin's, sliding his hands out of his pockets as he approached so that when he stood before them, it was clear he held no weapon.

He ignored her, keeping a steady, wary gaze on the two men. The testosterone flowed between the three so thickly she could almost smell it.

Petric, it seemed, had met him before, but he introduced himself again, showed his ID, introduced Macklin, all with a firm, follow-the-rules professionalism. Watching Gil closely, he added, "We have a warrant to search and if necessary, seize your vehicle."

Gil's dark eyes narrowed to slits. "Show me."

Petric handed the paper to him, and Gil cast his eyes across it before passing it to Kris. She glanced over it herself.

"It's all in order, Gil."

He nodded, so tightly wound that she half-expected something in his body to snap. But every instinct in her screamed that it was distrust, not guilt.

"Would you unlock your vehicle for us, Mr Gillespie?" Petric asked smoothly.

Gil fished keys from his pocket, unlocked the door, then stood back, arms folded in front of him.

The younger officer, Macklin, began to go through the contents of the glove box. From what Kris could see, it seemed to be mostly insurance papers, a torch, a cleaning cloth. Petric glanced into the back seat, then leaned in the driver's door to pop open the boot. The latch clicked open, and Petric strode around to open it fully.

"Oh, God," Petric groaned, just as a sickly, nauseating aroma wafted to Kris, tainting the cool freshness of the morning air.

A woman's naked body lay inside, bound, gagged and brutally beaten, dried blood from her slit throat splattered on her torso.

CHAPTER
THREE

Oh Christ, Marci, not like this.

Gil closed his eyes against the sight, willing it away, but when he opened them again she was still there, horrifically real in his vision, not some nightmare imagining.

He fought back the anger steaming into rage. He might have often wished Marci out of his life, but he'd never wished her dead. He'd done what he could for her, and it hadn't been enough. Either someone had got to her before she could leave or else stupid, stupid Marci had tried to play one lot off against the other for whatever she could get, and had lost, big-time.

And now she was dead, and in his car.

"Morgan Gillespie, I am arresting you on suspicion of the murder of Marcella Doonan."

He nodded, muttered "Yes" when Petric recited the standard caution and asked him if he understood.

Yeah, he understood all right. Someone was framing him for Marci's murder.

He dragged his eyes away from Marci's battered face.

The sergeant was pale, her skin against the blue of her uniform almost white. In her eyes he saw horror, and a million questions. But not the condemnation he'd been dreading.

"I didn't kill her." He spoke to the three of them, but saw only her. *Believe me, Blue.* "I know it might appear that way, but I did not kill Marci."

Kris swallowed, turned away, and he wanted to read her reaction, but Petric stepped between them, ordering him to put his hands up against a nearby tree, and as he endured the frisk and the cuffs snapping onto his wrists, he could hear only her voice, cold and hard, telling Macklin to keep away from the rear of the car, to avoid walking on any evidence.

The detectives' vehicle was too close to his own, so Petric ordered him in to the back seat of Kris's patrol car. Gil hauled in a breath, then another and another, the small space pressing in on him, and rage and frustration pounding in his head.

The wheel has come full circle; I am here.

Back in Dungirri. Back facing a jail sentence.

Sweat beaded on his forehead, trickled down his temple, but with his hands cuffed behind him he could not wipe it away.

The wheel has come full circle; I am here.

No, damn it, *not* full circle. He straightened his spine, unclenched his fists and stopped pushing his wrists against the confines of the cuffs. It might be some damned loop, but he wasn't back where he'd been. It was different now. *He* was different now. Not some wild, angry kid, powerless against a system he'd scarcely understood.

51

He'd done more than enough years in prison for one lifetime, and there was no way he'd let anyone send him back there. He needed to work out who had set him up, and prove his innocence.

Not far from the car, Petric and Macklin were talking in low tones, mostly inaudible. The few words he heard told him nothing. Kris was out of his sight, but he tuned in to her voice, in a one-sided phone conversation, arranging officers and forensic specialists.

The dappled sunlight falling into the car dulled to shade as she finished her call and joined the detectives, stopping just outside the car window.

"I don't know what you think you've got on Gillespie, but you're going to have to think again." Her voice wasn't loud, but her icy tone carried every word to him, despite the closed door and window. "His car was empty at eight o'clock last night. I know that because he gave me a lift into town, and I put two computer boxes in there. No body, no blood, no weapons, nothing. From eight o'clock he was in his room at the pub, until a posse of locals decided he was their evening's entertainment. From ten o'clock, he was down at the station with me and from midnight until six this morning he slept in my spare room, and I woke him every hour to make sure he wasn't concussed. By seven this morning he was in the café, with one of the world's most reliable witnesses, who will also testify that after he left there he was nowhere near his car until the moment he walked up to us."

Her back was to him, but he could see her in his imagination, defiant, eyes blazing, just as she'd been last night, facing down the crowd.

"So . . ." She paused for a fraction to take a breath, and continued clearly, as if she knew full well he could hear. "So, troublesome pain in the neck he may be, but I think you'll agree that there's not a whole lot of opportunity there for him to have found and murdered this woman and stuffed her in the back of his car, without anyone happening to notice."

Kris wasn't feeling friendly towards anyone in the frigging universe just now, so there was a certain amount of snarkish satisfaction in seeing the two men exchange a quick glance, clearly taken aback by her revelations.

Yep, definitely *not* what they'd wanted to hear.

Petric recovered first. "Gillespie stayed with you last night?" He raised an eyebrow. "Just what is your relationship with him, Sergeant?"

Oh, she'd been pissed off before, but now she was furious.

"There is no *relationship*, Petric. Just a purely professional concern for a possibly concussed citizen, when the nearest hospital is sixty kilometres away. Out here, the job doesn't finish when the shift ends."

"I merely asked out of concern for your safety." Petric's smoothness did nothing to ease her temper. "We have reason to believe that Gillespie was responsible for his ex's murder."

His ex? Shit, just what she needed — a violent murder involving an ex. *Gil Gillespie's ex.*

She recalled his face in those moments after Petric had opened the car boot. No, he hadn't reacted much, but the briefly closed eyes, the tightly controlled anger when he'd opened them again, suggested he'd had as much of a shock as the rest of them.

Well, time and the investigative process would tell if she'd read that right, or if she was a damn fool, taken in by a definitely not-pretty face. But right now proper procedure was her responsibility.

"I'm afraid you're going to have to cool your heels before you interview your suspect, boys. The Dungirri station doesn't have the facilities to detain anyone, so we'll have to take Gillespie into Birraga as soon as we can leave the scene here."

"But —"

She held up a hand and didn't let Macklin finish. "No buts. It may have escaped your notice, but this is the bush, not the city. And since I am currently acting Senior Sergeant for the Birraga command, I not only have overall responsibility for custody procedures, but I outrank the both of you."

She smiled sweetly, just to rub it in.

Oh, yes, she was in one *hell* of a bitch mood today. But they would damned well follow the rules, dot every "i" and cross every damned "t", because whoever had murdered that woman was not going to get off due to some procedural stuff-up.

"I've just called in extra officers from Birraga to guard the vehicle until Forensic Services get here from

54

Inverell. My constable will be here in a few minutes, and I want him to look over those footprints and tyre marks in the dust near the vehicle. In the meantime, you might want to talk with some of this gathering crowd, and find out whether any of them saw someone dumping a body in a car in the small hours of the morning."

She hadn't left them much to argue with, and they at least had sense enough not to try.

She would have preferred to talk to the group gathering on the corner outside the pub herself, rather than have strangers do it, but she had other priorities, and the two detectives headed towards the group with the air of men in charge.

A fly buzzed past her, and with the temperature starting to climb after the cool morning, she had to protect the body from both insects and prying eyes.

The guys at the corner probably couldn't see, but Jeanie stood on the other side of the road, Megan with her, and from the way Jeanie held her hand to her mouth, she could either see or guess what the open boot held.

Carefully, stepping in Petric's sharp-toed footprints in the dust beside the road, Kris returned to the rear of Gillespie's car. The woman . . . God, Kris didn't want to think about what she'd endured before she died. The rush of adrenaline-fuelled anger evaporated, and reaction slammed a nauseating punch to her chest at the sight of the battered body. Her knees threatened to buckle, and she had to struggle like a rookie cop not to throw up. She screwed her eyes shut for a moment to regain some control. She'd seen too many dead people these past two years. Too many that she should have been able to prevent. Too many people she'd known personally. At least *this* death was unconnected to those, unconnected to her, but the viciousness of it still rocked her.

She muttered a few choice swear words under her breath and made herself focus on the task at hand. She had a job to do, and puking and snivelling wouldn't get it done. She reached up with a handkerchief covering her fingers, and gently closed the boot, giving the woman the dignity of a little privacy, at least for the moment.

Gillespie sat in the patrol car, head up, staring straight ahead. A man she'd talked with, eaten with, allowed to sleep in her home. Her certainty that he hadn't put the body in his car didn't make him innocent of involvement, and she could no longer trust her own instincts.

She'd once thought she was a competent officer, until she'd discovered that she'd been face-to-face with a serial killer regularly over a period of years, seen him go about his daily business, spoken with him politely in passing, and never recognised his evil. Gil Gillespie could be anything — innocent, murderer, accomplice, instigator — and right now she just wished that he'd never come back to Dungirri.

The drive to Birraga was long and mostly silent. From where Gil sat in the back seat of the patrol car, he could, if he wanted, see the sergeant at the wheel, her face set in hard lines. In the front passenger seat, Petric made a few attempts at polite conversation with her, but she kept her responses brief.

His arms uncomfortably behind him, Gil mostly stared out the window, ignoring them all, especially Macklin. When he'd got in the car next to Gil, Macklin had given him the kind of grin that dared him to make trouble. Gil didn't plan on giving the man the satisfaction. He wasn't stupid, and he was in more than enough shit already.

The sergeant might have spoken up to the dectectives about his whereabouts last night, but he didn't expect to hear that again in court. Cops closed ranks and backed each other in public — if not willingly, then through pressure. If by chance she stuck to her guns, they'd crucify her. Gil hadn't heard all the conversation back in Dungirri, but he'd heard her angry retort, denying any relationship between them. The insinuations so soon meant Petric and his offsider had already started waving the hammer and nails.

When they finally arrived at the Birraga station — relatively new, and at least four times the size of the Dungirri police station — the sergeant waved Macklin and Petric through to the local detectives' office, and escorted Gil to an interview room, picking up a manila folder from a desk as she passed.

"The folder's got a list of legal firms in the region," she told him as she steered him to a chair, all briskness and business, although, for an insane moment, the brief brush of her fingers against his wrist when she keyed the handcuffs open almost drove business from his mind.

"The local Legal Aid duty solicitor is Kent Marshall," she continued, oblivious to his distraction. "His number is there, too."

The cuffs loosened, fell away, and he brought his arms forward and flexed his freed hands, as much to erase the lingering sensation of her touch as to relieve muscular stress. Disgust with his inappropriate lust loaded on top of his anger with the rest of the frigging world and gave the detached response he intended a bitter edge.

"If I asked for a recommendation, would I get an honest one?"

The flare in her eyes mightn't have quite reached thermo-nuclear strength, but her voice was pure cold fusion. "I believe in the law, and justice, Gillespie. That includes due process and representation."

Oh, well done, Gillespie. Question her integrity and join the queue of bastards making life hell for her.

With deliberate moves, she folded the handcuffs together, slid them into her trouser pocket, and tucked the key into its place on the belt at her waist. "Whether you need Legal Aid or not, I'd suggest Kent Marshall. He knows his stuff, is straight down the line, and won't waste your time and money, or ours."

Cop or no cop, he trusted her recommendation, simple as that. She might crack under pressure later, but for now she was dealing straight and honest with him. Not on his side, but not against him, either, just focused on seeking justice.

Surprise, gratitude, relief — he didn't know what it was, but before he thought twice about it he opened his mouth and said, "Remind me later that I'm not supposed to like you, Blue."

Her huff of breath held as much amusement as her death-glare. "If it turns out that you had anything to do with that woman's death, Gillespie, then you definitely won't like me."

"I didn't kill her."

He spoke quietly, held her gaze, and blue eyes drilled into his, undaunted.

"I figured that, since I'm your damned alibi. But arranging someone's death is as bad as doing the deed itself, in my book, and I'm not your alibi for *that*."

"I didn't arrange her death, either."

She leaned against the wall, crossed her arms and studied him. "'I've already dealt with Marci.' That's what you said on the phone last night, while we were in the car."

He grimaced, felt the small room closing in on him. Yeah, that would give any sane person more than enough reason for doubt. Throw in what little she knew about him and his past, and maybe he should be grateful she'd even taken off the cuffs.

He slid back the chair and stood at the window. The view of the police yard was fractured through the pattern of the security grill, but he wasn't looking for anything as stupid as an escape. Just the reminder, if not the reality, of space around him, beyond the crowding walls of the cell-sized room.

With the window at his back, he faced her again, acknowledged her doubt. "Yeah, I did say something like that."

"So?"

She shifted slightly against the wall, slid her hands into her pockets, the movement bombarding his senses with a rapid onslaught of contradictory impressions. The curve of hip, disguised by the masculine style of trousers. Slim waist, bulked by the uniform gun belt, loaded with the standard tools of the trade.

He slammed the mental door shut against everything but that belt and what it meant. Police tools, police trade, and he shouldn't for even a second let a misplaced, irrelevant and incredibly stupid lust make him forget it.

"Is this a formal interview, Sergeant?"

"No, the detectives will conduct the investigation. This is informal and off-the-record, because I'm a witness to your activities last night, and I'm trying to work out whether you're an innocent man or a murderer." She tilted her head slightly to one side, and continued just as bluntly, "So, how did you 'deal' with her, Gillespie?"

He drew in a slow breath, debated silently for a moment the best strategy. Until he knew where he stood — who had set him up, and how — he didn't plan on giving much away. Yet if he clammed up, avoided her questions, he'd give her even more reason to distrust him. Her alibi had to be putting her in a difficult position with her colleagues, but right now, that alibi was the nearest thing to a lifeline he had.

"I paid six months' rent on an apartment in Melbourne for her, and gave her a plane ticket to get there and some cash."

"Why?"

The question caught him off-guard. *Fucked if I know*, he wanted to say. Yeah, like that would go down well. Possible explanations raced through his mind, but none of them worked. He owed Marci nothing. And any debt he might have had to Digger had been more than repaid, years ago.

"Long story," he finally answered.

"She was your ex- what? Wife? Lover?"

"Hell, neither." At least *that* was easy to answer.

"That isn't what Petric thinks."

"It isn't what a lot of people think," he conceded. Damn Marci and her delusional games — and himself, for not calling her out on them more publicly. But then, it hadn't really mattered, until now. "We were co-owners of a hotel for a while. I bought her out years ago."

But even as he gave her the brief, bare-bones explanation, the full reality of the shit he was in started to hit him. His long history with Marci would provide more than enough circumstantial evidence of a motive for murder. She was the perfect target; the only thing most people would wonder about was why he'd taken so long to get rid of her.

Gil jammed a hand through his hair, turned to stare out the window, away from the sergeant's scrutiny. Christ, he needed to think, get his head around the possibilities, the timing. How had Marci's body ended up here in Dungirri, almost seven hundred kilometres from Sydney, in such a short time, when no-one — *no-one*, not even Liam or Deb, and definitely not Marci — had known he was coming here?

Tony Russo might have already been planning some move against him, but Tony couldn't have laid a finger on Marci while Vince was still around, and he couldn't have anticipated his father's shooting, unless he'd arranged it, or pulled the trigger himself.

But if this wasn't Tony's work, then it could be that Marci had tried to sell what she thought she knew. There were more than a couple of people she might have gone to, and if any of them had found out what Gil had done — if they *ever* found out what he'd done — then framing him for Marci's murder was only the beginning.

Whoever it was, they'd moved fast for everything to have happened within twenty-four hours. To a jury it would look quite plausible that Gil had come to Dungirri to dispose of the body somewhere out in the wilderness of the scrub, a wilderness he'd once known well.

Unless he could find some other evidence, then the sergeant's alibi was the only thing that stood between him and maximum security at Long Bay or Goulburn. *Except . . .* His hands curved into fists. What her colleagues could do to her was nothing compared to what Russo or others would do if she got in the way of their plans. None of them would blink at discrediting or eliminating a straight, honest female cop.

62

Something more than claustrophobia tightened around his chest.

That straight, honest cop was watching him, waiting for more of an explanation. But for all the gutsy attitude and the weapons on her uniform belt, she was just one woman. If they got to her, as they'd got to Marci . . .

The image of Marci's body flooded Gil's vision again, and he swallowed hard. Even if it meant cutting the lifeline, he had to give the cop an "out" and make her think twice about that alibi. *Protect her from them.* He didn't consciously think the words, just acted on them and started talking, damning himself.

"The truth is, Blue, that there'll be hundreds of witnesses who can testify that Marci spoke frequently about our 'relationship'. There'll also be a pub full of people who can tell the court that we argued in my office a few nights back and that I carted her, kicking and screaming curses at me, out of the pub. There are probably witnesses who saw me go into her place yesterday morning, and come out half an hour later."

"But you didn't kill her or set up her murder." He couldn't read in the flatness of her voice whether she believed him or not.

He wouldn't go as far as confessing to murder to keep her out of their sights. He looked at her without moving. "No, I didn't."

She pushed herself away from the wall. "I'll be back in a couple of minutes to book you in." Nodding at the folder on the table, she continued, "Choose a lawyer, Gillespie. You're going to need one."

CHAPTER
FOUR

The late afternoon sunlight shafted in through the office window. Kris checked her watch, then the times logged in the custody records. Time of arrest, time of arrival in Birraga, time of Kent Marshall's arrival.

It had been after noon before the detectives had begun interviewing their suspect. They'd had a few sessions with him — unsatisfying, it seemed, judging by the brief comments they'd made when they'd come out for breaks — but now it was getting close to five o'clock. With the time-outs allowed in the regulations, that made the four-hour questioning limit almost up.

She would have handed custody responsibilities over if there'd been someone else qualified to handle it. She'd bent the rules when she'd spoken with Gillespie earlier on. She bent rules sometimes — out here in the bush, there was often no choice — but she didn't bend her principles. She'd assured him the conversation was off-the-record, and she'd meant it. She'd kept right out of things since then, but now her responsibilities as custody manager had to kick in.

She found Joe Petric helping himself to coffee in the station's break room. Steve Fraser, the local detective liaising with them, was on the phone in his office, and

Macklin had gone out a while back and not returned as far as she knew.

"You've now got less than half an hour before you have to either charge Gillespie or release him," Kris reminded Petric.

"Yes, his lawyer has already pointed that out." He yawned, and added a second spoonful of coffee powder to his mug. They must have left Sydney sometime around midnight, and driven through the dark hours, so she almost felt some sympathy for him. Almost.

They might have progressed to first name terms during the course of the day, but she kept catching that whiff of a superior air under the professional courtesy and cooperation, the unspoken assumption that a uniformed country cop couldn't match a city homicide detective.

"Have you got any basis for charging him?" she asked.

"I've got a witness who swears he saw Gillespie and another man carry a body out of the back of the victim's apartment and put it in his car."

On the mental list of evidence she added a tick in the "Guilty" column. "What time was that?"

"About three o'clock yesterday afternoon."

She didn't need more than a moment to work out the significance of the timing.

"He couldn't have driven from Sydney to here in less than five hours. No way, especially with the direct road closed, no matter what speed he might have been doing."

"Yes, I figured that." Joe filled his mug with boiling water, before casting her a careful glance. "Are you sure about those times last night, Kris? You couldn't have been mistaken about when he arrived?"

She bit back a sharp retort. "Check the records, if you like. I logged a report of the accident when I called Adam back on duty, just before we went to get the vehicle. Then there was the call-out to attend the fight at the pub. That can all be verified."

"That's what I thought." He leaned casually against the bench, taking a slow mouthful of coffee. "Gillespie has a timed and dated credit card receipt from filling up with fuel at Mudgee, and will probably be recorded on video, too. Which means my witness must be mistaken about who he saw."

She silently filed that under the "Not Guilty" column.

"Mistaken? Or lying?"

Joe shrugged. "Why would someone lie about that?"

"Oh, I could think of any number of reasons." She ticked them off on her fingers. "To frame Gillespie. To send you off on a wild goose chase. To protect whoever did murder her. Or maybe even to be so obviously a lie, that you'd think him innocent."

"You don't think he is?"

"Hey, I'm just giving you a range of possible reasons. And it probably *is* logistically possible for a man to arrange someone else to do the dirty work, and then travel seven hundred kilometres to put the body in his vehicle, so he could dispose of it out here."

"Getting the local cop as an alibi could be a clever move." His eyes narrowed, thoughtful.

This time, she didn't hold back the retort. "Oh, yes, and he would have known that I was going to be so tired that I'd play dodge 'em with a 'roo and prang the car and be ready and waiting to check his empty boot and give him a nice handy alibi."

Joe grimaced at her heavy handed sarcasm. Point made, she dropped it for a more even tone. "Look, even if logistically it was possible, *logically* it doesn't make any sense. There's a thousand places within an hour of Sydney to dump a body where no-one will find it. So why would anyone bother to come all the way out here to do it? Let alone arrange two vehicles, and do a body transfer in the middle of town at night?"

As she made the argument, the common sense of it lifted a weight of anxiety, and the relief almost made her light-headed.

Joe rubbed the back of his neck and stifled another yawn. "We can't entirely rule him out, but you're right, it seems unlikely at this point. He knows more than he's saying, though. He's a cold bastard, never gives much away."

A cold bastard? She'd figured him for a loner with a thick layer of reserve, rather than cold — but then, there was a hell of a lot she didn't know about Gillespie.

"You've dealt with him before?"

"Yes, a few times. General enquiries, mostly. Last year I informed him of his father's death, and all he said was he hoped he'd rot in hell."

"If that makes a person a suspect, then you'd have to arrest at least half of Dungirri, including me. Des Gillespie deserved to rot in hell."

"Like father, like son."

She wasn't sure if Joe meant it as a question, a statement, or a challenge. She thought of Des, foul-mouthed, too ready to swing his fists at anyone who angered him or to shoot a straying dog the moment it touched his land, and she remembered Gil last night, offering her his car, using only defensive moves against the Barretts, refusing to press charges, making her dinner.

There might be a lot she didn't know about Gillespie, but each of those actions spoke volumes.

"No," she told Joe. "They're not alike at all."

They'd left him alone for a while. Gil sat in the rigid chair in the stark room, and mentally replayed the day, searching for any hint in the detectives' questions and comments that might help him work out what was going on.

He'd answered their questions as briefly as he could. Where he'd been, what he'd done, and when he'd last seen Marci. They'd tried to trip him up, but he'd stuck with the facts, coolly repeating his statements as many times as they'd asked the questions.

He didn't know enough about Petric or Macklin to even consider trusting them. Marci's threats gave him a good reason to be cautious, and the detectives' arrival in Dungirri was way too convenient for his comfort.

Had the crack and the booze fucked with Marci's brain so much that she'd really thought she could get away with selling him out to her dealer and his associates? Gil had warned her she'd be putting her own neck in a tight noose if she admitted to them that she'd told him about her cop clients. But it was a possibility that fitted this outcome.

Of course, there was a chance a client had just gone over the edge with her. She'd been desperate enough lately to get into kink, and there were some sadistic bastards in the BDSM prostitution scene. Or perhaps her crack-dealing, pimping boyfriend had got fed up with her.

But neither of those scenarios explained the presence of her body in his car, or the arrival of the police. His thoughts circled back again to Tony Russo. Tony had motive; with Vince out of the way he probably had opportunity; he had a network of connections he could lean on for information; and he usually had at least a few cops in his pocket.

Elbows on the table, Gil dropped his head forward and rubbed the tight muscles of his neck with both hands. If he could get out of here, he might be able to find some answers. But if they charged him with murder, he wouldn't get bailed, and he'd be shipped off tonight or tomorrow to the nearest remand centre. Dubbo, maybe, or Tamworth.

He knew the ropes now, and was tough enough and bastard enough to hold his own in a remand centre. In maximum security, if he couldn't clear his name, it would be a different story. Violent lifers with vengeance on their minds and no parole to look forward to could make a mess of a man, painfully and slowly. He'd just have to damned well make sure he never made it that far.

The door handle that definitely needed oiling squeaked its warning. He leaned back in the chair, readying himself for another round with Petric and Macklin.

Instead, it was the sergeant. Gil credited the small improvement in his mood to the fact that she was carrying a large paper cup, and knew he was kidding himself. He'd scarcely seen her since she'd processed him in the morning.

Expecting the same tasteless gunk that Macklin had brought in for him earlier, the heart-pumping aroma of real coffee that wafted under his nose as she passed the cup to him upped his mood a little further.

"Thanks."

"Can't have an addict getting the jitters," she said.

The light reference to his comment that morning was the closest thing to "friendly" he'd heard since he'd walked out of Jeanie's. He dragged in a deep breath of the coffee, then a taste. The liquid hit the back of his throat, and he looked forward to the jolt of caffeine kicking in, re-invigorating his brain.

"Your coffee is better than Macklin's."

"My fault." She shrugged carelessly. "I forgot to tell him where the good stuff is stashed. My apologies. The instant is so vile it probably constitutes torture to give it to a detained person."

It would be stupid to read anything into the dark humour of her comment, or into the fact that she'd brought him the decent stuff.

She sat on the end of the table. "So, how are you doing?"

She might just be following custody rules in monitoring his wellbeing, but the genuine question invited an honest answer. Gil could imagine a distressed or agitated prisoner pouring out their woes, giving her the opportunity to assess their risk level. Which was her job, of course.

He kept his answer brief and to the point. "I'm not going to harm myself or anyone else, Sergeant."

"Good. Still no after-effects from last night? Headache? Dizziness?"

"None to worry about."

She nodded, all business. "Anything else I should be aware of? Medications due? Other health issues?"

"You asked those questions when I arrived."

"Yes, I did. But being arrested can be stressful, and sometimes people don't think of things at the time that can later be important."

He had to respect her professionalism in ensuring the wellbeing of those she held responsibility for, the way she'd left it open, easy for him to raise issues if he'd needed to, without losing face.

"You can rest easy, Sergeant. As I told you, I have no allergies, drug addictions, medications or health problems."

Obviously satisfied, she stood and walked towards the door. "Detective Petric will be in to talk with you again in a few minutes. He's just taking a phone call. Kent is on his way back over."

"Any idea whether I'll be released or charged?"

Her relative ease with him gave him hope for the first time that day — he couldn't imagine her being even slightly friendly to anyone she believed a murderer — but her questions about medications suggested he might be in for the long haul.

She paused in the doorway. "It's not my investigation, Gillespie. That's up to the detectives to decide."

He hadn't really expected anything different. She might take a little pleasure in scoring a minor point against an arsehole detective over coffee, but where police work was concerned, he doubted she'd play games.

He didn't have to wait long before Kent Marshall returned, with Petric not far behind him. The Birraga detective, Fraser, came in too, but it was clearly Petric running the show, and Gil figured Fraser was only there as a concession to the locals.

He swallowed another mouthful of coffee as they sat, and Petric turned the recorder on and completed the formalities.

Petric leaned back in his chair, pretending casualness. "Where were you the night before last, between seven pm and midnight?"

Immediately wary of the change of tack in both manner and questions, Gil answered briefly, "Behind the bar at the pub, working."

"You have witnesses to confirm that?"

"Yes. It was a busy night. The new owner and a couple of his staff were there, learning the ropes. There was also a fair few regulars and two-hundred-plus other customers, in the bar and the brasserie."

Petric nodded, appeared satisfied, and in that same easy manner, asked, "When was the last time you saw Vince Russo?"

Shit, were they going to try to pin Vince's shooting on him, too? Gil kept his face neutral, his gaze steady on Petric. "I've seen Vince Russo only twice in the past five years or so. The last time was on Wednesday morning."

"Why? What was your business with him?"

He'd give them the truth, or at least the important parts of it. If Petric was one of the cops Vince had in his pocket, chances were he knew the answer to the question, anyway. And if he wasn't . . . well, he'd been investigating organised crime for a while, probably knew more than he was letting on.

"Marci was in debt to one of his son's associates. I gave Vince the money to clear the debt."

"Why give it to him?" Petric asked. "Why not to whoever she owed it to?"

"If Marci learned that I'd paid her debts, she'd have just racked up more."

"How much did she owe?"

"Twenty thousand dollars."

Fraser whistled low under his breath.

Petric didn't seem surprised. "So, you give Vince twenty grand, that night somebody shoots him, and then Marci turns up dead."

Wondering where the insinuation might be going, Gil replied coolly, "We both know that twenty grand is small change for Vince."

"And small change for you, too, these days."

Gil deflected the veiled question with a shrug. "I won't starve without it."

"I heard you got over fifteen million for the pub. That would be more than enough to pay for a few . . . 'favours'."

Kent Marshall paused in his detailed note-taking and raised his pen in protest. "If you wish to examine my client's financial records, you will need to obtain a warrant, Detective. And may I remind you that you have only ten minutes remaining before your time is up."

Petric tapped his fingers a couple of times on the table before he pushed back his chair and rose with a cordial smile. "Thank you for your cooperation, Mr Gillespie. You're free to go. Sergeant Matthews will sign you out and return your belongings."

As suddenly as that, it was over. This round, at least.

Gil exhaled a long breath. Petric mustn't have enough to charge him, but Gil doubted the man would drop him from his investigation. And whoever had tried to set him up wouldn't give up easily. But for now, walking out the door of that interview room as a free man felt like a victory.

Marshall gave him a few more words of general advice, shook his hand, and hurried away to another appoinment.

In the custody office, the sergeant passed the plastic bag containing Gil's personal effects across the counter to him, with a faint smile that might have had a tinge of relief.

"Check that everything is there, and then sign here that you've received them."

A cursory flick through the contents of his wallet was all he gave before he scanned the document and signed his name. He slid his wallet into his jeans, picked up his phone and switched it on.

"What will you do now?" Kris asked.

He hadn't yet thought much beyond getting outside, into space and air. His car and the gear in it had been seized for examination, and it would be ages — weeks perhaps, maybe longer — before he got anything back. The forensic people would go through his clothes, looking for blood or any signs of his involvement in the murder. They'd probably even go through his laptop, check his emails and other web activity.

In the meantime, he was stranded here, with only what he had on him. He was lucky they'd left him with the clothes he was wearing; although one of the forensic mob had looked him over during the afternoon.

"I don't suppose there's an express bus for Sydney tonight?" he asked.

The corner of her mouth twisted in a sympathetic grimace. "Sorry, next bus is Monday morning. Bus to Dubbo, then train to Sydney. Not exactly 'express'."

He swore silently. Monday. And today was only Friday. He ran through his options. Take his chances hitching out of town, find a hotel in Birraga and ask

Liam to drive up and get him tomorrow, or hang around another three nights, and take the bus. None of them appealed.

"Jeanie's phoned a few times, worried about you. She said that if you need a place to stay, you're welcome to use the cabin out the back of her place." With a faint trace of hesitancy, she added, "I'll be leaving here around six, if you want a ride back to Dungirri."

He could only think that Jeanie's trust and offer of accommodation had reassured Kris of his character. Another reason to be grateful to Jeanie. He'd seen her by the road, when they'd arrested him this morning, her obvious worry for him painful beneath his anger. The girl had been there, too. He still had to do something about her.

He added Jeanie's offer — and the sergeant's — to his list of options, and quickly dismissed the others. Dungirri wouldn't want to see more of him, but as well as seeing Jeanie, he had a couple of things he could do there before he left for good, like trying to find out for himself if anyone had seen anything last night, and making some financial arrangement with Jeanie for the girl. He could get Liam to drive up tomorrow, and they could be out of Dungirri in twenty-four hours.

Not totally sure if it was the right decision, he nodded anyway. "Thanks. I'd appreciate it. Anywhere still open that I could buy a change of clothes?"

"Robertson's will be open until five-thirty. And there's a new Target in the old bank building on the corner. But don't expect the kind of range you'd find in Sydney. If money is a problem, I can phone Captain

76

Tan from the Salvation Army and I'm sure they'll be happy to assist."

"Money's not a problem, Blue," he told her, more roughly than he intended.

The door from an inner office swung open, and Petric and Macklin sauntered through, hardly glancing at Gil.

"We're off, Kris," Petric said. "Thanks for all your help."

"Drive safely." She shook hands out of courtesy, but there was not a lot in the way of warmth, by Gil's reckoning.

That shouldn't have cheered him, but it did.

On his way out, Petric turned back, with that expression of polite concern that Gil was fast coming to distrust. "Oh, by the way, Gillespie, we just heard. Unfortunately, Vince Russo passed away this afternoon. He never regained consciousness."

Kris caught the flare of anger, quickly controlled, on Gil's face. Not good news then, as far as he was concerned.

Joe didn't wait for a response, just dropped that information as if it were an afterthought, and continued on his way. Afterthought be damned. Petric had to be playing some sort of game. She'd overhead him earlier this afternoon, telling Craig Macklin of the Russo guy's death. What the hell his strategy and purpose was, she had no idea.

She opened her mouth to ask Gil about Russo, but her phone rang and by the time she'd dealt with a night duty officer reporting in sick, Gil had left.

Needing some answers, she went straight to Steve Fraser. He'd been flat-out since arriving in Birraga on temporary transfer a month or so back, juggling the workload of two vacant detective positions, and her opinion of him wavered. She'd worked with him before, when he'd been called in on the two child abduction investigations that had shaken the area in the last couple of years. But those times had been intense, with a large team headed by a senior officer focused exclusively on the urgency of finding the children. The first time, they'd failed, and the repercussions of that failure still shadowed them all. The second time, they'd found the child alive — but not before people had died and officers, including Steve, were injured.

In the day-to-day of normal operations this past month, she'd found that, like Craig Macklin and a lot of other guys she'd worked with, Steve had the testosterone-charged cockiness not uncommon in the predominantly masculine environment of the police force. His flippant attitude bordered on exasperating at times, and his casual approach to paperwork and procedure had her tearing her hair out. Yet underneath the bravado she caught occasional glimpses of something deeper, and they'd established a friendly enough working relationship in the past month.

When she swung into his office Steve gave her his lazy, bad-boy grin — but along with it his full attention. She sat in the chair in front of his desk and came straight to the point.

"Who's Vince Russo, what did he die of, and what does he have to do with Gillespie?"

"He's a businessman. Successful and very wealthy, apparently. Gillespie had some dealings with him, and so did the dead woman. He was shot the other night in a car park and was in a coma until he died this afternoon. No witnesses or security camera footage."

"Is Gillespie a suspect?"

"Not that I'm aware of."

Her breathing came a little easier. "What kind of dealings did he have with Russo?"

"He's known him for a while. Some money changed hands recently. I don't know all the details. Probably legal."

"*Probably* legal?"

"Joe asked a few questions, but wasn't interested in pursuing it. The woman had run up some debts, and Gillespie bailed her out."

Rent on an apartment in Melbourne, money to get there, cash, and he'd paid off her debts.

"A regular bloody boy scout," she muttered.

"I'm not sure I'd bet on that," Steve replied dryly. "You want my advice, Kris?"

"You'll give it, anyway."

"Yeah. Look, leave it to Homicide, mate. It's their case, and they think the murder happened in Sydney and someone just tried to frame Gillespie by dumping the body here. The unofficial first impressions from Sandy Cunningham in Forensics support that theory."

"Did you talk with Adam? What does he think?" She had a lot of respect for Sandy, but she had a lot, too, for Adam's traditional knowledge and observation skills, learned from the elders of his community.

"He agrees. He and Sandy had a long discussion."

She'd seen Adam working with colleagues often enough to know that, despite his youth, he used his skills with tact and respect for others' knowledge. She must remember to mention that in his performance review, whenever they managed to find time to do it.

Steve glanced at his watch, and reached out to close his laptop. "Joe's going to follow up a few other leads down in Sydney, and I'll be surprised if we see them back here. Which suits me, because I've got more than enough on my plate already."

He unplugged the laptop, getting ready to leave, and although he wasn't hurrying her, she quickly asked the most important question.

"What do you think about Gillespie? Is he involved?"

"In either of the murders? Can't be certain at this stage, but I doubt it. Why?"

"I'm giving him a ride back to Dungirri."

His eyebrows rose. "Do you have to?"

"We arrested him, seized his vehicle and brought him here," she pointed out. "Kind of gives us a moral obligation since there's no public transport. And it's not as if it's out of my way."

"He could afford to buy a damn car and drive himself. Joe reckons he's worth fifteen million."

Fifteen million? *That,* she hadn't expected. The well-worn leather jacket, the plain old sedan — not the usual accessories for multi-millionaires. *"Money's not a problem, Blue,"* he'd said. Obviously not.

"Millions or not, buying a car, legally, at this hour isn't that easy, especially for a stranger in town. Do you think he's too much of a risk? I can easily make some excuse not to give him a ride."

"I don't think he's that kind of trouble. And I know you can handle yourself, Kris. I'm just a little wary of close-mouthed ex-cons associated with two murders in forty-eight hours." Steve glanced at his watch again, pushed his chair back. "Sorry, I've gotta get going."

"Got a date?" she teased.

He grinned back. "I wish. Nope, it's a meeting with the Community Services director about the Davies' case." The brief frown brought by mention of the child abuse investigation was quickly erased by one of his cheeky winks. "Mind you, she is hotter than hell . . ."

"She's also married to the works engineer at Council."

"Real tall bloke? Built like a brick shithouse?" He grimaced when she nodded. "Ouch. There goes that idea."

He shoved his laptop into his backpack, and followed her to the door. "Hey, Kris," he said as he flicked the light switch off. "Send me a text when you get home, okay? Just so I know you got there safely."

She agreed, because it made sense, and because his wariness had fed her own worry. Could she really trust Gillespie? She had so little to go on: his actions since she met him last night, Jeanie's opinion, and her own instinct, which could well be way off the mark.

The question hung in her mind while she finished the most pressing of the day's tasks. Just on six, the desk officer paged her and she grabbed her keys and went out to find Gil sitting in the reception area, a new kit bag at his feet.

The darker colouring around his bruised eye and cheek and the swelling of his split lip lent his usual shuttered expression an even rougher edge, but when he looked up and saw her, met her eyes, his attempt at a wry smile seemed a crack of connection and openness.

Most of her uncertainty evaporated. She was used to people in custody often being angry, aggressive. Yet in the whole day since his arrest, despite his evident frustration at the situation, he'd shown no hint of hostility towards her. In fact, he'd treated her with a simple respect, more genuine than Joe's performance of collegiality.

He'd dealt with the confinement and the questioning, and although she'd seen the tension in him, he'd been self-controlled, not taking it out on her or anyone else. Gil Gillespie might have secrets, but his behaviour provided no evidence that he had any intention of harming her.

She led him to the patrol car, and he slung his bag into the back seat. More than just a change of socks and jocks bulked its sides, but she didn't comment. The guy deserved some privacy after the day he'd been through.

The drive back to Dungirri was about as quiet as the trip to Birraga had been in the morning. At least this time, Gil sat beside her, his hands unfettered, although he still stared out the window, absorbed in his own thoughts.

82

Kris focused on the road ahead, the headlights cutting through the early darkness. The previous night's rain had gone, but wind chased intermittent clouds in front of the near-full moon hanging in the east.

Despite the million questions whirling in her mind, she didn't disturb Gil by broaching any of them. She needed brain space to think through the day's events, go over the few details Joe had shared and the information Steve Fraser had added, because no matter which way she'd looked at it all so far, it didn't add up to anything simple.

Instead of getting out of uniform and spending the night curled up in front of the fire with a good movie, she'd be asking some of her own questions around town. Dungirri might be small, and fairly dead after ten o'clock at night, but maybe someone had seen something. The ball committee meeting hadn't finished until after midnight, so she'd start with them.

She was approaching a bend in the road when Gil asked out of the blue, "Can police access mobile phone data?"

She felt his gaze on her, but she kept her eyes straight ahead, negotiating the bend. "Not without authorisation."

"How long does it take to get authorisation?"

"It depends. Can be pretty quick, if there's a strong reason. But there's formal channels to go through with the telco, and it's not instantaneous. Why?"

Beyond the hum of the engine, the silence stretched.

"Spill it, Gillespie. What's going on in that brain of yours?"

"No-one knew where I was," he said slowly. "So I'm wondering how both the police and the . . . how they found me."

"You must have mentioned it to someone — your employees, perhaps. Or the woman, Marci. You said you saw her yesterday morning."

"No. I told no-one. It was a spur-of-the-moment decision." The quiet certainty of his words rang of the truth.

"What are you suggesting, Gillespie?"

"I had my phone on the whole trip yesterday. I received that call when we were driving into Dungirri. I made a phone call from my hotel room. Two, I guess, since I accessed the internet through my phone. I can't think of any other way that anyone could have found out I was in Dungirri. Unless you put something on the police system last night."

She cast her mind back to what she'd reported, and how. "Yes, I did. I logged the incident in the pub, the Barretts' names and yours. If Joe had an alert in for your name, the system would have notified him. But that wasn't until around eleven o'clock last night. And it wouldn't explain how whoever put Marci in your car knew where you were."

"No." The single word said he'd already thought that far.

"Who's trying to frame you, Gil?"

She wanted an easy, straight forward answer. An answer that meant the problem could be identified, dealt with, and solved.

Instead, he exhaled a long breath and eventually replied, "I don't know. Could be any one of several options."

"Jesus, Gillespie, how many people have you pissed off?"

"Probably a few."

Yeah, and count her among them now. "How?" she demanded. "What *are* you involved in?"

His voice was quiet. "It's . . . complicated, Blue. Best you don't get involved."

"Too bloody late for that. Oh, shit," she added, as the beam of the headlights picked up a dark, ragged shape on the road, and she reduced her speed.

A huge branch, fallen across the road, shattering dead timber from one dusty side to the other — a real hazard if drivers failed to see it.

Frustrated and angry with the universe, she glanced in the rear-vision mirror as she flicked on the indicator and pulled over. They were on a long straight stretch of road here, and the lights of the other vehicle were pinpricks in the darkness a couple of kilometres away. She switched on the emergency lights as a warning, and reached under the seat for a reflective vest.

Gil was already out of the car, testing the weight of the heavy end of the main limb, while she thrust her arms into the vest.

"We should be able to move it," Gil said, "if you can take the lighter end of this part."

A few metres long, the branch was heavy, but as most of it was hollowed out by insects they managed, with a bit of effort, to lift it and carry it to the side of the road.

Shorter branches littered the bitumen, and Gil began picking up the pieces that were too dangerous to leave in the dark.

Kris checked the road behind them. The headlights of the other vehicle were getting quite close, so she took her flashlight out and stood in the middle of the road to wave the car down. It approached with some caution, lights on low beam. She couldn't really see what kind of vehicle it was, but as it came within a few metres, she stepped forward to go and speak to the driver.

The sudden glare of the car's lights blinded her, and she jerked her arm up to shield her eyes. The engine roared, the tyres screeched, and she dived out of its path as it raced straight towards her.

CHAPTER
FIVE

Dropping an armful of wood into the bush beside the road, Gil heard the scream of rubber, the dull thump of a body against a vehicle, and was already leaping back across the ditch as Kris hit the bitumen, hard.

She lay still on her side, among the debris from the tree, too small and fragile beside the bulk of her vehicle. He crouched next to her, fingers seeking a pulse in her wrist, scanning for blood or obvious trauma.

Paula had died.

He shoved that memory away. He found her steady pulse, saw her chest rise and fall in breathing. There might be internal injuries he couldn't deal with, but he knew more about first aid than he had years ago, and with radio and phones, help could be called.

Her eyelids flickered open, closed again, and she moved her arm closer into her chest. "Fucking bastard!" she said, and he breathed again, grateful for the normality of her voice.

"He won't ever again if I find him."

Damned stupid thing to say, but there was too much pounding in his head, relief and worry and anger, the anger the only one he had words for.

"Yeah. Me too." She opened her eyes again, started to roll over, but he put a hand on her shoulder to stop her, fumbling for his phone with his spare hand.

"Lie still, Blue. You've been hit by a car. You need an ambulance."

"No. It's okay. It didn't hit me. I just hit mine." Her crooked grin reassured him as much as the coherence of her words. "Misjudged my Superwoman leap."

"Forgot your cape, too." His mouth as dry as their attempt at humour, he ignored the pounding in his head and took her hand carefully, the flashing red and blue lights casting eerie shadows on the scratches and cuts along her palm and up her arm to her shirt sleeve. "You're going to need some patching up, Blue. A debris-strewn road isn't as soft as a trampoline."

"I noticed."

She tried to sit up, wincing as she went to put weight on her hand, and Gil put an arm around her back to help her into a sitting position.

"What hurts?" he asked.

"Everything. Just jarring and bruises, though. Nothing broken."

"Except your skin." It looked like she'd taken the brunt of the fall on her left arm, landing on a rough mix of gravel and wood splinters. Now she was upright, blood was trickling down her arm in several places. "Is there a first-aid kit in the car?"

"In the boot."

When he returned with the kit, she was standing up, leaning against the car, inspecting her arm. The day had been warm enough for short sleeves, but in the dark with the wind blowing the night had turned chilly. She shivered, her grazed skin coming out in goosebumps, and he took off his leather jacket and draped it around her shoulders.

"Get in the car. I'll get the worst of the splinters out now, and drive you back to Birraga hospital for the rest."

"There's no need for the hospital. Nothing major is damaged, and I just want to get home." The defiant tone cracked, and she jerked away, heading towards the driver's door.

He stopped her with a hand on her uninjured arm. "You're not driving, Blue. Either we get someone to come and pick us up, or I drive. Assuming it's not a hanging offence for a civilian to drive a police car."

She huffed in frustration before nodding. "You're probably right. And under the circumstances, the punishment for the offence is probably a pile of paperwork for me."

Her smile was clearly a strain, so he kept things light. "Only if your boss finds out. And I won't tell him."

"Thanks." Probably unaware she was doing it, she pulled the jacket a little more closely around her shoulders. "I need to phone Adam. The car might pass through Dungirri. Did you see the type of vehicle?"

"Not well. Dark, probably black. A large four-wheel drive. Maybe a Land Cruiser or a Patrol or something similar. Must have a fair bit of power, to have accelerated that fast."

"That's what I thought. I don't suppose you saw the registration plate?"

"No." He'd been too focused on her, landing hard on the road, to even think of looking at the damned rego. He'd probably relive the moment a hundred times over the next few days. "Now, get in the car, out of the wind. You can phone Adam while I'm taking that tree trunk out of your arm."

She sat in the passenger seat, and he crouched beside her, using the open door as a small protection from the wind as he took out the wipes and bandages from the first-aid kit.

Her conversation with her constable distracted both Gil and her from some of the discomforts of the task. While she briefly related what had happened, Gil inspected the damage to her skin. Her uniform had protected the rest of her body from significant abrasions and splinters, and the adrenaline and shock were probably masking the pain, but she'd be aching before too long.

He decided he'd just deal with the main sources of bleeding now — a large splinter, and a cut — and do the rest in Dungirri, with better light and some warmth and water. Or better yet, get someone more qualified than him to do it.

"Don't try to stop the vehicle, Adam," she was saying. "He tried to run me down, so it's too dangerous when you're on your own. I just want the rego number, vehicle type, and if you can get any idea of the occupants." She winced as Gil eased a three centimetre-long sliver of wood from above her elbow and pressed a dressing against the wound. "No, it's okay."

Gil caught her eye. "Is there a nurse or a doctor in town? Someone who knows the proper way to do this stuff?"

She nodded. "Adam, could you ask Beth if she's free? I've got a couple of scrapes she could look at. Thanks."

She finished the call, dropped the phone on her lap, and Gil felt her watching him as he swabbed the cut on her forearm.

Her attention unnerved him, making him too conscious of his fingers on her skin. Touching her should have been impersonal, detached. But there were parts of his brain that had missed that message, parts noticing the pale smoothness of her skin, the slimness of her wrist, and taunting him with impossibilities.

"We've got to stop doing this to each other, Gillespie," she said.

He swallowed, pretended to hunt for another swab without seeing a thing in the kit. First aid. Patching each other up. That's what she meant. Not . . .

"Yeah," he agreed. "Definitely gotta stop it."

Kris dropped her head back against the headrest while Gil put the first-aid kit away. She was cold, tired, aching all over, and struggling against the effects of shock. On top of a god-awful day that wasn't finished yet, it was enough to make her want to curl into the foetal position and howl.

Tempting though the idea was, it wouldn't solve a damned thing. She pulled Gil's jacket closer around her shoulders. In the rush this morning, she'd left her own uniform jacket at home, but she found the bulk of Gil's and the subtle male scent of him oddly comforting.

Comforting? She almost laughed at the thought. It definitely wasn't the first word that came to mind when contemplating Gil Gillespie.

And yet . . . he'd automatically gone to help clear the road when they'd first stopped, before she'd either asked or suggested. Even now he was kicking away the pieces of wood on the road, getting rid of the worst of the debris. Simply doing what needed to be done, capable and practical, without any grandstanding or complaining. Lifting a little of the weight of responsibility from her shoulders, or at least sharing it, for a short time.

She should get out and help, but her body rebelled against the idea of movement. He'd almost finished, anyway.

Cold air swirled into the car when he opened the driver's door and got in, sliding the seat back to accommodate his height. Turning on the ignition, he glanced over the dashboard, found the heater and turned it up to maximum.

He adjusted the rear-view mirror, and the side mirror, and she had to respect his caution.

"Anything I should know about driving this thing?" he asked.

"Just go lightly on the accelerator. There's a fair amount of power behind it."

He nodded. "How do you turn the emergency lights off?"

"Isn't it every guy's fantasy to drive a cop car with lights flashing?"

She'd been trying to keep it relaxed between them, but she heard his teeth grind.

"It's not my fantasy." There was nothing relaxed at all in his growl, and she sensed his withdrawal from her again.

Shit. Wrong words. Gil, with his obvious distrust of police, wouldn't get a thrill from that kind of thing.

She reached to the centre console, flicked a button and turned of the flashing lights. Now only the headlights shone into the blackness.

Gil kept a good ten kilometres under the speed limit all the way back. He'd left Dungirri this morning as a prisoner; having to drive a police car back in to town less than twelve hours later verged on bizarre. Despite the justification of the situation, Kris suspected her superiors might not look lightly on an ex-con under suspicion of murder being at the wheel of a police car. She hoped she wouldn't have to mention it.

On the edge of Dungirri, Adam's utility was parked by the side of the road, and the headlights picked him up standing near it, a dark jacket obscuring his uniform. She noted his sensible thinking in not using the police car, alone and without backup. If the thug who'd tried to run her down had a thing against police, at least Adam wouldn't be an obvious target.

"That's Adam," she told Gil. "Can you stop?"

Sparing barely a glance for Gil, Adam came straight to Kris's window when they pulled over, his usually cheery face creased with concern.

"You're really okay, Kris?"

"Yes. Any sign of the idiot?"

"Nothing. It's been dead quiet. He must have turned off on to one of the tracks. I'll stay out here a bit longer, though, in case he's lurking until after you've passed."

"Good idea."

"Beth is on her way to your place. I'll give it fifteen minutes or so here, then meet you up there."

The town was quiet as Gil drove through the few blocks. Lights from the Truck Stop and the pub were about the only signs of life, a few cars parked here and there, but the main street was even quieter than usual.

Kris doubted the black vehicle would come through town. It could have taken any one of half a dozen side tracks through the bush surrounding the town, might be almost back in Birraga by now, or miles away in any other direction. Their chances of tracking it down and charging the driver amounted to near-zilch, and that fact did nothing to improve her mood.

Her mood worsened still further as they approached the police station, and she saw the cars out in front of the Memorial Hall next door, its doors wide open and people milling around, inside and out. Of course, that's where a fair few town residents were tonight, decorating the hall for the ball tomorrow night — and now watching Gil Gillespie park the police car in front of the station.

"Shit. The working bee tonight. I'd forgotten about it."

His mouth a hard line, Gil didn't say anything.

Kneeling on the veranda of the hall, Jim Barrett paused in the act of hammering in a floorboard, and slowly stood up. Karl Sauer and a mate, loading paint tins into the back of a ute turned and stared, Karl taking a few steps forward, and from the window of the kitchen several female faces watched, new lace curtains pulled back for a better view.

"Maybe it's for the best that they've seen us," she said quietly. "Most people have enough sense to know that if I thought you were a murderer, you wouldn't be driving me around the countryside."

He still didn't respond. Staring at the hall, he unbuckled his seatbelt and opened his door slowly.

Kris climbed stiffly out of the car.

"Everything all right, Kris?" Jim called out.

"Yes. Had a close encounter with a road, at some speed. Some bloody moron tried to run me over. It's just scratches and bruises, though." Including a holster-shaped one on her hip that was now making its presence felt as she put weight on her leg.

Loud enough for the spectators to hear, she turned to Gil and added, "Thanks for everything. Gil. I really appreciate all your help today."

She couldn't exactly apologise for his arrest — that might get her into legal hot water — but she figured her words might convince the audience that he'd cooperated fully and was not under suspicion.

Beth emerged from the hall, her large first-aid pack weighing down one shoulder. She raised her hand in a casual wave to someone inside, carefully stepped over the floorboard Jim was fixing, and strolled across the grass to them.

"Walking wounded, I see," Beth said cheerfully. "I'm glad it's not worse."

"So am I," Kris answered dryly.

Gil came around the side of the car and, with a nod to Beth, opened the back door to retrieve his bag.

"Hello, Gil," Beth greeted him with quiet warmth, with none of the tension that was emanating from the hall. "It's good to see you again."

Of course, Kris thought, they'd both grown up in Dungirri, must have known each other as kids. Kris would have to ask Beth what she knew about him; although she couldn't really imagine sweet, quiet Beth and the hard-edged Gil having had much in common.

Gil didn't smile, but the wariness in him seemed to relax a little.

"Hi, Beth."

Out of the corner of her eye, Kris saw that the curtain in the kitchen had fallen back into place, and she heard Jim's hammering start up again. Good. The odds of another lynching tonight had just reduced. Maybe the renaissance of community spirit, led by the Progress Association, was having a positive effect.

With some reluctance, Kris shrugged off Gil's jacket and handed it back to him, the chill without it adding to her discomfort. She should get inside, turn the heater on, but he stood there with his bag, about to leave, and for reasons she didn't try to comprehend she wasn't ready to let him walk away for good just yet.

"It would be useful to have a witness statement from you, Gil, if you'd be willing to give one." A logical request. She hoped he wouldn't refuse.

He might have considered it for a moment, but eventually said, "Yeah, I guess so."

"Can you come back after you've taken your things to Jeanie's? Beth should be finished with me by then. If I can get the incident report finalised tonight, then Steve Fraser can get onto it first thing in the morning."

He slung his jacket over his shoulder. "Sure. If that's what you want."

The lack of enthusiasm in his voice spurred her to convince him. "I want to arrest him, Gil, and charge him. It could have been any one of my officers out there tonight. Half the time we're travelling alone, because we cover a huge region and there's not many of us. The sooner we get the information together and circulating, the better chance we have of finding him, and the safer my staff will be."

She paused to take a breath, a little surprised at her own passion and anger. Coming on top of such a tense day, maybe the near-miss had made her more on edge, more shaken than she'd realised. Yet he'd had to face more than she had — the brutal death of a woman he'd known, his arrest and hours of questioning.

She slowed her breathing and continued more calmly, "Gil, I can't do much about finding Marci's killer. That investigation is out of my hands. But I do want to find that driver, before he does someone real harm."

Gil seemed about to say something, then changed his mind. He nodded, and said simply, "I'll be back in a while," before he turned and walked off down the road.

From the looks he'd been getting from Jim Barrett and others at the hall, Gil half-expected to hear shouts or footsteps racing up behind him, but the only voice he heard was Beth's, urging Kris inside and into the warmth.

He'd probably never spoken more than a few words to Beth in his life, but from the little he knew about her, Kris was in good hands. Painfully shy and bookish as a kid, Beth had overcome her reserve enough as a young teenager to join the St John's volunteer ambulance in Birraga as a cadet. Hanging around the fringes of events in Birraga and Dungirri — football matches, the Birraga show, the Christmas festival — he'd seen her, always neat in her black and white uniform, part of the community in a way he'd never be.

When Dungirri had first hit the news, almost two years ago, he'd felt little more than a flicker of connection, only what he might have felt for any town facing such a tragedy. When it had made the news again last summer, with a second little girl abducted, it had been harder to put from his mind. Not because of the fact that his old man had somehow been in the wrong place at the wrong time — he still felt no sorrow about that — but because the child's parents were Ryan and Beth. Ryan was the closest thing to a mate he'd ever had in his youth, and Beth, with her shy nature and

98

huge doe-eyes, the kind of girl any half-way decent guy would want to protect.

The shadow of what had happened the previous time a kid was taken had hung over the long days of waiting, and Gil had found himself tuning in to almost every radio news bulletin. When he'd heard that the child had been found alive and unharmed, he'd done what he rarely did — poured himself a Scotch and drunk it, straight.

He'd never expected, all those months ago, that he'd ever set foot in Dungirri again. Until that lawyer had pulled a stool up to the bar a few weeks back and he'd discovered how much he really owed Jeanie, the idea of returning had never crossed his mind.

But now he was here, and what should have been a simple, fleeting visit to Jeanie had become as complicated as all hell. Maybe that's why his mind had strayed to things done and past rather than working on the present problems — Marci's murder, his arrest, the sergeant's near-miss. He had no answers yet, for any of them.

His steps slowed as he approached the Truck Stop. The teenage girl. *Megan*. Another complication. He still couldn't get his head around her existence, his brain constantly shying away from the "d" word.

He paused on the driveway, his hesitation not so much because he didn't want to see her, more that he didn't want to be seen *with* her. Someone might notice the resemblance, and it had to be far better for her if she never knew who he was. He'd set up a financial arrangement with Jeanie so that the kid wouldn't ever need for money, but other than that he'd steer clear of her. He'd made the decision on his walk this morning, and the day's events had only confirmed the sense of it.

A couple of empty cattle trucks were parked out front, and through the brightly lit café windows he saw it was Jeanie, not the girl, taking drinks to the drivers' table. They were the only customers.

He waited until she returned to the kitchen, then pushed the door open and went inside. The truck drivers gave him a couple of seconds of attention, but he didn't recognise them, and their interest passed after he gave them a curt nod.

Jeanie turned a couple of steaks on the grill, lifted a basket of chips out of the deep-fryer and propped it to drain before she saw him.

"Gil! Thank God. Come on through."

In the once-familiar kitchen, he dropped his bag near the back door out of Jeanie's way while she was cooking. She was reaching for a new can of pineapple, from a shelf almost too high for her, and he leaned over and got it for her.

"Thank you, Gil," she said, with the same warm, sincere smile that had gentled the wild kid he'd once been. Even after all these years, her simple gratitude still had the power to affect him, with an unsettling mix of pride in her approval and fear he'd disappoint her. Whatever was decent in him he owed mostly to Jeanie.

Busy putting together side salads, she cast a cautious glance across at the two diners and lowered her voice. "I was worried about you. I phoned Kris a few times,

but she wasn't allowed to tell me much. The woman —
she was someone you knew?"

"It was Marci Doonan."

Jeanie knew enough of his history to recognise the
name. "Oh, Gil, I'm so sorry. That must have been
awful. And then to be arrested like that . . ."

"It's okay, Jeanie. They released me a couple of hours
ago. The sergeant gave me a lift back." Keen to avoid
discussing things any further, he switched subject. "Is
that offer of the cabin still open?"

She shot him a sharp look, but didn't ask any
questions. "Absolutely. I've cleaned it out, and it's
ready for you. The key's in the door."

"Thanks. I appreciate it. I'll be out of your hair
tomorrow."

"Take your stuff out the back. The grill's hot —
would you like a steak for dinner?"

His stomach threatened to rumble. The sandwich
Macklin had brought him at lunchtime seemed a long
time ago.

"I can't stay just now. I have to go back up to the
station. The sergeant . . . there was some trouble on the
way back. Some bastard tried to run her down." He
heard the roar of the engine again, the sound of her
hitting her car, and swallowed hard, dragging his
concentration back to the present.

"She's hurt?" Jeanie's hands were already reaching
for her apron ties, ready to whisk it off to go and help.

"Minor scrapes, nothing major. Beth Fletcher . . .
Wilson," he corrected himself, "is with her at the
moment. But she needs my witness statement."

"Is there anything I can do?"

He almost said "no", then remembered the state of Kris's fridge. "Does she eat takeaway?"

Jeanie's frayed smile didn't erase the worry in her eyes. "Works burger. She reckons it's almost healthy."

"Better make it two, then. I'll go and put my bag in the cabin."

She had the burgers and onion on the grill before he was out the back door.

The cabin was a portable job of the kind used for accommodation in mining camps and the like. Two small rooms, each with a couple of single beds, on either side of a basic bathroom. It had been beside the Truck Stop, up against the fence, for as long as Gil could remember. Back when he'd worked there in his teens, it had only had occasional use — a family stranded by a car breakdown, an old guy wandering the roads on his bicycle seeking better shelter than his tent during rainy weather. People who, for various reasons, didn't want to stay in the pub across the road. Like himself. The bloke at the pub would probably throw him out if he showed his face in there again.

He left his bag on the floor, between the beds. There wasn't a lot of room to move, but the cabin would do fine for overnight. Outside, although the wind had dropped a little the air was still cool, and he pulled his jacket on. The branches of a large kurrajong tree in front of the cabin stretched over a wooden picnic table and bench, and he brushed a scattering of dead leaves off the bench and sat down, drawing in a few slow breaths of the fresh night air. So different from Sydney, out here in the dark. Only small sounds drifted, each distinct in the stillness — some eighties rock song playing on the jukebox from the pub; a vehicle a block or two away; a dog barking somewhere beyond the creek.

Jeanie would be a few minutes making the burgers, so he dug for his phone in his jacket pocket, and called Liam.

He didn't beat around the bush when his offsider answered. "Marci's dead," he said bluntly. "Her body was in my car this morning. A couple of Sydney detectives turned up with a search warrant and found her there."

There was stunned silence for a long moment, then, "Holy shit. How? Who would . . . ?"

"I don't know who, yet. As for how . . . it looked pretty bad. Not quick." His throat thickened and the words stalled.

"Jesus."

Gil heard Deb's worried query in the background, and Liam relayed the news.

"You left Sydney last night?" Gil asked, when Deb had finished swearing. "Are you at that eco-resort? North of Maitland, isn't it?"

"Yes. We stayed in Maitland overnight, came the rest of the way this morning."

"Good." That put them an hour or two closer than Sydney, though still a long way away. "Can you drive up and get me tomorrow? The forensic mob have taken my car."

"Sure. Where are you?"

"Town called Dungirri. Northwest of the state, past Narrabri. You'll need a fair chunk of the day to get here."

"But how did Marci . . . ? You didn't take her up there."

It was statement more than question. Liam knew him, knew there was bugger-all chance he'd spend any more time with Marci than necessary.

"No. I saw her yesterday morning at her place. But someone got to her after that, and must have tracked me somehow, and put her body in my boot during the night."

"What do the cops think?"

"They arrested me this morning." He hated even saying the words, kept it to a bare minumum. "But they released me this afternoon. They've gone back to Sydney."

"The guys who leaned on Deb yesterday wanted to know where you were," Liam told him. "My neighbour said I had visitors, too, but I didn't come home till late. Sounds like someone's out to get you."

"Tell me something I don't know. Better bring Deb with you tomorrow. She can share the driving, and I'd rather neither of you were alone. I'm staying at the Truck Stop. You won't have trouble finding it."

As he finished the call, his brain rapidly put a plan together. He'd go to Moree with Liam and Deb tomorrow, and buy a new car there. Then he'd send them on to somewhere right out of the way, maybe into Queensland, so he could go back to Sydney, find out who was screwing with him, and deal with it.

Yeah, that was definitely the plan.

He locked the door of the cabin and headed back over to the kitchen. The cooking smells of meat, bacon and eggs kick-started his hunger. Piling the layers of the burgers together with the speed and dexterity of years of practice, Jeanie tilted her head in the direction of the drinks fridge.

"Help yourself. Kris has apple juice."

By the time he'd selected a couple of bottles of juice, she'd wrapped and bagged the burgers.

"Tell Kris if there's anything she needs, she just has to call."

She refused the twenty-dollar note he held out to her. He didn't argue with her, just went over behind the counter, studied the cash register for a moment to work out the system, and then rang up a sale and put the money in the drawer.

She objected, of course, but he overrode her. "I'm not free-loading off you, Jeanie."

He glanced at the security monitor behind the register, and stopped still. The screen, divided into four sections, showed an image every second or so of the fuel pumps out front, the counter, the café, and the diesel pump to the side of the building — with the side street beyond and the hotel hazy in the background.

"Do you leave the security cameras running all night?"

"Yes. The fuel pumps are turned off at night, of course, but there were a couple of break-ins a few months back, as well as people driving off without paying, which is why I decided to put the system in."

"Is this recorded? Do you have last night's footage?"

"It's recorded onto the computer in the office. The young man from the security firm in Moree left some instructions on how to access it, but the only time I needed to, I couldn't work it out. I had to get Adam to help."

He resisted the temptation to go and look at the footage now. Far better if a police officer did it, following whatever rules they had about possible evidence.

"I'll see if Adam can come and take a look later, Jeanie. Just in case the camera on the diesel pumps picked up anything on the road. It's not in focus, but we might be able to get something off it."

As he walked up towards the police station, he didn't let his hopes rise far. On the screen, the road beyond the immediate focus area was indistinct. In the dark there'd probably be little that was discernible. But if there was something, anything, that would show evidence of who had dumped Marci in his vehicle, it could help the investigation and go towards clearing his name.

As long as he stayed out of jail, he didn't care what most people thought of him — except for a few. Jeanie's loyalty and faith in him hadn't come as a surprise, but the sergeant had to have her doubts about him. No matter what she'd said, no matter that she'd trusted him enough to risk offering a ride, she couldn't be a hundred per cent certain. He wanted her to be certain. He had bugger-all chance of earning either her approval or her respect, yet he wanted her to be convinced of his innocence in Marci's death. Some part of him argued that it was simply because he'd caused her enough worry she didn't need, on top of the load she already carried. Beneath the logic, he knew that was only part of the truth, but his thoughts shied uneasily away from acknowledging it.

The moon, close to full, provided enough light for him to avoid the main street, so to dodge the crowd at the hall he took the back way, turning up the side road and cutting across the empty paddock along the creek to reach the residence behind the police station.

Kris was on the doorstep, saying goodbye to Beth. She'd changed out of her uniform. In contrast to the masculine lines of her police shirt and trousers, the cream colour of the knitted Aran cardigan she wore over her jeans was softer, more feminine. Beautiful, with her red hair falling loose around her face. *Vulnerable*. The reminder of it twisted in his guts.

What if the idiot who'd tried to run her down had shown up last night, instead? When she'd been alone, without radio or phone, her car useless in the ditch. Or what if someone wanted to break into her place, do her harm? Her backyard extended to the creek, the fence that had once provided some privacy and security was no longer there. A couple of large eucalypts and some wattles created plentiful shadows. And he knew from using it this morning that although her back door had a deadlock, it had no peephole, and a deadlock was no use if she opened the door to anyone who knocked, which she probably did.

107

She was too dedicated, and that dedication put her at risk every day. If the psycho who'd murdered the kid had targeted her, she could have been killed, just like the others. That guy was gone, but there were plenty more murderers and thugs out there in the world, too ready to turn cop-killer.

And he couldn't do a damn thing about it — except leave town as soon as possible, and reduce the risk by keeping the bastards who were after him well away from her.

CHAPTER
SIX

Good. He'd come back. He'd said he would, but Kris hadn't been overly confident. He waited in the shadows a few metres away while Beth gave her last-minute instructions and said goodbye, returning her smile with a polite nod as she passed him.

The rich scent of grilled meat and onions wafted in the night air.

"Food." He stepped into the broader circle of light and handed Kris a paper bag. "Since you probably didn't fill up your fridge today."

She guessed the contents from its weight and warmth in her hand and her mouth watered. "Do I have you or Jeanie to thank for this?"

"Jeanie made them."

Another evasive answer — so, he obviously had some responsibility for either the idea or its execution.

"Thanks to you both. I'm ravenous. Come on in."

It was impossible to eat one of Jeanie's piled-high burgers with any degree of decorum, so she wouldn't try. She put out plates on the kitchen table, and tore a few large sheets off a roll of paper towel to serve as napkins.

"Eat while it's hot," she told Gil. "Then we can talk."

Strange to be sitting here, eating with Gil, the silence not exactly relaxed, but not uncomfortable, either.

Despite being there by choice, he still carried a degree of wariness, tension in his body, in his silence. After they'd eaten, she'd probably have to work to dig through his layers of secrets and complexities. Yet she had a strong sense that the little he'd told her so far was the truth. No wild stories, no contrived explanations, just some bare, basic facts. Maybe that's why she trusted him. And that highlighted the whole skewed nature of the situation; basically she trusted him — an ex-con with a dead body in his boot and questionable connections — and he didn't trust her, a police officer.

He was focused on the food, and made short work of his burger. With his large hands, he didn't have as much trouble keeping the bun and its contents under control, whereas she battled to keep shredded lettuce and the sauce-slathered rissole from escaping.

Sucking sauce from her finger, she glanced up and caught him looking at her, the flare of heat unmistakeable. And just as unmistakeable, her own body's immediate reaction: her pulse audible in her head, her breath suddenly shallow, her acute awareness of his strong, male physicality. Her long-missing libido flung the door open and flounced back in, all dressed up and raring to party.

Shit.

He scrunched the empty paper bag tight in his hand, and shoved his chair away from the table to walk over and toss it in the kitchen bin. His back still to her, he broke the silence abruptly.

"Jeanie's new security system — there's a camera that might have picked up something last night. She said Adam knows how to access the footage."

It took a moment for her brain to change gear. *Security system. Last night.*

"The camera on the pumps at the side? Shit, why didn't I think of that?" She dropped the remains of her burger on the plate, self-reproach killing her hunger. She should have remembered the security system. It might not have caught anything, but she should have thought about it this morning, and checked it then. Tiredness and shock weren't any damn excuse.

"The images probably won't be any good."

"We'll find out," Kris said.

Glad of something practical to focus on, she wiped her hands on a paper towel and found her phone among the stuff cluttering the table. Adam answered on the first ring. He'd called in at Jeanie's, who had already asked him to check the security footage.

"If there's anything useful, I'll make a copy and bring it over. Might take me an hour or so," he added, before he disconnected.

She glanced at her watch, slightly surprised it was only eight o'clock. What else did she have to do tonight? Text Steve to let him know she'd arrived home. Report the incident. Get Gil's witness statement. Then go out and knock on a few doors, find out who might have seen or heard something last night. There'd be no long relaxing bath this evening to soothe her aching body, no early night to catch up on her sleep. Just the work she was honour-bound to do.

Her thoughts were scattered, racing around in her brain, too slippery to catch and hold on to them all.

She made herself concentrate. As she lifted her phone again, its light bell tones announced a text message, the phone vibrating gently in her hand. Her mental list still forming in her mind, she distractedly thumbed the keys to access the message.

She had to stare at the letters on the screen for several seconds before they made any sense.

GilSP is ded. If U hlp him U wll B 2.

He shouldn't have brought the food. Sharing a meal with her again in her kitchen was just too damned . . . *personal*. Friends shared meals, and lovers, and he'd better bloody well remember that they were neither.

The sooner he got out of here, the better. He'd made a mistake in the car asking her about tracking phone calls. It had raised her curiosity and suspicions. She'd start on the questions again, just as soon as she'd finished with her phone. He'd have to think of some way to answer them that would discourage her, keep her uninvolved.

Discouraging a dedicated cop who genuinely worried about people, and about justice, wouldn't be easy. He could lie convincingly if he had to — and he'd had to, more than once in his life — but he preferred the truth. And in this case a brief version of the truth would probably be enough to convince her that she didn't need to be involved, that the action was in Sydney, not here, and that once he'd left tomorrow she and Dungirri could forget about him for good.

She was frowning at her phone, the text she'd just received obviously not to her liking. He saw the anger rise: her narrowed eyes, the hiss of an in-drawn breath, the slight colour darkening her cheeks. She pushed the remains of her burger away and stood up, sliding the phone across the table towards him.

"I am going to make a pot of strong coffee," she said, her voice cold and deliberate, "and then you are going to explain to me exactly what is going on."

If the coolness of her order didn't quite chill him, the text on the screen did.

"I should go, Blue."

"No." She dumped four heaped spoons of coffee in the plunger, and turned on the kettle.

"You'll be safer . . ."

"I'll be safer when I know what's happening and whether this is just someone playing silly buggers or something I really need to worry about."

As she moved past him to retrieve the coffee mugs they'd left in the drainer that morning, she met his eyes, honest and direct, and he wished for a moment that she was a weaker person, that she would go running scared from him, call in her colleagues for protection. But even out of uniform, in that soft cardigan, there was still the strong core of determination and commitment, and he sensed that she would never run from anything she considered to be her duty.

That knowledge made him all the more worried for her. "I'll tell you what you need to know, Blue. But then I'm leaving. Being with me puts you in danger, and I won't let you risk that."

"I decide what risks I take," she said, too calm for his peace of mind.

Reaching for her phone again, she dialled a number and reported the text message. Gil didn't know the abbreviations she used, but he understood enough to know that she'd requested a trace on the message.

"How long before you get an answer?" he asked as she dropped the phone back on the table.

"Depends. An hour or two. Maybe longer."

The kettle came to a rolling boil and she turned to flick it off. A grimace of pain crossed her face as she lifted it, her arm shaking and water splashing unevenly into the plunger.

He closed his hand over hers to steady it.

"I'll finish this. Go and sit down."

"I think I'll get some painkillers." Cradling her arm against her body, she headed to the bathroom.

He stayed where he was while the coffee brewed, leaning against the bench, relieved by the few moments alone. From outside, he heard a couple of car doors slam, the sounds of engines starting, vehicles turning on gravel. The working bee next door finishing up, he guessed, and hoped none of them had seen him come in here. It could make things more difficult for Kris than they already were.

If she wasn't too sore, she'd likely start with her questions soon, and he had no doubts that by the time he finished answering them, she'd be more than glad to see the back of him. If he could just explain in a way that didn't . . . No, he was who he was, not the kind of

114

man who had any business being kitchen-table friends with a decent cop.

He poured the coffee and placed her mug on the table when she returned, still holding her arm. She hooked a chair out with her foot and sat, stirring sugar into her coffee for a few moments before she tossed her first question at him, direct and to the point.

"Do you know who murdered Marci?"

He might not have been forthcoming in his answers during the day, with Petric and Macklin playing their smart-arse games, but he owed *her* straight honesty now.

"No. I've got suspicions, but they're just guesswork. I don't know anything for sure. There are too many possibilities."

"Marci had a lot of enemies?"

"She was in with some rough folk, Blue. She drifted from one man to another and they used her. She didn't have enough sense to take charge of her own life."

Not like you. The thought came unbidden. Marci, with her overdone make-up and tight clothes and all the artifice she'd learned in the sex trade couldn't have been a greater contrast to the woman in front of him, natural and beautiful without make-up, comfortable and confident in her self and her profession.

"Until the last year or so, she kept control of the booze, and didn't do much in the way of drugs. But her latest boyfriend's a dealer, and he got her hooked, pimped her to pay for it. He was connected to scum, and she was sliding down, way out of her depth. She's not young any more, not as attractive, so he was

115

pushing her into the BDSM scene. She thought . . ." He had to word this part carefully. "She thought she could sell some information she had, to pay off her debt. I warned her that was dangerous, for her."

He met Kris's long, appraising look without blinking. But if she guessed that the information Marci had involved him in some way, she didn't pursue it directly.

"You paid her debts, tried to get her out of Sydney. What was Marci to you, Gil? And what are the two of you caught up in?"

He hesitated, wondering how he could explain it all, where to start. "It's a long story," he said.

She curled her hands around her coffee mug and lifted it to her mouth. "Then start at the beginning."

The beginning. It seemed so long ago, the beginning of that part of his life, but it was where he and Digger and Marci and the Russos had first crossed paths.

He took a mouthful of coffee. "Marci was married to Digger Doonan, back fifteen years ago. Digger gave me a job as a bouncer and general dogsbody in his pub, when I'd been sleeping rough in Sydney for weeks after I got out of prison. The pay was a joke but I got food to eat and a cockroach-infested room to sleep in on the premises."

She listened without commenting, and he had another drink of coffee before continuing, "Digger was a Vietnam vet, but he never really got his head back together afterwards, and with the booze he was easy pickings. He held the deeds to the pub, but he'd got himself in too deep with the Russo family. They're big in the 'Ndrangheta in Sydney."

116

She leaned forward. "The 'Ndrangheta? The Calabrian *mafia*?" Her short laugh held no humour at all. "Oh, Jesus, my day just keeps getting better."

So, Petric hadn't tried to discredit him by telling her the seedier aspects of his connections. That made him wonder whether Petric was game-playing with his country colleagues, too. Or whether he just didn't regard them as important enough to warrant sharing with them significant information.

"The Russo family made their money from marijuana and cocaine in the 1970s and '80s," he explained. "Vince, the one who died today, pursued mostly legal interests after that — imports, investments, property development — and left most of the running of the illegal business to his brother, Gianni. At least, that's how Vince wanted it to appear. In reality, he exercised authority when Gianni crossed over what Vince considered a line. Gianni ran a tight territory, keeping control of drugs, brothels and pubs in his part of the inner south. Vince's son, Tony, preferred Gianni's style of business, and worked with him for years. It was Tony who oversaw Russo's interests at Digger's pub — drugs, girls, extortion."

Kris didn't say anything, her mouth tight and disapproving.

"Digger owed Tony, and Tony sent his thugs after him one night, just to put the frighteners on him, but Digger had a heart condition, and that's how he died."

"Was Tony charged?" she asked sharply. "Or his accomplices?"

"No. They didn't leave much evidence of anything but natural causes, and Tony cleaned up any messy questions by calling compliant cops to the scene, and a coke-addict doctor who certified that Digger had a heart condition and sky-high blood pressure."

Her frown deepened, but she merely said, "Go on."

"I'd been at the pub more than a year by then. I knew Vince a little. Thing was, he'd known Marci since she was a kid, had a soft spot for her, and he used to come and visit the pub sometimes. He had some control over Tony and kept him from squeezing Digger dry. In return, Digger lent me to Vince a few times when he needed a driver or an extra bodyguard."

That didn't go down well, judging by the hard look she shot him.

"One of the things I'd learned was that information could be more powerful than knives or fists. So I kept my eyes open, and watched and waited. When Digger died, it turned out he'd left the pub to Marci and me, a fifty-fifty split. Maybe he had the guilts because I'd been running the place for him for all of a few bucks every now and then. Maybe he figured if he left it all to Marci she'd lose it within a month. I don't know. The pub had been in his family for almost eighty years, and he was proud of that. But he didn't have any family of his own."

"Let me guess." Her tone was dry and cold. "Tony wasn't happy?"

"Tony was enraged. He wanted control of the pub, made all sorts of threats. But I wanted to run the

118

business on my terms, not Tony's. Turn it into something decent if I could."

"What did you do?"

"I made a deal with the devil. With Vince. I met with him, and let him know about the contents of a package locked up in a safety deposit box, and that it would stay there as long as Gianni and Tony and their dirty business stayed out of my pub, but if anything happened to me or the pub, the contents would be copied and sent to some senior police officers, the anti-corruption commission, and a few top journalists."

Her mug thumped down on the table. "Shit, Gillespie, what the hell did you have on him?"

He took a slow breath, knowing he was about to damn himself, steeling himself for the condemnation that would darken her eyes. For all that he expected it, the loss of her trust would leave a jagged emptiness inside him. He'd only known her for twenty-four hours, and he shouldn't care. It shouldn't matter to him. But it did.

With no choice, he held her suspicious look. "I had a video, proving he ordered and was present at the murder of a cop."

She'd been punched in the face once long ago, and his words hit with the same hard slam of betrayal, anger and nauseating shock.

"Oh, Jesus. You were there? And you never reported it? A murdered *police officer*?"

"He was no hero, Blue. The guy might have carried the badge, but he was up to his neck in corruption and vice. Drugs and kickbacks were only part of it. He was trafficking teenage girls — some of them only thirteen, fourteen years old. He and his mates made a mint from kids being raped and brutalised. Even Tony didn't touch that kind of stuff."

If he'd been defensive, making excuses, it would have fuelled her anger further. But his explanation was just that, an explanation, delivered with the weary tone of disillusion, and her anger faded a notch.

"That doesn't make it right."

"No, it doesn't. I couldn't have stopped it, though. If I'd tried, I would have just ended up on the slab myself. The guy had made the mistake of luring in a Russo girl, a cousin of Vince and Gianni's. However, it did give me a lever, later, to get the pub clean and out of the Russos' territory."

"And what if that evidence could have put them away?" she challenged. "Cleaned the streets of Gianni and Vince?"

"There would have just been somebody else move in. Tony taking over, or rival groups expanding their empires. Believe me, there are far worse criminals out there than Vince Russo, and one of them is Tony. Vince's honour and morals might have been skewed, but at least he had some, and he curbed his family's excesses. Besides, who would I have given the evidence to? The only cops I knew then were the ones taking kickbacks and running drugs."

She would have bristled at the criticism of her colleagues, if it wasn't for the bleakness in his words.

"You don't have a high opinion of the police, do you?"

"I haven't met many I trust, Blue."

"Do you trust me, Gillespie?"

He took a long time to answer, and she found herself stilling her breath, trying to read something, anything, in the midnight dark of his eyes.

"I don't think you'd be easily corrupted," he said eventually.

"Well, that's not quite the ringing endorsement I expected," she commented wryly. But she'd asked a question, and he'd answered it, and his frankness probably spoke more about his confidence in her than his words.

"What was the information Marci had?" she asked, getting back to the real questions at hand. "And why was it so dangerous?"

"She thought she knew who informed on two bent detectives, and figured their associates would pay for the name. But she refused to believe that since she gave the person the information to start with, they'd hold her accountable, too."

Kris quickly added up what she knew, and took a punt. "The person she gave the information to — the informant — that would be you, right?"

He stared down into his mug, then swallowed the last mouthful and put it on the bench beside him. The glance he threw her had more than a touch of defiance, as if he expected her to disapprove. "Yeah. That would be me."

The defiance left her wondering. Had he sold the information for money or other advantage? Or did he think she'd side with fellow officers, no matter how corrupt, and condemn him for informing on them?

Everything he told her left her with more questions than answers.

"Is that what you argued about? The night you carted her out of the pub?"

"She wanted a share of what I'd sold the pub for, even though I'd paid her above market value for her half, years ago. I said I'd help her out of the mess she was in, if she left Sydney and the boyfriend. She didn't like that, started making threats, and I told her not to be stupid."

"Some people might consider that kind of threat as a motive for murder."

He conceded the point with a small nod. "Some people might."

But he'd told her he hadn't murdered Marci, and she believed him. None of what she'd learned about him added up to the kind of man who would beat a woman to death to protect himself. Which still left the problem of who *had* killed her. Not to mention all the other questions raised by Gillespie's revelations.

Sorting through it in her head, trying to decide what she most needed to find out, what she needed to do, she absently lifted the mug to take a sip of coffee and discovered it already empty.

He noticed, lifting the half-full plunger in offering.

"No, thanks. Any more at that strength, and I'll be awake until Christmas."

The painkillers and the slug of caffeine had returned some clarity to her brain, and when she stood it was stiffness more than pain that she felt. She found a notepad and a pen under a pile of bills on the table, and passed them to Gil.

"I'm going to make a couple of phone calls. I want you to write lists," she told him. "Who might have murdered Marci, who might want to frame you. And since Vince Russo's dead and he has links with both of you, I want to know who you think could have murdered him, too. When it comes to murder, I'm not big on coincidences."

He took the pen and pad and didn't argue.

As she reached the door, she remembered something he'd said, and although it wasn't directly connected with Marci's death, she wanted an answer.

"You said you wanted to turn the pub into a decent place, Gillespie. Did you succeed?"

It wasn't much of a grin, but he'd been so tense and wary all day that the unexpected curve of his mouth, the light of pride in his normally guarded eyes caught her by surprise.

"Yeah, Blue," he said quietly, "I did."

The knock on the back door jerked Gil out of the momentary distraction of her smile and back to blunt reality. He cut in front of her and caught her hand just as she raised it to open the door.

"Find out who it is first," he warned her, releasing her hand quickly, too aware of its warmth on his skin, and not daring to interpret her quizzical frown.

His growl must have carried further than he meant it to, or sounded threatening, because they heard Adam's worried call, "Kris, are you all right?"

She pulled the door open wide. "Everything's fine, Adam. Come on in."

The young constable didn't relax or take his hand off the weapon at his hip until he'd given Gil a long, hard stare. Gil didn't blink.

Adam eventually relaxed enough to pull a rolled-up piece of paper from inside his jacket.

"What can you tell me about the vehicle that ran Kris down?" he asked Gil.

Gil repeated pretty much what he'd told Kris, out on the road. "Black or very dark in colour. Large four-wheel drive type — the size of a Patrol or a Land Cruiser. The way he accelerated, it has to be a powerful engine, and probably petrol rather than diesel."

"Do you know anyone who owns a vehicle like that?"

The edge of suspicion in Adam's cool cop stance and tone put Gil immediately on guard. "No. Why?"

"What's going on, Adam?" Kris demanded.

Adam tapped the paper against his fist, and then unrolled it and passed it to Kris.

"Jeanie's security system caught this vehicle around four this morning. This is the best image we have of it. They used the driveway to turn from the side street back on to the main road. But before that, it parked by Gillespie's car, and two people manoeuvred something large out of their vehicle and into his."

Kris sat down heavily in the nearest chair, and handed the photo to Gil.

The grainy image showed the vehicle side on, silhouetted by the streetlight behind. Gil didn't know enough about recent models to be able to pick the make from the shape, but it was definitely large and dark.

Watching for his reaction, Adam asked, "What's the odds of two dark four-wheel drives being involved in incidents on the same day?"

"Bugger all." Gil provided the unnecessary answer, and didn't bother keeping the bitterness from his words.

It hadn't been some smart alec local on the road tonight after all, and that knowledge doused the relief at there being evidence of someone else dumping Marci's body. Rage boiled in him, and he wanted to ram his fists into something, rip someone apart for menacing her. The threat to Kris was real, and he'd brought it on her. Whoever was after him had already come close to killing her.

But if the realisation had thrown her for a moment, Kris showed little sign of it now. She held out her hand for the photo, and when he passed it back, she briskly assessed it.

"Can't see anything distinguishing on the car. No roof-rack, aerials or markings. Did any of the other images show anything, Adam? Or anything identifiable with the people?"

"No. The shots across the road are too far out of focus. One bloke is a little taller than the other, that's about all I can tell. Might be able to get a height estimate if we can identify the make of car." He pulled a USB drive from his pocket. "Jeanie's printer didn't have much ink, but I copied the whole sequence of images."

"Good. Come into the office, and we'll take a look at them. You, too, Gillespie."

They crowded around the desk in her small office, and Gil tried to force his attention to the computer screen, and not the woman sitting at it. But standing beside her, closer than they'd been in the kitchen, he was all too aware of her — and of Adam, on the other side of her, who kept him under close scrutiny. Kris might have decided to trust him, but her constable had yet to make up his mind.

There were well over a hundred images, most too fuzzy to decipher any detail, and she flicked through them quickly. The dark shape of the vehicle pulling up beside his car. Two figures, little more than shadows near the cars. But then the camera had caught them at the back of his lighter vehicle, with a large smudge of white between them. Marci. The rage burned again, but he made himself watch. It took them too many frames to get her into his boot, and his imagination filled in the gaps, seeing them callous and disrespectful, manhandling her body to fit her into the awkward space, sickening him.

Kris's face was pale, her forehead creased in a frown, but she kept clicking through the frames as the reversing lights of the car flared in an image, then a headlight, side on, in the next. For several frames, it was out of sight, only a glow on the edge of the image indicating the turn into the Truck Stop, before the frame Adam had printed, of the whole vehicle in as much detail as they would get, right in centre front of the camera.

"Can you take it back a few frames?" Gil asked.

The diesel pumps stood sentinel in the illumination from the security light, only darkness beyond and the glow off to the right. Gil counted eight or nine frames.

"They stopped, out of the picture," Kris said. "But why?"

"Yes. That glow doesn't change. What's over behind the building?" Gil wracked his memory of parking on that side of the building last night and slammed his hand on the desk. "Christ, it's the garbage skip. They've dumped something in the garbage."

"Shit. Wait a minute. Let me check back a few frames again." Kris studied the screen closely as she reversed back a few more images. "There, see that?" She pointed at a lighter smudge on one of the figures. "It's almost like a reflection, or a shine, on something large that he's carrying."

"Plastic?" Gil wondered aloud. "Did they wrap her in plastic sheeting before transporting her?"

"They could have wrapped her in something," Adam said. "There were blood smear patterns. Vinyl or plastic would fit them. I never thought to look in the garbage skip."

"None of us did. We weren't looking for a murder weapon. There was no reason to think there might be something across the road." Kris leaned back in the chair, rubbing her temples with both hands. Overtired, in pain, with too heavy a load on her shoulders — a load that *he'd* put there — yet she pulled herself together within seconds, deciding the necessary action. "Adam, we'll need to secure the skip until Forensics can get back here. Can you go down, keep an eye on things while I call Sandy and see if he can come back tonight? I'll get a couple of guys from the Birraga night shift to come over as soon as they can."

"No worries." The young man's cheerful willingness to work even longer hours impressed Gil, and he didn't begrudge the copper's caution where he was concerned. Adam's loyalty and commitment lay with Kris and the police service, and she needed as much of that as she could get right now. "I'll just go grab a torch."

"I'll be down as soon as I can, Adam. I'll call Steve Fraser, too, and let him know of the developments."

Adam nodded and left the room, heading to the old cell-turned-storeroom, and Kris swivelled her chair round to face Gil.

"I don't suppose you saw anything to identify either of the people?"

"No. Sorry." He wished he could say "yes", give them a lead to go on, but the figures had been ghostly shadows, just hazy movement in the poor light. Even the closest image, near the diesel pumps, hadn't caught any recognisable detail of the two people in the car.

"I'll need you to work on those lists, then, while —"

Her words were lost in a thunderous roar of sound, smashing through the quiet night outside.

"What the . . .?" She was already on her feet and out the door, Gil right behind her.

A block down the road, brilliant orange flames leapt high in the sky over Jeanie's Truck Stop Café.

CHAPTER
SEVEN

Gil bolted ahead of her towards the Truck Stop, but she wasn't far behind him, despite dialling triple 0 on her phone as she ran.

The building itself was ablaze, but not the fuel tanks — not yet anyway. At the Rural Fire Service shed a few doors down, she could see lights on already, and she hoped their volunteer training dealt with the possibility of thousands of litres of exploding fuel, because hers sure didn't.

A few men were coming out from the hotel, two already running towards the RFS shed, and she yelled across the road, "Dave, evacuate the pub — everyone out and away from here!"

Adam caught up with her, and without stopping she ordered him, "Evacuate a whole block on all sides. Get those on this side down to the hall, and . . ." she thought quickly, not wanting residents of the side street and beyond walking within range of the fire and potential explosion, "the others over the creek and around to the hall the back way."

"But Jeanie . . ."

"I'll go for her."

The west end of the café was well alight, and when she followed where Gil had disappeared around the back, she saw the external stairs up to Jeanie's place had been blown off, along with half of the back of the building.

It was probably the gas cylinders used for cooking that had exploded, but she'd worry about the how and why later. Right now, Gil was climbing up the remains of the stair post, despite the flames eating at the old wooden building only a metre or two away, and the thick smoke swirling around them.

If Jeanie was in her place — and where else could she be? — then they had only minutes to get her out. It would take the volunteer RFS crew longer than that to get to the truck shed and gear themselves up.

As Gil swung onto one of the remaining floor beams, she started up after him, but he saw her and waved a hand towards the old cabin. Above the roar of the fire she only caught some of his shouted words: ". . . ladder . . . there . . . awning at . . . front."

He disappeared into the building, and with fear strangling her breath as much as the smoke, and fighting panic, Kris made herself move through the heat and debris behind the café until she reached the cabin. Gil must have noticed the ladder earlier — he couldn't have seen it through the smoke.

Firelight glinting on the metal helped her find it, propped against the cabin.

It was heavy, metal and big, but adrenaline helped her drag it around the front, skirting the fire to take it past the fuel bowsers to the side of the awning furthest from the worst flames.

In the middle of her terror for Jeanie and Gil, the stark realisation occurred to her that if the fuel tanks below her feet blew, at least her own death would be speedy.

The ladder in place, she scrambled up it, the corrugated iron of the awning already hot from the fire's heat, glass from Jeanie's large windows shattered all over it. The west end of the top floor was burning now — Jeanie's kitchen and bathroom. Kris climbed through the bedroom window at the other end shouting Gil's name, Jeanie's name, and coughing at the effort. In the smoke and the heat and the hellish whirling light, half her instincts screamed at her to get out of there. The other half drove her out of that room and into the living area, desperate to find Jeanie . . . and Gil.

Eyes and throat burning, she couldn't speak when Gil lurched from the kitchen, Jeanie's limp body in his arms, the garish light showing her white hair dark with blood. Coughs wracking his body, Gil stumbled, falling to one knee. Her own legs barely working, Kris pushed past him, slamming the door shut against the flames. With the wallpaper already curling on one wall, and the carpet smoking in the corner, she knew the closed door would only give them a few seconds advantage.

Gil was already struggling to his feet, and with one arm around him, she took some of Jeanie's weight. An upturned table blocked the window, so together they

132

stumbled to the bedroom, and she kicked the door shut behind them.

"You first," he croaked, nodding at the glassless window. "I'll pass her."

Jeanie weighed less than she did, but with oxygen-starved lungs it was a struggle to hold her when Gil handed her through the window. Her knees buckled, taking her down. At the same moment the back of the bedroom wall erupted in flames, Gil disappeared from her view and trapped, holding Jeanie, she could do nothing but shout his name.

She dragged Jeanie back a few metres towards the ladder, and then Gil was there again in the garish light, tucking something inside his jacket, clambering over the window frame, and insanely she wanted to cry and rage at him for scaring her.

He lifted Jeanie in his arms as Kris crawled the last metre to the ladder.

"Go." He gave her a small nudge with his foot.

Somehow she made it onto the ladder without falling, concentrating hard to get each foot onto one rung, then the next, feeling the ladder shudder as Gil moved onto it above her. And then yellow-clad arms folded around her, and Paul Barrett's voice said near her ear, "Nearly there," as he steadied her, and lifted her down the last rungs, then Karl Sauer in his orange SES overalls moved in to take Jeanie from Gil.

Her eyes burned so much she could hardly see, but she knew the body holding her upright as she coughed was Gil, his own breathing as ragged as hers.

"We need to get out of here, Sarge," Karl said. "Can you make it as far as Ward's?"

She nodded, and with Gil beside her, she pushed her heavy legs one step at a time away from the fire, following Karl hurrying down the road with Jeanie.

She didn't know if Jeanie was alive or dead, and that frightened her more than being in the midst of the heat and flame.

How could she bear to lose Jeanie? And how would Dungirri survive, if Jeanie died?

Gil felt like an old man, shambling up the road; the effects of the smoke seemed to be paralysing his muscles as well as his lungs, the effort to keep moving as great as if he carried a huge cement block instead of supporting one slightly built policewoman.

He'd never in his life experienced fear as strong as the dread that had gripped him when she'd appeared in the burning building. Seeing the car accelerating towards her earlier in the evening had been bad enough, but that had been over in a few moments. In the fire, the time had dragged like hours, each second endless.

Even now, she might not be all right, and Jeanie . . . Jeanie had to be in a bad way. The gash on her head, the lack of consciousness, and there were burns on her legs. He'd had no choice but to get her out of there, but how much had hauling her around worsened her injuries? He might have killed her.

Ahead of them, under the streetlight at the vacant lot beyond Ward's Rural Supplies, Beth Wilson leapt out of

134

an SES vehicle, and ran to meet the guy carrying Jeanie, starting her examination even before he laid her carefully on the ground.

Gil was too far away to hear their quick exchange, but close enough to see Beth start CPR. In the ten or so seconds it took to reach them, the man — one of the Sauer brothers, he thought it might be — had grabbed a defibrillator out of the SES vehicle, and Beth was giving instructions to place it.

Gil held Kris back, just held her, while Beth administered the shock to Jeanie's chest. There was noise in the distance, but here they all kept still, hardly daring to breathe.

When Beth gave a weak smile and set the defibrillator aside, he started breathing again, and coughing.

She glanced across at them while she attached an oxygen mask to Jeanie. "You two, sit down somewhere. Try to breathe slowly and deeply. We'll take a look at you as soon as we can."

"Will she be okay?" Kris asked.

"Her heart's beating again. That's a good start."

"I should help. I'm trained . . ."

Beth barely spared them another glance, but her firm order wasn't unfriendly. "So are Karl and I. You'll help most by sitting down with Gil, and letting me know if either of you develop any severe problems."

Karl waved a hand towards a rough bench against the brick wall of the Ward's building, and Gil pulled Kris down beside him, relieved to be able to lean back against the wall instead of making the effort to stay upright.

They watched in the streetlight and moonlight while Beth and Karl worked with calm and efficiency on Jeanie. Funny how the girl who'd been so shy she'd been nicknamed "Mouse" now gave orders to others without hesitation.

In the distance, he could hear the motor of the fire truck pumping water and the shouts of the crew at work. If they could keep the fire contained to the building, the fuel tanks would probably not explode, he figured. The fuel pumps would have been turned off for the night, and that should reduce the risk. They were far enough away here, and protected by the sturdy building if it did blow; further down, at the end of the main street, he could see the lights and the shadows of the evacuated people, milling at the hall.

Kris and Gil sat in silence for a while, listening, watching Beth clean Jeanie's head wound and monitor her while Karl cut away the remains of her trousers and treated the burns on her legs. Kris's breathing gradually eased and Gil's, too, became less of a struggle.

"There won't be anything left of the building," Kris said, her voice raspy but no longer gasping.

"No."

As if on cue, a rumble and a drawn-out crash signalled a significant collapse.

"Oh, God." She sniffed, cleared her throat. "It's been her home for fifty years."

"I know." It wasn't just smoke clogging his voice. He tightened his hand around hers, and then wondered when he'd taken hold of it.

He should untangle his fingers, let hers go, before anyone saw and made things difficult for her. He kidded himself that it didn't matter, that it was a normal reaction to the stress. Maybe she hadn't noticed. Or maybe with all the chaos and trauma, she'd forget.

"You care for her."

For Jeanie, Kris must have meant by her observation, but that wasn't his brain's first interpretation, and the words echoed in his head as an accusation.

"Yeah. I worked for her for a while." Those few words weren't adequate, but he didn't know how to describe what Jeanie had come to mean to him. How she'd shown him that there was a world beyond the hell of living with his father. How sometimes, in quiet times, they'd talked. Or rather, Jeanie had talked, and he'd listened. He realised later — years later — that in her own way, in her stories of her marriage, her life and community, she'd been teaching him things he'd needed to learn.

He still had hold of Kris's hand. He uncurled his fingers, reached inside his jacket, and drew out the photo of a young Jeanie and her husband that he'd snatched from her bedside table. The light from the moon shone on the silver frame, and the couple smiling out of it, and Kris gently took it from him.

"This is what you went back for?"

He nodded. "She doesn't have many photos of him."

And even fewer, now. So little to be left of a man's life. Aldo Menotti, who'd survived war and imprisonment and made a new life in a young country and winked when he'd snuck sweets into a small boy's hand.

That memory had stayed with Gil, but distanced, as though the small boy was someone else, because then Aldo had died fighting a bushfire, and not long afterwards the boy's mother had left, and there had been little kindness in his life after that.

"She'll be grateful to have it. So I might almost forgive you for scaring the hell out of me, Gillespie."

Jeanie *would* be grateful — if she made it. Beth didn't look quite so worried now, but she hadn't budged from Jeanie's side, and the small figure under the blanket remained motionless.

Jeanie had to be okay. He wouldn't dare imagine any other scenario. She'd come around any minute now, and although she might spend a day or so in hospital for precaution, she'd be fine, and he'd buy her a beautiful house wherever she wanted it, and she'd never have to cook another meal, or pump petrol, or do anything for anyone else again.

Sirens were approaching, their wailing eerie in the night. Soon two ambulances pulled up, and a police car, and the area began filling with people. Gil helped Kris to her feet, worried when she wavered, and led her straight over to an ambulance.

One pair of paramedics were already beside Jeanie, and the other pair, eager to work, took charge of Kris and Gil. Before he knew it, he had an oxygen mask on his face, and some sort of monitor pegged on his finger. They'd pulled out a gurney for Kris, and she was sitting on it, a blanket around her shoulders, giving instructions to two uniformed cops while the paramedics attached monitors to her and checked her over.

Adam appeared, and Steve Fraser, but Gil couldn't concentrate on their conversation with Kris because one of the paramedics assessing Jeanie came over to him. An older man, with an air of calm and experience.

"Can you tell me how you found her? Did you see what gave her the head injury?"

Gil slipped the oxygen mask down so he could answer. "In the kitchen, lying on her front. I think she must have got caught by the explosion, because the wall behind her was mostly gone, and there was debris around her." He thought back, tried to remember what he'd taken in of the scene in the rush to get her out. "There was a cupboard door open near her head. She might have hit that when she fell."

"Any idea how long she'd been there?"

"We heard the explosion from the police station. I ran straight there. So, I guess four or five minutes, maybe." It had seemed like hours, but logic said it couldn't have been. "I tried to cradle her head when I could, but there wasn't much time."

"Fire usually doesn't leave many choices. But you got her out alive, mate. That's what matters."

"How is she?" He didn't expect much of a detailed answer, and he didn't get one.

"She's holding her own. We'll know more when she's been assessed by the docs. Birraga hospital only has basic facilities, so we're calling in the rescue helicopter to take her to Tamworth."

He could go back to Sydney tomorrow via Tamworth, Gil figured quickly. Make sure that Jeanie had the best care, and everything she needed.

"Put that oxygen mask back on, mate," the ambo told him, as he headed back to Jeanie.

He hated the feel of the mask on his face, but took the advice anyway, taking a moment to adjust the straps to make it more comfortable. His head down, he saw legs in neat trousers passing, and he jerked his head up to see the back of a man, making a beeline straight for Kris.

Adam and Fraser both stepped aside when he approached, and the man put his arms around her, drawing her in close, and she rested her forehead against his shoulder.

When he turned his face to speak with Adam, Gil recognised him, and his lungs constricted again. Mark Strelitz.

Mark Strelitz, Dungirri's golden boy, who had almost died with Paula in the car accident all those years ago. Now a federal politician, highly respected on all sides of politics, and heir to one of the wealthiest grazing properties in the region. Rich, popular, intelligent and influential — the kind of man who could have anything he wanted. Including, it seemed, Kris.

Before Mark could notice him, Gil tossed the oxygen mask aside and walked away into the shadows.

140

★ ★ ★

For a couple of blissful seconds, Kris allowed herself to lean on Mark. He knew her well enough that she didn't have to pretend, and his sympathetic, supportive presence gave her the brief space she needed to regroup, to clear the buzzing in her head and focus on what needed doing.

So much to do, to organise. Mark dropped his arms as she pulled away.

"You shouldn't be here, Mark," she told him. "Emergency personnel only in this area. But if you could go up to the hall, and keep everyone there calm, I'd really appreciate it."

She could rely on him to do whatever was necessary. He'd proved that, again and again, through all the traumas of the past few years. A natural leader, people trusted him because he cared about the community and he was one of them.

"Of course. What do you want me to tell them about Jeanie?"

"They'll hear the helicopter when it comes, so tell them she'll be flown to Tamworth. Serious but stable is probably the best descriptor for now." She hoped. She'd worked with Beth and these two ambulance crews frequently enough over the years that she could tell the difference between worried and desperate. They were monitoring Jeanie closely, but her vital signs seemed to be holding steady. *If* the head wound wasn't severe, *if* the heart problem wasn't bad, she could still have a full recovery.

Kris concentrated on believing that. She'd seen any number of people who'd been seriously injured survive and heal. Steve had had a bullet in his thigh last summer, and now he walked with barely a limp. The summer before that, she'd endured the long ambulance ride to Birraga beside her friend Bella, attacked by a mob gone mad, and now Bella was fine, happier and healthier than she'd been for years.

So it would be all right, as long as she got off her butt and organised everything so the helicopter could get Jeanie safely to hospital. The oxygen mask still dangled around her neck, and she took it off, waving away the paramedic's protest as she hopped off the gurney.

With thick smoke blowing to the south, and a fire site still not totally secured, two of the best landing sites — the school oval and the showground — were too dangerous to use.

"Gary," she called over to the senior ambulance officer. "Tell the chopper to land in the stock reserve on the north side of town."

Karl Sauer and a couple of other SES volunteers waited nearby, not needed now that the ambulances had arrived, but keen to be useful. She asked them to arrange a couple of vehicles to light up a safe landing spot in the reserve. She'd already sent the two Birraga police officers to block each end of the main street.

"Adam, can you liaise with the RFS? As soon as it's safe, that whole site needs securing and guarding."

"You suspect arson?" Steve Fraser asked.

"Yes." She hated saying the word, acknowledging aloud that someone might have deliberately targeted

Jeanie. "There's been a few developments since this afternoon."

"Adam just mentioned that you'd run into some strife on the way home. Or that it ran into you."

"Close enough."

"What about Gillespie? Is this his doing?"

"Hell, no." She glanced around, having lost track of Gil, but she saw his figure not far away, dark in the shadows, leaning a shoulder against the back corner of Ward's, silently watching.

Alone. On the outer. She guessed he'd probably spent most of his life that way. Not the kind of guy comfortable in a group.

"Gillespie was with me when the fire started," she told Steve. "And he saved Jeanie's life."

"So you're his alibi. Again. Mightn't be wise to make a habit of that, Kris."

She felt her face harden, and studied him coldly. "Is that a threat, Steve?"

"No." He didn't shy away from her straight gaze. "It's an expression of concern. Gillespie's involved with some hard types, who could make things difficult for you."

"They've already tried. With a text message threat after the run-down-the-copper episode."

"Fuck." The vehemence of the swear word seemed genuine. "You should have phoned me, Kris."

"Yep, that was on my to-do list," she said dryly, "but other things intervened. I reported it — still waiting on the trace. So, have you got any contacts in arson investigation? I want somebody good on their way here right now."

"I'll make a phone call or two. You seem pretty sure it's arson."

"I'd much rather that it was an accident, and not connected to Marci Doonan's death," she answered, "but since the place contained two sources of evidence that might have helped us to identify who murdered her and dumped her, an accident is pretty damned unlikely."

CHAPTER
EIGHT

No-one was paying Gil any attention, and he could have just left — but to go where? With the cabin probably destroyed or at least out of bounds, he had nowhere to go. Besides, his main priorities now were there in front of him — Jeanie and Kris. He couldn't do anything for Jeanie, but he worried for Kris's safety. So, for the moment at least, he stayed on the edges of things and observed.

The paramedics hauled a gurney out of the back of one of the vehicles, and wheeled it towards Jeanie. Beth stepped aside, and the ambos carefully moved their patient on to the stretcher, arranging the oxygen and monitors around her.

Activity buzzed around the informal control post the area had become. There were brief discussions, hurried phone calls, and a few people came and went. One of the firefighters came to report, and Karl Sauer returned, then both of them went straight to Kris. Even with Fraser there, even with the ambos and each of the emergency services having their own senior officer, she seemed to be at the centre of everything. They all reported to her, or consulted with her, and she handled it with a down-to-earth efficiency.

And all the while she didn't forget him. With the light behind her, he couldn't see her face as she approached. But when she stopped beside him, her tired attempt at a smile came naturally enough.

"Would you like to see Jeanie before she goes? The helicopter's only ten minutes or so away."

The considerate gesture threw him for a moment. With so much else to attend to, she'd thought of him.

Did he want to see Jeanie? No, not lying still and helpless, instead of bright and healthy as she'd always been. But he owed her, and with the future so uncertain for both of them, he couldn't just let her go.

"Yes. Thanks." The words scraped in his raw throat.

Jeanie seemed tiny under the white blanket on the stretcher, her head and neck encased in a padded immobiliser, her face obscured by the oxygen mask.

"*You're strong enough to get through this.*" They were her words, after the committal hearing all those years ago, when they were about to take him to prison.

He wanted to tell her the same thing, but the senior paramedic hovered nearby, and he didn't know if it would be stupid to talk to an unconscious woman.

He laid his hand carefully on the bony shoulder under the sheet, and spoke to the paramedic instead. "Tell them to look after her. She's tougher than she looks. She's strong enough to get through this, and she won't give up."

"Yep, mate, she's a fighter." The paramedic grinned. "I've known her a few years. Bloody stubborn when she makes up her mind, our Jeanie. They're a good team at Tamworth, and they'll give her their best."

Gil took one last look at Jeanie, then went and found Kris, waiting while she finished giving instructions to one of the coppers.

"Is someone going with Jeanie?" he asked her. He hated to think of Jeanie going alone to a strange hospital, in a strange town a few hundred kilometres away. And he couldn't just leave the photo with her — it could too easily be lost, with no-one to look after it.

"There's no room in the chopper for an extra, but Dave Butler from the pub is going to drive his mother to Tamworth tonight. Nancy will stay with her."

Gil vaguely remembered Nancy, an older woman who'd spent most of her time in the pub kitchen, while her husband Stan manned the bar. Last night he hadn't picked Dave as their son — but when he'd left Dungirri, Dave had been just a kid of six or seven.

Kris touched a light hand to his arm. "Do you want to give her the photo, for Jeanie? They're close friends, and since Nancy lost her husband a few months back, she'll understand its importance and take good care of it."

Her perception, the way she answered questions before he'd formed them, despite all the other matters demanding her attention, impressed him yet again.

"Nancy's place is two doors down from here." She pointed back down the road past Ward's. "The fire's almost out now, so I let her go home to pack a few things. You can go and give it to her." About to turn away to where Steve waited to speak to her, she added, "Don't disappear, hey? We need to go over a few things later."

He nodded in agreement, although he didn't look forward to the prospect of "going over" things.

A flustered voice calling "Just a minute" answered his knock on Nancy Butler's door, but it was nearer two minutes before the outside light flooded the porch and the door opened.

When her red-rimmed eyes focused through the screen door on him, Nancy took a step backwards.

"What do *you* want?"

He wished he'd pulled the photo out of his jacket before now, because the way she was looking at him, she'd probably think he was going for a gun.

Anger brewed in him, but he reined it in. Given his reputation and his arrest on suspicion of murder earlier that day — the whole town would know about that by now — expressing his bitterness wouldn't do a damned thing to change their attitudes.

"Mrs Butler," he began, using the formal address in an attempt to allay her suspicion. "I managed to save a photo of Jeanie and her husband. I . . . Could you take it for her?"

He reached for the photo slowly, holding his jacket wide so she could see what he was doing. She inched the screen door open, took the photo, and yanked it shut again.

"You got this photo? When? How?"

"When the sergeant and I were getting her out of her place."

"You? But it was Karl who rescued her."

148

So, that was how the story was going around. No wonder, since it was Karl who'd carried her away from the fire, making the perfect picture of a local hero.

"Karl . . . helped. When he got there." He didn't downplay the man's contributions. No doubt Sauer would have walked into the burning building, too, if necessary.

"Jeanie will need some money. I'll give you what cash I've got." He pulled his wallet from his jeans pocket and found he still had three hundred dollars left. That would cover some nightdresses, a few clothes, enough to get her by for a couple of days until he made it to Tamworth, or made other arrangements. He held the notes out to Nancy. "Please get her whatever she needs."

Her lips pursed, the woman took the money, neatening the notes and folding them in half together.

"You can trust me," she said, almost as an accusation, as if she wanted him to know she didn't entirely trust him.

"I know I can." He spoke the truth. Nancy Butler didn't like *him*, but her affection for her friend would see to Jeanie's best interests.

The door shut firmly before he'd finished stepping off the porch.

The thwack of the rotors reverberated in Kris's head as the helicopter gained height and circled around to head east to Tamworth, with Jeanie on board.

If anyone asked why her eyes were moist, she'd blame it on the dust blown around by the chopper. But no-one asked. A subdued mood settled on the paramedics and the SES crew, now that their task was completed. With the fire reduced to embers, and under the constant watch of the RFS and the police, the danger had passed. From all reports, there wasn't much left to burn. She thanked the SES and ambulance crews for their work, and sent them home.

She walked with Beth across the paddock to her place. Neither of them spoke much, but it was peaceful, in a way, to have the few quiet minutes of space with a friend, where she didn't have to be in charge. The clear night air and the easy pace eased her breathing even further.

Ryan waited on the back veranda, taking Beth's hand as soon as she was in reach. "You look bushed, Kris," he said. "Do you want to come in for a bit?"

The thought of stopping for a while in undemanding company tempted her, but she regretfully shook her head.

"Thanks, but I've got to go and tell the evacuees at the hall that they can go home. Then get reports written, and the investigation started."

She headed down Scrub Road, back towards the police station and the hall. The gravel crunched under her boots, and although she had too much to do, she didn't hurry. She had a task that could use this time as she walked.

She flipped open her phone and dialled Bella O'Connell's number.

She'd first met Bella on a police training course in Sydney, four or five years back, and they'd quickly become friends. Although Bella worked then as a detective in Tamworth, she'd grown up in Dungirri and knew the area well. When young Jess Sutherland disappeared after school, one summer afternoon almost two years ago, Kris had recommended to the area commander that Bella be seconded to the police team.

That investigation had ended in disaster, with Jess murdered, and Bella seriously injured trying to protect a suspect. Yet she'd returned last year, and at least then the outcome had been positive — to a degree. Beth and Ryan's little girl, Tanya, had been rescued, relatively unharmed by her ordeal, but two local men had been murdered, their deaths adding to the toll of murders and suicides that had traumatised the town since the first abduction.

Kris only thought to check the time as the ringing tone sounded in her ear, realising it was past ten o'clock at the same moment as Bella answered.

"Sorry to call you so late, Bella. But something's happened, and I wanted to let you know before you heard it elsewhere."

"Is it Delphi?" Anxiety clear in her voice, Bella asked after her aunt, who lived a few kilometres out of town. "Is something wrong with her?"

"Delphi's fine. It's Jeanie, Bella. She's being airlifted to Tamworth hospital. There was an explosion at the café this evening, and she was injured." She explained quickly, giving what details she could about Jeanie's condition.

151

"I'll call the hospital first thing tomorrow," Bella said. "But the explosion . . . what happened? Was it an accident or suspicious?"

Despite Bella's resignation from the police force to pursue a research career, she still thought like a detective.

"Highly suspicious," Kris answered. "Arson squad is on its way."

"But who . . .? Why Jeanie's place?"

The breeze rustled the leaves in the trees by the creek, and in the moonlight a night bird of some sort flapped across the road in front of her.

"It's a long story, Bella," she said after a moment. "The short version is that Gil Gillespie came back to town last night, and inadvertently brought some Sydney mafia trouble with him."

"Morgan Gillespie? Des's son?"

"Yes. Did you know him?"

"Not well. I haven't seen him since I was a teenager. But you need to talk to Alec. I know he met Gillespie in Sydney, had some dealings with him. And if there's mafia involved, Alec might be able to advise you. He won't be home until late tonight, but I'll get him to call you in the morning."

"Thanks, Bella. Hey, how is everything with you two?"

She could hear the smile in her friend's voice. "Good," Bella said. "Very, very good."

Kris grinned at the phone as they finished the call, pleased to hear Bella so content. But she slowed her steps as Bella's earlier words came back, her thoughts whirling. *Dealings*. Alec Goddard had had dealings with Gil, in Sydney.

Before his promotion to the Commander's position on the north coast six months ago, Alec had led a team at State Crime Command in Sydney, specialising in organised crime. She'd met him — as had Bella — when he'd been appointed to lead the investigation into Tanya's abduction. In the harrowing days while they'd searched for the child and hunted a killer, Alec had earned Kris's respect — for his investigative skills and leadership of the police team, his interactions with the broader community, and for his integrity.

But as soon as the Dungirri case was over, and Tanya had been found, he'd been called back to Sydney for another major investigation. And Kris knew — because she'd followed the news almost as closely as Bella — that he'd wrapped up that case after arresting two corrupt police officers. The pieces were fitting together. Gil had passed on information about corrupt officers. Alec had had dealings with Gil. One and one had to equal two.

Yes, she definitely wanted to talk with Alec.

Maybe she'd get more background from him than she had from Joe Petric. Joe had worked with him, before Alec's promotion, and while Joe had said today that he'd come across Gil in general enquiries, he'd given no indication of more than that. He might not have known about Gil's information — Alec would likely keep the identity of an informant secret, especially in such a sensitive situation — but Joe had been less than forthcoming about other aspects of the circumstances around Marci's death. The lack of information might be no more than a touch of arrogance, a power-playing game to keep the local cops in their place.

But Kris could play that game too to get to the bottom of a crime, and with direct access to Alec Goddard, she intended to use it.

She turned off Scrub Road to take the short-cut across vacant blocks to the police station. Beyond the station, the hall was lit up, and between the hall and the creek a group of evacuees were usefully filling in time by erecting the marquee that had been hired for the ball.

It was mostly the younger guys involved. Sean Barrett, with a few beers under his belt, Karl's cousins, Luke and Jake, and the three Dawson boys all cheerfully argued about the process. Melinda Ward and Heidi Sauer resignedly held on to two of the corner poles as the testosterone flowed, while Angie Butler, mug in hand, propped up a corner of the hall, laughing and trading friendly insults with the lads.

Kris left them to it, and went inside. A few tables and chairs had been set up at the kitchen end of the large space, and someone had pulled out the urn and opened the Progress Association's tea and coffee supplies.

A couple of dozen adults sat around the tables, the majority of them well past their middle years. Most of the younger, fitter residents were out with the RFS and the SES, like Karl and Paul, and his wife Chloe. Jim Barrett and George Pappas were leading their assorted grandkids in a noisy game of blindman's bluff, but they

154

stopped when Kris walked in, leaving Andrew Pappas's eldest in charge of the game while they joined the adults to hear the news.

She declined Mark's offer of a seat. She wouldn't be here long, and if she sat down, she might never stand up again.

"Jeanie is safely on the flight to Tamworth," she told the group. "She's still unconscious, but her vital signs are reasonable. We won't know anything more until at least the morning."

"But do you think she'll be okay?" Joy Dawson asked.

Kris hesitated. She'd already given more information than the standard police report, but this was a small community, under pressure, and most of these people had known Jeanie for their entire lives. There'd be talk, and anxious worrying, and it would be better if it was based on fact, rather than speculation.

So she answered honestly. "I don't know, Joy. She has a head injury, and her heart stopped for a little while. She also probably inhaled a lot of smoke, and there may be other injuries we don't know about. It could all be minor, and she might be sitting up in bed in the morning eating breakfast, or it might not. There's simply no way any of us can know, at this point. We're just going to have to be patient and wait for news."

She heard footsteps behind her on the wooden floor.

"Did that bastard Gillespie start the fire?" Sean Barrett demanded.

She summoned up the energy to turn slowly and pin him with her glare.

"No, Sean, Gillespie didn't start the fire," she said firmly, to squelch any rumours. "He was with me most of the evening."

A slow, sly grin twisted his mouth. "With you, huh?"

The insinuation ignited her temper. Jim and Paul Barrett might be occasionally hot-headed and cagey around authority, but they both worked hard, and contributed to the community in their own ways, and she could respect them for that. Sean Barrett was another matter entirely.

She spoke coldly and deliberately, so there could be no misunderstanding of either the facts or her attitude towards his suggestion. "Gillespie was voluntarily giving his time to assist with a police investigation."

She turned away from him to speak to the rest of them. "You might not be aware that when we heard the explosion, Morgan Gillespie ran straight there, going into the burning building to rescue Jeanie, with no thought for his own safety. His actions saved Jeanie's life."

She let that sink in for a moment, watching the faces, the exchange of glances. The news certainly discomforted some of them, puzzled others. Years of prejudice was going to take some shifting.

"If any of you witnessed anything," she continued, "or have any information about how the fire started, I'd like you to come over to the station."

Blank looks and shaking heads answered the question.

156

"We'd just started playing cards," Tom Trevelyn said, indicating Jim and Frank Williams, the usual Friday night card crew. "Then we heard the bang."

"Eleni and I, we were watching TV," George Pappas volunteered. They lived behind the store they'd run for decades. "We too heard the bang."

It seemed that no-one had seen anything. Those who'd been at the working bee at the hall had either gone straight home or, like Jim and his mates, had gone to the pub.

She stifled a disheartened sigh. "Okay, thanks, everyone. The fire's contained now, and the RFS will keep watch on the embers all night, so it's safe for you to return to your homes. Thank you all for your cooperation in the evacuation. I know it must have been a worrying time for you."

She pulled her cardigan around her as she stepped out again into the evening air, the aroma of smoke that clung to it scratching her eyes. The post-adrenaline let-down had settled in, making her feel the chill more, and long for a warm bed and oblivion. But Adam and Steve would be waiting for her in the station, and there were too many questions that needed to be answered to even think about resting yet.

No-one had followed her from the the Wilsons' place. Well, no-one except him. Maybe she'd forgotten, or was disregarding, the threatening text message, but Gil wasn't. The situation had escalated far too fast to take any risks.

He waited until she emerged from the hall before he stepped out from the shadows of the gum tree in her backyard.

"You shouldn't be wandering around in the dark alone, Blue."

She waved her hand at the spotlights glowing from the eaves of the hall. "It's hardly dark. And it's probably a whole fifteen metres to my place."

"It's dark on Scrub Road," he pointed out.

"Not with a good moon. And there are a dozen houses along the road," she retorted with a sharp edge. But the edge blunted when she added, "Don't creep around behind me, Gillespie. I might mistake you for a thug."

He'd half-expected her to be angry. He'd known her less than twenty-four hours, didn't have any right to play the protector, especially for a capable police officer. But he couldn't shake off his fear for her, and wouldn't risk contemplating why it was so strong.

He changed the subject to more practical, logical matters. "The text message . . . could they trace the sender?"

"No luck. I got the report a short while ago. It was a pre-paid phone, owned by a Sydney school kid who lost it last week. The message was sent from somewhere in the Birraga area, but the phone's now gone dead, so we can't trace its whereabouts. They've probably tossed it in the bush somewhere, impossible to find."

Inside the station, the interview room seemed smaller with Fraser and Adam seated at the table. Claustrophobic, almost, particularly with both of them looking at him. Gil made his face expressionless, and wished himself anywhere but there.

Kris pulled out one of the two remaining chairs and sank on to it, with a steadying hand on the table. Gil reluctantly took the other, nearest the door.

Fraser took the lead, casting Gil a guarded look, but not objecting to his presence. "Adam's updated me, Kris, on what you discovered tonight. So we're all agreed that the circumstances of the fire are suspicious."

"Did you have a look at the site, Steve? Anything obvious there?"

"I'm no expert, and the place is still too hot to go right in, but the RFS guys think it started in the office, and there are signs of accelerant in that area. It's just as well Adam copied those images because the chances of there being anything salvageable from the computer are bugger all."

"What about the garbage skip?" Kris asked. "It was at the other end of the building."

"It's a heap of molten plastic," Adam replied. "Forensics might be able to get something from it, but it will take them a lot of time and processing."

"Shit." Kris closed her eyes briefly in frustration.

Fraser leaned forward. "Did you see anyone around when you were down there, Adam? Or you, Gillespie?"

"A couple of truckies," Adam said. "Nobody I knew. They left around the time I did."

"They were there when I was there, earlier on." Gil spoke for the first time. "They probably heard me talking with Jeanie about the security cameras."

"And me, too," said Adam. "In fact, when we were leaving, one of them asked me about the 'excitement' this morning. The news will be all around the district, and I didn't think of it as anything more than a casual query."

"Did either of you see who the trucks belonged to?" Kris asked. "A transport company?"

Gil hadn't noticed — the trucks had just been shapes in the dark — but Adam had.

"One of them at least was a Flanagan's truck."

Flanagan. The name hit Gil like a physical blow, and some of the puzzle pieces slammed into place in a recognisable picture, dark and threatening.

"Flanagan's?" he asked sharply. "As in Dan Flanagan?"

"Dan Flanagan and sons, these days," Kris answered. "Brian and Kevin are both involved in the family businesses. Irrigation equipment, earthmoving, harvesting and transport. Flanagan's Agricultural Company has a virtual monopoly for the entire region. And, with the drought bankrupting many graziers, Flanagan's has been buying up properties these past few years. Across the northwest, and in to Queensland."

"What do you know of him, Gillespie?" Fraser demanded.

"Flanagan got his start working for the 'Ndrangheta in rural Queensland in the early nineteen-sixties," he said, uncomfortable about drawing everyone's attention, but ploughing on anyway. "Extortion and blackmail were his main focus back then. He came here in the late sixties, and within a few years he was

160

managing a pretty large marijuana production network for the mob."

Kris frowned, studying him. "I've heard some stories about Flanagan and his family over the years, but nobody's ever produced facts, evidence or witnesses. Have you got anything more than hearsay to connect him with organised crime?"

He respected her for needing evidence, at the same time as he worried about all she didn't know.

"Flanagan is careful. Those who cooperate aren't pressed too hard; there can even be benefits to having someone as influential as Flanagan on-side. But he uses fear to keep people silent. Getting on his wrong side is dangerous, and he doesn't hesitate to act on his threats. I could suggest names of people to ask, but chances are they'd deny they know anything."

"So how do you know all this?" Fraser challenged him, folding his arms and staring. "You left here a bloody long time ago."

The challenge held an edge that made Gil even more wary. He gathered from a conversation he'd overhead in Birraga, that Fraser was usually based in Moree. But by the way Kris had described Flanagan's expanding business interests, nowhere in the northwest — and no cop — would be out of potential reach of his influence.

Steve Fraser displayed a brash confidence that bordered on arrogance, and an attitude that suggested he didn't have much time for authority. Not a combination that Gil felt inclined to trust. Fraser couldn't be suspected of passing on the information about the security footage, because Kris hadn't had

161

time to inform him before the fire, but he'd had plenty of opportunity during the afternoon to leak other details about the investigation — including the fact of Kris's alibi.

Still, both Kris and Adam seemed comfortable with him, despite the occasional hint of annoyance in Kris's body language. Annoyance, not distrust.

Gil had to rely on her judgement.

"My old man ran a portable sawmill," he explained, "so we worked all around the district, felling trees for landholders and sawing timber. Other than a 'donated' load of lumber every now and again, we didn't have much business with Flanagan, but I kept my eyes open and my mouth shut. I didn't go to school much after fourteen or so, but a few of the guys I'd known there ended up working for Flanagan. I saw them around here and there, and sometimes they didn't keep as quiet as they should have."

"So, what's the connection with the mafia? Last I heard, 'Flanagan' wasn't an Italian name."

Gil responded to the question, not Fraser's sarcasm. "There's plenty of organised crime run by Australians. But as far as Flanagan goes, I didn't find out all his history and connections until years later."

Not until the day he'd delivered a couple of cases of single-malt scotch to the Russo family Christmas party, and come face to face with Dan and his sons.

He met Kris's earnest stare for a moment before he transferred his attention back to Fraser, and explained. "I bumped into him when he came to visit his brother-in-law in Sydney."

162

"His brother-in-law?" The question seemed genuine. Fraser either didn't have a clue who Flanagan was, or he was a damn good actor.

"Yes. Dan's wife was Gianni Russo's twin sister."

CHAPTER
NINE

He should have left when the others did. There wasn't much more that could be done; the fire site was secure, guarded by Birraga police officers, waiting for the arson investigators and forensic team. Both he and Adam had given descriptions of the two truckies, and Steve Fraser would attempt to follow up those with the Flanagan Agricultural Company in the morning. No-one expected he'd find out much. Fraser had headed back to Birraga, and Adam had finally been ordered off-duty and home.

Kris tried to hold back a yawn as she closed the door behind Adam, and failed. She had to be near collapse from exhaustion, and she moved stiffly, wincing in pain from her injuries.

"I should go," Gil said.

"To where?" Her blunt question echoed his own thoughts. "If Jeanie's cabin isn't a heap of ashes, it will still be off-limits. And last time I looked your father's hut wasn't in any fit state to stay in. So you might as well just sleep in my spare room again."

"Is that wise?"

"Wise?" She raised an eyebrow. "Seems to me that given the threats and the day we've both had, it makes more sense than you staying alone in the pub, and me staying alone here. If anyone comes looking for us, or we develop any after-effects from the smoke, at least this way there'll be someone nearby."

There were still reasons why he should refuse — to protect her from insinuation and gossip, and from association with him — but only one overriding reason to stay: to protect her from harm.

Jeanie had almost died, and he still didn't know if the fire was set to eliminate evidence, or to punish her for supporting him. Maybe both. Kris had spoken out in support of him too many times already, and that information would have made it back to whoever was pulling the strings. With it likely that Flanagan's local resources were involved now, there was no way could he leave her alone and vulnerable in her house overnight.

He nodded and muttered his thanks, following her down the short corridor to her residence.

She raised her arm to lock the connecting door, sniffed at her sleeve and grimaced. "Sheesh. These clothes smell like a bad barbeque. And yours are probably the only ones you have. Toss them outside the door when you go to bed, and I'll run them through the washer with mine. If I hang them up tonight, they should be dry by morning."

It was a good plan, except for the fact that she was almost asleep on her feet. He stuffed his hands into his pockets and resisted the urge to pick her up and carry her to her room.

"You go to bed, Blue. I've worked nights for years, and I don't usually sleep until the bats go home to roost, so I'll stay up to hang out the washing."

She was tired enough not to argue. "I've got some old cargo shorts that will probably fit you. And I'll find a T-shirt. They're not much but . . ." She turned away, the words trailing off.

But it's better than wandering around her place stark naked, he finished the sentence in his head. Being naked anywhere near her would definitely be a bad idea.

Morning came far too early for Kris. The vivid dream of hot sex in the middle of a blazing building ended when the building collapsed, jerking her awake with a half-muttered cry. No need to question where *those* images had come from.

Her hair under her face smelt of smoke. Her pillow smelt of smoke. With an effort, she pushed herself upright in bed, every muscle in her body moaning in protest, with even her gut roiling, as if she had a hangover.

She hated mornings at the best of times, and this morning certainly didn't qualify as a good one. She'd feel better when she got moving, she promised herself, in an attempt to find the motivation to get up out of bed. It wasn't too much of a lie — she couldn't, at any rate, feel much worse.

The door to Gillespie's room was still shut and as she stumbled to the shower there was only silence in the house. Good. She might have a chance to become

166

human again before he woke up. The shower helped a little to loosen her stiff muscles, and afterwards she used up most of Beth's pot of bruise cream on the multiple bruises darkening on her body.

She studied her arms in the bathroom mirror. The bloody grazes and dark bruises would be blatantly obvious with her ball dress tonight. Just as well she had no ambitions of being the belle of the ball. The sooner the ball was over, the better, as far as she was concerned.

The official roster had her off-duty for the next five days, but she dragged on her uniform. Responsibilities and rosters didn't always coincide in a bush posting.

As she buckled on her belt, someone knocked loudly on the back door. Mindful of Gil's warning, she glanced out of the window. On the back step stood a young woman, maybe twenty-five or thirty, neatly dressed in black trousers and a softly patterned shirt, her long brown hair braided. Behind her, a younger man waited, Asian in appearance, also neat in trousers and white shirt.

"Have you got Gil here?" the woman demanded, the moment Kris opened the door.

The woman's glare almost matched her own, but even on a morning like today, Kris could summon her sergeant's stare to outdo the best.

"You are . . . ?"

"Deborah Taylor. Gil's my boss. Was my boss, I mean. Until the other day, when the new owners took over. Look, I know Gil," she rushed on. "He wouldn't have murdered Marci. Not that he didn't have more than enough reason to throttle the lying, conniving user of a bitch, and probably should have, but he never did. Okay, maybe a firm grip on her arm to escort her out of the pub sometimes when she was pissed and kicking up a stink, but nothing more than that. Ever."

"It's okay, Deb." Gil's voice came from behind, and the woman, Deb, audibly breathed a sigh of relief.

Sighing wasn't exactly what came to mind when Kris glanced around at Gil. She'd found clothes for him last night — a T-shirt, and Hugh's old hiking shorts, that he'd inadvertently left at her place that last weekend, years ago, that she'd never quite been able to toss out.

Maybe it was the white T-shirt that softened Gil's appearance, despite his rough, unshaven face. Other than yesterday morning's brief aberration, she'd only seen him in black. And maybe it was seeing him in her brother's old cargoes, temporarily jumbling her thoughts with old memories and grief, and not the sight of naked feet and calves and shorts riding low on slim hips that stole coherent words from her head.

Fortunately, he didn't have a muting effect on Deborah.

"Gil! Some guy down the road said you were here, that they should be locking you up."

"Everything's fine." He held up his hands to her view. "See, no handcuffs. Deb, this is Sergeant Kris Matthews. She hasn't arrested me, so there's no need to do your Doberman impersonation."

The laconic, dry humour and the absence of Gil's usual guardedness spelled friendship and affection, although probably not intimacy, since neither of them

168

made any effort to touch the other. Kris pulled together what she knew of the woman so far. His former employee. With a black belt in karate, who'd been attacked two days ago in her home. Pretty and assertive and fond enough of Gil to confront a police officer to defend him.

The young man stepped forward with an easy confidence and pleasant smile, his hand outstretched to shake hers. "I'm Liam Le. Please forgive us for calling in so early, Sergeant. We were worried about Gil."

Kris found herself smiling back at him. She didn't know what his job had been, but she imagined running a successful pub required at least one person with public relations skills, and this lad had more than enough charm for the three of them.

"I didn't expect you two until later today," Gil said bluntly.

Deb shrugged. "We left last night, as soon as we could after you phoned. We shared the driving, and stopped for a couple of hours by the road."

Loyalty. Kris added it to the affection and friendship she'd already noted. It spoke a lot for Gil that these two young people retained such a strong personal allegiance to him. She couldn't think of many people, other than Bella and Alec, who'd drive for eight hours overnight at the drop of a hat if she was in trouble.

She gave them a few minutes of privacy by heading outside to check the clothes Gil had hung out on the washing line the night before. The dry night and the early morning sunshine had done their job, and even the thicker pockets of their jeans were dry.

There was a stack of work waiting for her, and Sandy Cunningham and the arson investigator might already be on site, but she selfishly took the time in the freshness of the sunshine to unpeg and fold the jeans, T-shirts, underwear and socks, the cloth sunlight-warm on her aching hands, a small, simple pleasure in what would undoubtedly be a demanding day.

And now that he had transport, Gil would likely leave soon. The realisation left an emptiness, although his departure had to be for the best — for him, for Dungirri, for herself. The absolute last thing *she* needed was the distraction of an impossible man to highlight the loneliness of her solitary, workaholic life.

Maybe she should get a dog. Bella had Finn, a devoted, if at times dopey, German Shepherd who'd kept her sane through bad times and good. A dog like Finn would be good company.

She stifled a sardonic laugh. A dog. She was actually contemplating getting a dog. That definitely counted as a sign of middle-aged, single desperation.

She hoisted the laundry basket to her hip, and caught sight of Beth walking down the road towards her. She waited, poised there, idly watching a family of small wrens flitting around a low branch in the gum tree, until Beth reached her.

"Can you spare a minute, Kris?" Beth asked, the tiredness in her eyes undermining her wan smile. "We've got a bit of a problem."

Gil gave Liam and Deb a brief summary of the previous night's dramas, but all the while at least half

170

his attention was on the scene out the window. Standing at the bench, making coffee, gave him excuse enough to keep Kris in his sight.

It felt somewhat disconcerting — the contrast of the police uniform, and all it signified in his mind, and the quietly domestic, feminine stance with the basket on her hip; two images that didn't fit together in his experience.

But then somehow the two images slid together, melded, and he saw just Kris, police officer *and* woman, independent, strong and proud.

Whatever Beth was telling her, it wiped away the calm expression that had softened her face just a few moments before. But he read frustration, more than worry, in the way she huffed her breath out, and jammed breeze-blown hair behind her ear with her free hand.

"This Jeanie, I gather she's important to you, Gil?"

Deb's question dragged his attention back, although it took a moment for his brain to relate the words to Jeanie, rather than Kris.

"Yes. She gave me my first real job. And she helped me, when I needed it. She's . . ." He searched for words, couldn't find adequate ones. "She's the kind of person who holds a town like this together."

And two more of them were out there, in the backyard. Courage, he thought. But it was more than physical courage. Emotional courage and compassion, the strength and determination to stand with the community, long term, and to stand up to them too, when necessary.

"So, what's the plan?" Liam asked. "Do you have to stay here, or are we going back to Sydney?"

He mulled over Liam's question while he pushed the plunger down slowly. Last night, before the fire, the decision had seemed clear — he'd leave here as soon as he could. But later, lying awake in the dark, leaving didn't seem such a good idea — at least, not until he knew more about what he was up against, and whether the threat to Kris was serious.

He'd have more chance keeping informed about the police investigation by staying in Dungirri. If he went back to Sydney, he'd be working alone.

And, he acknowledged to himself, there'd be a certain amount of satisfaction in staring back at some of Dungirri's residents, showing them he had nothing to hide.

"I want to stay here for a day or so longer, see if I can get any info from the forensic reports on Marci, and on the fire. But I need to get a vehicle." He hated being trapped, reliant on others. "There's a chance I might be able to pick up something in Birraga this morning, but if there is a car dealer there, they'll probably close at noon."

"You can use my car whenever you need it," Liam offered.

"Thanks, but you'll need it yourself." Because Liam and Deb wouldn't be going back to Sydney with him. They could stay here for today, while he found out some more about what was going on, but he wanted them going somewhere else, safer, when he went back to Sydney.

Outside, Beth was leaving, and he held the door open for Kris.

"Any word on Jeanie?" he asked.

"She's okay. Awake, and talking, and with no major damage. They're a little worried about her heart, though. There could be some underlying problem. They're going to run some tests over the next few days." She let out a sigh. "I'm glad in a way. I'd been worried about her. She's been very tired lately, but she kept saying it was nothing. Now they'll find out if something is wrong, and treat it."

Whatever Jeanie needed, she'd have, he resolved. The best specialists, private hospital if she needed surgery. They could do amazing things these days with hearts, and although he still worried, it wasn't at the same level as before.

Probably unaware of it, Kris let out another huff of breath.

"There's other trouble?" he prompted.

She paused on her way through to the laundry, shifting the basket to her other hip. "Jeanie was catering for the supper for the ball tonight, and all the supplies and everything she'd prepared were at the café. With Jeanie in hospital and Nancy Butler with her, there's no-one with any experience in catering to organise replacement food, even if Birraga has things in stock. There's a meeting at the pub shortly to decide what to do, but since there's less than twelve hours now before the ball starts, I'm afraid they'll end up buying a stack of frozen party pies."

Deb echoed her, aghast, "*Party pies?*"

"Okay, it probably won't be that bad," Kris conceded, with an unsteady laugh. "This town can band together to produce food when needed, but barbecued sausages and Eleni Pappas's lamingtons aren't quite the supper Jeanie had planned." Her voice caught, and she turned her head away sharply, digging in her pocket for a handkerchief, her cheeks flushing red.

"I'm sorry." She blew her nose, shaking her head at herself. "It's so stupid. I didn't even want this bloody ball. But it was supposed to be something special, to build morale and community pride, and now . . . now I'm afraid that without Jeanie it will be a disaster."

Her voice cracking, she turned on her heel and left the room.

Since Gil had met her, Kris had been strong; resilient and professional in the face of murder, capable and focused in the terror of the fire. But now defeat and self-doubt sat heavily on her shoulders and shadowed her eyes, and he saw the cost of the long struggle she'd endured, providing leadership and hope through all the community's traumas.

When she'd first mentioned the ball the other night, the idea of a ball in Dungirri had seemed so ridiculous he'd dismissed it from his mind. Some country towns had an elegant social set, the type of people featured in country fashion magazines, people with wealth, position, social standing. Dungirri wasn't one of those towns. Mark Strelitz and his parents, wealthy landholders, came the closest. Beth's parents moved professionally in social circles, due to Harry Fletcher's

174

veterinary work in livestock research, and old Doctor Russell and his wife had always upheld old-fashioned standards, but the rest of the town was decidedly working-class, with more than its share of battlers. He'd bet that Mark and Doctor Russell were the only men in town who wore a suit to anything but funerals.

Funerals. There'd been too many of those in recent years, in disturbing circumstances, and it struck Gil that rather than some ridiculous aberration, maybe this ball was a desperate claim for community pride and self-respect — for something to celebrate, instead of mourn.

All the more reason for it to succeed. He didn't give a flying fig about most of Dungirri, but he did about Jeanie, and he worried about Kris. She already carried far too many burdens, and his arrival had only added to them. He wished he could reassure her that it would work out, that Dungirri people could turn things around, deal with the challenge positively and not go to pieces. He just wasn't sure if they could.

"Should I offer to help, Gil?" Deb asked in a whisper. "If you think I should, I will. If it matters to you."

If it mattered to him . . . It mattered to Jeanie, to Kris. Maybe that made it the same thing, for him. But her offer wasn't a simple solution.

"You're an outsider, Deb," Gil warned her, "plus you're connected to me, and most of them won't like that at all. Maybe letting them solve the problem themselves might be better."

The warnings only made Deb more determined. "I wouldn't tread on any toes. And unless you've got other plans for us for the day, I've got the time. Besides, I'm suffering from kitchen withdrawal. I haven't cooked anything for days."

"Don't get too excited. Remember, this isn't the city. The only decently equipped kitchen in town is now a pile of rubble. As for supplies, Birraga's sixty kilometres away, with one small independent supermarket that will never have seen at least half the ingredients you probably use every day."

"So?" Deb grinned with dangerous zeal. "I like a challenge."

He shrugged, and didn't try to talk her out of it. It would keep her occupied, out of trouble and, truth was, if anyone could pull it off — short notice, limited supplies, and strange, likely ill-equipped kitchen — it would be Deb. She had a rare blend of pragmatism and imagination and, unlike some chefs he'd known, her ego was healthy but not bloated. And she didn't just like a challenge, she relished it. Her energy and enthusiasm might even be enough to rise above the locals' prejudice over her connection to him.

Kris walked into the room, brisk and business-like, and passed him a neat pile of his clothes, without meeting his eyes.

Deb spoke up. "Sergeant, maybe I can help with the catering problem, since we're staying here for a day or two. I'm a chef. I've done plenty of catering for functions."

"Could you?" The wild hope shone in Kris's eyes for a moment, then dimmed. "But there's no supplies, and I don't know what the committee will want to do . . . There's only the pub kitchen, or the hall, and that's pretty basic. They might just go for everyone bringing a plate."

"How about I go along to the meeting, make the offer if it seems appropriate, and see what happens?" Deb suggested tactfully, and despite his reservations about the whole idea, Gil felt proud of her.

Kris offered to take Deb to the pub and introduce her, and Liam went with them. Gil had no qualms about Liam mixing with the locals; the guy had a natural, easy way about him, with a tact and diplomacy Gil rarely bothered with. People generally trusted Liam, and often talked openly with him; that had proved to be a useful skill, time and again. He'd probably come back with a good sense of the town's reaction to the fire, what they were saying and thinking.

The house fell silent after they'd left. Being in Kris's place, alone, didn't feel right, in spite of her invitation to make himself at home. On top of the disconcerting sense of intruding, the plans he'd made for the day kept changing, being revised, and the uncertainty and the risks hung over his head, with no clear way to deal with them. Combined with another bad night's sleep, it didn't encourage the best of moods.

Still, there was no point sitting around staring uselessly at the walls. A shower helped to clear the smell of smoke from his nostrils, and the steam and warmth must have relaxed smoke-strained airways, because his breathing came effortlessly afterwards. He changed back into his jeans and T-shirt, more comfortable in his own clothes than some other guy's shorts. Not his business who they'd belonged to.

With time to fill in before the others would be back, he sat at the table and pulled over the writing pad Kris had left there last night. Ripping a page off it, he turned it sideways and wrote four names as headings across the top — Vince, Marci, his own, and Jeanie. Under each of the headings, he jotted down names of people who might have a motive to harm them.

Before long, he had three or four possibilities for each of them — all capable of violence, all capable of killing, and all with significant resources. But it was their links that concerned him most. Each of the possible suspects had connections to the others. From whichever way he viewed it, he wasn't up against one person, but a web. Now he just had to work out who was the deadliest spider, and when they'd come for him.

CHAPTER
TEN

When Kris arrived at the Progress Association meeting with Deb and Liam, Angie Butler had just stepped forward, quelling the panicked chatter by offering to do the cooking, assuring everyone with a cheerful laugh that she'd learned a thing or two since she'd helped her mother in the pub as a teenager.

"It won't be anything fancy, folks," she announced, "but I probably won't poison you."

With the crisis averted, the committee dispersed, and Kris introduced Deb and Liam to Angie, who leapt on their offer of assistance with the down-to-earth practicality and acceptance that Kris had discovered was her natural way, in the month or so since she'd returned to Dungirri. Angie seemed to have no reservations about their connection with Gil; her only comment, when she learned why they were there, was thankfulness that Gil had been in time to rescue Jeanie. The three were much the same age, and Kris left them already on friendly terms, brainstorming menus.

Sandy Cunningham and the arson investigators had yet to arrive, so Kris returned to her place, hoping to grab a bite of breakfast before the day got too busy. As she pushed open her back door, Gil folded a piece of paper and tucked it into his pocket. The move was unhurried, and his carefully blank expression was innocent — maybe too innocent. Her fingers itched to get hold of that piece of paper.

She almost asked about it, then stopped herself. He'd shared a lot of information with her, and if the fragile trust she'd built up with him was going to hold, she needed to keep trusting that he'd tell her what he knew, when he was ready.

"How did the meeting go?" he asked her.

The kitchen bench gave her tired body some support. "There was some panicked talk about cancelling the ball when we got there, especially since most of the good cooks have hair appointments in Birraga for chunks of the day. But Angie Butler volunteered to take over. She's not a trained cook, but she pretty much grew up in the pub kitchen, and helped Nancy a lot before going to university. She was pleased, though, to have Deb and Liam offer to help — and I think a bit relieved."

"People weren't wary because they know me?"

"Most had gone by then. And as far as Angie's concerned, you're a hero."

It might not have gone quite so smoothly, she thought, if the others had not rushed off so quickly. Ironic how some of them distrusted him so much, yet a real evil had remained undetected for years, a trusted member of the community. But that was in the past now, and she had to hope they'd all learned from that experience. At least Beth and Ryan were on Gil's side, and they'd speak up for him. And the fact that he'd

180

saved Jeanie's life had to count for something. Once word got around about that, surely there'd be some respect for him?

"There may be a grumble or two later today," she admitted, "when people realise who's helped Angie, but since no-one else volunteered, they've got no grounds to complain."

He shrugged, unsurprised and accepting. From a few of the comments she'd heard since he arrived, he'd been as outcast as his father all of his life, long before Paula Barrett's death. A cruel thing for a boy to carry, and his lone-wolf wariness probably covered the scars. Yet she was becoming far too aware that he was capable of gentleness, and trust, and respect.

She'd seen that herself, these past days, and Deb and Liam had spent the walk to the pub providing her with glowing character references that confirmed her impressions.

"Is there a car sales yard in Birraga?" he asked.

"Yes, Birraga Autos, east end of the main street. New and used vehicles, but not a huge range. But if you're planning to buy a car, you probably want to know that Birraga Autos is owned by Dan Flanagan's son-in-law."

"Shit. There's nowhere else, I suppose?"

"Not in Birraga."

"F- Damn."

"Can you ride a motorbike?"

"Yeah," he said. "I ride."

"Ryan has a good one that he and Adam have just fixed up to sell. It's years old, but well looked after. Ryan hasn't ridden since his accident, of course, but

Beth uses it sometimes, when Ryan needs the car. Now they're selling it because they need the money."

"I might go and see Ryan, then."

"They live in the old O'Connell place, up on Scrub Road."

"I know." His eyes didn't shift away from hers.

Of course. He'd followed her last night from the Wilsons'. It must have been from some distance back, because she hadn't been aware of him.

She wasn't sure which annoyed her more, the fact that he'd done the he-man protective thing and followed her, or the fact that she hadn't noticed. Probably the latter, if she was going to be honest.

"I didn't need protecting last night," she told him.

"Someone had sent you a death threat. It was a dark road, and you weren't armed."

Before she could argue that she was a trained police officer, he shrugged dismissively and headed to the door.

"It's no big deal, Blue. I was walking down there, anyway." Having calmly claimed the last word, he left.

It occurred to her that she could have countered by observing that he was more at risk than she was, but by then he was already halfway across the back paddock.

Oh, well, they were both probably safe enough, walking around town in broad daylight. And with the supper crisis averted, she had to get back to her real job — make a few calls, and meet with Sandy and the arson investigators at the ruins of the Truck Stop. There were killers and arsonists to catch — if they could.

182

And after that, she'd have to look into Gil's allegations against Dan Flanagan, and find out once and for all whether one of Birraga's leading businessmen was, in fact, up to his neck in crime.

Gil heard voices around the back of the Wilsons' house, and he found Ryan at a small workbench on the veranda, fixing the leg of a doll's chair while his three little girls watched, keeping a steady flow of light chat, explaining what he was doing as he straightened and glued the broken timber.

The quiet family scene was a far cry from Ryan's larrikin youth and the toughness of his early boxing days. Despite the wheelchair, the musculature of his upper body suggested he kept in better shape than most men, and he'd been a force to reckon with the other night, dealing with the Barretts.

Ryan glanced up as Gil approached. The oldest girl immediately sidled close to her father, tucking her hand under his arm. Gil paused on the grass, keeping his distance, conscious that these kids had more reason than most to fear a strange man.

"Hi, Gil," Ryan greeted him with a broad grin. He pushed his chair away from the bench, and all three girls gathered tightly around him, staring at Gil with wide eyes.

"Hi." Gil nodded at the girls, but his experience with children was minimal at best, and he made these ones nervous enough without paying them awkward attention. He came straight to the point of his business.

"Kris tells me you've got a bike to sell. I'm in need of wheels, and a bike would do me fine."

"It's in the shed, if you want to have a look. But mate, I gotta say, she's near on twenty years old." As ever, Ryan dealt straight and honest. "Bought her in my first year of professional boxing. A damned good road bike, and I've looked after it, but you probably want something newer."

"It's registered?"

"Twelve months rego, new tyres and brakes." Ryan reeled off some more details, but Gil had pretty much made up his mind already. When he went into the shed, and pulled the tarpaulin off the gleaming bike, he knew it was the right decision. He'd ridden around Sydney for years on a bike like this one — sturdy, reliable, with guts and good handling, but not flashy or distinctive. A rider in a helmet on this bike could be almost anonymous. Especially in Sydney.

Ryan offered a couple of helmets as part of the deal, and Gil took the bike for a test ride a few kilometres up Scrub Road. Damn, he'd missed riding. With the fresh warm air, the smooth rumble of the engine, and the bush road straight ahead, the temptation to just keep going tugged at him. But he had business to attend to, and he reluctantly turned the bike around.

He made Ryan a good offer as soon as he pulled up in the driveway.

"That's more than I was going to ask for it," Ryan protested.

"It's worth it to me, and what I'd pay in Sydney." And the Wilsons needed the money more than he did, although he wouldn't trample Ryan's pride by saying that aloud. "If you've got internet access, I could transfer the money to your bank now."

The girls had moved under the shade of a large eucalypt, where a tea party seemed to be in progress. Ryan took him into a small study, where an old computer sat on a homemade desk, the shelves above loaded with a mix of management and kids' reference books. Ryan switched the computer on, and pulled over a chair for Gil, positioning himself by the window where he could keep an eye on his daughters in the backyard.

As the computer slowly hummed into life, silence sat between them. Ryan must be wondering — about Marci, about his arrest and release, about the fire — but he didn't broach any of these topics. He'd stuck up for him during the fight the other night, but that was before Marci's body was found. It said a lot for his trust in Kris's judgment that Ryan had invited him inside, was selling him the bike. Wheelchair or not, Ryan would have kicked him off the property the minute he'd arrived if he thought Gil was any danger to his family. Ryan might have run wild for a time, but he'd always looked after what he valued, and the protectiveness and care that had seen him help a painfully shy Beth to her feet when she'd tripped on her first day of high school was even more evident now, with his eyes straying to the window several times a minute, to check on his girls.

Gil was willing to bet that the same protectiveness meant Ryan would have his ear to the ground, and a fair idea of what was going on in the district. Ryan had never succumbed to the rougher, illegal stuff but, like Gil, he knew people who had, years ago.

Gil broke the silence. "Any idea who's in with the Flanagans these days?" he asked quietly.

"The Flanagans?" Ryan raised an eyebrow, cautious.

The computer screen finally flickered into life, and Gil started the browser. "A couple of Flanagan drivers were in the café last night," Gil explained. "I don't know what the cops think, but they're my prime suspects for torching the place."

"Shit." Ryan stayed silent for a moment, and again he looked out the window. Gil navigated to his bank's web page, letting Ryan take his time to choose how to respond.

"I don't know anything for certain," Ryan said after a few moments. "The Flanagans have taken more interest in the Dungirri area this past couple of years. The drought's hit everyone hard, and Dungirri's had its other troubles on top of that. A few of the blokes from here . . ." He swallowed hard. "There were suicides. And a couple of deaths that might have been, might not. Some people left town. Mitch and Sara Sutherland . . . after little Jess died, they sold up. They only had a couple of hundred acres, but Mitch's parents sold up their big place and left, too. Flanagan's Agricultural bought their properties, and a couple of others. They've got more land in this district now than the Strelitz family company has."

Gil let out a low whistle. The Strelitz family had been the local pastoral royalty for the last fifty years.

"The thing is," Ryan continued, "the last twelve months or so, the Flanagans have been investing heavily in improvements — new dams, fencing, sheds, and top breeding lines. Everyone else is tightening their belts, and some are on the edge of bankruptcy. So most of the casual and contract work round here at present is through Flanagan's. And most of the younger blokes who stay around are reliant on casual and contract work."

Gil understood the significance. That had been one of Dan Flanagan's strategies: make a youth grateful for some work, manoeuvre him into a couple of shady jobs, and then hold those over his head as a threat if he wanted out.

"So, who's working for them?" he asked.

"Who isn't, might be quicker. Two of Johnno Dawson's boys, and Luke Sauer — Karl's cousin — have been doing a lot of casual stock work. Luke's sister Ingrid works for the company office in Birraga."

The Dawsons and the Sauers had just been kids when he'd left. He didn't know enough about any of them to hazard any guesses as to their characters.

"Sean Barrett drives heavy equipment for Flanagan's earth-moving business," Ryan continued. "Paul's a fencing contractor. He's just finished a big contract on the old Sutherland property."

"And Jim Barrett?"

"Jim's managing one of the Strelitz properties, since Mark's parents retired to the coast."

Well that was one person, at least, who didn't work for the Flanagans, at least, not directly.

"What about Butler at the pub?"

"Dave? He only came back after Stan died a few months back. He works out on the gas fields in South Australia, makes damned good money out there. He'll be off again as soon as the pub is sold, or closes. Same with Angie, his sister. She does environmental surveys and the like."

Being only temporarily in town didn't mean they weren't influenced, but lessened the chance of it. Gil mentally moved them towards the bottom of the suspicion list.

"What does Karl Sauer do?"

"He worked for a phone company in Birraga, until they closed their local office earlier this year. He's been doing casual IT work here and there since then."

They ran quickly through the rest: Karl's siblings, at uni in Sydney; Andrew Pappas, health and safety officer for the council; his wife Erin, a vet working with Beth's father Harry; his sister, Lexi, a teacher in Birraga, along with Chloe Barrett.

That left only the older, retired people and the school kids. It struck Gil that of his particular age cohort — those now in their mid-thirties, once considered a demographic bump in town — there were few left. Ryan and Beth, Paul and Sean. Mark. Everybody else had either left, or died. Paula and Barbara weren't the only ones; a couple of guys had died in a railway crossing smash, and Ben Sutherland had been one of the suicides Ryan had mentioned.

The high mortality rate gave a strong sense of foreboding about his own future. So did the fact that half the working population of the town appeared to be employed by the Flanagan company.

He finished transferring the money to Ryan's account, thanked him for his help, and rode away on his new bike.

He parked in front of the pub, beside Liam's car. Across the road, the ruins of Jeanie's building lay, drab black and grey in the sunlight. The cabin still stood, scorched but mostly undamaged; his few belongings might be salvageable, after all. Assuming the arson investigators didn't seize them for examination.

A sombre group of police, including Kris, Fraser and Adam, and several men in overalls, were talking together under the kurrajong tree, while a couple of uniformed cops, their faces tight, dragged a blue plastic sheet across part of the ruins, at the office end of the building.

Damn, not a good sign.

Police tape cordoned off the whole corner, fluttering lightly in the breeze. He hesitated by the bike, undecided whether he should cross the road, try to find out what was happening, or whether they'd just brush him off.

Kris glanced around, saw him, and waved him over. She ducked under the crime scene tape and met him on the corner. Her eyes were dark in her stark white face.

"More trouble?" He nodded towards the splash of blue plastic.

"Yes. Somebody was in there, Gil. In the office. They found him under the rubble." Her voice shook, and she glanced away, swallowing.

"Do you know who . . .?"

"No. Nothing recognisable." Her pale face took on a grey tinge, and she closed her eyes briefly, but held herself together. "However, one of the cattle trucks is on a side track, about a kilometre down the road, and there's no sign of the driver."

And two and two made four, Gil thought bitterly. Setting fires was dangerous business.

"Did you see anything, Gil? Hear anything?" A note of desperation sharpened her voice.

"No." He'd been so focused on getting upstairs to Jeanie, believing her the only one in the building, he hadn't spared a thought for the possibility of anyone else being in there.

"I went past the office," she said, the words coming fast, her breathing shallow between them. "I got the ladder from the cabin. He might have still been alive then . . ."

"Blue, listen to me." He didn't dare touch her, with too many people around to see, but he used firmness and logic to defray the frenzied thinking of shock, give her something solid to hang on to. "By the time we got there, no-one was alive in that office. The gas explosion probably got him instantly — the cylinders were right outside. There wasn't a damn thing you could have done to save him."

She sucked in a long breath, blew it out again. "You're probably right." Casting a reluctant glance towards the tarp-covered area, she took another deep breath. "I'd better go back." Hands in her pockets, she straightened her shoulders. Toughness and vulnerability, wrapped in one bundle, her courage all the greater because she fought to overcome her own fears and susceptibilities to do her job.

She took a few steps away, before swinging about to ask, "You'll still be here later? You're not leaving yet?"

"I'll be around, at least until tomorrow."

Again, a brief nod, then she swivelled on her heel and strode over to her colleagues.

Gil met up with Liam coming out of the pub.

"I saw you ride up," Liam commented. "I see you've found some transport."

"Yes. Bought it from an old mate." He jerked a thumb towards the pub. "What's happening?"

"Deb and Angie from the pub have got it all organised. Angie's giving us accommodation for a couple of nights in exchange for the help. But the hotel kitchen's been closed up for a couple of months, since Angie's Dad died, so it needs a good clean. Which do you want to do — shopping for supplies in Birraga with Deb and Angie, or kitchen cleaning so it's ready when they get back?"

Gil weighed up the choices, made his decision quickly. "I'll stay here." He didn't want to go too far from Kris, because of the developing investigation, he almost convinced himself. Besides, he'd told her he'd be here. "You go to Birraga. But Liam, I want you to stick with Deb, and to keep an eye out for trouble."

"You think there'll be more?"

They would come for him, at some time, he figured. The attempt to frame him had failed; now the evidence of that was destroyed, they'd turn their attention to him directly. The death of the truck driver might delay things a day or two, giving him time to find out more about who and why, and then leave here so that Kris and others would be safe.

He answered Liam's question with a shrug. "Hopefully not today. Do you need money for the food? You can use the business account if you need to."

"No, it's okay. The politician bloke, Strelitz, he's put up the extra cash to replace the food."

Of course Mark Strelitz had covered the extra cost. And, Gil had to give him credit for it, probably without a political motive in his head. He belonged in the town, had always been a part of it, and he'd apparently followed in his parents' footsteps in generously supporting community causes.

Gil headed to the pub's kitchen with Liam, Maybe a couple of hours scrubbing benches and ovens would improve his mood. And maybe, if he spent the time thinking through the evidence, he might find some answers to this whole damned mess.

The flyscreen door banged against its wooden frame as he and Liam entered the kitchen, and at the sound Deb glanced over from the cupboard she was investigating.

"Gil's going to be chief cleaner," Liam announced with some relish, "while we see the metropolis of Birraga."

"Great." Deb grinned cheekily. "Always good to see the boss doing the dirty work."

If he'd been in a better mood, less distracted, he'd have come up with some dry retort. And if he'd been less distracted, he might have noticed the girl half-hidden by the open pantry door.

"Have you met Megan?" Liam asked, with a warm smile for the girl. "She worked with your friend Jeanie. She's going to help you clean the place up, and then be another kitchen hand with me."

There she was, smiling a hello at him, her dark hair pulled back from her face in a ponytail, the hairline peaking down on her forehead, just like his own. His . . . His brain still stumbled over the word.

He dragged his hand through his hair and managed to mutter some sort of greeting without really looking at her.

His . . . *daughter*. If there were any gods, they'd be laughing at him now. That the fumbling episode in the dark with Barb, all those years ago, could have resulted in *her* — this lively, pretty girl — seemed impossible, a bizarre joke on him.

And now he was going to spend the next few hours scrubbing with his daughter.

CHAPTER
ELEVEN

The one o'clock national news came on the radio as Kris parked outside the station. She'd been to the other side of Birraga with Steve, visiting the truck driver's wife who had reported her husband missing, and preparing her for the probability that he wouldn't be home, ever.

An hour later, she could still hear the woman's anguished cries in her head, and when she closed her eyes she could see the faces of three little kids, scared and confused, not yet old enough to understand why Mummy was yelling and sobbing.

Kris rested her arms on the steering wheel, letting her head drop onto them. How were you supposed to tell a grieving woman that she shouldn't see her husband's body? That there was nothing left to recognise of the man she'd loved, the father of her children, and the man she'd made love to? Of all the deaths Kris had notified in her career — and there'd been too many, this past couple of years — this was one of the hardest. Even if the man had deliberately set the café fire, no-one deserved what had happened, his wife and kids least of all.

She and Steve had drawn little information from the woman. Her husband had been driving off and on for Flanagan's Transport out of Jerran Creek for a couple of years, and they'd moved to Birraga three months ago. He'd had more steady work since then, four or five runs a week, with the occasional overnighter.

Nothing she told them gave them anything useful to indicate his guilt or innocence, motivation or associates. They hadn't been able to locate the other driver, either. According to the job sheets Karl's cousin Ingrid had given Kris from the Flanagan company office, there was only one truck scheduled for the run to transfer steers from a property west of Birraga to the old Sutherland property, not two. Ingrid had no clue who could have driven the other truck, and the manager of the transport division was off pig shooting for the weekend, and not answering his mobile phone.

Kris dragged herself out of the car and into her house, avoiding the station. For now, she was off-duty. At least officially. Steve would follow up the mystery driver and other issues during the weekend, but the Local Area Commander had taken one look at her overtime claim for the past couple of weeks and ordered her home.

It didn't mean she'd stop thinking and asking questions, but there wasn't much more she could do, formally, until the forensic, arson and autopsy reports came through. And even then Steve was in charge of the local enquiries, and Petric had control of the investigation into Marci's murder, so her role was technically only support and local liaison.

In her bedroom, she stripped off her uniform and pulled on jeans and a cotton shirt. The temperature had climbed today towards summer levels, with blue skies and no sign of rain, a precursor for a clear, warm night. That was one thing going right for the ball, at any rate.

At the hall next door, half the town seemed to be involved in final preparations for the evening. She walked in the other direction, down the road to the pub, the street pretty much deserted.

The bar was closed, a sign stuck to the door saying it would be open at one o'clock. Voices from the courtyard led her through the gate.

At one of the wooden tables, shaded by a large patio umbrella, Gil stood, making sandwiches with Megan, while she chatted away. Gil didn't appear to be contributing much to the conversation, but seemed almost relaxed, prompting Megan with a question when she paused.

So, the rapid shuttering of his face when he saw Kris had to be all due to her, and his sudden concentration on cutting cheese. Her own smile took some effort to maintain in response to that closure, and so she directed it at the young woman.

Megan cheerfully waved her knife in greeting. "Hi, Kris. Do you want some lunch? Eleni had some basics in the shop, so you've got a choice of cheese and tomato, or cheese and ham, or ham and cheese and tomato. With options on mustard."

"Ham and cheese, please," she requested. It wasn't much of a choice, but it would keep her going until supper tonight. Tomorrow, she'd have to see what else

196

the Pappases had in stock, because she hadn't had time this morning in Birraga to get groceries.

The long-term repercussions of the fire started to hit home. The pub no longer made food, and now with Jeanie's café gone, the Pappas's little corner store would be the only place in town to buy food. But the small store had struggled financially for years, and George was winding it down in preparation for retirement. Most people did their main grocery shopping in Birraga, at the independent supermarket where the range was better and the prices lower. But she wasn't the only one who relied on Jeanie's or the corner store when she ran out of essentials like milk and bread.

It would be another challenge for the Progress Association, after the ball. They'd have to find some way to keep the corner store business viable, to keep Dungirri feasible as a place to live. There she went, worrying about the town again.

Gil sliced through a couple of layers of sandwiches as though he'd done it many times before, and slid them on to plates. Megan picked up her plate and thanked Gil, leaving to go and finish off cleaning in the kitchen.

"Busy morning?" Kris asked, watching his hands as he reached for more bread, laid it out on the plastic board, and spread margarine over it. Watching strong hands deftly at work was easier than trying to read his face. Less confronting. Although, as her eyes drifted to his wrists and arms, and she saw muscles and tendons flexing as he sliced more cheese from the block, maybe not.

Sheesh, if men realised just how sensual a naked forearm could be, they'd never wear long sleeves. She dragged her gaze away, and pretended an interest in the gazania flowers in a nearby overgrown garden bed, trying to focus her mind on anything other than the attractiveness of his body. Like murder. Arson. Conspiracy. Threatened violence.

"The kitchen's ready to use," he briefly answered the question she'd almost forgotten asking, a whole ten seconds ago. "The others are on their way back from Birraga."

"Good. You've got time for a chat over lunch before they get here, then."

"Hmm."

She took that as agreement, and while he finished making the sandwiches, she went in the back way to fetch a couple of glasses of lemon squash from the bar, leaving some coins on the till to cover the cost. When she returned, he was sitting at the table, his food untouched in front of him, and hers on a plate opposite.

Someday she'd have to shout him a meal, instead of being on the receiving end of his culinary skills. If he stayed in town long enough.

She passed his drink over to him as she sat.

"None of the official reports are written up yet, but I've got some unofficial information you might like to know."

Normally, she took great caution sharing information with a civilian, but in this circumstance, she made the judgment call, for Gil's knowledge might be central to

198

them solving the crimes, and he'd demonstrated his willingness to cooperate, despite his reservations about police.

"The arson investigators believe the gas tanks were tampered with, set to explode. However, they think the fire began in the office. There's not much left of the computer, but what there is — well, what appears to be the lid of the CPU is separate from the rest, and there's a small pile of melted screws."

"They took it apart."

"Yes. And there's evidence of accelerant on the remains."

His eyes narrowed, and he dropped his voice. "How many people know you've got a copy of the images, Blue?"

She didn't answer his question directly. "The USB drive Adam copied them onto has been logged as evidence and locked up in the Inverell forensics unit."

"But you've still got a copy."

"Yes. And so, now, do a few others." She understood, appreciated his concern, and sought to reassure him. "I won't be a target for that reason, Gil. If anyone wants to get rid of the evidence, they're going to have to destroy a few computers and servers, here and in Sydney, to do so."

They might not stand up in court — the images were pretty blurry, anyway — but something on them might provide a lead.

"Steve and Joe both have copies," she told Gil. "They'll look over them, see if they can recognise anything."

199

"Is that wise?"

"Are you asking if I trust them?" she challenged him bluntly.

"Yes."

"I've worked with Steve a couple of times in the last few years. Look, he can be a bit of an arsehole sometimes," she said with brutal honesty, "but I think that's mostly an act, playing along with the macho culture the police force still has, as well as something of a rebellion against his Assistant Commissioner father, who is renowned for having absolutely no sense of humour. But Steve put himself in the direct line of fire several times last summer; I don't doubt his courage or commitment."

"What about Petric?"

"Petric, I only met yesterday. But he worked with Alec Goddard for a long time. I know Alec, and he doesn't suffer fools or liars." She looked straight at him. "I spoke with Alec this morning, briefed him on what's happened. He's a commander now, up on the north coast, but he was a senior detective in Sydney, and knows a lot about organised crime there. And I'm guessing he's the one you told about the corrupt officers, because he arrested Kevin Jones and his colleagues earlier this year."

His gaze dropped to the table, and he pushed his uneaten sandwich away, brushing at some breadcrumbs before he looked up again and answered.

"Yes. I'd met Goddard a few times, over the years. He was about the only one I thought I could trust."

She confirmed his assessment without hesitation. "I'd trust Alec with my life. I *have* trusted him with my life. He's one of the most honest, principled police officers I've ever met. Integrity could be his middle name."

And he'd proved it again, in their phone conversation, protecting the identity of his informant even to her.

"He didn't give you away, Gil, even when I asked, straight out," she assured him. "He insisted it was an anonymous tip."

"It was." Gil shrugged. "But I figured he guessed, anyway."

"So, you informed on Kevin Jones," she said quietly, "one of the most notorious criminals in the country, and you're still breathing, with limbs intact."

Gil acknowledged the fact with a tilt of his head. "For now."

She knew the reality as well as he did. Kevin Jones was locked up in the Super-Max facility in Goulburn, but even from there his orders carried weight. If he ever found out Gil was responsible for his arrest, Gil's life expectancy would be cut dramatically short. It was a threat that haunted Alec and Bella, too, and one of the reasons they'd moved north, away from Sydney.

Despite the sunshine, a chill settled on Kris. She didn't ever, ever, want to see Gil's body, dead. She'd seen too many dead people, and even the thought of his possible murder distressed her in ways she didn't have time to contemplate right now.

Waving a fly away from her half-eaten sandwich, she forced her thoughts back to the practicalities. "How many people know it was you?"

He was quiet, matter-of-fact, about it. "None, other than Goddard. Marci might have told what she suspected; but if so, I don't know to who — her boyfriend, who used to work for Jones's mob, or Tony Russo, or someone else." He hesitated for a long moment, searching for words. "Was there anything on Marci? Any clues in how she . . . died?"

Despite his uneasy relationship with Marci, his question still held concern for her as a person.

"I spoke with the Deputy Coroner after the autopsy this morning. Toxicology and samples will take some days at least to process, so there won't be a formal report for a while. But he confirmed that the estimated time of death was three on Thursday afternoon, give or take an hour or two." She paused, reluctant to relay the gruesome details. "You said she was involved in the BDSM scene?"

"Her boyfriend pushed her into jobs in it. She pretended she liked it, but she did it for money, not because she got a kick out of it."

Sympathy for the woman, and pity, made it harder to deal with the facts, yet they had to be told to find justice for her.

"There were extensive injuries, and multiple sexual assaults. That might have been a client, but . . . well, there's usually boundaries, safe words, role-playing the dominant and submissive, discipline rather than

202

violence. The injuries inflicted on Marci . . . they're more consistent with torture than discipline."

"She suffered?"

She wished she had a different answer. "Yes. The Deputy Coroner is going to call in a psychologist. There's a possibility that there's two types of injuries; one set suggesting precision and control, the other . . . not."

"Maybe two frigging bastards, then." He twisted off the seat, threw the remains of his sandwich with some force into a rubbish bin, and strode to the fence, his tense back to her.

She gave him time, gave herself time to regain some equilibrium. A magpie hopped up hopefully onto the table, and she pushed the plate with her uneaten food towards it, her stomach too disturbed for her to finish it. The magpie greedily poked into the bread, then dragged the ham from inside and proceeded to tear it into bite-sized pieces.

When Kris looked over at Gil again, he seemed to be watching the bird, but she'd bet he wasn't really seeing it.

"I should have made sure she left." Cold, hard anger echoed in every word. "I should have taken her to the airport myself, put her on the damned plane. If I hadn't been so bloody impatient with her, she'd still be alive."

"You can't take responsibility for her life and her choices, Gil. She was an adult, making her own decisions."

He shook his head. "No. She wasn't capable of making good decisions. Between her upbringing and the booze, she was so fucking screwed up . . . Her mother ran a brothel, auctioned off Marci's virginity when she was just twelve years old, had her working from then on. What kind of bitch does that to her own daughter?"

Kris's stomach twisted uncomfortably. She didn't have an answer for him. She didn't have answers for far too much she'd seen — like how a mob of otherwise normal, ordinary people could bash to death an old, defenceless man, or how someone could hold a gun to a small girl's head and pull the trigger. And she wasn't sure that answers would make any of it easier to deal with.

"It was Vince who took her out of there," Gil continued. "Married her off to Digger, so she'd have a home and someone decent to look after her. Except Digger eventually fell to the booze, too, and wasn't much bloody use to her, even before he died."

"Vince married her off?" The archaic notion caught her attention, and heightened her curiosity about the connection between the dead woman and the dead man. Two murders, so close together, made any connections important. Petric might know more than she did, but he hadn't shared his knowledge. "You mentioned last night they knew each other. Was she his mistress?"

"No. He had mistresses. He had a wife, too. Marci and him . . . it was weird. He kept in touch with her all those years. She flirted with him — she flirted with every man she knew — but he treated her like a little girl, not a lover. I sometimes thought . . ." He dragged a hand through his hair. "I mean, her mother told Marci her father was just a punter, and Vince just laughed the one time I asked him, but . . . is it possible to get a DNA comparison on them?"

"You think Vince was her father?" Kris's thoughts ticked over rapidly. A rich, powerful man, taking a long-term interest in a woman he treated like a child. It made sense, in a sick, twisted kind of way. But the pathologist might need something more solid than a guess before authorising a test. "How old were they?"

"Vince, mid-sixties, pushing seventy maybe. Marci a couple of years older than me. Vince would have already been married when she was born. Marci — she didn't actually look like him, but if she was his daughter, it would explain some things."

"Like?" she prompted.

He came and sat down again, opposite her. "When I made the deal with Vince, I remember he said as I left, casually, that he'd appreciate it if I kept an eye out for her. It wasn't part of the deal, not even a threat, just a comment. But when I saw him about her, the other day, he was grateful — he even said it — that I hadn't 'let her down'. I thought it was a bit odd, coming from a guy whose son hated her guts, was actively trying to destroy her life. If Tony suspected, too . . . well, that would be more than enough reason for his hatred."

"I'll request the DNA tests. But they take some time," she warned. "There won't be a quick answer."

He drew a piece of paper out of his jeans pocket — the one he'd hidden earlier — and flicked it open. After a quick review of it, he passed it across to her.

"That's the list you asked for. The possibilities. People with motives . . . the ones I'm aware of, anyway."

She scanned the columns, concerned by the number of "possibilities", and was startled to see a column for Jeanie, with a couple of names listed underneath it.

She trusted Gil's judgment, but they didn't make sense. Not for the Jeanie she'd known and become close friends with over the past five years.

"Why on earth are Dan and Brian Flanagan on *Jeanie's* list?"

He expected the question and answered it steadily, as though he knew she'd have trouble believing it. "She and Aldo paid protection money for years. Brian was the one who delivered the 'invoices'."

She shook her head. Protection money. *Invoices.* Shit, that belonged elsewhere, not here.

"How do you know this?" she asked, with a vain, wild hope that he couldn't prove it.

"Back when I worked for Jeanie for a while, I helped her put together enough information to hold over the Flanagans and get them off her case. I went with her when she confronted Dan."

Her mind struggled to grapple with the ideas — of Flanagan running protection rackets here in Dungirri; of Jeanie knowing about it, dealing with him, and yet never breathing a word of it; of her own ignorance of Flanagan's activities and influence. Yes, it might have been years ago, long before her arrival in the area, but it seemed things were still going on. There'd been a few rumours, but as far as she knew, every time she or her colleagues had had cause to contact Dan, he'd been the model citizen, squeaky clean.

She focused on one aspect, sought to make sense of it. "You did the same thing with Vince — found information to hold over him. So it was your idea to best Flanagan that way?"

"No. It was Jeanie who showed me how powerful information can be."

"*Jeanie* taught *you* how to handle the mafia?"

"Yes."

She screwed her eyes closed, wondering if the sun was addling her brain, but when she opened them again he was still there, looking at her, unsmiling.

"Please tell me you're joking."

"Sorry, Blue."

She hauled in a long breath, huffed it out. When Jeanie was fit enough, she'd send someone to interview her. Probably even go herself. But in the meantime . . .

In the meantime, she believed Gil. Despite the shock of it, what he'd told her was entirely plausible. Jeanie wasn't the kind of woman to succumb to bullying, and the old sergeant who'd been here then had not, from all reports, been a sterling example of a police officer. Jeanie hadn't liked him — she'd told Kris that, a while back — so it made sense that she'd have dealt with Flanagan herself. It made her wonder what else had gone on in the town's past.

The sunshine hadn't changed, the pub's courtyard was the same as ever, only Kris's perceptions had shifted, the shadows more stark. And she just had to deal with it, piece by piece, fact by fact.

"The information on Flanagan. What was it?"

"A package of information. Some Polaroid photos. A cassette recording of threats. Lists of dates, times, places. And maps and photos of a couple of hydroponic marijuana production areas."

"Do you still have the package?"

"I hid it out at the old man's place. It should still be there. But it's close on twenty years old, Blue. Not much good then, to be honest, as anything more than a bluff, and even less use to the police now. I doubt the photos and tapes will have lasted."

She pushed herself to her feet. "Let's go and find out."

CHAPTER
TWELVE

Gil wanted to give the new bike a decent run, so he rode out on it, Kris following in her own car. The Birraga road was quiet, only a single vehicle, a dusty white ute, heading into Dungirri. Not anyone he recognised.

Three kilometres out he signalled the right turn, taking the sharp corner onto the dusty track carefully.

Eighteen years since he'd been along this road. Anywhere else, it might have been a pleasant country lane. With eucalypts on either side, their branches reaching out to form archways above, shadowing the road, and between the trees the native bushes a mass of small spring wildflowers, white and pink and yellow.

But the track led past the old shack he'd grown up in, and he'd trudged along it too many times as a kid, desperately dredging up the courage to face the old man, never sure whether he'd meet violence or the hard stone wall of silence.

Even when he'd grown taller than him, filled out with some muscle, the violence hadn't ended, just changed. The old man gave up belting him, but he'd lash out sometimes, unpredictable and irrational, using anything to hand — timber, steel bars, tools. Gil had learned to be constantly aware, on edge, even in his sleep, listening for the rough catch of breath that heralded a swing.

Between those episodes, there'd been only silence. No conversations, no arguments, no acknowledgment of his existence beyond a sporadic growled order.

If it made a man a bastard to be glad his father was dead, then so be it — he'd wear the label. To pretend anything else would be hypocrisy.

He steered the bike cautiously along the track at a moderate speed, the corrugations in the dirt hazardous enough for four wheels, let alone two.

A kilometre or so along, a sharp bend followed old property boundaries, and the place came into view. On one side of the road, the large paddocks were cleared for grazing, only a scattering of trees here and there. On the other side, the old shack, more decrepit than he remembered it, stood shadowed by trees; beyond it lay two hundred remnant acres of the native bush. Land he technically owned, now, since the old man's death. Other than having his accountant pay years of overdue council rates, he'd scarcely given it a thought.

He parked the bike in the shade of a tree, outside the fence. Kris wasn't far behind him, and he waited for her, unbuckling his helmet, welcoming the fresh air on his face.

The gate swung open in the breeze, one hinge twisted off the gatepost. The shack seemed smaller than it had been, with more corrugated iron and rough timber patching up the old slabs. The junk around it had increased, though — a second ancient truck rusting away in the scrub, broken machinery, boxes of empty bottles and other rubbish. The outdoor dunny had collapsed on itself, and the corrugated-iron shed tilted drunkenly towards the tank stand, itself developing a definite lean.

The car pulled up, the door slammed, and he heard Kris's footsteps, felt her beside him.

"Is this the first time you've been back?"

"Yeah."

"Miserable place."

He agreed, but to admit it aloud might give the memories too much power.

The old lines appeared in his head again: *The wheel has come full circle; I am here.*

Here, but an adult now, not a kid. Strengthened by the lessons he'd learned, the hard knocks he'd survived, the life he'd built for himself through hard work and guts.

And he'd not only survived but succeeded, when all the old man had ever done was fail.

The last part of the quote echoed in his mind, but this time as a statement, and a challenge: *I am here.*

Kris beside him, he went through the gate and walked across the dry ground to the shack.

The corrugated-iron door, too, was already open, squeaking in the light breeze, and she hesitated, falling a step behind him.

"Were you here? After they found him?" he asked.

From what they'd told him, he could imagine what she'd seen; the man on the bed, rifle in his mouth, blood, bone, and brains spattered across the wall. Murder set up to look like suicide.

"Yes. I secured the scene, waited while forensics examined it, and until the Deputy Coroner came. And I returned later, with Jeanie, when she checked to see if there were any belongings or papers that you should have. There wasn't much at all."

"I know. She wrote and told me. You don't have to come in, Blue," he added.

"No. It's okay. It's just that — somebody's been here recently, Gil. We made sure the door was latched, wrapped the chain around it. And the table was upright."

His eyes had grown accustomed to the dim light inside, and he saw it wasn't only the rough table overturned; the old chair lay on its side, the ancient newspapers that had lined the walls were ripped in shreds on the floor.

"It's out in the bush, Blue, and the place has been empty for months. Between possums and hoons, I'm surprised it's not more beat up."

"I know. I drive past every now and again, keep an eye on it. But the door open — the gate open, come to think of it — it wasn't like that a few days ago."

Just a few days . . . *that* put a more sinister light on it. "You stay here, Blue. I'll take a look inside."

She placed a firm hand on his shoulder, stopped him moving forward.

"I'm the cop, Gillespie," she reminded him.

If he'd thought there was imminent danger, he'd have ignored her and gone in first, but all was quiet within, so out of respect for her — more so than for the uniform — he stood aside and let her go inside first.

The main room was a mess, its few pieces of furniture scattered, coals raked out of the fireplace, the rags that had covered the food shelves torn down.

In the small sleeping space behind the partition, the camp bed was overturned, the mattress slashed open, its kapok stuffing strewn on the floor. The drawers and doors of the cupboard that had once held their few clothes were pulled out, exposing the empty interior, and the filthy piece of lino under the iron washstand was ripped up, the chipped enamel basin tossed to the floor.

He followed Kris back in to the main room.

"Wanton vandalism? Or were they looking for something?" she mused.

"No grafitti," Gil observed. "Vandals usually like to leave their mark somehow. Which suggests a search."

He scanned the dingy room again, his gaze focusing on the food shelf against the wall. The contents had never amounted to much, and now there was even less. The vintage flour tin that he remembered was upside down, lid off, weevils rummaging in the flour tipped out from it. A lone ant nibbled around the edge of the treacle, dripping from the toppled jar.

Treacle . . . one ant . . .

"Blue," he said, keeping his voice low, pointing to the sweet, sticky mess. "There's only one ant. They were here not long ago. Less than an hour. Maybe only minutes."

She glanced at the treacle, and agreed with a brisk nod.

"Okay. Don't touch anything. We should go straight out. My phone's in the car. I'll report it."

Outside, the bright sunlight hit his eyes hard. He paused in the yard, studying the rest of the place, noticing now the jemmy marks on the shed door, the old seats dragged out of the dead trucks, green weeds poking out underneath them.

Not long ago at all.

In the distance, he heard a faint sound, what might have been a metallic clang, and he whipped around to look at the overgrown track behind the shack — and saw recent tyre tracks bending the grasses.

"Get out of here, Blue." He grabbed her hand and started running towards the car. "They're up at the other shed. They can't see us from here, but they will when they come back. We don't want them to see your car or they'll know we're onto them."

She stopped by the fence, hauling him to a halt. "I can't just run away, Gil."

She was out of uniform, without her belt or any sign of a weapon under her light shirt.

"Neither of us are armed," he argued, "and we don't know how many there are." He thought quickly, offered a solution, hoping things hadn't changed since he'd left. "Go up the road half a kilometre or so. There should be a grid, and a track along the fence line among the trees. We can leave the car and the bike there, out of sight, and go in that way; there's a slight rise, overlooking the shed, that should give us cover."

She considered it briefly, and agreed. "I'll call for backup on the way."

The sound of the engines couldn't be helped; they'd probably be heard by whoever was at the shed, but if they were lucky the intruders would be distracted enough not to register the distant noise, or at least think it was coming from the main road. The fact that they hadn't come to investigate it yet was a good sign.

The side track, an old closed road, was still there, the grid overgrown but passable. Kris's compact four-wheel drive eased over it, and she bounced her way about thirty metres along the rough trail before a fallen tree blocked the way. Gil pulled up beside her, turning the bike and leaving it where the car blocked it from view. If they needed to escape fast, the bike might be their best chance.

"Backup coming?" he asked.

"It will be a while. There's nobody closer than Birraga. We're on our own for now."

He led the way through the trees, the bush dry underfoot. They had to curve around to view the shed from the rise behind it, and it took some minutes of steady walking, the way hampered by pockets of undergrowth. Kris easily kept pace with Gil.

They didn't speak, but as they approached the slope, he signalled her to stay silent. Here, there was less undergrowth but more rocks, and they kept low, picking their way up the small hill, careful not to dislodge rocks or stones. Every now and again, the sound of voices drifted to them, the words indistinct, but definitely from the direction of the shed.

A few metres from the top of the slope, he dropped to the ground, scrambling the last part on all fours, crouching behind a huge tree stump for cover. Kris slid into place behind him.

The tree cover provided a patchy view of the clearing below the rise, two hundred metres away, where a dusty blue ute and a large black four-wheel drive stood in front of the wooden, double-bay machinery shed. The truck his old man had driven sat under the awning, the doors of the cab open and the seat on the ground beside it. Whatever they were looking for, they were going to some effort to find it.

A couple of guys emerged from the side door of the shed. One in black trousers and a dark sports jacket over a dark T-shirt, the other in jeans and a T-shirt, carrying a crowbar.

Two guys, two cars — but there'd been two in the four-wheel drive last night, and he'd be willing to bet there was at least one more man inside.

He pulled out his mobile phone and started taking photos. He didn't expect them to be clear at this distance, but anything was better than nothing. Kris took photos with her phone around the other side of the stump, her free hand leaning lightly against his shoulder for balance.

A clatter on the hill a short distance away startled all of them. The men whipped around, and as Gil hauled Kris closer behind the protection of the stump, gunshots cracked through the air.

Gil breathed again when he recognised the sounds of a wallaby or a 'roo racing across the slope not far below them. He heard laughter from the men, and another couple of shots, rowdy voices yelling encouragement.

Whoever was firing was both quick to draw, and took pleasure in shooting. Not the kind of thug he wanted to be caught by. He tightened his arm around Kris, shifting his kneeling position so that she was pressed between him and the tree stump, keeping her close into the cover it provided, protecting her. Her white shirt made too much of a contrast against the dull greens and browns of the bush; even an inch or two showing might attract the attention of the men in the clearing.

Tension in her body and the frown she directed at him told him she was not pleased.

When he dared another glance out, there were two more men in jeans and work shirts near the shed, conversing with one of the first two, and the guy in the jacket stood slightly apart, talking on his phone.

Gil recognised only one of them. He eased up on Kris, and she peered cautiously around, her arm snaking out with her phone, thumb busy on the key.

He leaned forward, whispered in her ear, "Far left. He was one of the truck drivers. Know him?"

She shook her head and mouthed, "Need number plates."

At this angle, they were side on to the vehicles, their rego plates not visible. But rego numbers might be a lot more useful for tracking down these guys than photos of unknown people.

"Stay here," he whispered.

He backed down the ridge a short distance, out of their sight, and made his way a couple of hundred metres along the slope, to overlook the vehicles from behind. There were no handy large tree stumps or rocks on top of the ridge here for cover; a low-growing, straggly shrub would have to do.

A car door slammed, and he hastened up the last few metres, silently cursing the thorns and spiders' webs as he crouched into place. Another door slammed, an engine started. Too many damned trees obscured his view. He had to get closer and quickly.

If the trees obscured his view, he'd just have to trust that they'd also block any view of *him*. If the men weren't looking this way — and he wasn't directly behind them so shouldn't be caught in their rear-view mirrors — he might just make it.

The second engine started, the driver's foot heavy on the accelerator, the noise loud enough to let Gil risk making a quick dash three-quarters of the way down the slope. Stopping by a large tree, a hundred metres or so away, he kept taking photos as the cars moved off, glad he'd bought a high-end phone, hoping the zoom function he'd never had reason to properly test would be sufficient to capture enough detail.

As they disappeared around a bend and into the trees, Kris stepped out from the bush, below where they'd taken cover, phone to her ear.

So much for staying put. Not that he was surprised — she was capable, and took her responsibilities seriously. She had been careful; he'd seen no flashes of white.

She finished one call and dialled another while she crossed the clearing to meet him by the shed.

"Delphi? It's Kris. I need your help. Can you go to your front fence, see if you can get number plates and descriptions on a couple of vehicles that might be going past? Black Land Rover and blue Ford ute. They just left Des Gillespie's place. I don't know which way they're going, but they could head to Birraga, past your place. At least one of them's armed, so be very careful — don't be obvious. Thanks, Delphi. I'll call you back soon."

"Good idea," he said as she disconnected. Delphi O'Connell's farm was about three k's further along the Birraga road, the farmhouse close to the road. If the men turned right at the end of the track, for Birraga, instead of left to Dungirri, then they'd drive right past her front yard.

She grinned wryly. "Delphi's as independent as ever, but you can always count on her when it matters. There's a patrol car coming, but it's on another road." She nodded over at the shed. "I want to take a look inside."

"Me too."

She seemed about to refuse, but changed her mind as if she knew it was fruitless. "Don't touch a damned thing in there, Gillespie. The guys in the Land Rover wore gloves, but the other two didn't. I want every fingerprint and scrap of evidence they left."

The men had used the side door, not the rusted roller doors at the front. Boltcutters had made short work of the rusty latch padlocking it. Kris used a handkerchief over her fingers and gripped the frame well above the broken latch to drag the door open.

Inside, it was initially hard to tell what was the old man's normal disarray, and what had been searched. Sunlight came through the grubby windows on the north side, dust caught drifting in its beams, the light casting a grid pattern from the wooden window frame onto the floor.

The workbench along the side wall was covered in tools and other junk, as well as possum droppings, dust and cobwebs. But a second glance showed the dust disturbed, the bigger pieces of junk moved aside, and the stuff from the shelves beneath the bench had been shoved up one end, some had fallen to the floor. The cupboards on the back wall were in similar shape. Beside them, vintage saws hung on nails on the wall, including the large crosscut saws Gil knew, too well, how to use.

The trailer with the portable sawmill his old man had eventually bought had few hiding places, but they'd been through the tool box. The other bay held a huge stack of cypress planks, the canvas tarpaulin that had covered it crumpled on the floor, the wood aged to a deep gold.

Gil surveyed the pile. It didn't look like there'd been much change since he'd laboured to stack every damned plank of it, years ago. At today's prices, that made thousands of dollars worth of timber sitting idle.

Kris gave a low whistle. "I'm surprised no-one's been in to steal this lot. Wonder how long it's been here, and why Des didn't sell it. I'm sure he could have done with the cash."

Gil didn't wonder. He'd long ago given up trying to make any sense of the old man's actions, and there'd always been plenty of rumours to discourage people from trespassing, most of them gruesome. Like the one about the old bastard murdering someone with the sawmill. As far as Gil knew, it wasn't true, but he didn't doubt the crazy sonofabitch could have been capable of it.

"Not many people know the shed is here," he told Kris. "It's a long way from the shack, out of sight. And he didn't ever invite anyone in."

"No, definitely not the welcoming sort," she agreed.

She dropped to a crouch at the end of the stack. "Someone's been down on hands and knees here, to see under the stack. I guess they thought you could tuck some photos and tapes in the spaces."

"But I didn't." He'd considered it briefly at the time, but deemed it too obvious, with not much point, since he'd expected the timber to be moved.

"Well, they obviously didn't feel like moving the lot of it to check."

"If that's what they're after. And if it is, they've taken their time coming to look for it." It still didn't make sense to him.

She rose to her feet. "Yes, but a lot's happened in the last forty-eight hours, Gil. Perhaps they didn't think you were a threat when you were in Sydney, but now you are. Or they might be worried that with Jeanie's place gone, she won't feel there's any reason to stay silent. Could be a lot of reasons. And we're only guessing until we find out for sure who 'they' are." She

221

scanned the rest of the shed. "So, where did you hide it? In here somewhere?"

"No. Outside. I'll show you."

On the edge of the clearing, he found the tree stump he was looking for — a giant of an ironbark gum, most of it felled generations ago, leaving only a metre-high stump of iron-hard wood. Picking up a small branch, he scraped away the few tough grasses growing near the base, and the thin layer of soil, to get to the rocks and stones he'd used to cover the hole he'd dug.

It had been night when he'd buried it, a dark night with only a sliver of moon, the wind in the trees on the ridge sounding ominously like distant vehicles, keeping him on edge as he worked quickly to avoid discovery. Now the sun was hot on his back, and Kris crouched beside him, taking stones from him as he levered them out. Yet despite the different circumstances, uneasiness wrapped around his spine as it had all those years ago.

His fingers scraped on fabric, and it wasn't long before he lifted the oil-cloth wrapped bundle out of the hole. He handed it to Kris without unwrapping it, and began to push the stones back in the hole again.

"See if it's still any good. Water might have got in, ruined everything."

He'd done the best job he could at the time, wrapping up the large plastic lunch box in plastic and then oil cloth, fastening the wrappings well with electrical tape. He finished filling in the hole while she unwrapped the layers.

He sat beside her on the ground, resting his arms on his knees, letting his gaze wander over the scene in front of him while she carefully took each plastic-wrapped packet out of the box. He knew what was in them, could still recall each photo, each map, and the cassette with its green label, dated with three dates in Jeanie's neat handwriting.

A swallow flew through a hole in the roof at the back of the shed, and he idly tried to remember whether he'd seen its nest inside, while out of the corner of his eye he saw Kris open the photo bag.

"Looks like the colours on the photos have faded, but the images are still clear enough," she commented, as she drew them out.

"Sorry. Archival-quality materials weren't to hand."

She flipped through a couple, then whistled low and long. "Is that what I think it is?"

He glanced at it to confirm which one it was. "Shipping containers being buried. For underground hydroponic marijuana crops. There's a pile of pipes there," he reached over to point, "for the watering system."

"Shit." She shook her head, still not quite believing. "Where is this? In this region?"

"North of here, on the river. It's marked on the map. Each photo has a date and code on the back."

"You ever consider espionage as a career, Gillespie?" she asked dryly.

He tilted his head so he could see her face. "Jeanie took that photo."

She stared at him for a moment, then broke into a laugh that held no humour. "I don't think I wanted to know that. You're one thing, but Jeanie . . ." She stopped abruptly, dragged her hair back behind her ear. "Part of me's having trouble believing that she knew all this, but never told me. But on another level, I can believe it's all true."

"It was a long time ago, Blue. Long before you came here. Flanagan left her alone after this, and unless she had more recent information, then there was nothing to tell you."

He gave her a little time to think that through, knowing her perceptions and beliefs had taken a battering with his revelations.

The swallow flew out of the shed again, followed by another. He frowned, tried to picture the roof of the shed from inside. The walls were timber but the roof was corrugated iron, on wooden rafters. There'd been no nest in the rafters, he was sure of it. No fresh bird shit on the floor. No birds swooping them when they went in.

He couldn't recall any sign of birds anywhere. He stared at the shed, recreating the interior in his head, the unlined walls and bare studs, the locations of the shelves and cupboards, the position of the windows, the way the sunlight had fallen across the floor, near the cupboards at the back.

Near the cupboards at the back . . .

It hit him then, what he'd never seen before. As a youth, he'd spent as little time as possible here. It was the old man's domain, and Gil had kept far away from him whenever possible. He'd stacked the timber at night, after a long day cutting it, hauling it from the truck out front to the shed by the light of a kero lamp, plank by plank.

But now in daylight, looking from the side, and with the years of renovations and rebuilding the pub sharpening his eye for proportions, he saw the inconsistency.

"The dimensions are wrong." He scrambled to his feet.

"What do you mean?"

"The shed. It's longer on the outside than on the inside. Not much — a metre at most. I'm going to check."

Kris started stuffing things back into their bags, but he didn't wait for her, jogging across the clearing.

He went straight to the back of the shed, outside. The tank that had once collected water from the roof was on a low stand near the corner, but the guttering on the shed and the pipe connecting it to the tank had long ago broken off. Brown marks on the wall, and a damp, grassy area below, showed where the water ran when it rained. Some of the wall boards had warped, been pulled out of place, riddled with damp and rot.

He broke one of them with his bare hands, but couldn't prise the whole board off far enough. There were a few pieces of rusting junk on the tank stand — he found a solid-looking piece of metal, and used it to lever the board out.

Definitely a cavity. He cursed himself. How he'd never known about it, for all those years . . . but back then, other than stacking wood, he hadn't spent much time in the shed, and he'd had other things on his mind. And it was big, so a metre or so didn't stand out as obvious.

Kris joined him as he levered off another board below the first one. He needed a bigger opening, enough light to see inside. The nails in the third board gave way, and Kris helped him tear it off.

And then he froze.

The floor level was visible, a few inches below. There were bones in the narrow cavity — human bones, a skeleton, only slightly scattered. And just below the dented skull, a plastic necklace strung with coloured beads looped behind the neck vertebrae.

He couldn't drag his eyes away. He heard Kris speak, had no clue what she said. There was only the bones, and the necklace, and his pulse pounding in his head and the anger rising and boiling until he felt as though his head might burst with the pressure.

She hadn't left . . . She'd never left.

"He killed her." He heard the words, didn't recognise the ragged voice as his own. "He said she left, but the fucking bastard killed her."

CHAPTER
THIRTEEN

Gil wrenched away from her hand on his arm, flung the piece of metal with all his strength into the bush, and strode away to the edge of the clearing, standing there, facing the trees, hands clenched stiff at his sides.

She didn't follow him immediately. She'd seen the remains, the childish necklace that only a mother would wear. She couldn't imagine the shock for him, after a childhood of cruelty, to discover this truth. A man as independent and proud as Gil would need a few minutes alone after this blow.

She brushed her eyes with the heel of her hand, and moved into duty-mode. Further into the cavity, she could make out a couple of bags beyond the skeleton, and what seemed, in the shadows, to be a stack of plastic boxes. The false wall obviously extended the full width of the shed, but in this part, at least, there appeared to be only the one lot of human remains.

Despite the dryness of the bones and the likelihood of the identity of them, it would take some time for an official confirmation, and she knew that the discovery of another body, connected to Gil, would only feed speculation and gossip.

She pulled her phone from her pocket and reported the discovery of the remains to the duty officer, and then phoned Steve's number and asked him to come out. Sandy from forensics was next. Already on his way back to Inverell, he grumbled that maybe he should move the office to Dungirri, before promising to be back within an hour or two.

With the official notifications made, she phoned Delphi again. If the vehicles had travelled that way, they'd have gone past her by now.

"No sign of the Land Rover," Delphi said.

The spark of hope she'd been holding on to sputtered and died. A dead end on that one, then. "And the ute?"

"A blue ute did drive past, and I got the number."

Kris didn't have a pen, or anything to write on. She picked up a stick and wrote in the dust as Delphi recited the letters and numbers to her.

"Thanks, Delphi. I appreciate your help." A thought occurred to her, and she asked, "On another matter, Delphi — did you know Des Gillespie's wife?"

"Gave her and the kid a lift now and then. She used to walk into town with him. Long time back, now."

"Do you remember when she left?"

She blew out a breath, as though she was thinking. "Must have been 'bout the same time Ruth died, bit before. Ruth taught the boy at school. I remember she was worried about him. But I didn't see him much after his mum left."

Ruth. Bella's mother, Delphi's sister-in-law. Kris knew she'd died of a snake bite, when Bella was in

228

kindergarten, around thirty years ago. And Gil was the same age as Bella.

"That's a great help, Delphi. Thanks."

Never one for unnecessary words or social chat, Delphi gave an indecipherable grunt, and hung up.

Kris phoned the Birraga station and requested a registration check on the ute's rego number. The constable only took a few minutes to look it up.

"Registered to a guy at Jerran Creek, Sarge, but he reported it stolen yesterday. He left the keys in the ute when he carried some cases of beer inside, and came out and it was gone."

"Damn." Kris kicked at a clod of dirt. "Any leads on who stole it?"

"Apparently not."

"Put an alert out for the vehicle, then," she instructed. "Let's hope they're stupid enough to keep driving it."

With the patrol car due to arrive at any moment, and Steve on his way, Kris crossed the clearing to Gil.

He stood still, staring out, his hands now thrust in his pockets, his spine rigid. He heard her approach, acknowledged her presence with a glance.

"I'm so sorry, Gil." It seemed such an inadequate thing to say under the circumstances.

He didn't respond immediately. She stayed beside him, looking out on to the dry bush, wishing she had something better to offer, wishing she could read what he was thinking and feeling, behind his stone-set features.

Birds sang among the trees, and the dappled sunlight danced on the ground as leaves moved in the breeze, the peaceful scene an unsettling contrast to the violence and trauma occupying their thoughts.

She knew little about his mother. In the time she'd been in Dungirri, people had only discussed Des Gillespie occasionally, and his wife had hardly rated a mention — other than someone commenting that she'd had the sense to leave him.

"I have to ask some questions, Gil. We need to investigate formally, confirm her identity, try to establish the time and cause of death."

He nodded, not looking at her.

"You believe the remains are your mother's? When did you last see her?"

"It's her." He spoke flatly, but with certainty. "The necklace . . . I made it for her. Mrs O'Connell, the kindergarten teacher, helped me. She, my mother, put it on straight away."

She found it hard to imagine him as a small child. Dark-eyed and serious, perhaps scowling as he worked to thread the beads, a solemn smile when she put the necklace on. The image made her eyes sting.

She asked, through her clogged throat, "Can you remember when she disappeared?"

"Maybe that day, the next. I would have been about five."

So young. Too young to be left alone with a man like Des. That matched what Delphi had said, but Kris still had to make him dredge up memories, get more facts.

"Can you remember her going?"

230

"Kind of." He sucked a slow breath in through his teeth, let it huff out. "She said we were going on a holiday, that we'd leave after dark. He wasn't there. It seemed to stay light for ages. She was wearing the necklace. I watched her put my jeans and pyjamas and the three books I had in my school bag. But I must have fallen asleep. In the morning, she was gone, and so was my school bag, and he just said she'd buggered off in the night."

He paused, gave a small shake of his head. "I believed him. Everybody believed him. I hated her for leaving."

Mentally, she cursed Des Gillespie to Hades, and everyone else ready to believe the worst of a woman, instead of asking questions.

"You were five years old, Gil. There's no way you could have known otherwise."

But that couldn't make it any easier for Gil. She'd worked enough domestic violence cases to know that a child would still blame himself and, now as a man — no matter how strong — he would still carry the scars, buried deep. Yet despite everything he'd been through, he'd made himself a man she respected.

"Do you remember much about her?"

He finally turned to face her. "No. I didn't want to remember." His brow creased as he thought back. "There's only a few bits and pieces, snippets of scenes. He belted her. She taught me to read." His mouth twisted up slightly. "She took me to Birraga once, to the library. I was amazed at all the books." He paused, frowning again. "But I can't remember what she looked like."

That he trusted Kris enough to share a memory or two from a time when he was so young and vulnerable, both surprised and touched her. She'd expected the stone wall, a grudging response to her questions, or rage against his father. The anger was there, no doubt about it, but constrained, simmering along with grief and guilt.

"Without photos, most people wouldn't recall a face after all this time," she said gently. "Especially not from childhood."

"Maybe." He didn't sound convinced.

"Her name . . . do you know it?"

"Jeanie and Aldo called her Anne. I don't have a clue whether they were legally married or not."

"Any relatives that you can remember?"

"No."

A woman named Anne, who might or might not have the surname Gillespie, who disappeared thirty years ago . . . Kris hoped there'd be a good DNA match with Gil, because otherwise they'd have a hell of a time confirming her identity.

The rumble of a car engine sounded in the distance.

"That's probably the backup arriving. Steve's on his way, too."

The patrol car appeared around the bend and parked beside the shed, and she left Gil and went over to greet the two constables. Gil needed some time to himself, and she had work to do — again.

There were more questions, of course. Gil sat on a stump in the shade, watching the investigation begin, and let them come to him with their questions. Fraser asked most of them, in his off-hand, careless way. When the forensic guys arrived, one of them asked a few more, his manner more serious and formal.

But after all the questions and the waiting, watching Kris and her colleagues at work, it was a relief when she told him there was little reason for him to stay any longer.

The ride back to town didn't so much clear his mind as numb it. The anger settled to a dull pounding and the words he uselessly imagined beating into the old man stopped going around and around in his mind. Useless, because the old man was dead, and there was nothing left to curse except memories.

He walked into the kitchen at the pub to find a whirlwind of activity, Liam and the girl, Megan, effectively filling in as kitchen hands for Deb.

"You're back," Deb greeted him with a quick grin, her hands in a large bowl of pastry. She nodded over to the sink. "The dishwasher's broken. You're it."

The routine work of scrubbing dishes occupied his hands, and gave his mind space to roam. Yet, instead of searching for solutions to the current threats, or going over the implications of his mother's death, he found his attention constantly drifting to the conversation of the others. Angie flitted between the bar and the kitchen, juggling serving customers with dessert preparation, grateful for the assistance. Deb gave orders, keeping track of multiple tasks being performed at once, allocating jobs to the others, providing guidance and answering questions. Liam had often helped out in the pub kitchen, and was accustomed to Deb's style of work. Megan's experience working for Jeanie stood her in good stead. She asked a lot of questions, intelligent ones, and she learned quickly.

Gil's efforts to take little notice of her failed, as they had earlier in the day. She'd chatted comfortably while they were cleaning the kitchen this morning, off and on, and he'd learned more of her story. He'd even — much to his own surprise — asked a question or two. She'd mentioned going off the rails and running away, living on the streets for a while after the death of her adoptive parents. But she'd pulled herself together well, and was trying hard to make the new relationship with her biological grandparents work, despite the differences between their old-fashioned, conservative ways and her experiences. He'd been impressed by her maturity and intelligence.

He was reminded of that now, as she worked in the team with Deb and Liam, sliding easily into their rhythms and ways of working, joining in the friendly teasing and insults as if she'd known them for years.

He still couldn't think of her as connected to him. His intellect knew it must be so, but his mind skirted the issue, avoiding the words, refusing to acknowledge it. He had too much else to deal with. Far easier to just put her in the same mental box as Deb and Liam — people he'd first met as teenagers, kids who'd had a damn raw deal, but had come up fighting for their dreams.

But then he reached around for more pans and caught the grin she shared with Liam — an innocent, friendly grin, with just a hint of lingering, of wondering — and the sudden jolt of worry for the girl, the instant protectiveness caught him like a thunderbolt.

He slid the pans into the water, drizzled on fresh detergent and started scrubbing again. Hard.

While Sandy and his team completed the examination of the shack and shed, Kris found Steve outside, putting the box Gil had hidden into his car.

"What did you think of the contents?" she asked.

He leaned against the car. "We have to send it to Petric."

"To *Joe?*" She didn't bother hiding her displeasure. "Shouldn't you be handling it?"

"He's in the specialist Organised Crime Unit for the state, Kris. If Gillespie's claim that Flanagan is connected with the Sydney mob is true, then it's already Petric's case."

If Gillespie's claim is true. The implied doubt irritated her.

"So you're not going to do anything about it?"

Unperturbed by her irritation, he shrugged carelessly. "I didn't say that. I'll make a few enquiries. But the fact is, Kris, this stuff is all twenty years or so old, and there's not proof of anything here. It's not even enough for a search warrant. Our few resources are better spent on higher priority cases than hunting for witnesses to lesser crimes that occurred two decades ago, that we'll probably never be able to prove."

"Cultivation of a cannabis crop and extortion aren't exactly insignificant," Kris pointed out, although she accepted she'd already lost the argument.

"No, but they're not murder, arson, rape or child abuse, either. And we've got all that on our plate at the moment, and more. I'll make a few enquiries, as I said, Kris. But given the drought, and the fact the river's scarcely flowing these days, I doubt anyone's trying to grow marijuana around here any more, hydroponically or otherwise. Most of the production's apparently moved to coastal areas in the last twenty years."

Oh, how she hated it when he was right.

"And what about Anne Gillespie? I spoke with Delphi earlier, and she confirmed what Gil said about the time his mother disappeared."

"I guess that gives us a date, assuming we can rely on Delphi's memory. I'll interview a few of the older people, see if their recollections coincide, and we'll check bank records and such to see if there was any activity after that, but it looks fairly straight forward. The skull had a significant blow. We'll have to wait for the autopsy report, and there'll be a coronial inquest, of course, but my guess is the guy found out she was leaving, and slammed her on the head with a heavy object."

"Poor woman."

"Yep. Some women sure pick 'em."

She saw Sandy strolling down the track from the shed, and they walked across to meet him halfway, the apricot-tinged light from the low-hanging sun mellowing the dusty colours of the landscape around them, beautiful despite the ugly history of the place.

"We're just about done," Sandy told them. "A few interesting things you'll want to know about, though. First up, we found a door into the cavity space — behind that big cupboard in the corner. Sealed up a long time ago, though. Second, those plastic boxes, they're full of food. Tinned stuff, mostly, but there are some grains. Or were, before the weevils got into them."

"Any idea of dates?" Kris asked.

"Before compulsory use-by and packaging dates. One of the tins of peaches has a price label of twenty-three cents, so at a wild guess I'd say early to mid-seventies."

"How much food is there?" Steve asked. "Are we talking stuff that fell off the back of a truck, or a stockpile?"

"A small stockpile. Maybe a couple of weeks' worth. Tinned meat, tinned fruit, tinned vegies. A fairly reasonable diet, to be honest."

"If you're going to stockpile food in case of some disaster, it makes sense to have a secret place to hide it, I guess," Kris mused. "Did you find anything else of interest?"

"A small suitcase with women's clothes," Sandy answered. "A kid's backpack with a few clothes and a couple of books. I'm guessing that he might have built the false wall to hide the food — some people had odd ideas about the Chinese or Indonesians invading, back then — but once the woman's body was there, he sealed it off. However, the really interesting thing . . ." He took a small plastic evidence bag out of the envelope he carried, "was this."

Kris turned the bag over to see its contents better. The remnants of a ribbon, with faded blue, red and yellow stripes. A round, tarnished medal. "A military medal?"

Sandy nodded. "Have to clean it up a bit more to check, but it looks like a Vietnam Medal, awarded to Australian service personnel who went to Vietnam. My uncle had one, which is why I recognised it. But it reminded me of something I noticed in the autopsy report on Des Gillespie last year. There was evidence of an old head injury, and a couple of tiny pieces of shrapnel still there."

Kris couldn't recall seeing the report; but then, things had been fairly hectic around that time. "You think Des was injured in Vietnam?"

"The medal suggests it's a possibility. Gil could do some research if he wants, find out if the medal was his father's and, if so, get hold of his service record."

If he wants . . . Kris didn't think that would be particularly likely. But maybe she'd make an enquiry or two herself. War service, a head wound . . . perhaps there might be an explanation for Des's violent instability.

"Well, I'd better get packed up," Sandy said.

"I'll wait until you're done," Steve volunteered. "Because Cinderella here has to go and get beautiful for the ball."

The ball. She hadn't given it a single thought for hours. She glanced at her watch and groaned. She had less than an hour to retrieve her car, get home, get showered, dressed and made-up, and be ready to stand beside Mark Strelitz and the organising committee to greet people. And, somewhere along the way, she needed to dredge up some enthusiasm for the event.

The town was quiet as she drove in — everybody else would be getting their glad-rags on, too, she supposed. As she got out of her car, a few bars of guitar music came from the hall, and a voice: "Testing, testing . . . is that working?" Someone must have assured him that it was, for it fell silent again.

Despite her lateness, she took the luxury of at least ten minutes for her shower, letting the hot water flow over aching muscles, giving her hair a wash. It would have to make do with a quick blow-dry and natural waves. She carefully lifted the plastic cover off the dress, but hesitated before putting it on.

Enthusiasm. She needed to find it from somewhere. Jeanie would want her to be cheerful about the evening. Most of the town would be there. Mark would be a pleasant partner. Ryan and Beth were having their first night out together in almost a year.

She slipped the dark blue silk off the hanger, drew it down over her head, and twisted to zip up the back.

But when she stood before the mirror, the thin straps and the fitted, low-cut bodice did nothing to hide the

239

bruises and scratches on her shoulders and arms, colouring up nicely after last night's incident, despite Beth's ointment.

She bit her lip in frustration. Why a ball, of all things? A picnic would have been so much easier. She could more easily have been enthusiastic about a picnic. She could have joined in the egg and spoon races, bobbed for apples, even been the target in a dunking machine. The locals would have paid up big to send her into the water, and it would have all been fun. She could have worn jeans, for heaven's sake, instead of this nightmare of an evening dress that was just not her, despite the earnest assurances of the salesgirl at the Birraga boutique.

She'd faced down riots and hardened criminals without flinching, but she'd never felt more like chickening out of something than she did right now. Sergeant's stripes and ten years of policing were kindergarten stuff compared with the horror of being on the official table of a small-town ball.

Music began to float in earnest from the Memorial Hall. She was almost out of time. Maybe if she just wore the sheer wrap that came with the dress and kept it on all night, no-one would notice the scratches and bruises.

She pulled back the skirt to buckle up her sandals and saw the indents on her ankles from the elasticised socks she'd been wearing all today.

"The height of feminine elegance," she muttered to herself. Just as well she hadn't gone for the dress with the side slits. The long, draping skirt of this one would

240

keep her sock-marked legs artfully concealed. She quickly applied some basic make-up, then grabbed the gold evening purse the boutique girl had convinced her complemented the dress, yanked the paper stuffing out of it, and stowed her key, her phone and some cash in it.

A knock sounded on the seldom-used front door.

"Coming," she called, adding under her breath, "ready or not."

Mark waited for her, effortlessly handsome in a well-cut black dinner suit, and he smiled, eyes sparkling, as he saw her.

"Gorgeous, Kris. Stunning." He kissed her on the cheek, and drew her arm through his.

Outside, dusk had deepened to night, the warmth still lingering from the sunny day. A half-dozen or so cars were already parked on the road in front of the hall, and here and there along the road couples and individuals who lived in town walked to the event.

Kris saw the hall itself, and gasped.

"It's . . . it's beautiful."

Hundreds of fairy lights, strung in lace patterns, draped down from the eaves of the old building, the new paint shining a soft white in the glow. The few large gum trees around the building were decorated with jewel-coloured lanterns hanging from low branches, illuminating outdoor tables and chairs; more of the fairy lights laced around the edges of the marquee behind the hall, two of its sides open to show the bar and the white, flower-decorated tables where supper would be set out.

For the last year or two, she'd hated looking at the place, with the constant, lurking reminder of its use as the police operations base through two long, traumatic investigations.

Now the transformation from a tired, old wooden building to somewhere picturesque and inviting seemed to hold out a promise, and for the first time in a long, long time she felt lighter, hopeful. Enthusiasm began to fill her, natural and unforced.

"They've done a fantastic job, haven't they?" Mark said, and although compliments were part of his politician's way, his pride surpassed mere politeness. "Just wait until you see inside."

They walked to the hall, arm in arm, and Frank Williams, chair of the organising committee, stood by the door and welcomed them with a smile that beamed so brightly it could have lit the room by itself.

Around every window, white organza draped gracefully; flower arrangements decorated tables set among the chairs around the edges, and the wooden floor, sanded and polished to a rich shine, invited dancing.

But it was the people who made Kris's breath catch again. Although still early, the organising committee and their partners had arrived, their usual casual working clothes replaced by formal outfits. The men stood inches taller in dinner suits and here and there a colourful brocade waistcoat. And the women . . . Beth, defying her childhood nickname, looked beautiful in a deep, rich red gown, Ryan holding onto her hand and bursting with masculine pride. Eleni Pappas, her gold

242

jacket embroidered with shimmering beads. Dainty Joy Dawson, elegant — and proud — in a dress from her native Philippines, the shaped organza sleeves a perfect frame for her face and her intricate hairstyle.

And — Kris almost didn't recognise her — Delphi O'Connell . . . in a dress. Kris couldn't remember ever seeing her in anything but patched work clothes, but there she was, in a simply cut but surprisingly elegant black dress, a string of pearls at her throat.

Keeping her arm through his, Mark drew Kris further into the room, and as they greeted people it struck her that all of them, like Frank, were smiling. Beaming. *Joyful*.

Kris hadn't seen so many smiles in . . . forever, it seemed. There had been too much sorrow, and confusion, and guilt to allow for joy to bloom.

"Jeanie should be here to see this," she said quietly to Mark.

"I'll call her during the evening," he replied. "And I'll send some photos to Nancy's phone, so she can show her."

She nodded, unsurprised by his thoughtfulness. It was just the kind of thing he did.

From the stage, Adam waved to her as he picked up his guitar, and within moments the band eased into a lilting folk tune, gentle but uplifting.

As Kris took her place beside Mark in the welcoming group, and guests started to arrive, she could almost begin to believe that the ball might really make a positive difference to the struggling community.

CHAPTER
FOURTEEN

Through the open door and windows of the pub kitchen, they could hear the music at the hall. Two bands, Gil noted, alternating sets. One an old-time dance band, with squeeze-box, keyboard, guitar and drums, the other a more contemporary folk band, putting their own harmonic twist on bush-dance classics.

Liam and Megan had taken the first batch of trays — the cold finger food — up to the hall earlier, on Megan's way to the Wilsons' to babysit for them for the evening. Liam hadn't objected at all when Gil had told him to take her there before coming back, and not let her walk alone.

Angie had her hands full in the bar with a couple of carloads of German tourists, as well as a few locals not attending the ball, so Deb had taken over the remainder of the cooking.

Now there was only the hot food to finish, some things already cooked and keeping warm, and a couple of final dishes to cook and serve fresh from the oven.

He hadn't told Deb and Liam much about the afternoon's developments. There had been little opportunity with Megan and Angie there, and now he decided to wait until later, when they'd finished for the evening.

While Deb rolled small spiced meatballs, Gil and Liam worked on either side of the centre bench to spoon filling into six dozen mini-quiches.

"The pub's for sale," Liam commented, with a casual innocence Gil saw straight through.

"No," Gil said flatly.

Liam grinned, and pretended he hadn't heard. "Angie and her brother came back to town to run it until it's sold, but their temporary licence expires soon, and they've both got other jobs to go to. If they don't get a buyer this month, it'll close."

Gil kept filling quiches and refused to comment. Liam had boundless imagination and optimism, and saw potential behind every "For Sale" sign — especially when attached to old buildings.

"A place like this could be developed into a sound business, with some planning and investment," he said, true to form. "Eco-tourism could be a drawcard, done well."

"I'm not going to buy the pub, Liam," he growled.

"It will be a huge blow for the town if it closes. But if someone with business sense invested in it, renovated it, it could be a solid success."

Some days, Gil admired Liam's cheerful and tenacious pursuit of his goals, despite the obstacles. Today wasn't one of those days.

He put down his spoon, laid his hands flat on the bench, and looked directly at the guy. "Liam, half of Dungirri is afraid I'm a murderer. The other half is convinced of it. That's not a good business basis for a community facility like a pub. And, as for minor renovations, the building needs gutting. The only bathrooms are shared, probably haven't been touched for forty years, and new plumbing's bloody expensive to put in, especially in a hundred-year-old building. The whole place needs rewiring. Electrics are probably a fire hazard, and there's no phone or internet in the rooms."

"You did all that and more in Sydney," Liam pointed out calmly.

"Yes, I did." And he'd worked damned hard, doing as much himself as possible to keep costs down. "But potential returns on the investment were much greater than anything you could possibly get here. This is way too far from Sydney to appeal to the weekend crowd. Most of the people who come out this way are either camping or caravanning, sticking to a budget. That doesn't leave a lot of room for margins that can earn a living and repay an investment."

Liam had the sense to shut up, but he didn't look at all defeated.

"Now you've done it, Gil," Deb commented. "Liam'll probably come up with a business plan within a week."

"Then he can find somebody else to finance it. It's not the type of business we agreed we were looking for." He didn't mean it to sound harsh, but he had too much on his mind to indulge in flights of fancy. They were used to his blunt ways, though, and neither of them pursued the topic as they finished up the cooking.

When everything was ready, Liam loaded his car with warm, foil-covered trays and left to drive up to the hall. After Gil washed the last few dishes, Deb brought a couple of schooners of beer from the bar, and they went into the courtyard to drink them.

They sat in companionable silence, as they'd done many times before. It had been their habit to meet over coffee in the morning, in the small courtyard behind the pub in Sydney, Gil letting the first kick of caffeine jumpstart his brain while Deb worked on the day's menus. She'd always let him wake up properly, get accustomed to the daylight, before she raised any issues they needed to go over before the day's trading began.

Gil took a sip of his beer, then stretched out his legs, and leaned back in the wooden seat, closing his eyes. He let his body relax, tired muscles appreciating the cessation of activity, his mind slowing down enough after the bustle of the evening to begin unravelling the multiple strands of worry that were still unresolved. One action was clear — when Liam returned, he'd tell both of them they were leaving in the morning.

He could hear Deb shifting in her chair, the muted clunk of her glass on the table each time she took a mouthful and set it down again. Still on the post-cooking buzz, she didn't slow down easily, either her hands or her mind.

Another swallow of beer, another clunk of the glass, before she broke the silence. "The police sergeant seems okay."

He didn't bother opening his eyes. "She's not your type."

"Oh, jeez, I know that. She's as straight as they come. But she's smart, attractive, and has the sense to know you're no murderer."

"Deb?"

"Yes?"

He only needed to open one eye to give her a warning look. "Do not even *think* it."

Instead of shutting up, she laughed. "You need to get yourself a life, Gil. Or a woman. Or both."

"I have a life."

She snorted. "A life? Until three days ago, you worked eighteen or twenty hours a day, seven days a week, for years. That's not what I call a life."

Only three days ago? Yeah, that was all, despite everything that had happened since then. And facing down the current threats wasn't what he'd call a life, either.

"When was the last time you slept with a woman?" She looked at him over her glass, her grin daring him to answer.

He could have told her to mind her own business, but they'd known each other for enough years that she probably could hazard a good guess at the answer, anyway.

"Not that long ago." A few weeks. A month or two. Maybe more. He couldn't really remember when. Some brazen, brunette lawyer who'd come on to him at the bar, hot and strong, and hung around till after closing and so he'd taken what she'd offered, hard and fast against his office door.

"The verb in that sentence was 'slept'," Deb retorted, as if she'd read his mind. "Not 'screwed'. Tangled limbs, under the covers, nice, slow, waking up together in the morning . . . that sort of thing, you know?"

Did he know? He dug around in his memory, came up with nothing. Sex, oh, yeah, he knew that. Healthy, uncomplicated, uncommitted sex. Anything else . . .

He reached for his beer, the liquid sliding down his throat smoothly. "Anyone ever tell you that grilling the boss about his sex life is usually a sackable offence?"

"You're not my boss anymore."

"No, I guess not. Just your future business partner. The one with the money."

She grinned cheekily. "And a truckload of empty threats."

Liam came out of the pub, a soft drink in his hand, and joined them at the table.

Gil straightened up, leaned his elbows on the table, hands clasping the schooner.

"Speaking of threats," he said, "I need to tell you about this afternoon. And first thing tomorrow morning, both of you are leaving here."

They objected, of course. They objected, and argued, and discussed, in low tones, that it had to be Tony responsible and how he might be exposed, and insisted that if Gil stayed, they should too.

"Listen, you two," he said finally, "Tony Russo isn't the only person with a vendetta." He rubbed some condensation off the glass with his thumb, and then told them the worst. "Last January, I informed a senior police officer about two bent detectives working with Kevin Jones. That info led directly to the arrest of the coppers and most of the Jones mob. The only person who knew it could have been me was Marci, and it's likely she leaked that before she died. If she did, then my life expectancy is now pretty darned short."

"Jesus, Gil," Deb said, "you informed on *Kevin Jones*? Shouldn't they be putting you in a safe house or something?"

"No. Going into protection means too many police would know, and it only takes one bent copper to leak that information. If I'm here, in the open, then they'll target me directly, and not use others to get to me."

For once, there was no sign of a smile on Liam's face. Despite his upbeat nature, he knew, even more so than Deb, the brutal realities of organised crime and the punishment for informing. As a boy he'd been forced to witness the execution of his mother and sister, a bloody message for his brother, caught between rival Vietnamese drug lords.

"That's why you want us out of the way." Liam spoke flatly.

"Yes. I'd prefer you left tonight, but you both look ready to crash, so first thing in the morning gives you a chance to get some sleep, and be more alert."

"There must be something we can do," Deb insisted. "Not just leave you in this shit by yourself. We're not *useless*."

"Disappearing for a few days will help me. Head out east in the morning, withdraw as much cash as you can from the first ATM you see, and keep your phones

250

switched off. If they do look for you, they'll think you're heading back to Sydney. Go north or south instead, and only use cash."

Reluctantly they agreed, and after a few minutes arranging methods of contact, he left them to discuss which direction to travel.

Some people might think it strange how well the three of them got along, with no blood relationship and no romance. Confident now in her career and herself, Deb was hardly recognisable as the bashed-up, runaway teenager he'd found on the pub's back doorstep, ten years ago. And ever since Liam had shown up five years back, offering to work in exchange for a meal, Deb had been one of his champions. Liam had returned the friendship with loyalty, and plenty of brotherly cheek. So, they'd look out for each other, those two, Gil had no doubt about it.

Which left him to look out for the other two people at risk through association with him. Convincing Kris to go would likely be impossible, and as for Megan . . . he had to hope that if no-one knew their connection, she'd be safe.

He left the pub through the side gate, avoiding the bar. Through the windows he could see Sean Barrett and a couple of mates at the pool table, a formal ball with the old folk obviously not their style. Although he could imagine them raising hell and getting smashed at a Bachelors and Spinsters ball.

He needed to stretch his legs, get some air and find some space to think. He could have taken the Birraga road, or turned on to Showground Road and headed out of town on one of the tracks into the scrub, but the music floated from the hall, and without consciously making a decision, he turned towards it.

Through the open door, Kris glimpsed a shadow moving among the trees on the bank of the creek beyond her place. The dark shape of a man, dropping down into a relaxed, comfortable bushman's crouch, watching from a distance.

Gil Gillespie. The one man in town who could never walk into this ball as if he belonged.

The hall suddenly seemed too crowded, too stuffy, and the cool night air beckoned. Kris murmured an excuse to the people she'd been talking to and slipped out the open side door, the skirt of her long dress brushing her legs as she crossed the rough grass between them.

"Quite the belle of the ball, aren't you?" That laconic tone of his drifted through the darkness as she approached.

"Give me a pair of jeans and a T-shirt any day," she retorted, although, just now, she did for the first time actually feel *good* in the unaccustomed sensuality of the evening dress, with the light breeze brushing skin not usually exposed. And she wasn't planning on examining that feeling too closely.

She couldn't see his face clearly. With a nod towards the hall, he asked, "So, are you and Strelitz an item?"

"Me and Mark?" She laughed out loud. "A politician and a cop? Not a good combination for anything other

252

than friendship, believe me. Diplomacy isn't my thing. And I'd want to arrest half his colleagues."

"What about the guy you were dancing with before him?"

He'd been watching her. Heck, he might have been watching any number of people, she reminded herself, to squelch the warmth coiling through her veins. He'd grown up in this town, knew most of its people.

"Scott? He's . . . nice. But he's also Ingrid Sauer's fiancée. Did you know her?"

He screwed up his face and thought for a moment. "Snotty-nosed blond kid with plaits? Or maybe that was her cousin."

She laughed lightly. "They've both grown up a bit, since then."

The music drifted across to them, muted at this distance, and she leaned against an old fencepost.

He still hunkered by the creek bank, and it struck her how surprisingly at ease in the bush environment he was, for a man who'd spent the past decade and a half in Sydney's inner suburbs.

And she couldn't, for the moment, picture him in the busy streets of the city, because he belonged here, in the dark stillness of the bush, as natural and untamed and complex as the wilderness around them.

The barking call of an owl echoed somewhere nearby, breaking into the easy silence that had fallen between them.

"You should go back inside to your friends, enjoy the party," he said.

"I'm not much of a party person. Besides, the company's fine out here for now."

He snorted. "Not many of them would agree with you." He said it carelessly, as if it didn't matter.

But it did matter, and she dropped the teasing banter and addressed the issue seriously. "It seems to me there's a lot of question marks over your supposed responsibility for Paula Barrett's death."

He was quiet for a moment. "How do you figure that?"

"I looked up a few records yesterday, Gil. It appears there was no evidence other than the blood-alcohol report, to suggest, let alone prove, negligence or culpability. Which leads me to suspect that there wasn't any, and that the report was falsified to nail you."

He rose, strolled a few steps away to stand with his back to the light coming from the hall, his face in shadow. "Cruddy investigation and record keeping doesn't change a person's guilt or innocence."

He might have been talking about the weather, for all the emotion in his voice. And yet . . . the controlled stillness of his silhouette convinced her that the don't-give-a-damn attitude was merely a hard shell of protection around a core that *did* give a damn.

"No, it doesn't. Nor does it make a crime out of a tragic accident." The dark, an unlit country road, and a kangaroo leaping out — she'd seen the results too many times, almost come to grief that way herself, and not just the other night.

He reached for a low-hanging branch, picked a leaf, and twirled the stem in his teeth.

"People don't like accidents," he said. "They always want someone to blame."

He was right, but it didn't make the situation right. "Sometimes no-one is at fault. Maybe they'll just have to get used to that idea."

"Don't go mounting a PR campaign on my behalf, Blue."

"Why not?"

He tossed the leaf to the ground. "Because it doesn't matter. I'm leaving here tomorrow. I don't care what they think. And because the less you have to do with me, the better. Tony Russo, the Flanagans . . . they're dangerous, Blue. They've already threatened you. They won't hesitate to do more."

"Are you trying to frighten me, Gil?"

"Yes," he said, blunt and hard. "You shouldn't have stood up for me, put yourself at risk. You should have run like hell from me the moment we met, Blue. You should run like hell from me now."

She held his dark gaze with hers. "I'm not running, Gil."

He stood unmoving in the night, his face still in shadow, his voice, when he spoke again, rough and low. "What if I told you that every time I see you, I imagine you naked?"

His attempt to frighten her with that tactic didn't work. If it had just been a line, it might have pissed her off, but the raw honesty only spoke aloud what they both knew and had been avoiding.

And maybe the night and the moonlight were stirring some wild part of her, eroding her usual caution, but she discovered that she wanted no lies or denials between them, just acceptance of who they were and what they felt. So she answered him with the same honesty. "If you told me that, I'd have to admit that it's a mutual distraction. I'm not going to pretend otherwise."

He started, then yanked his eyes away, muttering, "Jesus, Blue." He dragged a boot heel through the dirt, scoring two furrows before he stopped, threw her a look that was both question and challenge, and said, "Then you're as crazy as I am."

The return of the dark humour to his voice let her breathe again. It would be all right. Whatever "it" was.

Still with a metre between them, she inclined her head and watched him, teasing him lightly, "That's a novel approach to sweet-talk, Gillespie."

"I don't do 'sweet', Blue. Slow, sometimes. But definitely not 'sweet'."

" 'Sweet' is overrated."

Three seconds passed before he challenged softly, "Yeah?"

"Definitely." And she had no idea if she was flying out of control, or totally in control, but right now she didn't actually care.

There was nothing slow or sweet or polite about their kiss. Nothing gentle or tentative, just raw and insistent and demanding.

Her initial thought — while she was still thinking — was that she would like to kiss him. Two adults, mutual attraction, a natural response. But hunger flared instantly, as their bodies touched, a fierce need to take from him and give to him she didn't want to resist. She gave up thinking, let the wild heart of herself respond without constraint.

Heartbeat spiralling, her hands explored the contours of hard chest, shoulders and back that she'd dreamed about since that first night. As bold and possessive as his hands roaming her, heated against her skin and through the fabric of her dress, drawing them together for total contact from mouths to thighs. Desire and need and Gil became her only awareness.

Until he pulled back. Abrupt and hard, letting her go and twisting on his heel to move several feet away, leaning his hand against a tree while he dragged in breaths.

She tugged her light wrap around her, the air cool on her heated skin, words and sensations too jumbled in her mind to arrange in coherent shape.

He gave a hard, bitter laugh. "Christ. I need my frigging head read."

Definitely not sweet-talk, but before she could frame a reply, a crackle of dry leaves warned her of someone approaching, and she turned to see Mark standing in the moonlight.

"Everything all right, Kris?"

"Yes. Fine." Oh, yes, fine if she didn't count fractured breathing and the ground doing a rollercoaster impersonation underneath her feet. She dragged some semblance of politeness together. "Mark, do you remember Gil Gillespie?"

Mark nodded acknowledgment, and the two men watched each other with all the wariness of a couple of wild dogs circling. "Gil. It's been a long time."

Her blood pressure, starting to come down, shot up again as she realised the significance of this meeting between the two men. It *had* been a long time — eighteen years since they'd been in a car together with Mark's girlfriend, Paula. A night that had ended with Paula dead, Mark critically injured in hospital, and Gil arrested. No wonder Mark hadn't stepped forward and shaken hands with his usual courtesy.

"Yeah," Gil responded eventually. "A long time." And then he glanced across at her, closed and distant again, as though they hadn't just been kissing each other senseless. "Well, I'll leave you two to your party."

He turned on his heel and headed towards the trees, disappearing into the darkness.

He needed to walk. He passed the pub, took the side road down to the school, crossed the playing fields and jumped over the creek. Once out of town, the full moon lit the dirt track into the scrub, the shadows of the trees black against the silver light.

His thoughts scrambled, too many things going on, each strand spinning around and tangling with the others. Marci's murder. Vince's murder. The fire at Jeanie's. Jeanie hurt, in the hospital. The dead truck driver in the café. The search of the old place. His mother's skeleton. Megan. Kris. Kissing Kris and wanting to peel away her clothes and taste her and feel her and be inside her and forget every other damned thing in the world but the feeling of them together.

He groaned and hauled his thoughts back from that madness. What he needed to do was to sit down, go logically through each issue, work out a strategy, and then act on it. And those issues did not include getting physical with Kris.

A gap in the trees revealed a gateway, an access into a large, cleared paddock, gently sloping away into the distance. The gate was old and rickety, but the gatepost solid and devoid of barbed wire, so he hoisted himself up on to it, hoping the clear space and fresh air might help to bring some clarity to his mind.

As he looked out onto the peaceful, moonlit view it occurred to him how often he'd roamed the night landscape in his youth. As a kid, escaping his old man, he'd both loved the bush and hated it. Sanctuary and purgatory. Sometimes both at once. But once he'd learned its ways, grown tall and strong enough to be unafraid, he'd been more at home in the bush than in the dilapidated shack with his father.

Working long days and nights in the pub, he'd almost forgotten how the moonlight could shine, without the urban lights dimming it. And how black it could be, without moonlight or starlight, when clouds obscured the night sky. He'd sometimes roamed in Sydney, too, after close-up and the cleaning had been done, in the quieter hours before sunrise, his ingrained restlessness not always negated by hard work and long hours.

The wheel has come full circle; I am here.

The racing in his mind had slowed, and he accepted it now, as a statement without judgment or threat, an acknowledgment that this place — the bush, Dungirri, the plains beyond — was a part of him. Nothing would change that, no matter what happened, no matter where he went in the future — assuming he had one.

In order to have a future, he'd need to find some way out of the current problems. Logic. Strategy. Starting with one issue at a time.

His mother — not much he could do about that now, except arrange a decent burial for her, when the forensic lot finished with her remains. Maybe he could ask Kris to help him find her relations . . . No, he wouldn't be around Kris much longer. He'd track down his mother's family himself, have her buried where she belonged, if possible.

But first he had to get through the next few days. Which brought him to Marci's murder. On the list he'd drawn up for Kris, he'd written a few possibilities — Marci's boyfriend, a client, an associate of Jones and crew, and Tony Russo.

He didn't think it likely that Tony had actually killed her himself. The sex factor didn't sound like Tony's personal work. Violence, yes. Sex with it, no. But Tony was the one common link among all the names on all the lists. Whoever had actually killed Marci, Flanagan's network had been used to torch the café and destroy the evidence, and Tony must have called Flanagan in.

As to who'd killed Vince, Tony had to be a possibility, although presumably his alibi had been checked already. He was smart enough and connected enough to arrange an assassination, but why now, instead of five, ten, fifteen years ago? The relationship between him and Vince had been strained for years. Likewise, the Jones gang had always seen Vince as a rival, but why would *they* act now, when Kevin had been in jail for the last nine months?

If it was either Tony or a Jones associate, then something must have happened to trigger it. Gil cast his mind back to his meeting with Vince on Wednesday morning, trying to remember if Vince had said anything, indicated anything, that suggested a problem. He came up with nothing. The meeting had been brief, less than ten minutes, closer to five. He'd handed over the cash to Vince, explained what it was for, told him — told him, not asked him — to warn Tony off interfering any further with Marci, and let him know he'd arranged for Marci to go to Melbourne. Vince had asked if Marci had agreed to leave, and Gil had replied that he was working on it, and then he *had* asked, not told, Vince to speak with Marci and persuade her to go.

That had been pretty much it. Vince had been his usual self, greeting him with a degree of warmth Gil never returned. At the end, when Gil turned to leave, Vince had thanked him for keeping an eye on Marci, congratulated him on running a good business, and asked what he planned to do next. When Gil had shrugged and said he had no plans yet, Vince had smiled and said he hoped Gil wouldn't need the contents of his safety deposit box.

Which, when Gil came to think about it now, did seem a bit odd. In all the years since Gil had confronted him and laid out his terms, Vince had never once mentioned the safety deposit box.

Had Vince been trying to warn him he could no longer control Tony? If that was the case, then his own actions in involving Vince in repaying Marci's debt might have brought Vince and Tony into further conflict. He had no way of knowing — yet — but it raised the odds of Tony being a likely candidate.

He still had nothing definite. And he could either wait here in Dungirri for their next move — having sent Liam and Deb away — or he could go to Sydney himself and see what he could find out there. The latter seemed the better option. Dangerous, especially since he had nothing to hold over Tony, but then waiting around here was dangerous, too. Dangerous for him, but more so for Kris. The sooner he took himself away from her, the better for both of them.

The two bands combined to play the last waltz of the evening. As the first notes sounded, Frank Williams bowed before Delphi O'Connell and led her onto the floor, with more than a few interested people watching. Mark held out his hand, and Kris took it, slipping comfortably into the waltz hold and into the dance. Mark was an excellent dancer, guiding her around the room in perfect rhythm with the gentle melody.

The floor was crowded with couples and, as they danced, Kris saw Eleni's huge smile shining at George, Frank engaging Delphi in conversation, their hands clasped firmly, Paul and Chloe dancing close, eyes only for each other and, sitting beside each other, Beth leaning in to kiss Ryan.

Inexplicably, her eyes prickled with tears. God, she must be getting soft and melancholy in her old age, if the sight of happy couples could turn her to mush.

"It's been a successful night," Mark commented.

"It has," she agreed, grateful for a safe topic. "Thank you for your contributions — the food and matching the funds raised for Jeanie. I think people feel better for having done something for her tonight."

His hand tightened a little on her waist. "Do *you* feel better?"

"Me? Yes. It's nice to have everyone together for something positive for a change."

"So why are you still frowning?" he asked quietly. "And why are you being so polite with me?"

He was right, she was being polite. And their friendship was too solid, too important for her to shut him out like that. Mark was a good mate, her closest male friend, and one of the few men with whom she could relax and be herself.

"I'm sorry, Mark. I've just got a lot on my mind at the moment."

"Gil Gillespie got anything to do with that?"

She briefly considered evasion, and discarded the idea as both pointless and an insult to Mark, and to Gil.

"Yes. Events connected to him. And Gil himself."

He smiled, but although his eyes twinkled at her, she read a touch of sadness, too. "You like him."

"I . . . Yes, I do like him. I know you mightn't feel the same way, because of Paula, but underneath the tough exterior, I've found there's a lot about him to respect."

He broke eye contact, his hand tightening on hers as he manoeuvred them away from a crowded corner of the dance floor.

"There always was a lot to like. And I don't hate him, Kris."

"You were injured in the accident when Paula died."

"Yes. A head injury. I can't tell you anything about the accident, Kris. There's a hole in my memory. I don't remember a thing from a week before the accident, until the day I woke up in the hospital. I still don't remember anything."

"So that's why you weren't called as a witness." She'd noticed that in the court reports, but then Gil had pleaded guilty, and with the blood-alcohol report they wouldn't have needed anything more for a conviction.

But Mark might be able to shed some light on the recent troubles. He'd grown up in the district, worked for the previous local politician before he'd entered Parliament himself, and he knew a lot of people in the region, kept a finger on the district pulse.

"Have you ever heard anything about mafia activity around here?"

He raised his eyebrows, but didn't miss a step. "A few stories. Nothing ever solid. There was a marijuana trafficking bust, ten years or so back that people gossiped about, but nothing suggesting organised crime came out of the investigation, as far as I'm aware."

264

Crazy to be waltzing around with a handsome man, and talking about the mafia. She should just enjoy the moment, but she mightn't have another chance to talk to him before he went back to Canberra.

"Know anything about Dan Flanagan?" she asked.

"Hmmm." He frowned, guided her around a couple doing a slow-sway version of the dance. "How shall I put this diplomatically? A canny, successful business-man, with an excellent knowledge of the law — including its weaknesses and loopholes."

The music slowed to the final notes, and he twirled her around and finished with a gentlemanly bow.

Although the last dance signalled the official end of the ball, there seemed to be a general reluctance to finish the evening. Ryan and Beth went home to relieve their babysitter, Megan, as did some other parents. A few of the older people left, but others stayed and talked, sitting in small groups inside and outside the hall. The bar closed, but people lingered over their last drinks, and others were happy with soft drink or coffee from the kitchen.

Mark brought Kris a drink and she stayed for a while, but she was distracted, unable to concentrate on the social conversation, and when her phone rang in her purse, she excused herself with some relief. Steve's mobile, she saw, as she answered the call. And she'd missed a number of calls and messages.

"It's after midnight, Steve," she told him, straight up.

"I know it is, Cinderella. The ball's over and we've got trouble. I'm driving into Dungirri right now. Meet me at the station, and check your email. I sent your

265

photos from this afternoon to Alec, and he knows one of your guys. I'll see you in a few minutes."

Apprehension rising, Kris apologised to Mark and walked across the grass to the station, punching in the keycode and turning the lights on as she went inside. Their harsh fluorescent glare was a world away from the fairy lights of the hall.

She felt ridiculous, sitting there in her office in her silk dress and heeled sandals waiting for her computer to boot, but once it finished its whirring and she opened her email, she forgot all about the incongruity.

With the message, "*Is this one of the men you photographed?*" Alec had sent her an image. It looked like a detail from a surveillance photo, taken with a far better camera and zoom than her phone. A man's face, almost front-on, neatly cut dark hair, dark brows, straight nose, and a well-shaped chin, held high, with a confidence that could easily be arrogance.

She'd seen that angle of the head before, on the man in the dark jacket who'd casually fired off shots into the bush. She hit reply on her email, typed "*Yes. Who is he?*" and pressed send.

Five seconds later, her phone rang. Alec. He must have been sitting by his computer.

"Are you sure about the identification, Kris?" he asked, as soon as she answered the call. There was a knock at the door and, phone to her ear, she went to let Steve in.

"I can't be absolutely certain, because I didn't get close, but I'm pretty sure he's the one with the handgun, who gave orders." She waved Steve through to her office and flicked the phone to speaker. "So who is he, and why do you have his portrait on your computer?"

"Sergio Russo," Alec answered her question as she put the phone on her desk, between her and Steve. "Sergio's a distant cousin of Vince and Tony. He turned up in Sydney about nine months ago. We've got nothing solid on him yet, but we're seeing an increase in cocaine and ecstasy on the streets, in Sydney and all along the coast, and he's suspected by Interpol of connections to key players in a major Calabrian-run drug supply system."

She tugged her wrap closer over her chilly arms. *This is Dungirri*, she wanted to say. *We don't have mafia here*. But they did. Had for a long time, and she'd been oblivious. Now she had to deal with it, somehow.

"Kris, we can't prove it yet," Alec's voice continued, "but I'm damned sure the guy is a killer, and that he's behind a resurgence in the 'Ndrangheta activity in Australia. We put away Kevin Jones and most of his gang at the beginning of the year, and it looks like the Russos have moved in to fill the gap. Tony's never been particularly strong, but the remnants of the Jones crew had already gravitated to him, and now with Sergio here, and the new connections, they're knocking off the competition, or absorbing it. Sergio came up to the north coast a couple of weeks ago, and within days I had three dead dealers from rival gangs."

"And now Vince is dead, and the Russos have reason to think Gil is a threat."

Steve shot her a questioning glance, and on the phone there was a pause before Alec spoke. "Yes. He's a danger to them, Kris. Vince kept Tony in check for years, but in an odd way he seems to have trusted Gillespie. I don't know how much information Gillespie has, and neither do the Russos. But they probably know he's prepared to use what he has. Add that to Tony's long-held resentment of him, and they've got more than enough reason to want him out of the way."

Now she was cold, a bone-deep chill that had little to do with the air temperature.

"I've got to go, Kris," Alec said. "I'm expecting another call. Liaise with Fraser and Petric on this, and keep me informed. If I can help any more, let me know."

The phone fell silent, and the room seemed emptier without Alec's capable authority.

"Gillespie has more information against the Russos than what we got today? And am I the last to know about it?" Steve asked dryly.

"He had information against Vince," Kris said carefully. The fewer people who knew Gil had informed against the corrupt officers, the better. Even when it came to fellow officers. "That's how he got the hotel out of the Russos' territory."

"So that's what they've got against him. And why they're aiming to silence him."

She nodded. "What I don't understand is, if this Sergio Russo is now involved, and Tony's more powerful through him, then why not go straight for Gil?

Why the attempt to frame him for Marci's murder, why the search of his place?"

"If he'd been charged with murder, the likelihood is he'd have been punished in prison," Steve suggested. "The search — perhaps that was part of getting the local boys on-side. They're operating outside their familiar territory here."

It made a kind of sense. "Get the information compromising Flanagan, and Flanagan will put his resources at their disposal. But why not just act themselves? He hasn't exactly been hiding the past two days."

"He's been in police company most of that time," Steve pointed out. "But also, guys like this, they often want revenge, not just to get him out of the way. My guess is, they're looking for some way to punish him before he's executed."

CHAPTER
FIFTEEN

Gil came back into town on the southern edge, avoiding the hall. The moon rode high in the sky, and no more music carried on the light breeze. After midnight, then, he figured.

Coming past the school he heard voices, three or four of them, male, laughing and jeering. He couldn't see anything from the road. They must have been beyond the senior classroom, where a security light was on. He'd have ignored them, but for a shout and a strangled cry.

Gil walked faster, sprinting when there was another cry, and came around the corner as a girl — *Megan* — broke away from the four men, tried to run, but was quickly caught again and pressed back against the wall.

He roared, went straight in, grabbed the closest by his hair and yanked his head back, jerking him around to fling him to the ground. Two of them came for him. He got one in the face with his right fist, caught a weak punch in the head from the other, but managed to grab the guy's arm and wrench it down, twisting around him to ram him against the wall.

The fourth man — Sean bloody Barrett — had released his hold on the girl, and the first was already up off the ground, both of them advancing on Gil. The moonlight glinted on a knife in Barrett's hand.

"Run!" he shouted to the girl. She hesitated for an instant, then ran, disappearing around the corner. She had enough sense to go for help; all he had to do was keep these four from following her.

Barrett was strong, experienced and, Gil guessed, handy with a knife. The guy he'd knocked to the ground was young, not much more than a teenager, and lightly built. He made the mistake of grinning to someone behind Gil, a warning Gil took every advantage of. When the guy moved to grip his arms, he rammed his elbows back into soft flesh, doubling him over in pain.

Number three staggered a short distance away, nursing a broken nose, and the one on the ground behind him groaned and puked.

Which left Barrett and the lad — Gil thought it might be one of the Dawson boys — circling around him. The Dawson kid was a bit drunk; enough to make him brave, dull his senses a bit, but not enough to make him easy pickings. Barrett had drunk a few, too, he'd bet, but he was old enough to hold it well.

Dawson came first, barrelling in with a shout, trying to ram him down. More courage than sense, Gil thought, as he caught him by the shoulders, heaved him upright, and slammed his fist into his gut. The kid crumpled into a heap.

"Did you learn that in prison?" Barrett taunted.

"I learned a lot in prison," Gil replied. "Maybe you're afraid to find out how much, since you sent the boys in first."

Barrett's hand clenched on the knife, but he didn't take the bait. "You shouldn't have interfered in what doesn't concern you, Gillespie. We were just having some fun with the little slut. It's not as though she hasn't done it before. She's been on the streets."

Gil saw red before his eyes, rage threatening to blast a hole through his head.

"Don't go near her again," he ordered, through gritted teeth.

"Why? Cause you want to screw her? Sorry, Gillespie, but there's not much talent around here these days so I'm claiming her."

He could hear movement behind him, braced to deal with an attack, but he kept still, studying Barrett, watching his eyes. Dawson went for Gil's legs, tackling him, and he couldn't stop toppling, but he struck out as he fell, landing a hard kick, twisting so that he landed on his side and not his face, ready to take on Barrett as he leapt on him. Barrett slashed at his face with the knife, but Gil jerked his head away in time and caught a slice on the shoulder instead. A street-fighter would have plunged the knife in for the kill, but Barrett wanted to best him, to punish him, and thought he could. His mistake.

They rolled on the ground, wrestling for the knife. Gil had a grip on Barrett's wrist, keeping the knife at bay, until Dawson joined in, wrenching at his arm, giving Barrett the control for a swipe at his chest. The

272

blade burned on his skin, even as he pushed back hard at the weight of both of them on his arm.

There was a dull thud, and the kid's grip vanished. Barrett started, and Gil took the advantage of the split second of distraction and threw him, slamming a punch to his gut as he went over, disabling him long enough to get his knee on the knife arm and the blade out of Barrett's grip.

Pinning him down, finding his own breath again, Gil discovered he didn't need to keep the knife to Barrett's throat to hold him still. Barrett's eyes were on Megan, standing beside his head, a stout branch held aloft in her hands, ready to strike.

An absurd sense of pride mixed with anger in Gil's mind at the sight of her. Such a slight build, her loose, goth tunic top ripped at the shoulder and a mark on her face where one of the bastards had hit her. Yet she held her weapon like a young Amazon.

"I told you to run," Gil growled at her.

"I did. The police are coming. But you needed help." Still holding the branch steady, she glanced at the lad lying on the ground, clutching the back of his head. He groaned and moved, rolling on to his other side, and Megan breathed an audible sigh of relief.

They could hear cars pulling up out on the road, doors slamming. Two of the attackers — the first two down — headed off on unsteady feet across the playing fields. There was a shout from the road, and someone set off after them at a sprint.

Barrett started to shift, but Gil moved the knife back to his throat. "Don't try it," he warned. "Between me and her, you don't have a chance."

Barrett's glance flicked from one to the other, then back again. He took a long look at each of them, and grinned. "Well, holy fuck, hey?" He started to laugh. "Jeez, Gillespie, so it was you who laid the princess. What a fucking joke."

"Shut it, Barrett," Gil warned, but it was already way too late. People were there, had already heard. Someone gently shifted Megan aside, and Gil looked up and passed Fraser the knife.

He levered himself to his feet and stumbled a few metres away, out of the glare of the security light. Blood dribbled down his arm, and when he put his hand to the stinging on his chest, it came away covered in it.

He could hear Barrett playing the innocent, proclaiming they'd just been chatting when "Daddy there came in swinging like a mad man, raging about us talking with his little girl". Gil gritted his teeth, resisting the urge to go and slam a fist into Barrett's face, wishing he'd had reason to use the knife earlier and shut him up before this.

There were at least half a dozen people there now, another car arriving, and they'd all hear it. Barrett would make sure of that, and Gil knew how quickly the juicy gossip would spread through town. They'd brand Megan with the Gillespie stigma, and make her life hell.

And as soon as word got back to Flanagan and Russo, they'd regard her as the perfect way to get to him. He couldn't let that happen.

Kris arrived at the scene about three minutes after Steve, Adam and Mark, her evening dress replaced in those minutes by jeans, sweatshirt, boots and her uniform belt — far safer for active police work than a long gown.

The men had taken extra help from those still at the hall. Near the senior classroom, Steve held Sean Barrett against the wall, and Karl knelt beside Trent Dawson on the ground, his first-aid bag open. Adam and Mark were walking back across the grass, with two more between them. Outside the circle of the security light, Gil watched from the shadows.

Megan stood to one side, arms clutched around herself, her top torn, and Kris went straight to her. The girl buried her face against her shoulder, and Kris held her close, letting her take her time.

"Can you tell me what happened, Megan? Didn't Beth take you home?"

Megan straightened, wiped a shaky hand across her eyes, bravely trying not to cry. "Yes. But when I got up the drive, I realised that my keys were in my jacket, which I'd left in the pub kitchen today. I didn't want to wake the grands, so I decided to go and get it. It's only a block. But then Trent and Sean and the others came, and . . ." Her voice wobbled. "They'd been drinking, and I couldn't get them to leave me alone. And then Sean pulled out a knife." A sob escaped her, and Kris tightened her arm around her. "I was scared, Kris. I tried to get away from them but I couldn't. But then Gil arrived. I ran across the road, got Mr Trevelyn to phone you, and then I looked for a big stick, so I could help Gil. There were four of them against him, and I didn't know how long you'd be."

Long enough, thought Kris, with a sick wrench in her stomach. Four against one. Gil could have been seriously injured, or killed, in those few minutes, but for Megan's help.

"I hit Trent on the head. I had to. Sean and Gil were fighting, and Sean had the knife. And then Trent joined in and Gil got cut and . . . he couldn't hold off both of them."

Kris was focused on Megan, listening to her, putting together what had happened, so although she heard Sean's shout in the background, it took a moment for his words to sink in.

"Hey, Gillespie, I reckon I know someone who'll love to hear about your little girl."

Gil's little girl? It didn't make sense . . . until she remembered Jeanie, the other morning, worrying about Gil going off without a word, saying, ". . . *he was upset, shocked, about something I'd told him . . .*"

A hitherto unknown daughter? That would have been a hell of a shock, enough to send a man like Gil off for some thinking time. And Megan had just turned seventeen, the right age for her conception to have occurred prior to Gil's abrupt departure from town.

He hadn't said anything . . . but then, Kris realised, when would he have had a chance? If he'd only found out yesterday morning, the time since then had been packed with other, more urgent concerns. No wonder he wore that cautious emotional armour; Dungirri had dumped one blow after another on him ever since he'd arrived.

Megan had heard Sean, too. Maybe she'd heard more than Kris, or there'd been things said earlier, during the fight, as she drew back to see Kris's face and asked, "Is it true? Is he . . . my father?"

It was all there, in front of her — straight black hair, with the widow's peak point at the centre of her forehead, dark eyes, the Saxon cheek bones, softer on Megan but still evident.

How the heck could she answer that? Paternity was a damned delicate matter, and with only guesswork and not knowing the full story, she had to tread carefully. "He hasn't said anything to me, Megan. Let's wait until this situation is sorted out, and you can ask him later, okay?"

She'd make darn sure she had a word with Gil to prepare him before "later" came.

Beth arrived, called in by Karl. Satisfied Megan was unharmed, just shaken, Kris left the girl in Beth's care.

Steve and Adam, with help from Mark, had Megan's attackers under control and were going through their stories. Kris looked over at the four of them: Sean Barrett, Zac and Trent Dawson, and Luke Sauer.

What was Sean doing, hanging around with youths fifteen years his junior? Zac and Luke were around nineteen or twenty, Trent barely eighteen. She could bet who'd been the ringleader in this crime; but there'd be time enough to sort that out later. Adam was already on the phone, calling in backup from Birraga, and Karl had moved on from Trent, and was now giving his cousin hell even as he mopped blood off his face.

Thirty metres away, in the shadows, Gil stood looking out over the playing field instead of watching the others. He didn't turn around as she approached.

"What happened, Gil?" she asked from behind him.

He took a little time answering, his back still to her. "I heard voices, then she cried out, and I came round here and found the four of them attacking her."

"So you fought them?"

"No other choice."

No, she figured, there probably hadn't been — for him. He wouldn't leave a girl alone, undefended, no matter the risk.

"Are you hurt?"

"Not much."

Uh-oh. She put a hand on his arm. "Define 'much'."

"A scratch. Or two." He turned, and she saw the ripped T-shirt, the wet cloth sticking to his chest, the blood on his arm, but as she gasped and moved forward to inspect the wounds, he stepped back abruptly. "Don't!"

He might still be on edge from the fight. From the wounds. From seeing Megan attacked. And was likely in pain, perhaps even a touch of shock.

She purposely played down her concern. "Really, Gillespie, if that's a scratch I'd hate to see a gash."

"It's not deep. Look after Megan. She needs to get home."

"I'll get her there, very soon. But you need that cut looked at."

He attempted to dismiss her worry with a wave of his blood-smeared hand. "It can wait. I'll wipe the blood up with something." He lowered his voice, spoke urgently, without any trace of confusion from his injuries, "Blue, she isn't safe. When word gets out, they could go for her."

"It's true then? You're her father?"

"Yeah." He nodded wearily, as if still trying to convince himself. "Dates are right, circumstances right. And the resemblance is strong."

Police training didn't cover what to say to a man who'd recently discovered an almost-grown daughter. "Congratulations" didn't exactly cut it, and sympathy could be awkward, not knowing the circumstances and never having met Barbara Russell. So she gave him what she could, and what he needed — some knowledge about the girl.

"She's a good kid, Gil. She's had a tough ride these past couple of years, but she's trying damned hard to make things work."

"I know." He stared down at his hand for a moment, then wiped it on the bottom of his T-shirt. "I don't know any fucking thing about being a father, Blue. I grew up feral . . ." Self-disgust loaded his words. "I scrounged, stole, hunted, did whatever I needed to survive. I stayed with the old man because I didn't belong anywhere else. How can I be any good for her?"

The fact that he trusted her enough to reveal his self-doubt made Kris's heart strangely tight. "Maybe the same way you've been good for Deb and Liam, Gil. They respect you, think the world of you. Seems to me you've already got some experience in building a family of sorts."

He snorted. "I didn't do much for them. And now I've dragged all of them, including Megan, into danger."

"That's not your fault. But I agree — there is a risk. Gil, the guy in the black jacket this afternoon . . . You didn't recognise him?"

Instantly suspicious, he stared at her. "No. Why?"

"Alec Goddard knows of him." She briefly explained Alec's revelations about Sergio Russo.

"Fuck." He repeated it a few more times, anger and self-disgust loading it. "I'd heard a few rumours, but I've been too busy these past few months to check into them."

He stared up into the night, fingers rubbing his temple while he thought. "I have to get them away. Deb and Liam were going to go in the morning, but they need to take Megan. Now. Tonight. Take her home, Blue, and pack some clothes for her. I'll be there shortly."

She caught his arm as he started towards the pub. "Gil, you can't just take off with her like that. You need those gashes seen to, and I need to get statements from both of you, so we can charge those louts with assault. And we need to think this through, work out the safest course of action for all of you."

He hesitated, reluctant, the desire for immediate action showing in his clenched jaw and arms.

More people had arrived, standing around gawking at the four attackers, and at Megan. Johnno Dawson berated and argued with Steve while Joy, still in her dainty ball dress, wept beside her sons.

Kris had to go and help Steve and Adam keep things under control until backup came and they could move the lads out of there and send them into Birraga for questioning and probable charges.

"I'll ask Beth to take Megan home, and stay with her until I can get there," she told Gil. "Do you want to go with them, or do you want to wait at the pub? Beth or Doc Russell should be able to patch you up, if you go with them."

"I'll go with her."

"Megan heard Sean," she warned him. "She asked me about you, whether it was true. Are you ready for that?"

"No," he said bluntly. But he walked across the grass to his daughter, anyway.

She stood for a few seconds and watched him go. Then she gave herself a mental shake and went to deal with four drunken louts and their irate parents, and a crowd that might just as easily side with the lads as with the police.

CHAPTER
SIXTEEN

It was a strange walk, that half block down the quiet street from the school to the Russells' large house, set back from the road in a couple of acres of garden gone wild. Megan walked between Beth and him, and none of them spoke until they'd reached the gate in the stone wall. After Megan opened the gate for them, she paused, fidgeting with the latch.

"Gil . . . what Sean said . . . Is he right? Are you my father?"

For all he'd known it was coming, the question still hit him hard, made him feel as if the ground beneath him had turned to quicksand. Answering it meant either lying, or taking a path through the quicksand he could never turn from. He couldn't lie. He glanced for help, for guidance from Beth, but she'd wandered a short distance away, and was carefully studying a flower she couldn't see properly in the dark.

"Yeah, it sure seems that way." He tried for casual, but the tightness in his throat made it sound strained. "Dates match up. You might want to do the DNA thing, but looking in the mirror's probably almost as convincing."

"Do you . . . do you mind?"

"*Mind?*" He didn't understand what she meant, at first.

"The grands wanted a sweet little girl," she said in a rush, "and instead they got me, their worst nightmare."

"Jesus." How was he supposed to respond to that? He didn't do this stuff. Personal stuff. He had no frigging clue how to deal with it, with her and his own damned inadequacies. He hunted through his head for words that could explain. Honest words that she could trust. "Look, mate, I'm still trying to get used to this whole idea. But yes, I mind that I never knew, until yesterday. I mind that I got Barb into trouble, when I never meant to. And I mind — in fact, it's really starting to piss me off — that I'll always have to wonder what you were like as a little kid, that I didn't get to watch you grow up. But as far as minding that you're who you are, well, if I can ever properly get my head around the idea that I'm a father and you're my . . ." he almost said "kid", but swallowed it and made himself use the *other* word, "my daughter, then I reckon I'll feel proud of who you are, and glad that you're not some obnoxious teenage brat."

He blew out a breath as he finished, instinctively looked around for some kind of escape. Over by the rose bush, out of Megan's line of sight, Beth gave him a thumbs-up sign.

Megan smiled up at him, a genuine, warm smile, her eyes sparkling.

So, he'd managed to navigate the first five minutes of parenthood without totally screwing up. Now he just

283

had to keep doing it for the rest of his life, however long that would be.

Ahead of them, the veranda lights switched on, and a moment later a series of lights illuminated the semi-circular gravel driveway.

"Who's out there? Is that you, girl?" the old man's voice called.

"Yes, Grandfather, it's me." Megan began to walk briskly up the driveway, Beth by her side.

Gil followed more slowly. Better to let Beth explain the attack on Megan first, before he explained . . . well, himself, and why he was here, and that he'd brought danger to Megan and that he had to see her safe.

He'd be the last person Doctor and Mrs Russell would want to see. Even if they didn't know — if Barbara had never told them who'd fathered her baby — it wouldn't make much difference. Edward Russell hated him on principle, with all the vehemence of a self-righteous social and moral superior, and had done his best to ensure Gil's conviction, well before Barb could have known that she was pregnant.

The man stood in the doorway, leaning on his walking stick, while Beth walked up the steps, her arm around Megan's shoulder. Gil caught a glimpse of movement in the background, Esther Russell, presumably, who'd always hovered behind her husband.

"Doctor Russell, Mrs Russell, Kris Matthews asked me to bring Megan home. Unfortunately, there's been an incident."

There was little sign of the old, shy Beth in her calm, professional manner and concise explanation.

284

"Gil Gillespie heard the attack, and fought the men off," Beth said. "It's likely he saved Megan from a much more serious assault."

"Morgan Gillespie?" Doc Russell almost spat the name. "I heard the criminal was back in town."

Gil stepped up on to the veranda and faced the doctor. "Yes, I am back." He'd have argued the "criminal" point, but in a ripped, blood-soaked black T-shirt and with a two-day growth of beard, he fitted the image too well. He probably should have cleaned up first, although chances were it wouldn't make much difference.

Closer, now, he saw that the doctor hadn't aged well. Under the woollen dressing gown, he seemed frail, and the walking stick a necessary aide rather than an affectation. Even with its support, he seemed unsteady. But his opinions hadn't mellowed, despite the frailness of his body.

"You stay out of my house. I won't have vermin in here."

"But Grandfather, you can't," Megan protested. "Gil's my father."

The old man stared at him for long seconds, his face twisting with rage. "You?" he bellowed.

Gil deflected the blow from the walking stick with his forearm, pain cracking along it and up to his shoulder.

Beth moved quickly, taking the stick with one hand, gripping the doctor's arm with the other, both to steady him and restrain him. Esther came forward to put an arm around her husband, shooting an apologetic look at Gil.

"Perhaps we should go inside," Beth suggested in a firm, polite tone that made it an order, rather than a suggestion. As the doctor started to object, she spoke over him. "I'm sure you don't want this discussion taking place on the doorstep where all the neighbours can hear."

The implied threat worked. The doctor turned his back on them and stomped inside. Esther smiled at Beth, and at Gil, somewhat nervously. "Please, come in, Beth, Gil. You prefer 'Gil' to 'Morgan'?"

"Yeah — yes. Thank you." As surreal as the courtesies seemed under the circumstances, he found it impossible to contemplate being ill-mannered to the delicate elderly woman.

"Gil sustained some injuries protecting Megan," Beth told her. "I was hoping we could use your bathroom to clean him up? And I think perhaps Megan could do with a soothing hot drink?"

"Thanks," he muttered to Beth when Esther showed them into a guest bathroom, and produced facecloths, towels and a first-aid box from the cupboard, before she hurried off to make hot chocolate.

"This will give the doc a few minutes to cool down," Beth said. "I'm sure you could have him charged with assault, if you wanted to."

"Jesus, no." He took his T-shirt off, with some pain in his shoulder, and waved at his chest. "I can do this myself."

She gave his chest a quick, professionally detached look to confirm his assertion, and left him to it.

He took his time. The cut on his shoulder was only a couple of inches long; the one on his chest about six inches. They both stung like hell when he washed the blood away with warm soapy water, and stung again when he applied antiseptic. But they weren't deep, and they'd stopped bleeding. He washed out his T-shirt in the basin, watching the dirty water swirl away, rinsing it again, then wringing it out as hard as he could before he pulled it back on, damp.

He had no more reasons to delay.

And he still had no clue how he was going to explain that he needed to take Megan away to safety, tonight.

"Come in, Kris," Esther said with a determined brightness. "We're just having hot chocolates. Good for calming the nerves. Would you like, one, too?"

Inside, in the living room with its beautiful, worn décor, the strain was obvious. From his wing-backed armchair, Edward Russell dominated the group, disapproval radiating from him as he glared at Gil, just entering the room. Beth and Megan sat on a brocade couch one would never dare to curl up on, sipping from delicate china tea cups.

And on the ornate timber mantelpiece, a large portrait of Barbara, in her university graduation gown and cap, watched over all of them, her smile not making it to her eyes.

The grandfather clock in the corner sounded a single sonorous chime. One in the morning, and Kris wanted to be anywhere else but here.

Gil shot her a silent plea for help.

"We have a problem," she said, as soon as she'd confirmed that Megan was okay. "The police have reason to believe that Gil's safety may be in danger." Edward's "*hrmph*" conveyed satisfaction rather than any degree of sympathy.

"Due to the unfortunate incident earlier, the relationship between Gil and Megan is now public knowledge. This means, Megan, that we now have some concerns for your safety, too."

Entering the room with another cup, Esther gasped. "Oh my goodness."

Edward growled and muttered something about criminals, but Gil just said quietly to Megan, "I'm sorry, mate." She smiled back at him, slightly nervous, but trusting.

"I've spoken with Detective Sergeant Steve Fraser" — Kris mentioned Steve as a deliberate tactic for dealing with the chauvinistic doctor — "who will be here shortly, and we believe that it would be prudent to move Megan to a secure location until this threat is resolved."

"Are you suggesting I can't look after my granddaughter?"

Of course you can't, Kris answered silently. Barely mobile even with the aid of a walking stick, the man could be no match for the average thug. But she noted he referred to Megan as his granddaughter — he'd not done that in her hearing before — and figured that underneath the bluster and the defiant male pride, he did care about the girl.

288

"I know that you would do your best to protect her," she said tactfully, "but we do feel, at this time, that it would be safer for all of you if Megan was elsewhere."

"But you can't take her away," Esther protested. "She's just a girl."

"I'm seventeen, Gran," Megan said gently.

"We hope it would not be for long, Mrs Russell," Kris assured her. Just days, she hoped, but that was being optimistic. It might take longer than that. People sometimes spent months in safe houses, even longer. Months without contact with their families and friends. At least Megan wasn't a witness, waiting to testify. She could return home as soon as the immediate threat was over.

"Go and pack some things, hon. We need to be quick. We'd like to get you out of here and well on the way before it gets light. Perhaps you would help her, Mrs Russell?"

That got Esther doing something useful, and avoided her questions, but the doctor sat in his chair, clearly fuming, and Gil still lurked in the doorway, the energy between them positively fiery.

"Who's going to chaperone her?" Edward barked. "And if you think that cur's going with her, then she's staying here."

Kris held up a hand to silence Gil. "Appropriate arrangements will be made for Megan's care and wellbeing, Doctor Russell. You have my word on that."

What they'd be yet, she didn't know. Her quick conversation with Steve after they'd seen off the police van with the arrested men hadn't covered any details.

Lights swept up the driveway, and Beth answered the door, letting Steve in. His masculine presence — and he played it just right — took the wind out of some of the doctor's doubt and hostility.

Kris's phone rang and she excused herself, leaving Steve to continue appeasing the old man. She wasn't surprised that Gil followed her out on to the veranda. Her conversation with Adam was brief and to the point. He was with Deb and Liam at the hotel, and she asked him to stay with them until she got there.

As soon as she'd disconnected Gil spoke insistently, "No police safe house, Blue. It's too risky. I'll look after her and the other two myself."

"And that's *not* risky?"

"There's no bureaucracy. In the police system, too many people know. The information can leak."

Fatigue sapped her patience. "Not every police officer is bent, Gillespie."

He kept his cool better than she did. "No, they're not. But it only takes one."

Right at this moment, she didn't have the energy to argue, even if she could have marshalled a case to convince him otherwise.

"As it happens, Gil, there's nothing available in this district at the moment. Unless Steve's come up with something, our choices are limited. We could drive for a few hours, find a motel or a cabin in a caravan park somewhere away from here, and maybe organise something better in a day or two. Not ideal. But there is another option."

"Which is?" His eyes narrowed, cautious.

"Mark Strelitz has plenty of guest accommodation at his homestead. He's hosted a couple of delegations of Iraqi agricultural officials and other visiting dignitaries, so the homestead has the latest in security systems. It's probably the most secure place outside the Birraga cells for a couple of hundred kilometres around here. Mark's flying back to Canberra for meetings on Tuesday, but he's happy for us to use it."

"What about his employees? There'll be too many people about."

"He doesn't have many. The manager and his wife — she's the housekeeper — are the only ones nearby, but they're away until Tuesday. They've both been vetted by the federal police. The yards, the sheds and the manager's office where the station hands work from are a kilometre or more from the homestead. They won't know anyone's there."

He leaned both hands on the veranda railing, studied the garden beyond, unconvinced.

"Gil, I think it's the best option, at least for a day or two. I'm officially off-duty for the next four days, so I'll come, too. That will keep Community Services off my case for sending a minor off with people she hardly knows, as well as providing some extra protection."

"You trust Strelitz?" he finally asked.

She held his gaze. "Yes, I do. We can take Megan, Deb and Liam there straight away, get them inside while it's still dark. If you all stay inside, then no-one will know who's there."

"How many people know? How many people have you talked to about this?"

"Steve and Mark. That's all. Adam's with Deb and Liam now, but I've just told him we're planning to go to a police safe house."

"Keep it that way. No-one else. Not even Adam." His fingers tightened around the railing. "We need to think of a strategy to get there without anyone realising what's happening."

She'd already given some thought to that. "I'll drop you back at the pub. You go in and be ready to leave at the same time as Deb and Liam."

"And you?"

She stepped back, watching his face. "How about I give the town something extra juicy to gossip about to distract them? Mark's gone back to the hall to help with the clean-up. I figured I'd go back home, pack a bag and then, for anybody who is watching, Mark and I can put on a convincing performance of affection before we leave in our respective vehicles for his place."

"They'll believe that? You and him?" The roughness in his voice betrayed his dislike of the idea.

And it did seem fickle and insensitive to be suggesting an attraction to one man, when only a couple of hours back she'd been kissing *this* one. But if she could make use of the speculation and the intimations that had been dogging her and Mark for at least a year to keep people safe, then she'd do it.

"Karl Sauer's been running an unofficial betting book for months that half the town's in on, so they'll want to believe," she explained. "Mark and I were partners at the ball, so it will seem natural. The story going around town tomorrow will be that, after a romantic evening, we've finally succumbed, and Cinderella is spending her days off with the prince. That will explain my absence, and keep everybody perfectly happy."

"Strelitz will play along?"

"Yes. We're good mates, and he'll do whatever's needed." She knew Gil well enough now to recognise that his stony, closed expression served as a shield to disguise emotion. And while she'd been using duty and responsibilities to effectively keep from examining her own feelings, she couldn't pretend that nothing had happened between them.

She laid her hand over his on the wooden veranda rail. "Gil, Mark and I are friends, that's all. If I was involved with him — or anyone else — I wouldn't have kissed you."

He didn't move a muscle. "It didn't mean anything."

Oh, didn't it just?

She wasn't sure, herself, what it meant other than that they both suffered from a bad case of lust for each other; but lust could be fun, in the right time and place. She'd have to worry some time later about whether they'd do anything more about it.

"Well, meaning or not, I just thought you should know that."

The homestead was the kind of place Gil had imagined Mark would have. A century-old home, tastefully renovated with contemporary, understated luxury. Nothing showy or extravagant, just comfortable style and excellent quality in everything, from the paintwork on the walls to the handcrafted timber furniture.

Wealth, position, family connections, respect: Strelitz had all that and more. He'd grown up in a close family, in an environment of privilege — the antithesis of Gil's experience.

Gil didn't begrudge him that. The man worked hard, always had done, and used his position and his wealth wisely. He'd earned a great deal of respect in politics, widely regarded as a man of integrity and perception. From what Gil had read and seen about him since he entered Parliament, the reputation was deserved.

But Gil had never been sure if he believed Mark's claim of amnesia about the accident. It was . . . *convenient*. Very convenient. For Mark, anyway. Not so for him.

Now that he'd seen Mark face to face, he was beginning to believe the amnesia might be genuine. Mark's courtesy remained, even more polished in his maturity, but there was an uncertainty, a caution, and questions in his eyes beneath the warm welcome, as if he wasn't sure how Gil would react to him.

Not that it made any difference. The past was long gone, unchangeable, and irrelevant to Gil's current concerns. Concerns he had to deal with.

The homestead was quiet. The rest of them had gone to bed, finally, settling in rooms in the guest wing. Too wired and too worried to sleep, Gil wandered restlessly up and down the long veranda of the guest wing, bordering one side of a terrace.

The moon was close to setting, and the sky in the east lightening up to a pearly grey. Weary, Gil sat in one of the wooden terrace chairs and leaned back, stretching his legs out in front of him. He would *not* think of Kris, would not imagine her lying in the single bed in the room she shared with Megan. Nor would he imagine her flirting with Mark outside the hall.

They'd joked about it, afterwards, Kris and Mark. They'd been subtle, they said, but were sure there'd have been a burst of gossip explode right after they left, providing a convincing scenario for Kris's absence from home for a couple of days.

But Gil didn't think it had all been play-acting on Mark's part. The man could hardly keep his eyes off her. Well, good luck to them both. It wasn't any of his business what either of them did.

He had to concentrate on deciding what to do once he got to Sydney. The revelation that Sergio Russo was now involved with Tony's operation — or vice versa — cast a different light on matters. He needed to go back through what he knew, see if there were any hints or clues there to guide him.

The aroma of coffee made him force open his eyes — and shut them again against the brightness. Disoriented, his brain full of sludge, he sat up straighter, dragging open his eyes again.

"Sorry to wake you, but you'll wreck your neck, sleeping in that chair, Gillespie," Kris said cheerfully, handing him a mug. "Here's your morning caffeine fix."

Gil wrapped both hands around the mug and dragged in a deep breath, hoping the smell alone might magically clear his brain and give him the equivalent of a few more hours' sleep. The sun only just topped the trees, so it couldn't be too late. An hour or two since he'd drifted off, then, no longer.

She sat in the chair next to his, contemplating the view while she drank her own coffee. The terrace overlooked the garden behind the house, and down across the brown paddocks to the river, winding among trees. They were miles from neighbours, the Strelitz property covering tens of thousands of hectares.

"It's so peaceful here," Kris commented.

The very peace, the pleasure of sitting quietly with her, put him on edge, made him want to push her away.

"You could probably sit here every morning, if you wanted to. Mark loves you."

She turned and studied him over the edge of her mug, those blue eyes serious, and instead of disagreeing, she nodded.

"Yes, he does," she said frankly. "Mark loves women. Beth, Bella, me, and plenty of others. He has an incredibly chivalrous nature, and he honours and respects women, and likes their company." She smiled wistfully, adding, "If King Arthur ever shows up again, Mark should be one of the first knights he recruits."

Gil wasn't into fairy tales and romances, but her description fitted the man, summing up his uncommon qualities, his driven nature.

"Late last year, the night after Bella and Tanya were rescued, after the debriefs and the press statements and

296

the internal investigators' questions were finished and it was all, finally, over, Mark turned up at my place, with a bottle of scotch. We sat on the floor of the lounge room, and got drunk together. After the hell of the year we'd endured, and the tensions of the previous few days, we both needed it." She took a slow sip of her coffee. "There's very few people I could have done that with."

The stark statement hit him with the reality of the personal cost of her job — having to be seen to be capable all the time, of needing to show strength and leadership even when she struggled to deal with the horrors her job exposed her to.

He realised, for the first time, how alone she must sometimes feel. She disguised it effectively with dry humour, a no-nonsense, kick-arse attitude and more balls than most men had, but underneath the public face lay a very human, empathetic woman who cared deeply about others.

"Some day," Kris continued, looking out over the view, "Mark will marry a woman who is his match, socially, intellectually, emotionally, and he will love her in a way few men do. I hope she will give him some balance, something to live for beyond duty. But that woman won't be me, Gil. He's an honoured and very dear friend, and damned good company, but that's it." Her easy grin broke through again, and at the same time broke through a corner of the dark cloud of his mood. "No stars in the eyes for either of us, or celestial choruses, or heaving bosoms. Just a rare and good friendship, and gratitude for it."

Very rare, in his experience. And he wasn't as convinced of Mark's non-interest as she was. How could any man with blood in his veins not want her? Even now, in long cargo pants, boots and a long-sleeved T-shirt, her hair still damp from her shower, she was as sexy as hell. Last night, in that curve-hugging blue dress, she'd completely fused his brain.

It had been utter madness, kissing her. Madness in letting it happen in the first place, and lunacy in not stopping it once they'd started. Because even just the memory of the taste of her, the wild heat of touching her, was going to keep him crazy from here on, craving what he couldn't have, more powerful and real than any drug.

He focused on the river in the distance, dragging his thoughts away from those moments, trying to visualise and feel water, cool and murky, water-weeds and mud and nothing in the slightest way sensual.

It didn't work. Only getting right away from her might have a chance of deadening his distraction. He drained his coffee mug and abruptly stood up. "I'll go and take a shower." It was as good an excuse to leave as any. And after his shower — his *cold* shower — he'd make whatever arrangements needed making to keep the others out of sight and safe, and then get on his bike and ride to Sydney, to find a way to end this nightmare, permanently.

A magpie warbled in the garden, and Kris jerked out of her daze. Not a good idea to fall asleep in this sunshine with skin as fair as hers. Not that she couldn't have

298

done with the extra sleep — it must have been four in the morning before Megan had talked through her thoughts enough to sleep — but there were things to do. Questions to answer, crimes to solve, so that Gil, his friends and his daughter could move on with their lives without fear.

In the homestead kitchen she put a fresh pot of coffee on to brew. Before retiring to the coast, Mark's parents had enjoyed entertaining, and the size of the renovated kitchen reflected that. Mark had updated it further, and now granite, timber and stainless steel blended together in a modern, practical workspace that nevertheless complemented its historic origins. If the woman Mark eventually ended up with was a cook, she'd love this room.

She sat at a circular table near the large windows overlooking the terrace, took out her phone and switched it on. Gil and she had stressed to the others last night not to turn their phones on, just in case someone had access to phone company data and could track them here, but according to their cover story, she was supposed to be here.

The phone bleeped with a message. Steve's brief text read: *Call me asap*.

Steve answered almost immediately. "Look, Kris, things have hotted up overnight. Petric's been on the phone. Vince Russo's solicitor was shot dead last night in his office. A security camera shows him being escorted in at gunpoint by two masked men."

Gil walked into the kitchen, and she held up a finger to alert him. He'd shaved, she noticed, the dark shadow he'd carried on his chin since yesterday gone, and he wore a new black T-shirt, fresh from its packaging, the fold lines dissecting his chest.

"Vince's solicitor?" She tried to give some clue to Gil about Steve's news. "But what's his murder got to do with Gillespie?"

"It wasn't the only thing that happened last night. Another solicitor's office was ransacked, complete with the safe-room door being detonated," Steve continued. "Turns out Gillespie is one of his clients. A storage unit recently rented by Gillespie was also firebombed, and they're still putting out the fire. And Kent Marshall's office here was broken into around six this morning."

Not good. Any one of those would be bad enough, but all of them together — all linked to Gil — spelled even more serious trouble.

"Any clue why they're targeting Gil's solicitors?" she asked Steve. "This can't be about the box he dug up yesterday, can it?"

"No. Petric got on to the dead solicitor's secretary this morning. Apparently Vince made a new will, a month or so ago — she remembers because she and another PA were called in to witness it. There were three copies. One held in the safe room in the office, and Vince took the other two with him."

"They're searching for Vince's will?" She saw Gil's head jerk up suddenly. "But what does that have to do with Gil?"

Even as she asked the question, an answer came that made some sort of sense. *Marci.* If Marci really was Vince's daughter, and Gil had looked out for her all these years, there could well be clauses in the will that his legitimate son would want to see destroyed.

"Looks like someone thinks that Gil has one or both copies and they don't want them to see the light of day. Tony's got a watertight alibi, of course, but Petric is pursuing enquiries along that general line. Kris, you need to warn Gillespie. And get him to contact Petric urgently."

She disconnected, and gave Gil a quick summary of the news.

When she finished, he turned without a word, stood on the edge of the terrace, looking out, and only the rigidity of his shoulders gave away his tension.

"Do you know anything about Vince's will?" she asked. "Do you have it, Gil?"

"I've never seen Vince's will," he said slowly, as if he were working it through. "Vince never said a word to me about it." He turned to face her, dark eyes meeting her eyes. "But I think I know where it is."

CHAPTER
SEVENTEEN

I hope you won't need the contents of your safety deposit box in the future.

Vince's words at their last meeting finally sort of made sense. The will had to be there — although how Vince had known which bank, and where the key was, Gil could only guess.

Damn Vince for his machinations and manipulations. A man was dead because of them, and others now in greater danger. If he'd not left everything to his son, as Tony expected, he should have had the guts to say it to Tony's face, long ago.

"You know where the will is?" Kris repeated.

"Yes. I have to go to Sydney. Today." Although he wouldn't be able to get into the bank until tomorrow morning, he realised as he spoke. But there were a few people he needed to see, information to search out. At some stage he'd need to put in a claim for what had been lost in his storage unit, but that was the least of his worries. Books, clothes and a few pieces of furniture could easily be replaced, when he needed them.

"We should tell Petric you're coming," Kris said. "Get him to arrange protection for you, safe custody for you and the document."

"No." His vehemence made her start. "I don't trust Petric," he added, quieter.

Cool blue eyes watched him. "Have you got a reason for that?"

He shrugged, sought to explain. "Nothing solid. The convenience of their arrival the other night. The fact that he's been withholding information from you. The fact that he now wants me to contact him, so he can find out where the will is."

"What information has he been withholding?"

"Sergio Russo. You sent him the pictures, didn't you? The ones from the shed? If Goddard recognised him, shouldn't a detective working in Sydney specialising in organised crime have known?"

She thought that over, nodded, accepting the possibility. "I could ask Alec what he thinks. He worked with him for years."

"And hasn't for months. A lot can happen in that time, Blue. It doesn't have to be wilful, a change in character. There's plenty of cops dancing to someone else's tune to keep their families safe. Or because they've been hooked on something minor, and then the crims reel them in."

"So, what will you do when you get the will?" she asked.

"I'm not sure yet. See what's in it. Take it to a court or something, make sure there are plenty of copies made." Or destroy it, he thought. Vince's estate couldn't be worth people's lives.

She moved to the next veranda post and turned to face him. "It's too dangerous for you to go to Sydney alone."

"It's better if I do."

"No, it isn't. I'm coming with you. Two is better than one, and it might be handy to have a police officer on hand."

"Megan needs you to look after her."

"Mark's security system is excellent, and she has Mark, Deb and Liam to look after her. Which is a hell of a lot more than you have, and why I'm going with you. The last thing Megan needs is for something to happen to you."

He dredged for more excuses. "I'm riding the bike. You won't want to go that far on the back of it."

She waved a dismissive hand. "I've ridden further than that."

"It's dangerous, Blue. I don't want you put at risk."

"If I wanted to play safe, Gil, I'd never have joined the police force. Or . . ." She smiled, an honest, wistful smile that wrapped around his heart and made it hard to breathe, "or kissed you. But since I've chosen to do both, don't think for a moment that I'm going to let you go alone when there's probably a contract out on your life now. Nor . . ." A shadow crossed her face. "Nor am I going to just stand by and not take whatever action I think is necessary to protect this town. I failed them once. I'm not going to do it again."

He should argue, refuse, anything but agree to let her walk into the lion's pit with him.

But while the protective male part of him raged to keep her safe and defended, the part of him that respected her — her courage, skills, strengths, choices — knew that to deny her would be to deny who she

304

was, and what she needed to do. And the truth was, he wanted her by his side. He wanted to survive, and her presence *would* even up the odds. But if it came to the worst, he would sacrifice himself to prevent her being harmed.

In the end, they decided to travel via Tamworth, and see Jeanie. It made for a longer journey by several hours, but with the bank not open until the morning they had time to spare.

It was sheer bloody torture, having her behind him on the bike. For the first few kilometres, on a dirt track, he took it easy, giving them both a chance to become accustomed to the bike and each other, matching their movements as they leaned to take the curves. She'd ridden a lot in her youth, she'd told him, and adapted quickly. He'd ridden a lot, too — but rarely with a passenger. Her hands rested on his hips, and he felt every movement of her fingers, every slight alteration in pressure, even through his jacket.

After the detour loop to keep off the main local roads, they emerged on to the highway about thirty kilometres below where the Dungirri road joined it. At the first town, almost an hour later, Gil turned off the highway, cruising down the two blocks of the main shopping street, and pulling up in front of the only bank he could find. He glanced around as he got off the bike, but the street was dead quiet. Nothing much happening on a Sunday, other than a couple of teenagers coming out of the milk bar a block or so down.

He slid off his helmet, and withdrew as much cash from the machine as each of his accounts permitted for a single day. Kris had her card out, but he handed her a wad of cash and told her to put her card away.

"You're supposed to be at Mark's. We don't want anyone tracing you through account activity. From here on, we use cash only."

They rode on. He kept around about the speed limit, not wanting to attract attention. There wasn't a lot of traffic, and most of it was trucks — semi-trailers, a few B-doubles, the occasional road train. Easy enough driving, despite the distance. Too easy, because he needed to keep alert, stay awake and focused.

To distract his thoughts from the woman behind him, he kept his brain busy with mental calculations while he kept watching the road. How much fuel he had left. How far to the next town. How long it would take to reach it. When those calculations proved too easy, he did a mental review of his investments, their likely earnings given various scenarios of interest rate variations, share value movements and dividends, and how much he was willing to invest in his next business venture with Deb and Liam.

A few hours and several small towns passed before he ran out of things to calculate. By then, he'd estimated everything he could think of — from the goods value and haulage costs of the trucks that passed, to the money Flanagan might have made over the years through extortion and drug distribution. He hated those kinds of numbers.

The only calculation he was truly interested in was one plus one. He and Kris. Naked. Together . . .

He dragged his brain away from that equation. Desperate for the continued mental diversion, he started working out a rough financial plan for the hypothetical purchase and renovation of the Dungirri pub. Definitely hypothetical, the way the numbers kept coming out in negatives.

Road signs eventually appeared, announcing Tamworth, around the time his mental exercises ran out. They stopped for food on the outskirts, talking little as they quickly ate. They circled the hospital a couple of times before parking, checking for anyone watching the entrances, but saw nothing obvious. Nor did Gil notice anyone suspicious as they walked down the long corridors, only hospital staff constantly on the move, and a few visitors here and there. If anyone was watching who visited Jeanie, they were damned good at being inconspicuous.

Sitting up in bed, in a private room, Jeanie looked pale, but she was pleased to see them, stretching out her hands to take theirs despite the tubes that dangled from her arms. Gil squeezed her fingers softly, worried about the needles stuck into her hands, not sure what to say. Seeing her awake and alert was a relief, but she was still weak, too fragile, tiny against the pile of pillows.

Kris leaned over and kissed her on the cheek. "You gave us a scare, Jeanie. I'm glad to see you looking better. How are you feeling?"

Jeanie smiled at both of them. "Tired, but okay. The doctor says one of my heart valves has a problem. I thought I was just getting old, but she says that with a new valve, I'll be fitter than ever. I'm to rest here for a few more days, and then they'll probably send me to Sydney for the operation."

Perching on the edge of the bed, Kris asked, "Nancy's been looking after you well?"

"Yes. She's just gone for a walk, to get some air. She said . . ." Jeanie's fingers gripped tighter around Gil's . . . "She said I have you two to thank for getting me out of the fire. I don't remember it, but thank you." Her eyes brimmed with tears, and she squeezed his hand again. "Thank you, both of you, very much."

"I'm glad you don't remember it, Jeanie," Kris said. Then she grinned, made light of it, "Because I think I dropped you there, at one point. Just as well Gil has more muscles than me."

Jeanie chuckled, a pale shadow of her normal laugh, but a sign that heartened Gil. She let go of his hand and waved at a chair in the corner. "Pull that up, Gil, and sit down beside me."

Carrying the chair over, he glanced around the room properly for the first time. On the chest of drawers beside the bed, the photo of Jeanie and Aldo had pride of place, in front of a bunch of flowers. A couple of other flower arrangements sat on the shelf on the side wall, where Jeanie could see them, and a long cotton robe hung on the cupboard door, a pair of satin slippers nearby. Although he hadn't doubted Nancy, it was good to see she'd bought nice things for Jeanie, and given her the photo.

Jeanie saw him looking in that direction, and smiled at him. "Thank you for saving that, Gil. I would have missed it a great deal."

"Were you insured?" His voice sounded rougher than he meant it to be. "If you need anything, I'll arrange it for you."

"It was all insured — the building, the business, the contents. I'll have enough to get by. That's all I need."

She'd have more than the basics, if he had anything to do with it. But he didn't argue the point. Despite her brave face, he could see her tiring. They shouldn't stay too long.

Kris must have noticed, too. She took Jeanie's hand in hers. "Jeanie, I'd like to ask you a few questions, but only if you're up to answering them."

"I thought you would."

"Have you any idea what happened? How the fire started?"

"No, Kris, I'm sorry. Adam and the customers had gone. I locked the money in the office, and did the normal close-up things — shutting off the pumps, checking the kitchen, locking up — and then I went upstairs. I was going to make a batch of friands for the ball, so I turned the oven on to heat up. I remember getting the recipe book down from the shelf, and putting the kettle on for a cup of tea, but that's all."

Jeanie reached for the cup of water on the tray table, and Gil refreshed it from the jug and passed it to her.

Kris waited until she'd had a few sips. "The customers — Adam and Gil said they saw two truck drivers when they were in there. Did you know them?"

"One of them had been in a couple of times. Sam, his name was. I don't remember his surname. Pleasant man, not long moved to the Birraga area. The other man, I didn't know him." Jeanie creased her forehead in thought. "Sam called him something, one of those names that might have been a first name or a last name. Let me think what it was . . ." She took another sip of water. "Clinton. That's it, because I remember thinking he didn't look like Bill Clinton."

The names didn't ring any bells for Gil, and if they did for Kris she gave no sign of it. Nor did she tell Jeanie that one of them had died.

"That's a great help, Jeanie. Now, I've just got one more question. Gil's told me about the trouble you had, years ago, with someone wanting protection money, and how you dealt with that. Can you tell me if you've had any threats, or other trouble, recently?"

Jeanie glanced between both of them. "You think it wasn't an accident? I thought maybe I'd just left the stove on."

"We don't know yet, Jeanie," Kris said gently. "We're still waiting on the report from the forensic examiners. But I want to make sure I check all possibilities."

"There's been no more trouble. Not for years. They've got more business interests, these days, so small concerns like mine probably aren't worth their bother. Plus you're there, now Kris, and Adam, and

310

both of you are much better officers than Bill Franklin ever was. He turned a blind eye to a lot of goings-on, back then."

She let her head fall back on the pillow, clearly tired.

Gil signalled to Kris, and she nodded. They'd asked enough, found out the most pressing answers.

Kris kissed Jeanie on the cheek again. "We'll go and let you rest now, Jeanie. I'll try to come down and visit you in Sydney while you're there."

Gil leaned over and kissed her on the cheek, too, her smile more than reward for the unaccustomed display of affection. "Take care of yourself. And let me know if you need anything at all."

They didn't talk until they were well away from the ward.

"Sam and Clinton — are the names significant?" he asked her at last, pushing open a door out of the building.

"Sam Weston was the victim. There's been nothing about a Clinton, but at least we've got a name, of sorts, for the second driver now. I'll get Steve to look into it." She frowned, stopped abruptly. "Did you believe her? About there being no more trouble?"

He thought back before he answered. "Yeah. Mostly. Maybe there were some threats after I left, but not recently. She's right in that her business is small, compared to their other operations. Her turnover can't be much, so extortion wouldn't be worth their while."

He pushed away the other possibility that gnawed at him. Nobody had known about him going to Jeanie's that evening except Kris. Even if the truckies had heard

Jeanie mention him staying in the cabin, things had happened too quickly for the fire to be a punishment for aiding him. And it was far more logical that the drivers had been sent to eliminate the evidence. He just had to believe it.

The late afternoon sun slanted across the road as they left Tamworth. They took back roads, not the highway, winding through the Liverpool Ranges on roads with little traffic. Nobody followed them. Most of the time, there were no vehicles at all in sight.

Worry about Jeanie occupied Gil's mind for the first hour or so, distracting him from thinking about Kris, behind him on the bike. But after a while, the torture ramped up again, and as the time passed and the twilight darkened to night, Kris filled his every thought, every moment of awareness. He tried to think of the reasons why him and her would be a bad idea, but his body rejected all of them. He rounded a wide bend, and she shifted slightly against him, her chest brushing his back. Two leather jackets, his and hers — Mark's, he reminded himself — didn't dilute the effect, or what his imagination did with it.

He gritted his teeth and rode on, hoping for a straight road until the next town. Fifteen minutes, he figured. There'd probably be a 24-hour or at least a late-night service station there, lights and people and fuel and food, and a chance for them both to get off the bike, stretch their legs, and give his body some respite from the sensual torture.

By the time he pulled in at the fuel bowsers, his teeth ached from clenching so long. Her hand rested on his shoulder for balance as she swung off the bike. Taking her helmet off, she stretched her neck side to side, and then gave her head a shake, waves of red hair blowing around her face, the bright lights overhead throwing glittery highlights in it. *Beautiful*, his brain thought.

She unzipped the front of Mark's too-big jacket, the leather falling back a few inches to reveal a glimpse of skin-hugging black knit. His brain stopped thinking. He hooked his helmet on the handlebar, reached for the pump, concentrated on undoing the cap on the tank, putting the nozzle in — and then kept his eyes straight ahead because that was just too damned symbolic.

"Do you need coffee? Or food?" she asked, oblivious — he hoped — of the way his thoughts were running. "Shall I go in and order something?"

"Yeah. Something quick. And Coke. There's still hours to go."

"We should stop somewhere, in an hour or so, get a few hours' rest. Neither of us had much sleep last night. We can leave early in the morning, and still be in Sydney by the time the bank opens."

He tried to come up with good reasons for not stopping to rest, and then settled on the truth.

"It's not sleep I want, Blue."

Her smile bloomed, danced in her eyes, and she slid a hand under his jacket and stepped close.

"Me neither."

Two words, one touch, and almost all his determination went out the window.

He clung on to a last shred of restraint. "This is crazy, Blue."

She cupped a hand against his chin, no longer teasing, the caress and the expression in her eyes more intimate than any of his sexual encounters.

"Is it?" she challenged softly.

"You're a cop. I'm a . . ." He left the sentence dangling, struggling to find the right descriptor for the taint of prison, for the darkness of his life.

"Person," she supplied. "And last time I checked, consensual sex between two single people who like each other was not a crime, legally or morally." But she stepped back, took her hands away, and he wanted to grab them back. "You tell me if you want it, Gil."

In answer, he pulled her to him, kissed her hard for a long moment.

When he let her go, she stepped back just enough to see his face, her own flushed, her breathing as fractured as his own.

"So, we can find somewhere here or, if we travel for another hour to Lithgow, we can leave an hour later in the morning."

Here, his body thundered. *Here, now.* But some element of his brain squeezed a reminder in between the thunder that he hated early mornings.

"Lithgow," he said, trying not to regret it. "We can make it that far." *Maybe*, he added to himself. And there had to be a few places they could pull up between here and there if they couldn't.

"I'll go and pay for the fuel," she said with a grin. "You might want to see if there's a condom-vending machine in the gents'."

314

He did want to. There was. By the time she came back from paying, he was beside the bike, waiting for her, watching her easy stride as she walked towards him.

"Can you drive this thing?" he asked.

"Yes."

"Good." He slid his hand into her hair, bent as if he was going to kiss her neck, and instead whispered into her ear, "Because I'm so distracted I can't focus on the road."

She laughed, throaty and low, planted a quick kiss on his mouth, and swung her leg over the bike in a smooth movement that turned his blood to steam.

By the time the lights of Lithgow were in sight, she was gripping the handlebars so tight she half-expected them to crumble any moment.

Nothing like straddling a bike, up close to a man she found intensely attractive, to get a girl in the mood. Except she'd passed "in the mood" after the first fifteen minutes. The last few hours she'd progressed through teeth-grinding frustration to incoherent silent screaming.

The only thing that kept her halfway sane, and able to keep steering straight, was the worry about what lay beyond, in Sydney, and her fear for Gil. She didn't want to lose him. She knew herself, and her relations with men well enough to recognise that the bone-dissolving physical desire was about way more than just sex. Yes, she *had* missed sex, this last couple of years, but she'd had other things on her mind. And

315

there were few men around who could get over the whole female cop thing and who she could like enough to have a comfortable relationship with.

Gil . . . well, Gil sure wasn't *comfortable*. Beneath the surface, Gil was raw and wild, powerful and rare. Exhilarating and dangerous — drawing the wild part of her to him, and there'd be no half-measures for either of them.

His hand slipped underneath her jacket, underneath her T-shirt, caressing her waist, gliding up her spine, and she had to concentrate very, very hard to keep the bike steady.

She turned in at the first motel she saw. Decent, but not flash enough to need a credit card. Perfect for their situation. She was wired so tight she was almost surprised the metal door handle of the office didn't give off sparks when she opened it. She'd registered, paid, and had the room key in her hand within minutes.

"Room fourteen," she said to Gil outside. "At the end. I'll meet you there." She needed, for just a few seconds, to walk. The space. A chance to breathe, if she could. Just like when she used to go abseiling, the few moments of stillness and quiet before the push off into thin air.

He pulled into the parking space just ahead of her, had their bags off the bike before she'd finished unlocking the door, and followed her inside.

The moment he closed the door, dropped the bags on the floor, they reached for each other, mouths hungry to taste, to connect, to explore, even as they shed their jackets and lifted T-shirts to find skin. She

316

indulged herself, loving his mouth, loving the feel of firm stomach and chest and shoulders beneath her fingers, loving the heat of his hands discovering her. But hands on skin wasn't enough. She wanted her clothes off, wanted his clothes off, craved skin against skin and losing herself in that bliss. She wanted to be herself, fully and wholly, and to peel away his reserve and find the strong, giving man beneath it.

They broke the kiss, breaths coming hard, and she grinned at him as she pushed his T-shirt up.

"Too many clothes, Gillespie."

"Yeah." He peeled it off, dropped it on the floor, then hooked his thumbs back under her shirt, lifting it breathtakingly slowly, watching her face as he did. She raised her arms, pulled it over her head, and let it fall on top of his.

"Black lace," he muttered, running a single finger down the edge of her bra. "Have you got any idea what black lace does to a man, Blue?"

"I can take it off," she offered.

"No. I will. Eventually."

"So, we're doing slow, are we?"

"Slow. Fast. Both."

Slow, and what his fingers were doing with it around the lace edges might have her begging, real soon now, for *fast*.

She hitched her fingers into the top of his jeans, drew him closer. "There's still the clothes issue."

His mouth — that delicious, kissable mouth — curved wickedly, and her heart did a slow-motion somersault.

"Nothing wrong with this garment," he murmured, bending his head to her, setting his mouth to the thin lace, lips and tongue skimming, tasting and sucking through it.

Nothing slow-motion about her heart rate, now, either. Need filled her, fractured her breathing, and she fisted her hands in his hair to hold him there.

He moved lazily from one breast to the other, as if with no need to hurry, but his fingers quested at her jeans, unbuttoning, sliding inside, stroking and discovering and lighting wild fires in her belly.

The muscles of his back rippled under her hands, hard and strong and beautiful to touch, and she wanted to reach more, find more of him. She kissed his forehead and he raised his head, eyes dark with desire.

"I think," she said against his mouth, "that we're getting to a fast bit now."

"Fast, hey?"

She punctuated it with teasing kisses. "Jeans. Boots. Off. Fast. Now."

Fast worked. They both discarded jeans, boots and underwear and in moments, were together again, how she wanted it, skin to skin, without barriers. Except she'd never *wanted* quite this much, more than just an attractive man, *this* man, complex and challenging, drawing her heart as well as her desire.

She edged him backwards to the bed, and he dropped on to it, drawing her down so that she straddled him. His hands on her shoulders, foreheads together, they both watched as she rolled the condom on him, and she could feel his pulse kick up another notch, matching her own.

But when she would have moved, he held her still. For a long moment, they breathed together, ragged and uneven, and although her blood pounded and every skin cell registered exquisite sensation, in a strange way the pause centred her, grounded her, so that this was real, every timeless second significant and precious.

Gil took her face in his hands, his thumbs stroking her temples with devastating delicacy.

And into the silence, he said with simple honesty, "You scare the hell out of me, Kris."

Kris. Not "Blue" or "Sergeant" or any other distancing nickname, and the beautiful, soul-deep gift of his trust, moved her with its intimacy.

She ran her fingers lightly over his lips. "*We* scare me, Gil. But I'm still not running."

She brushed his mouth with hers, kissed him with tenderness and need and all she wanted to give, until the heat spiralled almost beyond bearing and her body, twined with his, demanded completion. She lowered herself onto him, held the searing connection of his gaze, and made love with him, body and soul.

Gil lay awake for a long time, Kris's head on his shoulder, legs tangled together, his arm keeping her close as she slept.

CHAPTER
EIGHTEEN

They hit the peak commuter traffic heading from the Blue Mountains into Sydney.

She hadn't missed this, Kris thought. City traffic, millions of people threading their way through dense, built-up streets, packed in to suburbs and office blocks and shopping malls, open space and trees few and far between. And although she'd grown up in the city, she was no longer at home here.

Gil rode carefully but used the relative freedom of the bike to weave between the cars when he safely could, and with no accidents or delays on the M4, they made reasonable time into Sydney. He took them through the inner south suburbs, zig-zagging through back roads, with frequent glances in the mirrors — making sure no-one followed them. He had to collect the key before they went to the bank, he'd explained earlier.

He cruised past some old terrace houses, unrenovated and long past their best years. Kris kept an eye out, checking that everything appeared okay, and that no-one, as far as she could tell, was watching for them. Gil clearly knew the place and the area, and he turned into a lane, then back along a narrow alleyway to pull in to the small backyard of one of the houses.

"It's a hostel, for homeless men," he explained to Kris as they got off the bike and removed their helmets. "A priest called Simon Murchison has run it for years. A good bloke. The pub is a street over that-away." He jerked a thumb over his shoulder.

Two men sat out in the morning sunshine on the back steps, one of them breaking into a grin when he recognised Gil.

"Hiya, Gil."

"Hiya, Phil," Gil said, with a rising, sing-song intonation and an answering grin, as though the rhyme was a regular greeting.

Phil's grin grew broader still, with the eager, child-like friendliness of intellectual disability, and Kris noticed again this gentle side of the usually taciturn Gil, not often seen.

The other guy hardly looked at them — drugs, or alcohol, or mental illness taking its toll, she figured, like so many of the men who found their way to hostels like this.

"Is Father Simon in?" Gil asked Phil.

"Yeah, Gil, he's inside. He's got plaster on his arm."

Kris didn't like the sound of that, and neither did Gil, from the worried look he threw her as he hurried in the door. He knew his way through the house, and she followed him down a passageway and into an office — where the jeans-clad priest, his left arm in a sling and bruising on his face, sorted one-handed through papers and files strewn all over the floor. A couple of broken wooden chairs were piled in a corner and a damp, blackened patch on the carpet still gave off a smoky scent.

Probably well into his fifties, with dark hair speckled grey, the priest greeted Gil warmly and rose, obviously with some pain, to his feet.

"Excuse the mess. We had some visitors on Saturday night."

"Are you okay?" Gil asked.

"Yes." Despite the pain, his eyes lit with humour. "The intruders and I had a meaningful discussion involving some solid objects and a certain amount of yelling and thumping until some of the residents heard and came to dissuade them from staying. My arm and a chair had a close encounter, but they're both broken cleanly."

Gil indicated the files and papers on the floor. "They were looking for something?"

"So it seems." Simon cast a questioning glance at Kris.

"This is Kris," Gil introduced her, making no mention of her surname or occupation. "She knows what's going on."

The priest shook her hand firmly, with a friendly, curious smile that said he'd noticed the omission, too. But there was clearly liking and respect between the two men, and trust enough that he let the omission pass.

He beckoned them to sit on an old leather sofa, and propped on the edge of his desk.

"I left you a couple of voice mails yesterday. I presume you've heard about Vince Russo?" he asked Gil.

"Yes, I know. My phone's been off the past day or so. Have you heard anything more about Vince, beyond the official line?"

"Not much. Rumour has it he was shot from some distance, twice in the chest. Police searched a nearby building, apparently."

"A planned assassination, rather than an argument, then," Gil observed.

Which made Kris wonder why Joe Petric hadn't shared that piece of information — and to wonder why a priest knew more than she did.

Simon tilted his head slightly. "If the rumour's true."

"Had you seen him, lately?"

"As it happens, yes. He called in a few times a year. The last time was only a couple of weeks ago."

Simon knew Vince? Kris glanced between the two men, saw that this was no surprise to Gil.

Gil stayed focused on the priest. "And?"

"We talked a while. He made a generous donation to the hostel. Then he asked me for a favour." Simon looked directly at Gil, spoke candidly. "He gave me a document envelope, asked me to make sure you got it if anything happened to him. Suggested that I might know somewhere secure to put it. But he stressed it might be safer for you if you didn't know of its existence until . . . necessary."

"So you put it in the safe deposit box." Gil's voice was even, controlled.

"Yes. It seemed the most sensible thing to do. He assured me that the documents couldn't harm you."

Kris made the connections. Simon had the key. Simon was the person Gil had been relying on to circulate the incriminating information about Vince, if anything happened to him. Except Vince had either known that, or guessed it.

She couldn't quite work out the relationship between Simon and Vince, but at some level at least, the priest trusted Vince enough to accede to his wish without telling Gil.

"You accepted his word?" she asked him.

"Given the nature of our conversations over the years, yes, I believed him. But I can see you find that puzzling. You know something of Vince's reputation, then?"

"A little." Like murder. Like drugs and extortion. Like fathering a child and allowing her to grow up abused. Not things Kris regarded as forgivable.

Simon shifted a little on the desk, took some of the weight of his broken arm with his good hand.

"There's a lot I can't tell you about Vince. Some things he told me in confidence, some things I truly just don't know. But I do know that he was a complex man. He grew up in a world that you and I could probably never understand, with its own moral structure and beliefs about strength and power. It's not the kind of world that encouraged conscience or compassion, but Vince gradually developed both. So he faced a choice: denounce what he knew, become an exile — more likely a corpse — or work from

324

within, using his strength and power to ameliorate the excesses and slowly change his world. He chose the latter."

"That doesn't make him a frigging saint," Gil said, with a sharp bitterness.

A sad smile crossed Simon's face. "No argument on that from me. But nor was he quite as black as his reputation. He cultivated that, to appear strong and invincible. It worked — at least for a time."

"Until Sergio Russo arrived," Kris observed, putting more puzzle pieces together.

"He didn't mention names, but I hear talk out there, and there's been an increase in activity. And while it seems that there's more drugs on the street, it's also more tightly controlled — more professional and hardline. There's a lot more fear now than there was this time last year. Vince had concerns about the future — including his own."

"Do you know what's in the envelope?" Gil asked.

"No. But I can guess. He felt it time to put some matters right. And he had a great deal of respect for you, and faith in you."

Simon went to an old metal filing cabinet in the corner, pulled out the top drawer, and reached in with his right arm, groping on the inside of the cabinet top at the back.

After withdrawing his arm, he tossed something to Gil, who caught it with one hand.

"I put a small magnet on it. No-one ever thinks to look up," he said, with a cheeky schoolboy grin.

He saw them out, and they found Phil admiring the bike. While Gil spoke with him for a few minutes, Kris hung back.

"How did you two meet?" she asked Simon, quietly.

"I found him on the streets, when he was out of prison with nowhere to go. I knew Digger at the pub around the corner needed help, so I introduced them. Gil made a good job of the pub, Kris. Turned it from a total dive into a great venue and a good business, with a responsible alcohol policy and no gaming machines."

"So I gather." She'd heard similar from Deb and Liam, and the fact that he'd sold the hotel for so much, without it having a gaming machine licence, testified to the soundness of the business.

"You've not known him long?" Simon asked, with that same restrained curiosity he'd shown earlier.

She considered a vague answer, then dismissed the idea. "A very long, intense few days," she said honestly. "I'm a police officer, from his old home town."

"Ah. I did wonder." He took a business card from his shirt pocket and passed it to her. "If you need me for anything, please don't hesitate to call. Kris . . ." He paused, watched Gil for a moment, both respect and affection showing on his face. "Gil's had to be hard and tough to survive. But there is a great deal of compassion and gentleness in him, too, and I hope some day he finds a way to express it."

Compassion and gentleness — yes, he had those qualities, and she'd seen glimpses of them. How to get through his armour remained a challenge, though, and

326

would be at least until the current threats were overcome.

Gil shook hands with Phil, beckoned to Kris, and strapped on his helmet. With a quick farewell to Simon, she joined Gil on the bike, and they rode cautiously out on to the lane, pausing to check for anything suspicious before turning on to the road.

A few suburbs away, in a main shopping street, Gil found a parking space in front of a café, across the road from the bank.

"Wait in the café and keep a lookout," he suggested. "This will take me ten minutes or more."

Half a dozen tables in the café were already occupied, but there was still a vacant table by the large, open window, with a good view of the front of the bank. She sat there and watched the people going into and coming out of the bank, the people on the street, all the activity around, anything for signs of a threat.

Other than a couple of men engaged in a lively conversation on the corner, she could see no-one who appeared as though they could be keeping an eye on anything, and when the guys in the corner moved off she relaxed a little.

The waiter brought the coffee she'd ordered, and she was stirring in sugar when footsteps stopped beside her, two hands leant on the vacant chair, and Craig Macklin said, "Hi, Kris. In town to do a little banking, hey?"

Every sense went on full alert.

"Hello, Craig," she said coolly. "What brings you here?"

327

Macklin sat down at the table, nodded towards the bank. "We thought we'd better keep an eye on the place. Make sure that if Gillespie turned up, nobody else did. I didn't know you were coming down with him. It's good to see you again."

Thoughts flitted through her mind as she assessed his words. Too many unanswered questions. "We" — who was "we"? Joe and him? His unit? How had they known Gil had a safety deposit box? How did they know it was at this bank? And how did they know Gil was in Sydney?

Okay, the last might have been a good guess, but the other questions needed answering, so she asked point-blank, "How did you know Gil uses this bank?"

"His lawyer told us. When it became clear what they'd killed the other lawyer for, we figured we'd better put some protection on the bank. Don't want any more mob hits, in broad daylight or otherwise."

That sounded reasonable, but she still had an inkling of doubt. It was . . . too neat. Perfectly logical . . . assuming that Gil's lawyer had been convinced that he or others were in such danger that he had to divulge confidential client information.

"So, what are you doing here with Gillespie?" Craig asked. "Steve Fraser said you were off having a long weekend with your boyfriend."

"Change of plans," she replied, determined to keep any information she gave him to a minimum. Maybe she was catching Gil's distrust, but the inkling of doubt scraped in her head like fingernails on a chalkboard, too loud to be ignored.

328

"Where are you going to go? Gillespie needs protection — they want both him and the will. We can organise a safe house for him."

"Thanks, Craig, but no. We'll make our own plans."

He leaned forward, spoke low and urgently. "Look, Kris, you need to be careful. The people after Gillespie — it's not just the old local mafia now. The new guys — Sergio Russo and co. — they're big players internationally. They've got access to resources we can only dream about, including all the cutting-edge technology. They eat cops like us for breakfast."

A warning or a threat? Impossible to tell.

"Or they bend them. So we're going to fly under the radar for a while." She stood, dug in her pocket for money, and dropped a five-dollar note on the table to cover the coffee she'd scarcely sipped.

He followed her out. "You're not suggesting . . .?"

She put her helmet on, started the bike. "I'm not taking chances, Craig. Too much doesn't add up."

She didn't wait for his response. Gil emerged from the bank, and she caught a break in the traffic, did a U-turn, and picked him up. As she glanced back to pull out into the traffic, she saw Craig already talking on his phone.

The road they were on led into the city, but Kris didn't stay on it. Gil held on, the large manila envelope tucked inside his jacket, as Kris wove through inner-suburban streets, taking many twists and turns until they were sure they weren't being followed.

Gil had seen Macklin with her, had held back inside the bank to keep from distracting her, only leaving when she'd started the bike to make the pick-up smooth. He'd known something wasn't quite right when the manager of the safety deposit area showed definite nerves around him. But it took time to go through the procedures, unlock the box, and check the contents.

The cardboard box he'd put there, almost fourteen years ago, was still there, apparently untouched, underneath the document envelope Simon had deposited. With no use for the box now that Vince was dead, he left it there, taking only the envelope. He hadn't opened it in the presence of the manager. He didn't particularly *want* to open it. Whatever it contained couldn't be good news, irrespective of Vince's assurances to Simon. And Macklin's presence near the bank was unlikely to be good news, either.

Close to the city, Kris drove into a multi-storey parking lot, and up the ramps to the roof. No-one followed them in. She parked near the exit ramp, but with a view of the ramp leading onto the roof.

She pushed up her visor. "Do you think this is safe enough, for now?"

He dismounted, yanked off his helmet. "Yes. What was Macklin doing there?"

She hung her helmet on the handlebar, shook out her hair. "Making sure there was no trouble if you turned up at the bank. That's his story, anyway."

A good cover story, except for one fact. "No-one but Simon knew which bank."

That didn't surprise her. "I asked how he knew. He said your lawyer told them."

"Bullshit. He didn't know. More likely they accessed my bank accounts, tracked the payments for the box."

"That's what I wondered. I got a definite whiff of week-old fish. I don't know whether it's Craig himself, or Joe Petric, or someone else manipulating them, feeding them information, but I refused Craig's offer of a safe house for you."

He took the envelope out of his jacket, turned it over in his hands. The sun burned warm on the concrete around them. He flipped the envelope again, reluctant to be drawn in to whatever Vince had planned.

She leaned against a concrete column, nodded at his hands. "You need to open it, find out what's in it, and then we can decide what to do from here," she said.

Yeah, he knew that. His pocket-knife made short work of the seal, revealing two smaller envelopes inside. His gut clenched, and he was mightily tempted to tear them both into shreds, unopened.

He handed one to Kris. Opened the other himself. Unfolded several sheets of paper, headed "The Last Will and Testament of Vincenzo Francesco Russo". He skimmed the standard legalese, and focused on the bequests.

A bequest to the hostel Simon managed, and large gifts to several other charities.

An allowance for his ex-wife, for her lifetime.

An allowance for his former mistress.

A more generous allowance for his current mistress, plus the apartment she lived in.

331

Nothing too surprising in those — unless it was that there were only three women named. Maybe his other mistresses hadn't meant as much to him. Or maybe they'd already had enough gifts from him. Vince had been insanely wealthy, his legitimate investments and development projects far exceeding the drug money that had originally seeded them.

Gil turned the page, and the next item leapt out at him: *"To my natural daughter, Marcella Doonan . . ."*

Although Gil had already suspected, anger blurred the confirming words. How could Vince have watched her live the life she had and have done nothing all those years? He'd let her be used by others, by just about everyone. Her *father*. Jesus, Gil wanted to throw up. He leaned over the parapet, sucked in some traffic-tainted air. All the generous bequests in the world couldn't make good Vince's sin — even if she'd lived. But Vince was too bloody late.

"Gil? What's wrong?"

She was by his side, her arm clasping him as if she thought he might fall.

He shoved the pages into her hand. "The bastard definitely was Marci's father. He knew it all along."

She skimmed the first page, slowed on the second, and whistled when she saw the sum of money Vince had bequeathed to his daughter.

As if five million dollars could have changed anything for Marci, Gil thought bitterly. She'd have gone through it in no time, been preyed upon by others. And she would still have sold her body, because that was the only value she'd ever learned to place on herself.

"Gil." Kris clutched the pages, her hand shaking. "Gil, did you read on?"

He read it over her shoulder, and it wasn't just the shaking of her hand that made the words hard to follow.

"To Morgan Gillespie . . . the properties listed in schedule A appended to this will . . . all my shares in San Damiano Enterprises . . . and the remainder of my estate after all bequests are distributed."

CHAPTER
NINETEEN

He couldn't get his head around it. The bastard had left property and shares to him.

"He's mad," he argued. "There has to be some catch. Maybe they're derelict, or on a uranium dump."

Kris flipped over the page, scanned it. "Gil, I don't think there are many uranium dumps in Point Piper. Or Double Bay. There's got to be twenty or more properties listed here, and they all sound — well, *significant*."

He didn't look at the list. The twisted truth was sinking in. Luxury apartment and housing developments had been Vince's interests these past ten years, and Gil could guess some of the addresses on the list — and some of the prices they'd be valued at.

He slammed a hand against a concrete pillar, the sting of the rough surface proof he wasn't asleep, caught in some hellish nightmare. He gave a harsh laugh. "No wonder Tony wants this, and wants me dead."

"Yes," Kris agreed. "If he's seen a copy, or the solicitor told him its contents, he'll be livid. Did you read this bit? 'It is my explicit wish and instruction that my son Antonio and my nephews' — he lists four including the Flanagan boys — 'do not benefit in any way, now or in the future, from my estate.' "

"Fuck." There wasn't much else to say. That clause on its own amounted to a death warrant.

She checked around for anyone in the vicinity, lowered her voice. "Gil — the other envelope. It's dates, places, details of cocaine shipments and distribution, ecstasy manufacture, money laundering. I didn't read it all, but I'm betting it's Tony's and Sergio's operation. With this kind of information, we could put together enough evidence to arrest and charge them."

He'd forgotten about the other envelope in the shock of reading the will — but it was almost as much of a bombshell.

"Vince wanted his son convicted." Gil thought through the implications. "And he wanted me to be the one to carry the can for it."

"Or maybe he trusted you, more than others, to do the right thing."

Her interpretation didn't make much difference. It still lumbered him with a huge responsibility, and a huge risk. Why the hell couldn't Vince have given the cops the information directly? Why involve him?

As the first angry reaction passed, two reasons occurred to him. Because he knew that Gil would follow it through — he'd find a way to make sure the information got to uncorrupted cops and didn't get buried. And secondly — Kris mightn't approve of this one — in Vince's world, information could be leverage. And he might yet need that kind of leverage.

She tapped the documents with her knuckle. "We need to copy these. We need to know if the will is legal, if it will hold up in court, and we need to know more about Vince's estate, and San Damiano Enterprises. I know someone who can give us expert advice."

"Listen, Blue, we have to be careful. I need to get you safe, away from me, until I work out how to handle this."

"Gil, the person I'm thinking of is my father. He's a barrister. We can trust him completely. He won't do anything that will endanger me. And his chambers are here in the city."

Gil thought quickly, putting together the first steps of a plan.

"Okay, we'll ask him about the will. But the other . . . I want some copies of it, but I don't want anyone to know about it, yet. I want to read it thoroughly first. When we act on it, it will have to be done quickly, and be well coordinated. I don't want anything leaked or even hinted at before then."

How he'd act, he wasn't sure yet. It would depend on the contents, the level of detail about the operations — and it might depend on the barrister's opinion of the will. Not to mention depending upon how long he survived, now that word could be out that he had the will.

Kris drove them to another car park, in the business end of Macquarie Street, and together they walked up the block to her father's chambers.

The décor of the reception area spoke, in no uncertain terms, of money. Parquetry floors, solid timber front desk, leather lounge chairs, original artworks on the walls. Behind the desk a man in his thirties, in dark suit, white shirt and tie, suggested "security" rather than "secretary" — an impression backed-up by Gil's quick scan of the foyer. He counted at least three security cameras, noted the security doors beyond the area and the monitor not entirely hidden by the high desk-front.

Kris strode up to the desk with straight back, head held high and an air of confidence anyone would be hard pressed to rebuff.

"Please inform Mr Matthews that his daughter Kris is here, and the matter is urgent."

The security man gave them both a good once-over as he made the call to advise of their presence. Leather jackets, bike helmets, no appointment — they probably ranked high on the guy's risk scale, Gil figured. If Kris hadn't mentioned she was Matthews' daughter, they would most likely have been politely escorted out.

Kris paced while they waited. It was subtle — more of a stroll, pretending to examine the artworks, but he knew her now, recognised her restlessness, the unusual tension. She faced criminals without a flinch, had dealt efficiently and logically with all the dramas unfolding around them, yet the prospect of seeing her father unsettled her.

It suddenly stunned him how little he knew about her background. She'd been in Dungirri five or six years, worked outback for longer than that, and her father was a barrister — that was about the extent of his knowledge. He knew her character — her toughness,

her compassion, her courage, the ethical core of her —
yet he had no clue what influences had shaped her,
what her life and experiences had been before the past
few years in Dungirri.

The gilt board listing the members of the chambers
only gave him one more piece of information: the
second name from the top, presumably ranked in order
of importance, listed *John Matthews, QC*.

Gil didn't know the finer details of the legal world,
but he did know a Queen's Counsel was not just a
barrister, but a senior one, recognised by his peers —
and appointed years ago, before they'd changed the
designation to Senior Counsel.

He didn't have to wait long to meet the man. The
automatic doors beyond the reception desk swooshed
open, and Matthews strode out, a commanding
presence in an impeccable business suit.

"Kris! What a pleasant surprise! I had no idea you
were in Sydney," he greeted her, kissing her on the
cheek, but not, Gil noted, hugging her.

"Hi, Dad. Sorry to burst in on you unannounced.
Can you spare me fifteen minutes? I need some urgent
advice on a serious matter."

"Come through. This morning's case got postponed,
so I've got a little time. And your friend . . ."

"Morgan Gillespie — Gil." Gil held out his hand and
returned the man's assessing look and his bone-
crunching handshake.

Gil noted the security as they followed Matthews —
the swipe-card controlled door from the foyer into an
area of meeting rooms and junior offices; discreet

cameras; another swipe-card entry into a corridor of offices.

The office he ushered them into was designed to impress, with an antique oak desk, a matching large table with velvet-upholstered chairs, and a couple of leather armchairs in an alcove. Bookshelves lined the walls, loaded with legal tomes, the shelves nearest the desk also holding an array of photographs.

He picked a teenage Kris in a family portrait, laughing with a red-haired brother, another brother disapprovingly serious, and a much younger sister, dark-haired and pretty, between her parents. Kris had her mother's colouring, but there the resemblance ended. Impeccable make-up and hairstyling highlighted her mother's looks, but he discerned little of character in the portrait. Whereas Kris — and her brother — glowed with life and energy.

In another photo, with a twenty-something Kris in police uniform, she was flanked by her parents, her sister, and the serious brother, all looking proud. Her police academy graduation, he guessed, and wondered briefly where the laughing brother was.

Matthews invited them to sit at the table, offered them coffee and, when he learned they'd had an early breakfast on the road, went to the phone on his desk and ordered a light lunch to be delivered.

Gil left it to Kris to begin, and she did as soon as her father had joined them at the table.

"Dad, this matter has connections with a police investigation, but I need to stress that I'm here on a personal basis, not official."

"Are you in trouble?" he asked sharply. "Accused of something?"

"No, not that," she assured him. "And neither is Gil. But some connections of Gil's have been murdered, and there is a distinct possibility of police corruption in the investigations. I believe his life is threatened, and more so since we found this a couple of hours ago." She took the will out of the envelope, unfolded it, and passed it across to her father.

He withdrew a pair of reading glasses from his pocket, unhurriedly read through the document, pausing only to call "come in" when a knock came on the door. A middle-aged woman wheeled in a trolley with an assortment of gourmet sandwiches, cheeses, fresh fruit and coffee, laid them out on the table, and departed again with a warm smile but no comment.

Kris passed Gil a plate and napkin. "Eat," she ordered in a low voice. "I don't know when we'll get another chance."

He needed the coffee more than the food, but he put a couple of sandwiches on his plate.

Matthews finally laid down the will and set his reading glasses on top of it.

"The testator was a friend of yours?"

"No." Gil didn't care how blunt it sounded. "I knew him, but he was no friend."

"Ah. Nevertheless, it appears to be a substantial inheritance."

Gil held his gaze. "One I don't want."

"Have you heard of Vince Russo, Dad?" Kris interjected. "Do you know anything about him?"

340

"I've heard the name, but I never met him. There was an item recently in the newspaper about his murder. I understand he was a successful businessman, predominantly involved with residential property development."

Funded by dirty money, Gil wanted to say, but didn't. Matthews was a senior barrister, the kind very careful with his words, and Gil had learned over the years to tread equally as carefully with lawyers.

"We need to know a few things, Dad. First, if the will appears legitimate and legally binding, and whether that stipulation about the exclusion of his son and nephews could be contestable. And secondly, if it's possible to find out through public sources, more about San Damiano Enterprises."

Matthews strolled to his desk and made a brief phone call. "Adrian, do a search on San Damiano Enterprises. Bring what you find to my office within ten minutes. Thank you."

Returning to his chair, he leaned back, clasped his hands behind his head. "Regarding your first question, assuming the document is genuine, it appears to be comprehensive. Everything is contestable, of course; however, given the explicit exclusion, and the recent date of the will, I would be surprised if a challenge resulted in an amendment to the legacy. There would have to be a strong argument. I presume the son and nephews are not minors, with a reasonable expectation of parental support?"

"No, they're not minors," Kris replied.

"What if I don't want it?" Gil asked.

Matthews steepled his fingers, studied him. "You would be free to dispose of the inheritance as you wish, of course. Although if the assets are as considerable as they appear, I would strongly recommend consultation with a good tax accountant. I take it you believe the son should inherit? Or his daughter?"

Gil shook his head. "Marci's dead. She was murdered the day before Vince. And Tony . . ." He glanced at Kris, unsure how to express it in exact, lawyerly terms.

"Is under suspicion of complicity in both murders," Kris said.

"Ah. So your reluctance is due to . . .?"

Gil pushed back his chair, strode to the window and watched the blue sky beyond the skyscrapers while he carefully put his words together.

"The source of the original money. The risk to people who . . . matter to me. And I don't need it. I've got plenty, and what I've got, I've earned . . . legitimately and above board."

Matthews nodded slowly. "I think I understand. I don't pay a lot of heed to rumours, but that doesn't mean I don't hear them. I have heard a number of rumours regarding the Russo family, over the years. And the more recent ones . . ." he eyed his daughter, "they have me worried for you. For both of you."

"I have to do my job, Dad," Kris said gently. "You know, getting the bad guys off the streets."

He gave her a fond smile. "Yes, my girl, I know."

A knock sounded on the door, and a clerk brought in a file.

"San Damiano Enterprises, sir. This is what I've found so far. I'll keep looking, if you like."

"Yes, please do so."

Gil itched to look over the barrister's shoulder as he flicked through the dozen or more sheets of paper. Instead, Kris pushed his untouched sandwiches towards him, and he ate a couple of mouthfuls while Matthews read, and washed them down with rapidly cooling coffee.

Matthews looked over his reading glasses at them. "It's a private proprietary company. Russo was sole director and shareholder. Financial reports aren't readily available, but assets appear to include another large property portfolio. The company is also listed as a shareholder in a considerable number of publicly listed companies, and as a significant donor to charity."

Gil swallowed a swear word. There went his hopes that San Damiano was simply a valueless holding company.

Matthews went to the computer on his desk, typed in a few words, and scanned the results. "I thought so. I'm assuming Russo was Catholic. San Damiano is the church where Saint Francis of Assisi had a vision of Christ instructing him to 'repair his house'. From what you've told me, the name of the company, and the will, suggests that he was seeking redemption, or trying to right wrongs."

That accorded with Simon's comments earlier, but it didn't make Gil any happier about the result. He heartily wished Vince had left him right out of his bid for salvation. Getting someone else to dob in his son didn't amount to much redemption, from Gil's perspective.

"That reminds me," Kris said, obviously thinking of the same thing. "I need to copy some documents. Can I use your copier, Dad?"

Her father opened a connecting door through to another office. "Madeline will help you if you need it."

And that left Gil alone with her father. He felt the man's considering gaze, turned and confronted it.

"I don't suppose you could persuade her to go somewhere safe, or stay with you?" he asked the older man.

"If you've known my daughter for long, you'll know that no-one can persuade her against what she believes is right. Least of all me."

There was sadness in his words, and obviously some history, but he continued without giving a chance for questions. "The people who matter to you . . . is she one of them?"

Gil didn't lie. "Yes."

The man ceased to act as a senior barrister, became simply a father. "Is there anything I can do?"

"Keep silent, for now. Don't mention to anyone — not even others in the family — that we've been, or what we've discussed. I'd suggest that you also put your security people on alert. I doubt we were tailed here, but someone may make the connection between Kris and you."

Unless the Russos really dug about for Kris's history, he hoped her common-enough name should keep her family out of it.

Kris returned with a small stack of envelopes. She passed one to her father. "That's a copy of the will. Could you keep it secure? And this too." After an instant's hesitation, she covered her father's hand with hers. "If I'm not in contact within forty-eight hours, Dad, please copy the contents, and have it sent by secure courier to the people whose names I've written inside. It's important."

"I will." He kissed her on the forehead, and then drew her into a brief hug. "Be careful, both of you. And next time you're in Sydney, plan on a little time with the family, hey? Your mother misses you. And Royce and Steph."

Royce and Steph, Gil noted. Not Royce, Steph and . . . ?

She was quiet in the lift going down, subdued.

It was too risky to discuss Vince and their predicament in a public lift, even if they were alone, and even riskier to put his arms around her, for the same and other reasons.

"Do you see your family often?" he asked.

She shook herself out of her thoughts. "Not a lot. They never come out bush — can't understand why I live there — and I've been a bit busy the past few years to spend much time here." She made an attempt at a grin. "Definitely not a city chick any more."

"Are your siblings here?"

"Yes. Royce is a financial analyst, he works a block or so from here, and Stephanie's a fashion editor for a glossy mag."

345

"In one of the family photos, there was another brother. He looked like you."

Her face clouded, and he regretted asking, but she answered the question, her voice flat. "That's Hugh. He died. He saw a woman being assaulted outside a pub, went to help her, and was shot by the assailant. Hugh was twenty-one."

And she'd have been maybe nineteen or twenty, he guessed, and very close to her brother. "Is that why you became a cop?"

"Partly." She smiled wistfully. "Partly to annoy my father, who wanted Hugh and me to go into law. Dad and I haven't always seen eye-to-eye on what constitutes justice. But mostly because I wanted to do something positive for the world, which didn't involve sitting behind a desk all day."

The lift pinged to announce the ground floor, and the doors slid open.

"Where to now?" she asked.

"Back to the bike, then straight to Dungirri," he decided.

The uneasiness that had dogged him since reading Vince's will ratcheted up further. They had to stand a better chance away from the city, where Tony and Sergio didn't have the same resources, and didn't know the environment as well. Tony wouldn't rest until he had the will; if he wasn't already on his way to the Dungirri district to join Sergio, he would be as soon as word got back from the police that Gil had it.

It was just on noon now. He and Kris could be back there this evening. He could move Megan and the

346

others to somewhere more distant — maybe enlist Mark's help to do so.

And then he'd prepare to face Tony and Sergio.

It was well past dark when they rode through Dungirri. The town was quiet, only a few regulars' cars in front of the pub, no-one out on the streets. They didn't stop. Kris took the Birraga road out of town, heading to Mark's place.

The moon, two days past full, was rising behind them, casting shadows that mixed, among the trees at the side of the road, with those from the headlight. She wanted to crawl into a bed, curl up beside Gil, and sleep for at least ten hours. They'd taken it in turns driving, but there was little rest in being a passenger on the bike, and she knew they were both on the edge of exhaustion. A couple of brief stops for fuel and food had kept them going, but she counted now the remaining distance to Mark's place — twenty kilometres on the Birraga side of Dungirri.

Seventeen, when she passed the turn to Gil's father's place. Fifteen, when she passed Delphi O'Connell's farm, a light still on in the front room. Five, when she approached the turn onto the dirt road leading to Mark's.

Ahead, two vehicles swung out of the road, turned towards Birraga, tail lights disappearing into the darkness. She idly wondered which property they'd come from — there were three or four down the fifteen-kilometre road.

As she decelerated for the turn, a flash of light in the sky beyond the trees caught her attention. She slowed right down, trying to catch it again. A shooting star? A plane? A few properties around here had airstrips — Mark's included — but planes rarely landed at night out here, except in an emergency. The light in the sky swung around, too manoeuvrable for a plane, more the motion of a helicopter — and from the direction of Mark's place. Helicopters only flew around here at night in an emergency, too.

She rounded the corner, took the speed up as far as she dared on the dirt, and raced to Mark's.

CHAPTER
TWENTY

The steel gates at the entrance to the property dragged crookedly on their hinges, bent and twisted, and the intercom unit set into the brick gatepost hung by a wire, the others cut, the metal smashed by something heavy.

Kris killed the bike's engine, coasting in to the shadow of nearby trees.

When they'd left Sydney, she'd taken her police weapon from her backpack and tucked it into the back of her jeans, as a precaution. Now she drew it, waving Gil into the cover of the old pine trees lining the long drive. They moved quickly but with caution up the drive, staying in the shadows of the trees, Gil, unarmed, close behind Kris.

There were no lights on in the house, and no vehicles outside it. While the possibility that the chopper had been at some other property had occurred to her, it didn't explain the busted gates, the lack of lights — or the open front door.

"If the emergency chopper had picked up someone, there'd be at least an ambulance, and probably police vehicles here," she whispered to Gil. He nodded in agreement, his eyes hard and cold.

As they came in sight of the multi-car garage beside the house, her suspicions of something sinister were realised. The doors were open, the cars — hers, Liam's, Mark's — riddled with bullet holes, windows shattered, tyres blown apart.

A voice came from the house, and she caught Gil's arm as he surged forward, but let go when Mark stumbled out on to the veranda, torch in one hand, propping himself up against a post for steadiness, his head bleeding as he yelled into a phone.

They raced to him as he demanded ambulance and police, reached him as he shook the phone in disgust. Dazed and not quite with it, he slid down the post to the wooden floor. "This phone's not working. Old one — they smashed the others."

She had her phone out, cursing the time it took to turn on, at the same time trying to examine his head wound and check his responses.

Gil went straight inside, calling for Megan, Deb and Liam, Kris didn't hear any answering calls.

"What happened, Mark? Where are the others?"

"Cars. At least eight men, with weapons. Balaclavas — couldn't see who they were. Then the helicopter landed. They took the girls. Tried to stop them but . . ." He indicated his head. "Rifle butt. Hard. Liam's down — shot I think."

Her phone beeped to announce its readiness — at last — and she dialled the emergency number as she took the torch, ordered Mark to stay put, and ran inside, searching for Liam.

350

"I'll need both police and ambulance," she told the operator. "Two women have just been abducted from the home of Federal MP Mark Strelitz, twenty kilometres west of Dungirri in northern New South Wales." She briskly gave the address, added when the operator sought more details, "The Birraga police know where it is. I'm their sergeant. Tell them the abductors are in a helicopter, which headed west or southwest about ten minutes ago. There are two casualties on the ground, so put me through to the ambulance operator now."

Finding the main rooms of the house empty, she stepped out on to the terrace, and in a sweep of the torch she caught sight of Gil out in the paddock beyond, kneeling on the ground beside Liam.

"Two males injured," she told the ambulance operator as she ran across the ground. "One with blunt force trauma to the head, conscious and talking but dazed."

Blood. Blood on Liam's chest, and on his thigh. Blood all over Gil's hands, as he pressed against the two wounds. Her brain registered it, reeled from it, even as her training kicked in and she kept speaking clearly to the emergency operator.

"One with multiple gunshot wounds to chest and upper leg, significant blood loss." She switched to speaker phone as she knelt beside Liam, dropped the phone and the torch on the ground as she tore off her jacket and T-shirt, and bundled it against the wound in the side of his chest. Gil's large hand pressed down on it, and she reached for Liam's wrist. "Pulse is weak,"

351

she said, loudly enough for the phone to pick up. "Patient is not conscious. We'll need the rescue helicopter."

His tone polite and calming, the operator started to ask more questions, but despairing at the delay, she spoke over him. "I'm a police sergeant. I know serious injuries when I see them. Just get that chopper in the air now, and ambulances on the way, and then we can do the rest."

Liam's lips moved up a fraction, and his hand moved slightly under hers. When she glanced down, she saw he'd given her a thumbs-up sign. Relief made her eyes blur, but it didn't lessen her worry by much.

Grim-faced, Gil told Liam to "Hang in there, mate. We've got you."

Kris continued reporting to the operator, responding to his questions, checking Liam's leg wound. A bullet wound, blood loss, but from what she could tell, no main artery hit. She knew damned well that this far from help, Liam wouldn't have stood much chance if that had been the case.

She heard car engines approaching, saw headlights arc across the garden. Worried it might be the abductors returning, she quickly flicked the torch off, drew her gun, and with a signal to Gil to stay with Liam, she ducked around the side of the house to check, yanking on her jacket as she went.

Two police cars pulled up in the driveway outside the house. The officer's torch beams caught Mark, slumped against the post, and one swung around and blinded her as she approached.

"Kris!" Adam exclaimed, dropping the light from her eyes.

"One of you get a first-aid kit around to the back," she instructed. "Someone else see to Mr Strelitz. Ambulance and chopper are coming."

"Yeah, we heard," Adam said, as the other officers hurried to act.

"How did you get here so quickly?" she asked. It could only be a few minutes since she'd called, nowhere near long enough for two cars to come from either Dungirri or Birraga.

"The security firm in Moree alerted us. An alarm went on very briefly, then stopped, and they couldn't get on to anyone by phone, or access the system. When you called, the operator relayed the call. We didn't see any sign of the chopper, but we came from north of here, we were attending a domestic. You weren't here when it happened?"

"No. Gil and I just arrived back from Sydney. We saw the chopper from the corner of the main road."

He raised an eyebrow. "I wondered why you hadn't returned my call this morning."

"Why? What happened?" she demanded, dreading the answer. Adam wouldn't call her on days off without good reason.

"The magistrate released Sean Barrett and the other blokes on bail this morning."

She closed her eyes briefly, silently cursed the magistrate. Mark had said there were about eight men in the vehicles, presumably another couple in the helicopter. Sergio, the Flanagan sons, Clinton the truck driver, the two others who'd been with Sergio at the old Gillespie place the other day — that made six they could reasonably suspect were already involved. Armed, prepared to shoot, and definitely dangerous.

And now the magistrate had released four more men with a grudge against Gil — and Megan — some of whom had existing connections to the Flanagans, all of whom had mates in the wilder, rougher parts of the community, bored and disillusioned by long-term underemployment and lack of money. Chances were, Sergio and Tony would have plenty of potential recruits, keen to see some excitement.

Paramedics bustled around Liam, examining him, setting up a drip, getting a briefing from the senior constable who'd joined Gil in looking after him.

Seething with anger, frustrated by their collective helplessness — there was no news, yet, on where the helicopter might have landed — Gil gritted his teeth and watched the paramedics work on Liam.

More police arrived, including Steve Fraser, and Gil heard Kris giving him a brief summary. One of the ambulances left again, with Mark, its siren wailing in the night. As it dimmed down the road, Gil heard the *thwack* of rotors in the distance, and before long the rescue chopper landed in the paddock, bringing with it another flurry of lights and activity.

Kris came and stood beside him, her hand on his shoulder. She'd found another T-shirt, discarded her jacket somewhere along the line.

"How's Mark?" he asked.

"They're taking him to Birraga for X-rays and monitoring. The rescue helicopter can only take one — they'll come back to Birraga for Mark if he needs it."

She heaved in a deep breath, her fingers tightening on his arm. "They were organised, Gil. A planned operation. The phone line and power were cut. They stormed in, heavily armed, and one of them at least knew the operation of the security system, took out the battery backup. They rounded them all up, held them at gunpoint, and collected up their mobiles and smashed them."

That matched the few phrases Liam had muttered, in between apologies for failing Megan and Deb, as he wavered in and out of consciousness.

Four unarmed people, against almost a dozen, some with semi-automatic weapons. Liam — bright, too-young, too-loyal Liam — could die, doing what Gil thought he should have been there to do: protect them. Deb would take the same risks. The thought of what they'd been through — of what still might be happening to Megan and Deb, wherever they were — snapped his control.

He spun away from Kris, belted his fist against a tree.

"We shouldn't have left them here," he raged. "It's my fucking fault for leaving them here, unprotected."

"You think I feel any better about it?" she snapped back, her own temper flaring. "This wasn't a few thugs. They could have dealt with that. It was a bloody paramilitary-style extraction, planned with inside information. So it's no good either of us blaming ourselves, no matter how much we damned well want to."

Lights suddenly came on, bright compared to the flickering torch beams, a security light shining into his eyes so that he had to blink.

"Good — power's back." Her voice was brisk, focused again after that outburst. "We'll meet in Mark's office, get the search for them underway. I want your input, Gillespie. It's probably more useful than thumping things," she added dryly, before she turned and walked away.

He took a short time to calm down, then found the water tank and washed Liam's blood off his hands. When he stood in the doorway of Mark's office a few minutes later, Kris was well underway, rolling off instructions to the ten or so cops in the room.

"Jake, get on to Harry at Birraga Air Charter, see what he knows about helicopter pilots in the district, and any choppers or pilots visiting. And then check with the properties around the region that use choppers for mustering. Adam, phone around the local graziers, see if you can get a path on the chopper. They'll likely have heard it, might be able to give us a better idea of direction. And find out if they know if Mark's had any visitors the past two days. Kate and Todd, check the manager's cottage, the outbuildings, and the old shearers' quarters down by the woolshed for anyone there, or signs that anyone's been watching the place. Trisha — the security firm at Moree — find out everything they've logged over the past two days around

356

this place. I don't think the full system was running, but find out what was."

She would cover it all, he knew. She'd efficiently go through all the possible sources of information, pull together every fact, keep searching and asking and hunting as long as she needed. Because she was a damned good cop and a dedicated one, who cared about the people she'd sworn to serve.

But she couldn't do the one thing he could do. The one thing that might have a chance of getting Megan and Deb released, unharmed.

He turned and left the house.

He could hear the rescue helicopter preparing to take off behind the house, but he didn't go that way. He dialled directory assistance while he walked down the drive and received the number by text just as he reached the bike.

The moon shone in a clear sky overhead, dimming out half the stars. Waiting for the phone to pick up, he searched for the constellations he'd watched as a kid, alone in the dark.

"Flanagan, it's Gillespie. Tell the Russos that I have the will. They can have me and it in exchange for the women. Use this number to arrange a time and place. No cops, because I know you've got a mole. Just me and the will."

He disconnected as soon as he finished. Leaving Kris's bag by the road, he drove away into the darkness.

CHAPTER
TWENTY-ONE

The bastard had left, and he wasn't answering her calls. Every hour, she left a message — first angry, then worried, then pleading — and her heart leapt every time her phone rang, but he didn't respond.

The only thing she had was the note he'd left in her jacket pocket: *Look for the informant. I'll be in touch. G.* Look for the informant. A whole lot easier said than done. Look for an informant, while at the same time trying to locate a helicopter and two abducted women, with a small force of police in a huge regional area where she wasn't sure who she could trust.

Adam's enquiries traced the noise of the chopper to an area southwest of Birraga, but there the trail ended. Whether that meant it had landed in the area, or flown further on, they had no way of knowing. In the interview room in the Dungirri station, she and Adam studied maps spread on the table, trying to match scraps of information that might or might not be relevant to find some sort — any sort — of pattern.

Steve had emailed scanned copies of Gil's maps from years ago, and the photos and notes, and she looked through the printed pages, identifying properties on the larger survey maps, comparing them with the lists she had of current Flanagan-owned properties. There were at least fifteen of the latter, and she didn't know if the list was complete. It was also likely that not everything they had an interest in was directly registered under the Flanagan Agricultural Company.

Properties in the outback areas beyond Birraga tended to be huge, and a few landholders used helicopters for mustering and other work. Harry at Birraga Air Charter gave them a list of the ones he knew, but they were all smaller aircraft, not large enough to carry four people. Still, she cross-matched that data against the Flanagan properties . . . and came up with nothing.

She closed her eyes, bit her lip, trying to keep from howling like a little girl from exhaustion and despair. Megan was out there . . . somewhere. Just seventeen years old, and vulnerable. Kris hoped she and Deb were together — Deb would do her best to look after her.

But they were both reliant on her to find those responsible, locate the hiding place and organise a rescue. She'd failed before. Little Jess Sutherland was lying in a grave, murdered. Tanya Wilson had survived, but no thanks to her.

Look for the informant, Gil had said.

But if she hadn't recognised a murderer when she'd seen him in the street almost every day, how could she hope to identify an informant when she had no evidence?

They waited until six-thirty in the morning to call him. The first rays of sunlight slanted through the timber gaps in the deserted shearing shed he'd hidden in, not far outside Birraga, and he woke from his doze with a start when his phone rang.

"It's a deal, Gillespie," an accented voice said in his ear. "Ten o'clock this morning. On the Tarlinton Road, five kilometres west of Dog Creek. Just you and the will. If we see even a hint of anyone else, we will shoot the hostages."

The click of disconnection sounded in his ear.

Tarlinton Road. He pulled up the GPS maps on his phone, checked the location and distance. About twenty-five kilometres southwest of Birraga, in an isolated area a long way from major roads, and with few properties around.

They weren't planning on making anything easy, but he had some time to prepare. He slid open the back of his phone, removed the SIM card, and replaced it with one of the ones he'd salvaged from the smashed phones at Mark's house.

Megan's, he discovered, when he switched the phone on again. She had Kris's number programmed in already. And Liam's, he noted, with some surprise. Fast workers, these modern kids.

He selected Kris's number, and hit the call button.

She answered immediately. "*Megan?*"

"No, Blue. It's Gil. Using Megan's card in case they're tracing mine. Can you be on the Tarlinton Road, five k's west of Dog Creek, at ten-thirty? I'll text you the coordinates. Just you, in an unmarked car."

"I know it," she said. "Where are you, Gil? Are you all right?"

"I'm fine. Any luck?"

"Nothing definite. I can't pin anything to anyone or any place. Steve interviewed Dan Flanagan, but he was at a function in Birraga last night, with fifty witnesses, and swears he knows nothing. His sons are apparently pig shooting in Queensland."

"So he says."

"I can't disprove it, yet. And I don't know who knew Megan was at Mark's." She sounded weary, had probably worked all night. "There's no evidence of visitors, or staff near the homestead, and I won't be able to talk to Mark until later today."

"Steve might have told them," he suggested. "Or Adam."

He watched a spider walk across in front of him in the silence.

"Not Adam," she eventually said, firmly.

She didn't say, "Not Steve." He didn't think it would be Steve either, but he couldn't be sure. Steve had access to information, was in touch with Petric and Macklin, had been involved in the investigations from the start, and knew where Kris had taken Megan.

But most of the town probably knew Kris had gone to Mark's, and it wouldn't have been too hard to guess Megan was there, too. It didn't narrow the field down, much.

"Why don't you go through the information from Vince?" he suggested. "See if there's anything there that helps."

"I've just started on that."

"I'll go through my copy. I'll let you know if I come up with anything. Listen, Blue, gotta go. I'll see you at ten-thirty. Be on time, but not early. And don't tell a soul — not until we've got this worked out."

After disconnecting and turning the phone off, he let his head fall back against the wall. He wouldn't see her at ten-thirty. He'd either be with the Russos, or dead on the road. But all going well, she'd find Megan and Deb, and he'd have to trust her to track him down, too.

He crossed the sandy causeway over Dog Creek in plenty of time, the rivergums along its banks creating a brief space of shade before he was out on the sunlit road again. Here, an hour west of Dungirri and its scrub, the flat plains stretched into the distance under a huge sky, the paddocks cleared for grazing.

Deep ridges ran along either side of the unsealed road, where graders and each passing vehicle had pushed the fine rust-red sand. Down the middle of the road ran another ridge, maybe six inches high, guaranteed to send the bike skating or sliding, if he veered into it.

He watched the odometer and stopped just on the five kilometres from the creek. There were no trees along the road here — nothing to interrupt the view in all four directions. Nowhere to hide, nowhere to run. They'd chosen the place well.

He hung the helmet on the bike, left his jacket draped on the seat, and the key in the ignition. He took only his phone, and the envelope with the will.

He caught a glint on the road ahead, and strolled towards it while he waited. A dead lizard was flipped over onto its back in the sand, its light underbelly shining white in the sun. A few ants had already found it, and more would find it soon, devour it, stripping away the flesh bite by bite. Or one of the larger birds, grateful for an easy lunch.

The sight of it found a small chink in his calmness, and he suppressed a shudder. He would do what he came to do and, if it worked, Megan and Deb would get away safely. If it didn't work . . . if it didn't work, he wouldn't feel the ants, and Kris would be along to find him, soon enough.

A plume of dust appeared in the west, and he waited on the road, some distance from the bike.

They only brought one vehicle — the black Land Rover. It stopped thirty metres away, and Sergio got out, a pistol in his hand.

"I'm pleased that you followed instructions, Gillespie," he said.

"Now let's see if you can, Russo. Let the women go, and let them walk to the bike. Once they're there, I'll walk to you." He held up the envelope with one hand.

"And if I don't like your instructions?"

"My thumb is hovering on the 'send' button of a text message, to a senior police contact, advising that a certain freighter about to dock in Sydney is carrying a shipment of cocaine."

"I could shoot you now, Gillespie."

"If you raise your arm, I press the button."

He forced himself to keep calm, keep still. It would work within seconds, or not at all.

"Release the women," Sergio ordered.

Three men hauled them out of the back, and they stumbled, blindfolded, hands bound. One of the men cut the ties around their wrists, and Sergio himself ripped the blindfolds off.

"Walk to the motorcycle, ladies. Do not go anywhere near Gillespie, do not stop, do not talk. Have I made myself clear?"

They nodded, then Deb put her arm around Megan and started guiding her away.

Gil remained motionless. They crossed to the side of the road, to keep their distance from him, but as they came closer, he saw the bruises on Deb's face and arms, the raw red marks on Megan's wrists.

"Get away," he mouthed, and Deb gave a minute nod. If she'd been by herself, he might have had an argument, but with Megan to protect, she'd do the right thing.

As soon as Deb and Megan reached the bike, the men came at him. He raised his hand with the phone, growling, "Wait until they leave."

He couldn't risk taking his eyes off the men. He heard the bike start, the engine rev. And he heard engine sounds alter as it started to move. He waited a second or two, then lifted his thumb from the phone.

They didn't give him any more time. They rushed him, tackled him to the ground, shoving his face into the sand. He tried to twist away, but a boot slammed into his gut. Pain screamed through his body, his head and, somewhere in the middle of it, he heard a shot, then another. They dragged his arms behind him, cuffed them and hauled him upright. Panic giving him strength, he fought them, needing to turn, to see down the road.

"Let him look," Sergio ordered. "It will give him plenty to think about, while we wait for my cousin to join us."

The bike lay on its side on the road, Megan and Deb sprawled nearby — silent, still heaps on the blood-reddened sand.

CHAPTER
TWENTY-TWO

Despite Gil's calm, almost casual, voice when he'd set up the meeting, Kris's uneasiness kept building. He wouldn't have set her up to go into danger without warning, but the sense that something was wrong couldn't be ignored.

According to the clock in the unmarked police vehicle, she crossed the creek at twenty past ten. She'd shifted into four-wheel drive earlier, the deep, sandy ridges on the road a hazard. She glanced again at the dark clouds gathering on the western horizon, their ominous colour a vivid contrast to the rest of the blue sky and the sunshine, gold on the dry paddocks. The forecast storms were on their way; with luck, she'd be off this road before it turned into a quagmire.

Four kilometres past the creek, she started looking out for Gil and his bike. When she saw a figure waving in the middle of the road, she thought for a moment that it was uncharacteristic of him. And then she saw it wasn't him . . . Deb slumped to the ground as she stopped. Kris leapt from the car and ran to her, then saw the blood on her hands, on her shirt, and covering her lower leg.

"Kris! Thank God it's you," she gasped, gripping her calf. "Megan's shot. In the back."

The unease solidified into outright fear, but Kris pushed it down, made herself focus on the here and now.

"Is she alive? Where? How far?"

"Just up the road. I was going for help, but shit, it hurts."

"You've done well, Deb. Let's get you into the car."

Kris helped her to her feet, half-carried her to the car, and guided her onto the back seat.

"Slide back if you can, and put your leg up on the seat. The higher it is, the better."

She found the first-aid box and pulled out dressings. She tore open packets, pressed a couple of dressings against Deb's leg. "Press as firmly as you can, Deb, and hold it there. I'll call for an ambulance as we go." Then she asked the question she dreaded hearing the answer to. "Do you know where Gil is?"

"They took him. He exchanged himself for us. He tried to get us a chance to escape on the bike, but the bastards fired before we'd got far. Megan was hit, and then me, and I lost control of the bike. We went down. I told her to stay still. We didn't move until the car drove off. It was a black Land Rover, but I couldn't get the number."

Kris nodded, made her way back to the driver's seat, thoughts racing, screaming between terror and anger, cursing Gil at the same time as she wanted to shake him and hold him and yell at him for making her so damned afraid she almost couldn't cope.

Her hand shook as she gripped the steering wheel and turned the key in the ignition. But she managed to keep her voice clear and steady as she radioed in to report the shooting, and request paramedics.

Eight hundred metres down the road, she found Megan . . . She was conscious, in pain from the wound in her side, and rapidly, Kris assessed, going into shock. She pushed back Megan's top, quickly located the entry and exit wounds, an inch or two from the side, just above her waist, and desperately tried to remember what anatomical parts were where.

"It hurts, Kris," Megan whispered.

Kris took Megan's cold fingers in hers, brushed her hair from her face with her other hand. "Sshh, Megan. Lie as still as you can. There's an ambulance on its way. We're not far from Birraga, so it won't be long."

Fifteen minutes it took, before they arrived. Fifteen long, lonely minutes during which she did the little she could for Megan, questioned Deb some more and briefed her colleagues on the situation by radio, giving orders and forcing herself to think professionally and objectively, as though the man in the custody of the Russos was simply a citizen, and not the man her heart cried out for.

She kept being a cop, doing what she had to do, holding the saline bag for Megan until the second ambulance arrived with more paramedics, supervising and liaising and thinking and planning while she did so, because letting herself fall apart would fail Gil and all the others she was responsible for.

Deb had hung Gil's jacket on a dead tree branch above in an effort to provide a small amount of shade for Megan, but after the ambulances finally departed, and while her colleagues were busy on the radio, Kris unhooked it from the branch, hugged it to her body, and tried to pretend that the warmth in it was Gil's.

Bound tightly at wrists and ankles, with a thick hood tied over his head, Gil lay on the floor of the vehicle, relaxing his body as much as the rough road allowed, and listening to everything the five men said. He didn't give himself a whole lot of chances, but he intended to take any single one that presented itself, and the more he knew, the more prepared he'd be.

He didn't, couldn't afford to, let his thoughts go to Deb and Megan. If he did, he'd lose his concentration, maybe miss his chance, and no way would that help them. If they were alive, Kris would find them. If not, he'd grieve for them after he killed Sergio Russo. Either way, he needed to be alive, and ready to act.

The men didn't talk much, but Sergio made a phone call to Tony, talking quickly in Italian. Gil guessed a word here and there, similar to English words, but the only one he really knew was "Dungirri".

They'd certainly been in the vehicle long enough to be getting close to Dungirri, although they'd stayed on dirt roads, not sealed ones, and taken many turns. Reality was, they could be anywhere within a seventy-k radius of Birraga.

They stopped at last, after a long, bumpy track, and the men dragged him from the vehicle, laughing when he hit the ground. Ignoring the bruising, he took the chance to scrape his fingers over the cool ground, identified leaf litter rather than bare dirt, broad leaves as well as fine needles. He breathed in deeply and slowly, got faint scents through the cloth that might have been the native cypress, and the white and pink spring-flowering bush he'd never known the name of. All of which suggested somewhere in the bush, on the Dungirri side of the scrub.

Two pairs of arms grabbed him and hauled him to his feet. Something firm pressed against his temple.

"We're going to free your feet, Gillespie, and you're going to walk. Just remember I've got this Glock in my hand, and if you do anything stupid, I'll use it. Your extremities first, I think, because my cousin does want you to be alive when he gets here."

They marched him across some flat, sandy ground, and into a building. A large shed, he thought, because of the way the voices echoed, and the swallows that shrieked around their heads.

"There's some narrow steps, now," one of the men said. "Don't lose your footing, Gillespie."

He made it down the first couple of metal steps before they pushed him the rest of the way. He twisted, landing mostly on his side, his arm scraping on the cement floor. They jeered, of course, while his arm and shoulder throbbed with pain. He heard the clang of a metal door and as they kicked him and told him to get up, he realised where he was: walking into a buried shipping container, about twenty-five kilometres north of Dungirri.

The emergency department at Birraga hospital buzzed with people working and speaking in low, urgent voices, against a constant background of electronic beeps.

Kris sat on the hard chair by Deb's bed, in an alcove at one end of the department. They'd given Deb painkillers, seen to her leg, and Kris kept her occupied by going over the details of the night for any more information she had about identities, locations, and the intentions of her captors. But Kris turned most of her concentration to the curtained bed at the other end of the area, listening for the lilting accent of the new emergency doctor, only recently arrived from India, or the Scottish brogue of Morag Cameron, the local general practitioner. Neither of them spoke loudly, though, and there were only snatches of information from the nurses and technicians who went in and out.

When Morag finally emerged from behind the curtain, Kris sprang up and went to her.

"How is she?"

"She's stable, but there's still some internal bleeding," Morag explained, succinct as ever. "We'll airlift her to Tamworth. They'll have theatre teams ready. Can you inform her next of kin?"

"Her father . . ." Her mouth dry, she swallowed, made her voice normal. "He's been abducted. I'll have someone inform her grandparents."

She went outside, into the garden beside the building, where she could hardly hear the beeps and where the perfumed roses drowned the hospital smell. The storm clouds were overhead now; along with the scent of the roses, the air carried the scent of rain, not far away.

Beth had stayed with the Russells overnight, so Kris dialled her mobile number, spoke with her briefly, glad she could rely on Beth to handle things at that end. She would find someone to drive the Russells to Tamworth if they were fit enough to go.

Steve Fraser swung out of the ward block on the other side of the garden, and crossed over to her as she hung up.

"I've just been speaking with Mark," he told her, after she'd given him the latest on Megan and Deb. "Gotta love a politician with a gift for faces, names and voices. We might have IDs on a couple of the men. I'll follow up the leads now."

"Good." She nodded, although a voice inside her head argued that they needed to know where, not who. "I'll go back to Dungirri. Half the town's been working for Flanagan properties in one way or another, and I'm going to interrogate the lot of them if necessary." *Especially Sean Barrett and the Dawson boys*, she added to herself.

"Okay. Keep in touch, let me know what you learn." He turned to go, then remembered something. "Petric and Macklin are on their way back. Seems Tony Russo left Sydney this morning, heading this way."

Desperate not to waste valuable time, she had one of the constables drive her back to Dungirri, using the forty minutes in the car to go over notes and maps and make phone calls, including one to Adam.

"Get together as many people as you can at the hall, Adam. Tell them I'm giving an update. After the meeting, we're going to have to find and interview Sean, and the Dawson boys, and Luke Sauer. Don't say anything to alert them. I don't want them disappearing."

Her phone bleeped during the call, and when she retrieved her messages, Alec's deep voice greeted her.

"Kris, I've been in touch with some colleagues in the Federal Police, specialists in drug importation cartels, and they're on their way to Dungirri. They're already investigating Sergio Russo, so give them whatever you've got on him. You can trust them, Kris. Oh, and I've notified your Commander about the Feds, so the protocol's dealt with."

Bless Alec for his thorough professionalism. She hoped the Feds had more information than she did, and were willing to share it. She'd give them a copy of Vince's notes, see what they could make of them.

Wind gusted leaves and small branches across the road ahead of the car, and large drops of rain plopped onto the windscreen.

"Storm's catching up to us," the constable observed, glancing into the rear-view mirror. "I hope the rescue chopper got away okay."

Another thing to worry about. Kris lifted her phone to call and check, but Ghost Hill was coming up on their left, and there was no signal.

Then the rain fell in torrents, and even above it and the engine noise they could hear the thunder rolling. Water sheeted across the road, and the constable slowed the car, driving with care. She was young, this constable, only a few months out of probation, showing promise but inclined to under-confidence in her abilities.

Kris suppressed an impatient sigh and focused on the maps again. The storm would pass, they'd get to Dungirri, and then she'd confront the town's residents at the meeting, see what she could get from them. And if Sean Barrett and mates didn't show, she'd go hunt for them.

She compared the list of Flanagan properties with the survey maps again, but this time, using a pencil, she shaded in the rough locations.

By the time they reached the edge of Dungirri, the rain had eased — Dungirri usually missed the best rain — and she'd identified a possible pattern in the locations of the properties. The Flanagan landholdings predominantly feel into two loose clusters — one, southwest of Birraga, with considerable frontage to the Birraga River, and the second group, expanded to a large area in recent years, northwest of Dungirri, edging the scrub in places, with parcels of land incorporating Dungirri Creek, Friday Creek and up to the eastern, upstream end of the Birraga River.

She tapped her pencil against the map, thinking. Last night, the helicopter's path had headed to the southwest. This morning, Gil had met with Russo in the same general area. It suggested that they'd holed up somewhere in that vicinity overnight. Deb had been blindfolded the whole time, but she'd mentioned hearing hordes of cockatoos squawking this morning, and they tended to congregate in the open plains, more so than the scrub area.

If they'd gone southwest last night, Kris doubted they'd stay long in the same area. So, if they were using one of their own places, they might — *might* — be closer now, somewhere within a forty-kilometre radius of Dungirri. That still made a damned huge search area, and no clues, yet, to pin them down.

And she could be wrong. They could be anywhere — heading for the Queensland border, going back to Sydney, over to the coast, or any other direction. There were too few police resources in this vast, sparsely populated region for effective road blocks, even if they'd been able to put them in place straight after Gil's abduction.

She gnawed on her lip, trying to keep a lid on her panic. Gil was out there, somewhere, and Tony wouldn't let him live for long.

CHAPTER
TWENTY-THREE

Adam and the local community networks brought together a good proportion of the town's population in the hall, despite the short notice. Kris strode through them to the front of the room. In stark contrast to Saturday night, tight expressions and subdued talk reflected the apprehensive mood. The talk died when Kris reached the front and faced them.

Someone had set out some chairs for the older people, and Beth sat in the front row, between Esther Russell and Eleni and George Pappas, holding Esther's hand. In the second row, at the end, Delphi O'Connell sat beside Frank Wilson. Sauers, Dawsons, Barretts — a few from each family were there but not, as far as she could see, Sean, Luke or the Dawson brothers.

Desperate not to let the air of fear and distress undermine her own shaky composure, she launched straight in to what she had to say.

"You will all be aware that there have been a number of serious incidents in the area this week. Several locals have been seriously injured, as well as two visitors. I can report to you that Mark Strelitz is likely to be released from hospital later today. Liam Le, one of our visitors, was also injured while trying to stop an abduction, and remains in a serious condition in Tamworth hospital. Megan, the Russells' granddaughter, and Deborah Taylor, another visitor, were both released by the abductors this morning, but were shot as they left the scene. Deborah's injuries are minor, but Megan is currently being airlifted to Tamworth, in a critical condition."

Esther Russell cried quietly into her handkerchief, and Kris added, on a softer note, "I am sure Megan, and Doctor and Mrs Russell, would appreciate everyone's prayers and positive thoughts."

She gave them a moment. A couple of heads bowed, others whispered to each other. George's worry beads rattled softly as he moved them through his fingers.

"Folks, I'm not going to beat around the bush. Highly organised criminal elements from Sydney are working with local people, and they are armed and dangerous, and not averse to murder. This morning, knowing the risks, Morgan Gillespie exchanged himself for Megan and Deborah. We have grave fears for his safety. We need to find him quickly, and I need your help for that."

"Why should we help Gillespie?" Johnno Dawson said, from the back of the room. "Isn't it his fault all this shit's happened?"

She saw red before her eyes. Blazing red fury raged in her head and burned, for long seconds, her capacity for coherent words.

"No, Johnno," she said finally, not caring if her words towards him were scathing, "it is *not* his fault. If you want to condemn a man, then have the guts to do it on hard, factual evidence, not blind prejudice and lazy gossip. Gil Gillespie is no criminal."

Johnno had wilted under her gaze, and a couple of his mates had subtly moved away. Good.

She turned her attention to the rest of the room. "However, speaking of criminals, I'm aware that some of you may have been forced to turn a blind eye to illegal activity, to not ask questions. Some of your sons, and maybe your daughters, have been drawn in to criminal activity. Maybe they got out of it. Maybe they haven't."

She took a deep breath, scanned the room again. "We've been through dark times these past few years. But on Saturday night, we gathered in this hall to celebrate the good things in the community, to build hope for our future. We don't have much choice about drought and economic downturn and climate change, but we can do something about crime. There's a cancer in this district, and it needs to be cut out, now. This town deserves better than that. We deserve better than that. Some of you have information that may help save the life of a man — a good man. I'm asking you for that information. Talk to me, give me a slip of paper, email me, text me — I don't care. Just tell me or Adam what you know."

She left them on that plea. Walked back to her office, giving them time to think and talk and decide to take the risk of telling the truth.

And she hoped to hell they would.

They no longer grew cannabis in the shipping container. They took his hood off just before they thrust him into a small, barred cell in a far corner of the space, and he took the chance to study his surroundings. The size surprised him, until he realised it was double width, maybe five metres wide, two containers with adjacent walls removed, of the longer type — ten maybe twelve metres in length. Storage shelves lined one wall, half-filled with boxes and crates and a pile of old pipes, and a metre-high stack of boxes sat on a pallet towards the other wall.

His captors left, clanging the main door locked, and a second later they cut the lights, so that he was plunged into total, black darkness. With his hands cuffed behind him, feeling around the cell was awkward, but he took it slowly, counting bars, learning the shape of the bolt-lock, using his hands, shoulder, face to feel over as much of the two ridged walls as best he could. His nose told him there was a bucket in the corner, emptied but not cleaned. Gil purposely avoided contemplating the fate of the previous occupant.

Other than the bucket, there were only walls, bars and floor. He slid down to sit on the floor against the wall, making himself as comfortable as the circumstances allowed, stretching his legs out in front of him.

There was no light at all, not even faint sounds from above. The metal door of the container was heavy and noisy, and would give him plenty of warning when they came back. And they would come back, when Tony arrived.

Gil closed his eyes, rested his head back against the wall. Sleep would be the best thing. Sleep would give him strength, sharpen his senses, increase his chances.

He didn't let his mind drift to things he couldn't do a thing about. Instead, he thought of Kris, remembered the gift of lying with her, wrapped around her, peaceful and calm. He didn't even think of sex, just that stillness, the complete trust and closeness of being with her.

He kept the calmness when he woke to bright light, some time later. He pushed himself to his feet, was standing upright when the door at the end scraped open.

They strolled in — Tony, Sergio, Sean, and another man — the second truck driver from the café, before the fire. Clinton. First name or last name, it didn't matter — he was muscular, and had the face of a thug.

He calculated his chances of taking them all on, making it to the open door beyond, but with cuffed hands the equation came out negative, in the suicidal range, and he decided he'd prefer to endure and wait for other options. As Sean and the truckie sauntered towards him, and Tony dragged a heavy metal chair into the centre of the space, Gil sent a quick thought towards the open door.

Now would be a good time, Blue. Any time about now.

Paul and Jim Barrett arrived at the station within minutes of Kris getting there. In the interview room, she sat opposite them and asked straight out, "Is Sean involved in illegal activity with the Flanagans?"

Jim stared at his clasped hands on the table, but Paul shifted uneasily on his chair. She had an answer. She let

380

the silence grow, waiting for them to fill it. Paul cast a glance at his father, didn't get any response.

"I think he is," Paul said. "I don't know for sure. I don't see him much lately. He works for the company, a legit job, but this past few months, he's been throwing around money. And . . . he's changed. More swagger. He used to spend time with me and Chloe and the kids, but now he hardly ever comes. And when he does, it's not like it used to be. Not . . . easy."

Jim lifted his face and, for all their previous run-ins, it hurt Kris to see the pain in his eyes.

"I was glad when he got the job with Flanagan. I thought he'd stay, not move away," he said roughly. "But he's grown hard and arrogant. I don't know what he's doing, who he's with, and I don't ask because I know I'll hate my son if I find out."

"Do either of you know where he is now?"

Jim shook his head. Paul hesitated, then spoke up again. "I don't know where he is. But while I was working on the old Sutherland place the last few weeks, I often saw him drive past in the late afternoons, heading north on the Hammersley Road."

Kris thanked them, saw them out, then came back and studied the map. North on the Hammersley Road. That could lead to five of the Flanagan properties, but it ran roughly parallel to Scrub Road, kilometres apart, and a few tracks linked the two. That broadened the area considerably and brought another three properties into contention.

Her phone rang. Steve, on his way to Dungirri. He told her Petric and Macklin were due to arrive shortly, that they'd agreed to meet in Dungirri.

The station's front bell sounded, and she answered it to find Karl on the doorstep, clutching several sheets of paper. He spread them out on the table in the interview room, gave her a wary grin.

"I'm not going to tell you how I got this data, and it's best if you don't ask, okay?"

She nodded, very cautiously, knowing he'd worked in IT for a phone company, until recently.

"Believe me, I wouldn't normally do this," he said earnestly. "But I can't do nothing if someone might die because of it."

He pushed a map towards her, different from the survey maps she used. "I hate saying it, but I think Sean is involved. He used to be a mate, but he's . . . well, he's not, now. Anyway, as of ten minutes ago, Sean — or his mobile phone — was somewhere in this area, between these three towers."

It was still a large area, but it covered the area north on Scrub Road, corresponding roughly with Paul's information.

"Sean may not be where Gil is, though," she thought out loud.

"No, on it's own, it's not significant. But I skimmed over some other data, and the number Sean called yesterday morning, probably around the time he was released, was this number" — he tapped one of the printouts — "and that phone is now in the same area that Sean's is in. What's more, that phone — let's call it

382

phone A — has been regularly called by phone B, which was in Sydney last night, and which is now in roughly the same place as Sean's and phone A."

Tony. Phone B had to be Tony, and phone A Sergio.

"Before you ask what you're not supposed to, no, I can't narrow the area down any further," Karl said. "But I know someone who might know if there's a specific place out that way."

"Luke?"

"Yes."

"Will he talk?"

Karl grinned and stacked his papers together. "Between your police glare and the threat of my cousinly thumps, probably."

They found Luke at home, and he needed no thumps, threatened or otherwise. A night in the cells, and the reality of the charge of aggravated sexual assault against Megan had frightened him enough to change his attitude, and made him eager to cooperate.

"There is a place Sean hangs out," he told them. "I haven't been there, dunno where it is exactly, but he said there's a cool house, with a home theatre and spa and all, but the guy that owns it doesn't live there any more, so Sean uses it sometimes. He reckons there's a freight container, under a shed. He reckoned he might use it, you know, to make stuff."

A freight container.

She raced back to her office, grabbed Gil's old maps and photos, found the relevant map mark and compared it to hers. Not a Flanagan holding. Not

383

currently, anyway, but it was in the right area and maybe the owner was a partner, willing or otherwise.

It didn't matter. She'd found Gil, and now all she had to do was set up an operation to get him out of there.

They tied him to the chair. It went against the grain, not to fight them, but that unequal equation made it too much of a risk. If he created trouble, they'd kill him in an instant.

Sergio leaned against the wall, idly observing while Tony stood in front of Gil, the will held high, and put a cigarette lighter to it. The paper curled, burned upwards, eating the paper.

"My father thought he was clever, but this is what his schemes have come to. A pile of ashes."

"Did you know she was your sister, Tony?" Gil asked.

He dropped the will to the metal floor, watched the last of it burn. "That whore?" He spat on the ashes. "She got all she deserved. I made sure of that. But it's your fault, Gillespie. You shouldn't have interfered, got Vince involved. He got angry, tried to tell me what to do, then he shouted his dirty little secret and said she'd get more than me. So she had to die, and before him." He snorted. "You know, people pay to do a woman like that. Instead of costing me, I made money on it."

Gil kept his face impassive, despite his revulsion. Tony's slip answered some questions, and Sergio's relaxed observation answered a couple more.

Tony hadn't killed his father. Sergio was the cool one, the planner, and must have arranged or carried out the assassination without involving Tony. But with Vince on life support, Gil guessed Tony had panicked, desperate for Marci to die before their father.

And Sergio had stepped in to clean up the mess, dispose of the body, implicate another. He had to have a reason for indulging his far less effective cousin.

"So, let me guess, Tony. You didn't find Vince's will until Saturday, is that right?"

Tony kicked the pile of ashes with his shoe. "The copies are destroyed, Gillespie. There is no will. I'm his son and I'll inherit. I'm going to enjoy spending my money."

No, thought Gil. Sergio will wait long enough for you to get it, and then he'll probably kill you for it. For all Tony's anger and violence, Sergio was the far greater danger.

Oblivious to anything but his own desires, Tony gave a twisted grin. "And the other thing I'm going to enjoy," he continued, "is watching you die. You cheated me, Gillespie. You took what was mine. That requires punishment, and I've been waiting a long time to see you get it. And since Sean here has long desired to belt the shit out of you for killing his cousin, I'm going to let him."

Sean stepped forward, a wide smirk lighting his face, a heavy metal pipe gripped in both hands like a medieval sword. "We might take this nice and slow, Gillespie. Make the pleasure last."

Gil exhaled a slow breath through his nose. He could endure this. He was strong, healthy, and he had plenty to survive for. He brought an image of Kris to his mind, and focused his thoughts, his energies on two words: Endure. Survive.

The pipe slammed into his gut and pain exploded, searing through every nerve in his body.

CHAPTER
TWENTY-FOUR

The good thing about Federal Police agents arriving on one's doorstep, Kris discovered, was that they could make a lot happen in a short space of time. She had the sense their own investigation was advanced, close to the point of moving in. Whether it was the extra information in Vince's detailed notes, or the fact of a hostage and the Russos in a known place that tipped the scales, she didn't know, but they decided the time was ripe. Phone calls flew, and the approval for a joint operation came quickly.

But the unsettling aspect of a hastily convened operation was that Joe, Craig and Steve were automatically part of the team. Not knowing, not being able to trust them, left her grappling with continued trepidation. The station was too small for the dozen officers called together; they gathered instead around a table set up in the hall, the late afternoon light casting a grid of shadows from the window frame across the documents spread before them.

"We've raided these types of facilities before," the senior agent, Caitlin Jamieson, explained to the team. "There's usually only one entrance. With a hostage inside, that makes it risky. Tear gas is the best option.

The next best is cutting the power, throwing them into the dark."

"The tactical response group usually does this type of operation," Kris pointed out. "We don't have tear gas, night vision goggles or sharp-shooters."

"Can you get the TRG here in half an hour?" Caitlin asked. "I don't think we can afford to wait much longer."

"Not a chance. It'd be three hours, minimum, before they could be here." Steve drummed his fingers on the table. "But if we cut the power and go in with torches, we'll have the advantage of surprise, and glare. I was with tactical for a while, and I think it's the best chance we've got."

"Any other options?" Caitlin asked the group. "Right, what do we know about the buildings, the area, and who is there? Do we have any recent aerial photos?"

Kris spread out a few photos on the table. "It's on the edge of the State Forest, and they did an aerial survey a year or two back. We've got this shot here, with the house, and the various outbuildings. I've compared it to Gil's photos from when they were burying the container, and the placement of the buildings in the background of that image." She indicated a large rectangle on the aerial photo, some distance from the house, not far from a thick band of trees and a reasonably sized dam. "I'm fairly certain it's under this machinery shed. If we approach from these trees, here, we'll have good cover, and any view from the house will be blocked by the shed itself."

★ ★ ★

An hour later, as the sun set, Kris scanned the shed and surrounds from the cool shadows of the trees, and breathed in the scents of the bush. The still-damp leaf litter below her feet, not yet dry after the storm. The fresh scent of the cypress trees around them. Something sweet-smelling. Another bank of storm clouds was rolling in across the sky, dark and flame-edged from the setting sun, the rumblings of thunder becoming louder, more frequent. With luck, the thunder might cover any noise they made.

Nothing moved around the house or the outbuildings. She could just see, across the clearing, the second team was in position, ready to go in to the house. Near her, waiting for the signal, Caitlin, Steve, Joe and Craig made only the slightest noise: breathing, the brush of fabric, the soft crunch of leaves as they shifted their feet.

Kris slowed her own breathing, made herself aware of her body, present in it. The familiar weight of the Glock in her hand. The less familiar bulk and weight of the bullet-proof vest. The soles of her feet, firm boots, firm ground beneath them.

The soft beep on Caitlin's phone gave the signal, and Kris set out across the open ground with her colleagues, quickly, quietly, heading towards Gil.

Ten.

This time the pipe dislocated his left shoulder, maybe smashed it. The fresh blast of agony blazed thought from his mind, sent him spiralling, drowning, and he was almost too weak to fight back from it.

Survive.

It hammered in his head, along with the screaming pain. He couldn't let go of it. He had to hold on, not let go.

Survive. Endure.

Ten. He'd survived ten. There'd be a space before eleven. Maybe a fist or two, a kick, but a space before the next pipe blow. Sean gave him that space, gave him time to fully experience each agony before adding the next one.

He wondered if they'd go for his legs next.

Probably.

The voices drifted, the light swirled around dark spots in front of his eyes. Someone laughed.

He felt his mind slipping, fought it, clawed his way towards the swirling light, struggled to drag together a coherent thought.

Now, Blue. Now would be a really good time . . .

They burst through the door, Steve in front, the rest of them in quick succession, fanning out immediately in the space, torch lights running a rapid scan to count and locate occupants, Steve shouting to them to drop to the ground.

Four, Kris counted. Four, plus Gil, slumped too-still in a chair in the centre of the bigger-than-expected space. The light from the torches cut wild arcs around the walls, constantly shifting. People shouted, and gun shots exploded, deafening in the reverberation against the metal.

Someone charged her, and she dodged, bringing her fists down on him as he passed, sending him sprawling. Then the torch was torn from her left hand, the force of the bullet that hit it convulsing up her arm. It felt like a dead weight as she lifted it to grasp her gun with both hands.

Through the surreal, slow-motion madness of noise, firing, and confusion, she heard Gil yell her name. In a sweep of light, she saw the gun pointed at her . . . Gil, still bound to the chair, charging, throwing himself at the man . . . the sharp jerk of their bodies, and the two of them falling, smashing against the wall.

She started for him. In the corner of her vision, she saw another gun raised, directed her way.

She spun around, squeezed the trigger, and shot Joe Petric.

CHAPTER
TWENTY-FIVE

It didn't fall quiet when the firing stopped. The ringing in her ears continued, and the pounding of her heart, both competing with all the other sounds — groans, swearing, Caitlin giving orders, handcuffs clicking into place.

The overhead lights flickered on, and Kris holstered her gun, crossed the floor and knelt by Gil. Still bound to the chair, his arm at a crazy angle behind him, his hand smashed, he lay sprawled over a man she assumed to be Tony Russo. A large pool of blood spread beneath them.

Too scared to even think, she lightly pressed her fingers to Gil's neck, seeking a pulse. At her touch, he opened his eyes, and a rush of light-headedness made the room sway in front of her.

"Gil."

His mouth curved a little. "Blue."

She blinked the moisture away from her eyes to see more clearly, looked him over to identify his injuries. She didn't dare move him, or untie him, until she had some clue what was damaged. His skin was too pale and cold, and the marks on his face would definitely bruise. His arm was a mess. At his waist, his hitched-up

T-shirt exposed long red marks. She couldn't tell if his legs, twisted under the chair, were okay or not, but they'd carried his weight in his mad charge against Tony. The blood beneath them was Tony's, and he was quite dead.

Gil's eyes had drifted closed again. She touched the only part of him she dared to, brushing a finger against his lips. "Hang in there, Gil. Paramedics will be here any minute. We had them waiting not far away."

"Good," he murmured. He didn't open his eyes, but his mouth made that small curve again. "Metal pipe. Ribs are broken, this time."

The dry reference to their conversation after the pub fight, an age ago now, almost made her howl.

His forehead creased, as he suddenly remembered something, and he forced open his eyes, searched her face. "Megan? Is she . . . ?"

"She's doing okay, Gil. Deb and Liam will be fine, too."

He moved his head in a nod, closed his eyes again.

A hand dropped onto her shoulder, and Gary the senior paramedic crouched beside her.

"What have we got here, Kris?"

She had to blink tears from her eyes again, made herself concentrate on a sitrep. "Repeatedly bashed with a metal pipe. Multiple fractures — left arm, ribs, I don't know what else. Pulse is weak, skin cold. Probably internal bleeding. He's been conscious, and coherent, until just now. The guy beneath him is a gun shot wound, deceased."

"Thanks, Kris. We'll take it from here." Gary already had his box open, was pulling out equipment, and another paramedic joined him.

Kris struggled to her feet, moved out of their way. The room seemed full of people, with the second police team and paramedics adding to the number. Sergio Russo and Sean Barrett were cuffed, under Craig's and Adam's guard. Another man lay on the floor, dead. And Joe Petric half-sat, leaning against the wall, breathing heavily, but swearing very capably at a paramedic. A bullet-proof vest might stop the bullets penetrating, but it didn't stop the impact hurting.

With all the urgent tasks being dealt with, she couldn't, for a long moment, think what to do.

Caitlin and Steve saw her standing there, but it was Steve who reached her first.

"How's Gillespie?"

"Alive," she said. "But critical."

She bit her lip, hard. She was a police sergeant. She wasn't supposed to cry on duty, in a room full of people.

Caitlin stopped in front of her, hands on hips. "Are you injured?" she asked briskly.

"No."

"Good. Then perhaps you can tell us why you shot Detective Petric?"

Kris straightened her shoulders and met the agent's hard stare evenly. "Because he was about to shoot me."

The rescue helicopter made the flight out from Tamworth again, and carried Gil away.

394

The remainder of the evening blurred into a series of interviews, statements and reports at the Birraga station. The search of the property revealed drugs and weapons — cocaine in boxes stacked in the container, semi-automatic rifles in the house. On top of that, two deaths in a police operation, injuries, an officer shooting another — it all had to be investigated, documented and analysed.

Kris expected to be suspended. However, as the hours passed and the interviews and investigation progressed, the evidence against Petric began to mount. The Feds already had information pointing to a leak. Craig expressed concerns about some of Joe's behaviour, inconsistencies and procedural violations that had raised questions in his mind.

Kris had just emerged from an interview with Internal Affairs officers around ten that evening, when Steve met her in the corridor and took her into his office. "Joe's just confessed," he said. "They found a text message on Sergio Russo's phone, warning of the raid — from Joe's phone. We're lucky that there's not much phone signal in a metal box underground."

She didn't feel any pleasure at the revelation, only relief, and nausea that a once-respected officer could have betrayed them all.

She'd been in meetings and interviews almost constantly for hours, with no news of Gil.

"Has there been any word from the hospital? Is Gil in Tamworth or Sydney?"

"They took him to Sydney. I know he survived the flight. But Kris, you need to know — the Feds, they're putting him into witness protection. As of tonight. They've got Sergio and Petric, but they've still got one hell of a mop-up operation to run. Gil's a valuable witness, they can't risk Russo's associates getting to him."

Witness protection. She sat down heavily on the edge of the desk, gripped its edges. It would be a private hospital somewhere, a false name, and 24-hour security. As soon as he was well enough to be moved, they'd probably take him interstate to an anonymous house or apartment.

But she wouldn't know where. For his safety, she wouldn't be able to see him, talk to him, have any contact whatsoever. It might be for months. It might be for years. And if the investigation against the Russos left loose ends, it might be forever.

She knew the process, knew it was the logical, most responsible course of action to keep Gil safe.

She just never knew how much it would hurt.

CHAPTER
TWENTY-SIX

Two months later.

Gil flexed his hand, the warmth of the sunshine on it easing the stiffness and aches.

"Are you sure about this, Gil?" Caitlin Jamieson demanded. His minders had called her in for a last-ditch effort to dissuade him.

"You've said yourself that you've got plenty of hard evidence against Sergio. I'm a minor witness, with only old, insubstantial evidence against Tony, and therefore of no real use to your case. You know that as well as I do."

She gave a soft groan, but didn't argue the point.

He closed his fingers around the coffee mug, lifted it without needing his other hand. Progress. Definitely progress.

"You do understand that once you leave here, your protection arrangements cease?"

"Yes."

"What will you do?"

He kept forgetting that his left shoulder no longer shrugged. "You know how it is. Places to go, people to see."

People to see.

Two months almost starved of news, and he'd learned something about himself: some people mattered to him. In those first few weeks, once he was conscious, he'd harangued the Feds enough that they'd passed on a few snippets. Jeanie's valve replacement surgery had gone smoothly. Liam would make a full recovery. Megan, too. Internal Affairs had declared Kris's shooting of Petric to be self-defence, clearing her of any wrongdoing. But simple facts weren't sufficient.

He put the mug down, and rose to his feet. His bag was already by the door. With his good hand he lifted it, his weaker one strong enough now to grasp the door handle.

"Good luck, Gillespie," Caitlin called, as he walked out of the apartment, into freedom.

He took the bus to Birraga, paying for two seats to give sufficient room for his healing body. Nevertheless, the long journey tired him; by the time the bus stopped in the centre of town, late in the afternoon, stiffness had set in, and his whole arm ached, each part with its own particular set of pains and discomfort.

The walk the few blocks from the bus stop to the police station helped ease some of the stiffness, but the aches remained. Healing, as far as he was concerned, took far too damn long.

He stopped on the corner near the police station, dropped his bag to the ground, and let his old-man body rest a moment or two. He'd had the whole long

398

bus ride to think about this meeting, but now the moment had come, uncertainty made him pause.

Much could change in two months. He hadn't contacted her since he got out, hadn't told her he was coming back. Hadn't told anyone, yet. Just a phone call to the Birraga station this morning to find out her roster, and whether she'd be here or in Dungirri.

He'd see her, and that was the extent of his plans. His future was wide open for him to choose — he had the resources for any business, any city or country he wanted, and no financial need to hurry to decide. His own money was enough. Sometime soon, he'd have to deal with Vince's legacy, come to grips with it, make arrangements; but that could wait a little longer.

"She's out at the moment, mate," the constable at the front desk said. "Should be back in half an hour or so. About six. Can I give her a message?"

He scrawled a note for her and left it with the constable.

At a café in the main street, he ordered coffee, and sat at the table outside, under the shade of the awning, idly watching the activity around.

Most of Birraga's shops and businesses closed at five or five-thirty, and the winding down of the day was evident in the cheerful conversations and exchanges along the street as shopkeepers started closing up, people passed on their way home, or popped into a shop to buy some last-minute things before closing time. People knew each other here. They called each other by name, stopped for short chats, or simply waved at each other in passing.

Mark Strelitz made slow progress down the other side of the road. In neat moleskins and shirt, he fitted in, part of the country community, respect evident in the way people greeted him, stopped for brief conversations, some casual, some clearly more related to business, community or political issues. His easy warmth and courtesy showed, even when an old man stopped him, directly across the road from where Gil sat, and engaged him in some topic about which the old man obviously held passionate views.

But when Mark glanced across and noticed Gil, his face changed, his initial shock shifting to a worried distraction as he hastily finished his conversation, shook hands, and hurried across the street. Gil rose as he approached.

"Gil! I didn't know you were back."

Mark's handshake was firm, polite as ever, but his eyes seemed . . . older, Gil thought. Troubled, under the social polish.

"I just arrived."

"It's good to see you. Everyone was worried, for a while there. You're well?"

Small talk had never been Gil's strong point. "Much better."

"Great to hear." Mark stopped, shifted uneasily, and the easy confidence evaporated. "Gil, would you have a few minutes? There's a matter I've been wanting to discuss with you."

Alarm bells rang in his head. He felt tempted to make some excuse, but if the "matter" concerned Mark and Kris, he didn't want to hear about it. Yet the man

400

did seem worried. Perhaps there'd been ongoing issues from all the arrests and charges.

"Yeah, I guess so. I've got nowhere to be until six."

"Thanks. My office is just round the corner — shall we go there?"

Mark's staff had gone home, the electorate office deserted but for the two of them. Gil accepted a cool drink, and followed Mark into his private office, taking a seat at a low table opposite him.

Mark looked down at his hands, at the glass in them, and took a long breath before he began. "Gil, I need to ask you about the accident, with Paula. I've never regained my memory of it, the medicos think I probably never will. It's just a black hole in my head. But the thing is . . . ever since the other month, when you were here and I had that concussion, I've had dreams, quite often. Always the same — a bloody kangaroo glaring at me in the headlights, a horrendous crunch as we hit the tree." He paused, his shoulders hunched, and took a swig of his juice, as though it were a strong spirit and he needed to fortify himself.

Then he looked Gil straight in the eye. "The scene I see — it's always from the driver's seat. I was driving that night, wasn't I?"

Gil stood abruptly, walked to the window and gazed out at the sky, no clue how to handle this. He'd buried it, long ago. Accepted the way the cards had fallen, and moved on.

"It's just a dream," he insisted.

"I have to know for sure, Gil. I don't know if what I'm dreaming is a fragment of memory or just my

401

imagination. I don't remember anything between my birthday the week before, and waking up in the hospital. But seeing you again, the concussion — one of them's triggered something in my head. The dream keeps coming again and again and again, and I need to know whether it's real or not."

"Leave it, Mark," Gil growled.

He heard Mark rise from his seat, come a few steps closer. "Can you swear to me that you were driving, Gil? Can you do that?"

Gil turned to face him, searching for words to dissuade him from this path. "It's ancient history, now. Just let it be." He knew as soon as he'd said the words that they weren't the right ones.

Mark closed his eyes and leaned his head against the window frame, a single quietly spoken curse escaping his lips. When he finally opened his eyes again, Gil expected to see anger or fear but there was only calmness, acceptance, and Mark simply said, "Why?"

Gil recognised the question but didn't answer, the silence stretching between them. Confirming Mark's suspicions wouldn't help anyone, and after all this time the truth might be more damaging than the fiction.

"Damn it, Gil, why?" Mark demanded. "Why did you tell them it was you?"

He let out the breath he was holding, slowly, carefully. "I didn't. The old sarge — Bill Franklin — was the first one there, and by then I'd got you out of the car and was doing what I could for Paula. I couldn't get to her through her door so I was kneeling in the driver's seat, and Franklin just assumed at first I'd been driving. Then Paula died at the scene, and they didn't know if you'd make it, and everyone was angry, and although Franklin knew by then it was you, not me — well, I guess he figured it was better to blame the feral kid than the town favourite."

"But why didn't you say something?"

As if it would have been that easy. The differences between his own experiences of the world and Mark's made a chasm.

"I was just a kid, outcast, and way out of my depth." With Franklin's hand on the back of his head, slamming his face into the table. "It was . . . made clear to me that I was to carry the blame. And then the first night in the remand centre, the threat was delivered — comply, or Jeanie would suffer. I thought I had no choice. The days went by, and you never said anything to contradict the story. No-one would have believed me, without your backup, and I couldn't risk anything happening to Jeanie."

And Gil had not known then, still didn't know, whether the deception was all Franklin's and Doc Russell's doing, with a favour or two from Flanagan, or whether others had knowingly participated.

Mark dropped his head in his hands, shaking it, grappling to comprehend. "Gil, I wish I knew what to say. 'Sorry' is nowhere near enough."

"You don't need to say sorry or any other shit. It's done and gone years ago, and you weren't involved. They stuffed up the rigging of evidence, and the conviction was quashed. I don't have a record. There's nothing to fix. There's no bloody *point* in bringing it up after all this time."

"There is if it was my fault," Mark insisted quietly. "Had I been drinking, Gil? Was I drunk?"

Gil ran a hand through his hair, searched for an answer. He still had no clue, to this day, whose blood they'd tested — except that it hadn't been his own. Trust bloody Mark to ask the awkward questions.

"You weren't drunk," he said and that was honest, because he could still remember Mark's cheerful, unslurred voice. "I was hitching, and you offered me a ride. I was only in the car ten minutes or so before the smash. Paula had a bottle of something, offered it around, but you didn't have any."

"That doesn't mean I wasn't already over the limit."

"I saw no sign of it." That, too, was honest — although maybe not enough to deter Mark from pursuing it. "Look, Mark, the accident was just that, an accident, no-one's fault. Not yours or mine or Paula's or even the bloody kangaroo's fault. So don't go being all high-minded and doing anything stupid."

Mark's half-smile didn't wipe the grim look from his eyes, the one that had aged him ten years in the past half-hour. "Don't worry, Gil — I didn't get to where I am by doing stupid things."

Kris parked behind the station, went in through the back door, and headed down the corridor to her office, glad her shift was almost done.

Jake had left a message on her chair and she flicked open the folded sheet of paper as she sat.

404

Arrived on the bus. Will come back around 6pm. G.

She grinned and might have kept staring at the paper and grinning stupidly, except she glanced at her watch. Six-ten. She refrained from dancing down the corridor to the reception area — just. But her boots were definitely lighter than they'd been for a while.

He was there, waiting, standing reading one of the posters on the wall, his back to her. Jeans, dark blue shirt, kit bag on the floor. His left arm hung a little stiffly at his side, but even as she watched, he flexed his hand a couple of times, with what seemed like a good range of movement.

Weeks of worrying and wondering, and frustration at simply not *knowing* faded into a wild jumble of relief and pleasure.

She leaned her elbows on the counter. "Good to see you upright, Gillespie."

He turned, stayed where he was, his careful, expressionless mask only holding for a couple of seconds before the corner of his mouth quirked.

"After ten hours on the bus, it feels good to be standing up, Blue."

God, she'd missed the dry humour, missed hearing that nickname in that laconic voice. Missed the sight of him — and more.

"You planning on visiting Dungirri? There's been a few people worrying about you. No news has been hard to deal with."

"Cuts both ways, Blue. Been wondering about a few people, myself."

Not much clue there on which specific people, but she could guess. That careful lack of expression had to cover emotion he wasn't sure how to reveal.

"Come on through to my office, then, and we can catch up on the news." She smiled on the last word, let it hang suggestively.

With a brief flash of a grin, he nodded, reached down with his right hand to pick up the bag on his left side, and grimaced slightly with the twisting, lifting movement. The blunt reminder of the trauma he'd endured cast a shadow on her joy. He'd been through too much, might not be ready for, or even want to continue, what they'd shared months ago. Things had to be different, now.

"How's the recovery going?" she asked as she led him to her office, trying to keep matter-of-fact, trying not to remember the horror of him broken and battered, close to dying.

"I had a very good surgeon, and my arm's better than they thought it would be."

And he still didn't move quite as easily as he had, she noticed, as they sat down in her office. But given the extent of his injuries, that wasn't surprising, at only two months down the track.

She left her door open, out of habit, but there were others around, passing in the corridor, and it didn't seem the right moment to close the door and get . . . well, personal with him.

"Liam and Jeanie and Megan — are they okay?" he asked, glancing out the door himself, keeping things neutral. "I only got the very basics out of the Feds."

At least she could reassure him, and despite her frustration at not being able to touch him, maybe it was better to update him on developments and news before they dealt with the personal. "Everyone's fine. Jeanie's staying out with Delphi at present. Deb's fine. Liam's made a full recovery, and so has Megan." She paused, not quite sure how he'd take this next bit. "She asks every time I see her if there's been any news of you."

He looked away, swallowed, but he didn't make any comment. She didn't push him.

"So, I gather the Feds think there's no more danger for you?"

"They've got more evidence than they need. They don't need me as a witness. So I told them I was leaving." He rubbed at his left hand. "I read in the newspapers that there's been a number of arrests around here, lately."

"Yes. There's been a team working on it. Sean Barrett provided enough information about this end of the Russos' distribution network for us to raid another property and the business office, and arrest and charge Brian and Kevin Flanagan and a number of others on trafficking, money laundering and extortion charges. Flanagan Agricultural Company has been placed in the hands of administrators, pending the outcome of the case."

"And Dan?"

She knew he'd ask. "Apparently, he officially retired from the company's board a couple of years ago, and declares he has no knowledge of any crimes. We haven't been able to find enough evidence to charge him, yet.

But his power is broken, Gil, especially with his sons arrested. He's put his house in Birraga up for sale — it wasn't a company asset — and is on the Gold Coast, where the Feds are watching him."

Gil rose, paced to the window. "Do you think . . ." He paused, took a moment to continue. "Sean, the Flanagan brothers — I imagine I'm not their favourite person, and they'll still have connections outside. Too many people were hurt because of me, Blue. I don't want that to happen again."

She didn't dismiss the fear. It explained his hesitation, the holding back from her, in spite of the signals she'd given him. He'd been through hell, almost losing the people he cared about; no wonder he was cautious.

"Gil, I can't promise you that nothing will happen. But I can tell you that I believe the risk is low. Sean pleaded guilty at his committal hearing. I believe there's genuine remorse there. As for the Flanagans — their influence is gone. Once they were exposed, it made a big difference — here in Birraga, and in Dungirri. A lot of information poured in. We can't use all of it, but the point is that people are standing together, against them."

"So, if I were to stick around here for a bit, Jim Barrett's not likely to stalk me in a dark alley?"

If I were to stick around here for a bit . . . her heartbeat gave a little skip. Oh, she definitely liked the sounds of those words.

"Jim's not going to stalk you, unless it's to apologise," she assured him quietly. "He and Paul were

408

shattered by what Sean did. I think their disgust and disappointment played a part in Sean's remorse."

Gil leaned against the window sill, hands in his pockets, dark eyes honest and direct. "I'm not sure I can forgive him yet, Blue."

She saw again the image of him surrounded by paramedics, remembered her choking fear as they'd battled to keep him alive. "I don't think I can, yet, either," she confessed, holding his gaze. "So I understand that you can't. However, since neither of us is into vengeance, Sean's safe enough, and we can move on with our lives."

She glanced at her watch. "Speaking of lives, since it's six-thirty, I'm now officially off-duty for four days. I can offer you a lift to Dungirri, if you'd like it." She grinned, let her expression convey the extent of her invitation.

He gave a slow smile in return. "I would like that. Thanks."

She kept the mood light and teasing, although her heart raced and underneath the lightness she wondered, slightly desperately, where the nearest private place might be.

"Good. We might even make it in time for dinner at the pub, where there is temporarily a really good chef, who is waiting for her business partner to reappear. Her cooking is definitely better than mine."

His eyes danced. "Why does this not surprise me?"

She switched off her computer, picked up her keys. "About the chef, or my cooking? On second thoughts," she added, "don't answer that."

"I suppose there's a temporary barman, too?" he asked.

"Yes. They were between jobs, and Nancy Butler offered them the work. They've been doing a great job."

She didn't tell him about the business options Liam and the town were exploring. There'd be time enough for Gil to consider them, to see what would be workable, to decide for himself whether he wanted to invest — financially or emotionally — in Dungirri.

Tonight, at the pub, he would discover how the tide of the community's attitude towards him was already turning. It might help to convince him.

"Megan will be pleased to see you," she said. "She's very keen to get to know her father."

"I'm not sure I'll ever get used to the idea. It still scares me." Standing there near the doorway, he reached out, his battered fingers crooked, but gentle, as he brushed her cheek with the back of his hand. "It's not the only thing that does."

His honest words, his touch, broke her thin control, and she no longer gave a damn about protocol.

She closed her hand over his, kicked the door shut, and moved in close. "But you came back, anyway."

His arms wrapped around her, held her tightly. "Yeah, Blue," he said, his mouth close to hers. "I came back."